Born in South Africa and raised in a small fishing town on the West Coast called Saldanha Bay, Simon grew up with a love of the movies. Ultimately this was a love of story telling. After moving to England at 21 and over the next decade working mostly as a Projectionist, it finally became a love that he was able to put into practice.

BENEATH

For my Mom, who has always been my number one fan,
and the reason why I knuckled down and wrote this thing,

For my Dad, for inspiring me to write my own stories in the first place.

I would like to thank everyone at Austin & Macauley for believing in my book and giving me this amazing opportunity.

Also, my friends and family for their encouragement and support. Particularly my parents, of course, but also my sister and my brother-in-law for always having a spare bed set aside for me when times got tough, and for always making me feel right at home.

And also for Stephanie Woolley, for her help in the early stages of trying to get this book read by the right people, and for her advice, which ultimately led me in the right direction.

Simon Wood

BENEATH

AUSTIN & MACAULEY
PUBLISHERS LTD.

A CIP catalogue record for this title is
available from the British Library.

ISBN 978 1 84963 215 7

www.austinmacauley.com

First Published (2012)
Austin & Macauley Publishers Ltd.
25 Canada Square
Canary Wharf
London
E14 5LB

Printed & Bound in Great Britain

CHAPTER ONE

1

Cold. Well, not warm enough. At least not for Jack. Hell, he'd just have to drink it – he wasn't prone to packing a back-up flask. The night air was cold and his car didn't have a heater, but he did have his smokes. Life wasn't all bad. He pulled out his pack of Camels. Only fifteen in the past two hours. He fingered the last five in his pack. He took out number sixteen and lit it. Better enjoy them, he thought. He wouldn't be able to just step out to the corner store and buy more.

Jack looked over to the low rent apartment complex where the Cartwright family were staying. The cigarette was going down well. It was the same old dump he'd seen a million times before, just with a different name. This one's he couldn't make out. He'd dealt with the low lives that lived there almost all his adult life. They were all the same. The cigarette was going down very well, and so was the coffee as it happened.

The street in front of *nameless building* was not busy, but Jack did notice the young girl standing on the sidewalk not doing too much of anything. Round seventeen, eighteen. New to the game as far as he could tell. Still very pretty. Still this side of used. He wondered if Cliff's view of the back was as interesting.

2

The closed sound that came out was not the scream she was panicking for. The tightening fingers were warm and wet. She knew it was blood. Her father's, her mother's, her brother's, hers? She tried to scream again. Nothing. Nothing but darkness around. Everything was rushing through her mind at once.

Another wet hand was now on her thigh, sliding up. She had just lain there frozen. The small sounds. Nothing – just bump in the night stuff. She thought about the breaking glass. She had known something was wrong then. When the door finally opened to her room she'd just stayed where she was. No amount of will could move her – not even a little.

The warm, wet fingers came between her legs. With their touch they sent a jolt through her, breaking through all the terror and forcing her body to react. She began to thrash and kick, desperately trying to get the bloody hand away. She tried to scream for him to stop but the other hand just squeezed harder. Spots of shimmering yellow were added to the darkness around her. He was going to rape her and kill her, she knew it, she couldn't stop. She continued to writhe and kick. This time her one foot connected with something. A groan sounded. The new most terrifying sound she'd ever heard.

There came a rush of cold air over her face. She couldn't tell if it was before or after the sudden slamming pain. The ringing in her ears replaced all capacity for thought. Warm blood flowed down into her eyes and her kicking stopped. The darkness around her was being replaced by a different kind.

3

God, he hated these bullshit assignments. Number seventeen was tasting even better. Why the fuck were they out here? Cartwright was playing them, he had no doubt. Nobody really had any doubt. How the hell did he end up working this kind of shit detail? Taken off a real job, one that he was getting somewhere on – an answer to the question that he could practically taste – and then he gets bundled into this one. And it wasn't that he didn't like Cliff, but he didn't like being kept in the dark. Why here? Why now? Why did they care? Bullshit.

"Jack, come in."

Speak of the Devil. Jack snatched up his radio and pressed in the button at its side.

"Cliff. What's up?" He waited.

"You been inside to check on our guests?"

"No I haven't."

"Do you think you could do that for me now then?"

"Sure… Why not?"

"Thanks."

Check on them. If there was any real worry they'd be in a safe house and he'd be camped outside their door. And that's where they had been – in a safe house, until he'd pulled them out. Fuck it. Probably just phasing them off the books. Another few days of rotating men around them before giving them the boot and telling them they were on their own. *But what about the hidden money, you say?* I guess we'll take our chances. Fucking bullshit.

Jack tossed number seventeen out the window and then wound it closed before opening the door and stepping out. He closed the door and stood for just a second pressing his fists into his lower back. With some crunching clicks his spine seemed to re-align. This was something he found himself doing more and more. He looked over to the building to see the seventeen, eighteen-year-old girl still standing there. He was pretty much obscured from her vision, as he'd parked the car in the darkness below the broken lamppost, but she was in his line and would see him as soon as he stepped onto the road and let her know that he was there.

One – two – There it was. A small grin came over Jack's face as he began crossing the road, heading for the front door of *'nameless building'*. His casual stride was not aimed in her direction, but he could tell that his presence was making her nervous. Mid-way his direction changed to face her.

4

Cold. She wasn't in bed anymore. She began forcing her heavy arm forward. She could feel that it was the floor that was cold. Her hand came to her forehead. She touched it carefully. Most of the blood was sticky now rather than wet. She tried to force herself to remember what was happening. She slid her eyes open.

They began to burn. Blood had pooled into both of them.

Where was he?

"Oh no. Mom. Jesus."

Tears flooded her eyes. The burning became worse. There was light. No direct source that she could latch hope onto, but she could see. She recognised where she was. It was the bathroom. A groan escaped her lips as she curled up on the cold tiles feeling the aching pain between her legs. She moved a shaky hand down there. Gently, she eased it in between her tightly clamped thighs. Her panties were gone and there was blood. Hers for sure this time. Her breathing began to quicken. Faster, faster. She couldn't slow it down. The panic was overcoming her.

One, two, three – she was on her feet and out the bathroom. Maybe he was gone. Left her for dead. She came to a stop as soon as she felt the wooden floor of the short corridor beneath her feet. Her breathing was coming out in sudden bursts as she tried to control it and keep it quiet. She let her eyes adjust to the darkness. The front door was to her right and the window to the fire escape, across from her. The window. One, two … Her knees gave and she thumped to the floor.

The small crumpled figure on the couch was her brother. Dead. Dead as a door nail. Deader than the deadest of all. The yellow spots were coming back. Tears brimmed up in her eyes again. She quickly wiped them away before the burning became too bad. She shook her head from side to side. It made her head hurt but it also made the yellow spots go away. Her eyes traced up to the couch again. She was glad she couldn't see him properly and turned her head away before her eyes adjusted any more to the darkness.

5

"What's your name?"

"Calista." She dragged on her cigarette smoothly.

A cool smirk told of her street-smart confidence. Her bruised cheek and the finger marks on her neck could have told the same or a different story. He was still fixed on the latter.

"Calista?"

She nodded, "Yes. Why?"

"Yeah right. What's your name?"

Another smirk. Less cool.

"What do you want it to be?"

"How about Jane Doe? More appropriate."

She didn't get it. She smoked on her cigarette again.

Jack gave her a smile. "How much?"

"For what?"

If not for her clothes, he might have bought this response. His gaze drifted down to her legs. They were thin.

"What happened to your knee?"

"Occupational hazard."

17

He had to laugh. Her cool composure was back. He looked at her breasts behind a tight red top. Small. Small breasts, skinny legs.

"A hundred dollars. For sex."

He looked at her face when she spoke. He was beginning to doubt she was even seventeen, eighteen years old.

"Go home Jane."

"What? What do you mean?"

"What's your name?"

Her cigarette seemed to slip from her fingers. Whether she meant to drop it or not it was too late now. It flew onto the road, caught by a gust of wind. He could just imagine her scuttling after it, desperate to take a few more drags from her last cigarette. Bought along with three other singles from the corner store. When he looked up at her again, her hand was holding an open pack of Marlboro Lights. Delicate fingers sliding out what looked like number six or seven. She put the cigarette between her lips. Using her hands to shield the wind, with the open pack of Marlboro Lights assisting, she lit the cigarette. Jack noted the stylishly small Zippo. Already putting her earnings to good use. Lighter, smokes, booze, drugs, clothes, fuck the food.

"My name's Frankie, okay. You happy now?"

"Frankie?"

She sighed. This was clearly starting to get old.

"Yes, Frankie. That's what my friends call me."

"Your friends, huh? Still see any of these friends?"

"Jesus Christ, man. What the fuck is this? A hundred dollars for sex. Do you want to fuck or what?"

Jack knew this was no good. He should be in the car drinking cold coffee. Not potentially making a spectacle of himself on the sidewalk in front of 'nameless building'. Time to end this, go inside, give Cartwright some shit, come out and smoke another one.

"No. I don't want sex."

No more time wasting for her. Things to see, people to do, bills to pay.

"Then I'm out of here." With a tight-shouldered turn, Frankie began her quick paced, small stepped strut off. "Fucking asshole."

Jack stood for a second to watch her leave. Too bad, he thought. Nice enough girl. Starting to harden, but still nice. He turned forward to finally go in but then turned to take another look. Small tits, skinny legs, nice ass. He went inside.

6

The blood glided off the blade onto the old rag he had brought along for that exact purpose. The knife had just gone in and out, twice, so easily. He was amused by the ease he had done all this with. Maybe he would feel guilty tomorrow but he doubted it. He had too much to do. Too much to plan for. He was a busy, busy man.

The stupid little bitch had just sat there. To kill her after she had passed out would have been boring. God, there it was again. He was starting to surprise himself. Just a quick two-step – yanked her up and then the rest was history. She had managed to get out a scream that time but he didn't think any of the neighbours could have heard it, or would have cared if they had.

One, two, three, four, everyone accounted for. BAM. Rapping against wood. The front door was directly behind him. He looked to the crumpled figure on the couch. Too much time wasting with the girl. Sloppy.

7

Jack waited. "Oh for God's sake." He knocked again. "Come on Cartwright, I don't got all damn night."

Jack looked at his watch. He turned his head, glancing down both sides of the corridor. Walls recently painted. Some kind of dull yellow. Maybe green. The wooden floors were still in good shape. Only three of the overhead lights were working. The other two were smashed. No glass on the floor beneath them. He smirked, almost turning his nose up, wondering how long it had taken before anyone had bothered to clean it up.

Jack reached forward and took hold of the door handle. As soon as the cold of the steel hit his hand he paused. What if? He flung his coat aside and found the handle of his Glock nine. He hesitated before drawing it from its holster. Did he really want to walk in there with gun in hand to find them all sitting there just watching TV too loud? He couldn't hear the TV. Jack turned the handle and as the door gave he pulled out his gun. Through the crack he could see the blackness of the apartment. Something didn't feel right. He pushed the door further in. He didn't have his radio on him. If something was wrong, the only way he would get help is if he fired off a shot.

Jesus, they were probably all just in bed asleep. This thought didn't ease the grip on his gun. He swung the door open. Still all black beyond the door. Jack took a step towards open doorway, his gun trained against the darkness. This was no good. He thought of Cliff round back. It would be better with some back up. He took a step back. What good would Cliff do in a situation like this?

He wasn't even an action man, he was a pencil pusher. Out here on guard in a blacked out assignment with a fucking file clerk for back up.

"Cartwright." He didn't want to call out too loud.

"Who's there?"

Jack froze, surprised by the sleepy voice. He didn't know how to respond. Another pause.

"It's me."

"Shit man, just come in."

The voice from the darkness sounded croaky, like Cartwright had just woken up. And although all this made sense, Jack's hands were starting to hurt from his ever-tightening grip.

"Turn on the lights."

…three, four. There was light. This eased Jack only a little. Still no

Cartwright in sight. He took a step forward, finally entering the apartment. It looked cluttered. The back of the two-seater couch was facing the door. He didn't know why, but this didn't seem right.

If he had looked around a bit more, Jack might have seen the raped and murdered daughter slumped against the wall to his left. Her white nightie with its picture of a castle in the clouds, now red with blood. Her blood, for sure.

Jack looked to the right. There was Cartwright finally. His relaxation was instantly dashed by realisation. Not Cartwright. He didn't hear anything. There were two flashes but no sound. Jack realised he couldn't hear anything at all. Nothing. No movement, no breathing. He didn't hear his gun fall and he didn't hear his body slamming to the floor.

CHAPTER TWO

1

Kathy Radley walked through the huge open building trying not to get irritated by all the rushing faces anxiously pushing past her. She was just glad to be off the plane and to be able to enjoy the feeling of having a behind again. The ever-talkative Cindy was yammering into her ear via her cell phone. Kathy was already regretting calling her.

She was back home in New York a day early, which meant that her replacement seat on her rescheduled flight had to be a coach one, from which she was still stiff and aching. Trouble, trouble, trouble, but from what Kathy could surmise it could all wait until tomorrow. She said her goodbyes to the still yammering Cindy and cut the conversation off. Kathy saw the luggage conveyor and made her way towards it. The spot-faced boy who'd told her where it was had been right, so the only person she could blame for taking so long to find it was herself.

In a day early, so no brother around to greet her and take her to his home. She had thought of calling David from the plane but decided against it. She wasn't really sure why. The fact was that he was undoubtedly very busy and also it would be nice to surprise him. Kathy grabbed her two bags and headed for the, thankfully obvious exit.

* * *

The sky was clear and the day was hot. This was one of the things that she had missed in the three years she'd been away. The street was heavy with traffic and the air was cluttered with noise. This she had not missed. Kathy closed her eyes and rubbed her fingers at the bridge of her nose. A headache was coming on. Another thing she could only blame herself for. Too many drinks on the plane. She raised a hand and was happy to see a cab pulling off towards her almost immediately. A young black man came out and took her bags. Kathy opened the back door and climbed in as he put her bags in the trunk.

2

Andrew pulled to a stop in front of Roseberry Homes, a decaying apartment building on the wrong side of town. He climbed out and freed his brown leather jacket before closing and locking the door. There were two marked police cars there already and he recognised one of the two unmarked ones. He went inside.

* * *

The receptionist was being questioned by one of the flat foots. Andrew pegged him as around thirty-eight and still trying to dress like a twenty year old. Andrew walked through the area, made up of dull browns and dingy beiges. He headed for the stairs.

"Listen, my friend, I was sleeping so I can't know."

Andrew smiled to himself. The 'as old as I feel' reception clerk couldn't help but act, sound, look and feel guilty. He probably didn't know anything, but having a cop that close was forcing up the defences.

"So you never saw anyone out of the ordinary?" The young flat foot continued to do his job.

"I was asleep. Sleeping." Andrew pegged the accent as Russian.

"Okay, you didn't see anyone, and nobody else who was here saw anything?"

"How you don't ask them for fuck's sake? I don't fucking know."

Their voices eventually disappeared as Andrew made his way up the stairs and headed for the fifth floor.

* * *

On entering the fifth floor apartment, Andrew had to close his eyes. All the curtains were open and the heavy light of the day was in stark contrast to the darkness of the buildings stairwell.

"Detective Bates. Good of you to show."

Andrew opened his eyes and blinked them into focus. He saw Bill Dudley standing in the centre of the room looking at him. Bill was everything his low easy voice suggested. Short, fat and balding. He was wearing better glasses these days, but Andrew still saw the black thick rims when he thought of him.

"Well, I thought it couldn't hurt to make an appearance."

Andrew made his way over to Bill, looking around as he went. Two uniforms standing off to the side not doing much of anything. Andrew had a hard time believing they'd already finished questioning the neighbours. The rest of the players were part of Bill's forensic team. Andrew took a moment to watch one taking pictures of some young girl slumped against the wall. Lots of blood. She couldn't have been older than fourteen.

Andrew rounded the centralised couch to come stand next to Bill. He was greeted by the sight of a small boy curled up on the once green seat cushions. They were now mostly a kind of dark brown. Bill held out a pair of latex gloves like the ones that he was wearing. Andrew took them and slipped them on.

"Jesus."

"I said shit." Bill smiled.

Andrew just looked at him. Bill shrugged it off and went down on his haunches followed by Andrew.

"Throat cut. Twice, if you can believe it." Bill indicated to the horrific mess of a wound.

Andrew stood back up, deciding that he didn't need to be that close to the front line.

"How many victims?"

Bill stood, "Four. Mr Cartwright in the bedroom. The boy. Mrs Cartwright in the kitchen, and the girl." Turning to look at Andrew, Bill's eyes widened dramatically, "That's all we've got on this lot as well. Cartwright. The name was in the ledger downstairs and they only just checked in yesterday."

"Checked in to be murdered, huh?"

"Looks like. You on this alone?"

There it was. Andrew was surprised that it'd taken this long for Bill to start digging.

"No. David's not in today, but he'll get caught up when I see him."

Bill nodded with clear dissatisfaction at this answer. Andrew headed him off before he could fine-tune his question.

"Any idea how it all happened?"

Bill was still nodding, "Um, yeah. I'm not positive about the order, but it looks like the boy first on the couch." Bill began to walk and Andrew followed. "The mother in kitchen."

Andrew looked back. "What about the girl?"

"No, she was last." Bill went into the kitchen.

Andrew stepped through the open doorway past Bill to see what he was looking at.

Bill continued. "Mrs Cartwright. See the defensive cuts on her hands and forearms?"

Andrew nodded as he examined the ragdoll form of the woman in her mid-thirties lying on the kitchen floor. The edge of a small table across her chest. Broken dishes and left over takeaway food all around. The cuts on the forearms and hands were deep and surrounded by dark lines of dry blood. With her skin as white as it was, these lines seemed like splinter cracks extending from the wounds. Her throat was uncut but her hair was slick and matted with blood.

"How was she killed?"

Bill turned back to the entrance of the kitchen and Andrew stepped to his side.

"She must have come out of the kitchen to see him kill her boy. Then when he came for her, she went for the knife."

Andrew nodded, watching Bill's short-stepped, half-done mimicking of the events.

"She got the knife and ran for the kitchen. The killer grabbed the first thing available."

Bill indicated to a golf club bag against the wall. He then pointed out the seven-iron lying on the floor. Its head was covered in blood. Turning back into the kitchen, Bill carried on with his dissection of the events.

"She grabbed for the table and took it down with her. You can see the smears of blood where her hands were."

23

Andrew looked, noting the two smears.

"You can also see where the knife landed."

Bill carefully stepped forward, negotiating the debris scattered across the floor. Andrew stayed where he was. On the other side of the victim Bill went down on his haunches above a small selection of blood streaks and speckles.

"If you can see, there's a small blood print of the point of the knife."

Andrew leaned forward to try and get a better look. It didn't help and was still all just streaks and speckles. He'd take Bill's word for it.

"Where's the husband during all this?"

Bill stood up. "That's a good question."

"That's why I asked it."

Bill negotiated his way back to Andrew and the two exited the kitchen. They headed towards the entrance of the dark corridor, which Andrew guessed lead to the bedrooms. Andrew stopped Bill, looking towards the young girl.

"What about her? How do you figure she was last?"

"She was raped. The only one." Bill walked over to the girl with Andrew close behind. "She was killed here but she was raped in her bedroom first. And maybe in the bathroom too."

Andrew shook his head, but only a little. Fourteen years old. Over and out.

"And the killer? Do we have anything on him? Fingerprints?"

"Not even a bloody footprint." Bill paused. "We haven't finished dusting yet, but I wouldn't bet on finding the killer's prints. He would have been wearing gloves. This may all look like seemingly sloppy shit, but I think the killer was careful and knew what he was doing."

"Anything strange, other than the obvious?"

"Did you see the door?"

He had. "No sign of forced entry. So either he had a key or they knew him."

"There's also this." Bill walked up to the couch with its back facing the door. "You see this? The rug under the couch."

Andrew looked at the rumpled and displaced rug half under the couch. "The couch was turned around. Why?"

"You got me."

"Okay, what about Mr Cartwright?"

* * *

The curtains were still closed inside the bedroom, so again Andrew had to blink his eyes into focus. The photographer was busy taking pictures of Mr Cartwright's large frame. which was sprawled across the bed. The repeated flashes meant that Andrew had to continuously refocus his eyes.

Cartwright's body was on its back. His eyes were closed and he looked like he was simply taking a long overdue nap.

"Was he asleep or something?"

Bill pointed to the empty bottle of Scotch on the bedside table. "Drank himself unconscious, apparently."

"That's seems strangely inconvenient."

"You're telling me. We'll get the blood work done and see what we see."

"How many wounds?"

"Eleven. Chest, stomach, and then one in the throat."

"So twelve?"

"No, sorry. Eleven includes the throat."

Bill took a moment before continuing. He brought his big left hand up to his head and ran it through his almost non-existent hair.

"I don't know. Maybe I'm wrong. Maybe the killer got in and snuck past the boy and mother and killed the father first."

Andrew didn't respond. He didn't think Bill had it wrong. He was a master of detailing crime scene events. If he said it happened this way, then that was good enough for him.

Bill continued, taking off his glasses to clean them as he did. "I'll have more to tell you once the autopsy's done."

"Okay, thanks Bill. I'll talk to you later then." Andrew slipped off his latex gloves.

"I'll get those for you." Bill took the latex gloves from Andrew.

"Thanks." Andrew turned to leave.

"Um, so this thing with David last night."

Andrew sighed turning back, "Yeah?"

"Does that mean the case is over or…"

"It was never ours to begin with Bill. We're just about the older brother. The rest was all Detective Wieze's deal."

"She was here, by the way."

Andrew's heart sank. He didn't want to have to deal with her.

"When?"

"Like forty minutes maybe, before you arrived."

"What did she say?"

"Nothing. She must have heard you were on this, cause she left soon as she saw you weren't here."

* * *

Inside the main living room area of the apartment, Andrew walked over to the two uniformed officers. He was starting to get a headache. He rubbed his eyes before coming to stand by them.

"Morning."

"Detective."

Andrew noted the officer's smug tone. He checked his badge. Officer Bishop. He was tall, blond and around twenty-two, Andrew guessed. And if appearances were anything to go by, dumb as shit. A ladies' man that never got the ladies.

25

"Have you finished questioning the neighbours?"

"Not yet. We will though, in a minute."

Andrew could tell this dumb shit wanted to smile. Andrew looked at Bishop blankly. Officer Townsend, who was next to Officer Bishop, was maybe just as dumb but not as tough. Two dumb flat foots giving him shit. He didn't need this.

Officer Townsend spoke. "We'll go finish up now sir."

Andrew looked at him. He liked this little brunette even less. Twenty-four, maybe twenty-five, but still a mama's boy. Andrew didn't know why people like this became cops.

"That's right. You will. Right now."

He looked at Bishop. After looking back for a moment of essential defiance, Bishop walked past Andrew and headed for the front door. Andrew watched them as they left. He remembered Bishop. Andrew smiled to himself. No wonder Bishop didn't like him.

"Andrew."

Andrew turned to face the voice with sour recognition.

"Jenny." He wasn't sure how that came out.

There she was, standing by the window. He should have ducked out of there the second Bill had mentioned her name. She started her graceful stride over. Things could have happened between them, and seeing the way the sunshine was lighting up that easy brown skin of hers, Andrew was feeling that pang of regret at knowing now he'd never get the chance.

She had the voice too. "You know what I heard this morning when I got into work?"

"I was going to call you but it only just happened. I..."

"You don't care at all, do you?" Her tone didn't change. "It wasn't your case, it was mine. That fucking partner of yours certainly made that clear often enough and now he's..."

She trailed off. Nobody wanted to say the words, not even her.

"Look, Jenny, nobody knows what happened yet so why don't we just cool it for now. We've still got Damon and..."

Her tone ratcheted up. "That idiot isn't worth shit to me. He was your boy. It was Garver who ran the show." She leaned in. "And nobody knows what happened? Are you joking? He went there to find him. And if you think your case is gonna hold up after this...." She trailed off, shaking her head. "It'll be thrown out as soon as the judge hears about it and then neither of us will have what we want."

Jenny turned to leave. "I'll see you in court.

3

The only light she had in the apartment was coming from David's nice big television. That was the best way to watch the tube. That, and wearing comfortable clothes and having a really, really comfortable couch. She had the clothes. Sleeping shorts and her stretched, frayed and holey sleeping shirt. The couch wasn't really that comfortable, but after raiding her brother's bedroom for blankets and pillows, she had made it tolerable.

The show on television wasn't one she knew. She probably didn't know too many anymore when she thought about it, but she was enjoying it. It was some drama series about a group of young friends living in the big city and going through life's growing up angst. It was funny and quite sweet.

Kathy reached for her drink which was easily accessible from the glass coffee table after she had rearranged the furniture for her perfect entertainment comfort. She had switched from coffee to beer about half an hour before. The primary result of this was more toilet breaks, but she could live with that. She put the beer back and reached for her lit cigarette. After a stretch to get it, she decided the ashtray needed to be just a bit closer.

She used the tips of her fingers to slide it towards her. Once satisfied that it was close enough, she brought the cigarette to her mouth and breathed in her favourite poison. She blew out the smoke as she tried to mentally recount the cigarettes she'd had that day. None on the plane and none in the cab. She settled on about ten or eleven. Not too bad. She didn't want to think about the day before when there was no plane trip to cut into her dirty little habit. But eleven was okay. She'd have to keep it a bit lower. Doctor's orders. Well, doctor's orders were to quit, but what the hell did he know.

The last thing in the world Kathy saw herself doing was quitting then. Too much stress in her life. And it was all to start a day early thanks to Giovanna suddenly having to jet off to go do another face-to-face massage job on some nervous money men. Not that her own time in France organising and fine-tuning future publication pipelines, coupled with sorting the final details of her own de-immigration back to the States and bla de bla was exactly an easy going time. Either way, she'd be back in the deep end come the morning, but for now she could sip beer and breathe in nicotine.

4

David slipped one of the nameless tapes scattered throughout the glove compartment into the car's tape deck. He had thought of getting a CD player but then that had evolved into that iPod thing and now he just couldn't be bothered. The tape deck was good enough. He had a CD player at home and could easily make tapes for the car, although that was another thing he had never bothered to do. He just listened to the radio or the same old shit he had in the car. Maybe he'd make some tonight, but he doubted it. David was looking forward to a quiet relaxing night in. He hadn't slept in it had to be near enough 36 hours.

David pressed play and eased back into his seat. He was tired. Tired of work, and sleepy, and just mentally spent. The song started. David slowed the car to a stop for the red light. Deep Purple. Nice. A little Rock to keep the neurons pumping enough to keep him from ploughing into a bus load of pregnant nuns, or something like that.

A young oriental woman walked past the front of his car. David watched her as she went. Straight black hair. She couldn't have been an inch over five feet. Not slim, but she still looked good in her blue jeans and black mid-thigh coat. She turned to look his way. He wasn't sure if she could see past the darkness of his windscreen, but she flashed a smile. David smiled back and almost waved. She was pretty. Small eyes and a fairly wide jaw, but she had a prettiness that David found so new. She looked ahead again and continued on her way.

David looked at himself in the rear view mirror. He needed a shave. The past 36 hours hadn't been kind to him and his edges were looking a little rougher than usual. It was an old man's face looking back at him and one that he barely recognised anymore. Salt and pepper hair looking a lot saltier nowadays.

The light turned green and David pulled off to continue on his way. It started to rain. A few drops at first, and then a decent steady flow. David watched the night pedestrians as most rushed to escape the potential downpour. Some paid it no mind and just carried on with what they were doing. David was glad to be in his car. He didn't like being caught in the rain anymore. He was reminded of the gash on his hand and with that it began to throb. The bandage around it was brown at the top with dried blood. He imagined that it would be stuck to his flesh and trying to change it would mean re-opening the wound.

* * *

David leaned against the wall of the elevator as it made its way towards his floor. God, he didn't know that he'd be able to make it to his bed. The couch was an idea. The rug by the door? The hallway carpet before the door? The elevator floor? Maybe the bed. The elevator doors opened and David slogged out and turned to the side which he hoped headed in the general direction of his door.

He was tired. He found his door and then found his keys. As soon as the door began to open, David heard voices. Soft voices that he couldn't make out. People talking – the TV. He put his hand on his gun and took a step forward. The voices cut out and he stopped, hesitating. What had Phil yelled at him?

"Dave?"

He recognised the voice, but whose was it? His head was full of sleep.

"Kathy?" He quickly stepped in and turned on the lights.

The apartment lit up and he saw his kid sister springing off his misplaced couch and quickstep towards him. She was smiling. He walked to meet her. This was strange, and when they reached each other that strangeness became obvious. Kathy broke the pause and hugged him and he hugged her back. It felt right but it still hurt to know that it wasn't the norm anymore. David eased off but his sister continued to squeeze. It was good to feel, and David felt his tension wane at this act of what felt like true affection.

She let go and looked up at him. She didn't speak. She just smiled. David never knew how to respond to these kinds of silent moments. He didn't know what to do at all. Now that the initial joyful hug was over, what did he say?

He hadn't seen her in three years. Hadn't spoken to her in over a year, except when she called to say she was coming down. All he could do was smile back and hope for her to break it open and get it started. Kathy lowered her head and patted David's chest three times before stepping back. This awkward moment was turning into an awkward marathon.

"You first," Kathy said, limply raising her hand at him before shifting into a hands-on-hip stance.

"Hmm," David said taking a moment. "Have you been smoking?"

"Aah." His sister turned away waving a dismissive hand in his direction.

David found himself smiling as he watched her head towards his couch. She grabbed her beer and came walking back towards him.

"I've been drinking your beers."

"Just so long as there's some left for me."

David eased out of his coat, being careful not to snag his bandaged hand as it ran through the sleeve. He hadn't noticed her leave but now she was back and dutifully holding a freshly opened bottle of beer for him to take. He did and took a sip. It was nice, but the first swallow made his eyes water and his nose burn. His tired body rejecting the late night invitation to stay awake.

He pulled the beer out of his mouth mid-way through the second sip. David quickly swallowed what he hadn't dribbled over the floor and then quickly went for the foaming beer pouring from the bottle. Once containing the situation David looked back to his sister. She was smiling her usual smile, the one David didn't know how to respond to. He switched the bottle to his left hand and then shook the right to rid it of its thin beer coating.

"Thanks. I needed that."

"You're welcome. Still wearing those dull suits and ties every day." She was looking to the grey coat that he'd chucked onto the small table by the still open front door.

David turned to close and lock the door. "This is my detective uniform." When he turned back, she was walking away from him, headed towards the television.

"Come, let's sit. Talk."

She turned her head to briefly smile at him after saying this, which seemed to make the awkwardness that they'd been chipping away at disappear. If only briefly.

He followed on and took a more prepared sip from his beer. "I see you've made yourself at home already."

David stopped in his steps, remembering his gun. His sister was already on the couch waiting for him to join her. He pulled his clip-on holster easily from his belt and put it on the counter of his open plan kitchen as he walked past. His eyes went up to see what was on the tube, but stopped at his sister's long deep red hair. He smiled to himself and continued forward. He had missed her.

Kathy spoke again as David walked between her and the TV, making his way to sit next to her.

"You been at work? Pretty late." Her eyes traced his progression from his body blocking her view to him sitting down next to her.

"Paper work. The dreary side of being a cop." David watched her watching him and once seated he caught her eyes and she looked away.

She sipped her beer and he sipped his.

"So Phil let you in?"

Kathy turned her head back to David. "Phil?"

David opened his mouth to clarify but Kathy continued.

"Oh, the guy at the front desk. The... how would you call it? The receptionist? Yeah, he said that you said I was coming." Another smile. "So he was ready for me."

"Good." David gave a satisfied nod and turned back to the TV.

Kathy's eyes were still on him. He could feel them. He turned his head to look at his sister again. Her eyes stayed fixed on him for another quiet, unflinching eternity.

"It's great to see you, Dave."

He didn't want to speak. He stopped a smile before it developed. He had to leave her to control the moment. She then closed her eyes and with the tip of her tongue, pulled her lower lip back and bit down. Her eyes opened. Her stare was no longer piercing, but saddened. If only a little. It scared David to think how much his sister had changed over the past three years. He didn't know her anymore. Still, she seemed better.

"I'm sorry I haven't been in contact with you."

"You're here now," he smiled.

"Yes, and it's not just because of the shows and the whole thing. I..." She stopped and David saw the reflection of the TV in her eyes, "It is why I came down, but I wanted to see my brother. You know that, don't you?"

David took her hand in his. "I know that." He squeezed her hand and let go. "You're here. We can see each other now."

Kathy's expression suddenly changed as she reached out and grabbed David's bandaged left hand. She held it up, looking at it closely.

"What happened to your hand?" She touched carefully at the darkened bandage.

David eased his hand free of her gentle grip. He held his hand in the other, carefully caressing it with the lengths of his fingers. It saddened David to see that Kathy was unconsciously doing the same to her own scarred left hand.

"Nothing. Just a scrape from a fall."

His sister was staring at him again. It was the truth. Sort of. He was beginning to remember how tired he really was. He hadn't slept in 36 hours.

5

Andrew looked at his watch – 01:47 in the morning. It had been a long day.

Bill was faffing around with one of his little helpers who seemed like the weight of the late night was resting on her eyelids. They'd been fucking around for ages. Andrew hated being stuck in this narrow cluttered place. All the space was taken up by small metal tables not big enough to hold more than one piece of whatever it was they were – computer equipment of some variety – and maybe a cup of cold coffee in a Styrofoam cup. And, of course, the rest of the space was taken up by huge metal shelves filled with boxes and vials and... Andrew sighed and reached for his cold cup of coffee and took a sip which he instantly regretted.

He didn't have to be here. Bill had told him it would be a while but there he sat on his awkward stool waiting to hear if the man who had been stabbed had been poisoned to boot. That was the word that had brought Andrew down to the lab. *Poison*. Not enough alcohol in his blood to knock him out. Not by a long shot, according to Bill, so it begged the question: Why didn't he act? Save his family. Why'd he just lie there waiting to get stabbed?

His blood apparently wasn't giving anything up, but Bill was checking that little bit that was still left in the bottle which they'd found by his bed. Andrew, unthinkingly, sipped his coffee again. That was it.

"What have you got for me, Bill? Give me something."

Andrew slid off his stool and chucked his next to full Styrofoam cup in a bin that was just far enough away for the action to leave a streaked mess across the floor. The black haired little helper looked at him and he looked back. She looked away.

"You're the one who bolted down here, Detective. I would have thought you'd have something better to do on a Saturday night."

Bill was right. He didn't need any interesting work in his life at the moment, not with their last case still lingering in court, and now made that much more interesting in itself with what his partner had done. But then soon as this new one had stopped making logical sense, he'd spread himself all over it like a rash.

"Make that Sunday morning now Bill. You said you had something for me over the phone and then it changed to almost, and now here we still are."

Bill let out a tired sigh as he leaned back in his chair. "I'm not sure. There's something in this but I can't isolate it. Go home. Tomorrow I'll have it all broken down and I'll have something for you then."

Andrew rubbed his eyes. "Any theories?"

"Just the original one. Poisoned, but I'm thinking poisoned just to knock him out. Not to kill him."

Andrew nodded giving this a second to sink in. "Okay." He turned and grabbed his jacket. Time for bed.

CHAPTER THREE

1

Time to get up – Time to get up – Time to get up! Andrew slammed his hand down onto his bedside clock trying to shut it up. On the second slam the repetitive alarm cut out. Seven-thirty already. It felt like he hadn't slept at all. What day was it? The ceiling began to blur and then went black. Roughly ten seconds of cognitive thought before sleep would have him. With a heavy groan and a heavy head, Andrew sat up whilst still keeping his eyes closed. They didn't want to be opened and he didn't want to disappoint them, but… He opened them and swung his legs over the edge of the bed. The wooden floor was cold. Rubbing his eyes, Andrew tried to remember why he had to be up this early. It didn't come to him. For now he'd have to just take it on faith that there was a good reason and get ready for whatever the day had in store for him.

* * *

Now with a strong cup of black coffee in his hand and a fresh shower under his belt, Andrew began to take in the world with a clearer head. He strolled from his small kitchen back to his bedroom and began sorting out his clothes. No court appearance today, which Andrew was getting well and truly tired of, but the lawyers had called him last night demanding that he be in to see them bright and early.

They were, of course, pissed off that no one had been in contact with them and they had to hear about the whole thing through the grape vine. They said they couldn't get hold of David either, which didn't surprise Andrew as he'd been trying that all day. It was a mess and now it was time to go in and see if it could be cleaned up. Andrew didn't think it would hurt their case even if Detective Jenny Wieze did, and she would undoubtedly be waiting along with the lawyers for his arrival. No, it was a mess, but the evidence against old Garver Harris' brother was solid. He wasn't going anywhere but down.

2

Kathy yawned deeply as she draggingly stomped her feet to the living room. Her yawn finished, she decided to give herself another arms out stretch to see if it would be as satisfying as her last, and it almost was. As she turned into the kitchen, her eye caught sight of the mess she had left behind in the living room. A coffee cup, five beer bottles and an ashtray surrounded by ash. She would clean it up – the mess wasn't that bad. It wasn't like she was an annoying house guest who comes in and takes over but doesn't lift a finger to help. She was family, and family is owed a little slack. Besides, she was going to clean it up. Though, first things first. A cup of coffee.

Kathy reached around opening the various cabinets in what she was beginning to realise was a very nice kitchen. She grabbed the essentials – coffee, sugar, milk from the fridge, all the while thinking just how nice the place actually was. Doorman downstairs and a big apartment upstairs. Uptown too.

She knew why David had the place but the thought of it had crept up on her and made her heart twinge. She'd left soon after her brother's divorce and it hurt her to think that maybe it had all been because of her. She filled the kettle and clicked it on. One, two, one, two? No. She decided against it and only took the one cup off its hook. Her brother had looked shattered and would probably need his sleep. Okay, kettle on, water boiling. Time for a smoke. Kathy walked over to the mess she'd left behind to see if she could see where she had left her cigarettes. As she arched her neck and trained her eyes towards the coffee table she…

"Ooh shit."

Kathy bared her teeth seeing the thick deep groove on the finished hard wood floor. It seemed to start from the couch's original position and ended somewhere underneath it.

"Ooh shit."

She looked towards her brother's bedroom. A flush of heat was going through her as she began to feel like one of those annoying house guests. Then, thankfully, she spotted her cigarettes.

* * *

Kathy decided to skip the shower portion of the morning, as she'd had one the day before to wash away her plane journey and also to get out and on her way without having to meekly get into it with her brother. Her meekness would just have to wait for later because she hadn't been able to cover the groove. So she'd have to wait and see what she would see. He probably wouldn't give a shit anyway, and obviously she was going to pay for it. Kathy noticed the cab driver look away as she caught his reflection in the rear view mirror. She pulled the door closed and secured her seat belt.

"Where to?"

* * *

Kathy Radley had always loved the world of fashion. From when she was a tiny little girl with her Barbie dolls, mixing and matching their outfits, to a teenager when she would rebel against the current flavours, in the trendiest way possible, of course.

She loved it even more now. She loved the back scratching and backstabbing. A world of big egos and bigger paychecks. From the bitchy models to the foppish designers to the sleazy photographers to the money grubbing agents. Yes, this was a sick, sick world where excess was the name of the game and reality didn't ever enter into it. She loved it.

33

As a teenager, Kathy had wanted to be one of the beautiful people walking the white line and shining iconically on the glossy pages. But while she was pretty in her own strange way with her deep red hair and freckly white skin, it just wasn't the right kind of pretty, and she could never quite get thin enough. She was also too short.

As a young woman preparing to go to college, she had come to terms with the flawed look God had seen fit to burden her with. So, she had figured, with her keen ability to mix and match which she had nurtured since childhood, she would be a designer. Besides, she didn't want to be one of those self-centred bitches anyway. But she quickly realised that she was cack handed with a pencil – God and his funny ways, clearly getting a kick out of testing her. So when college came around, she had decided to study the deeper side of things. If she couldn't do any of these things herself, she could damn well judge those who thought they could.

* * *

As she walked into the lobby of the luxurious hotel housing all the various degrees of people who had flown in to be part of the fashion event of the decade as she liked to think of it, the stress and exhilaration of the world she had chosen to live in hit her like a sudden but welcome wave. The small jittery figure that was Cindy Tao spotted her instantly and quickly rushed over in her permanently panicked way.

"Kathy, Kathy." Cindy reached her and continued hyperventilating out her words. "Thank God you're here!"

"Hello Cindy."

"Yeah. The hotel guy says there's some trouble with some of the rooms. Some double bookings and Lyle Tadworth is threatening to walk if they don't sort it out. He says if anyone tries to put him in another hotel, the hissy-shit's gonna hit the fan."

"He said that?"

"Yes. Why are you smiling?"

Tadworth, a foppish designer on the rise. Kathy led them walking further into the lobby.

"He's not pulling out of anything. This is his big chance to make his mark, and he knows it."

"Well, the troubles don't end there." Cindy shuffled through her papers trying to ensure she got all the quotes exactly right. "No one's been able to get hold of Gabe. His assistant said he disappeared two days ago, and now Katrina Mile is apparently trying to pull out of wearing Carvell's showstopper."

"Why?"

"She says it makes her ass look too big."

"Someone should tell her big butts are in."

"Very funny. What about Gabe?"

34

"It's still morning. Give him a chance to sober up. He'll be in."

Kathy watched the various degrees arguing amongst themselves and shifting their blame to their underlings. Chaos was all around as was to be expected. Part and parcel of an event like this. A fashion parade held over two weeks with three main shows in three different locations. She was a little concerned about Gabe as he had let her down before, but he was the best, and the best was exactly what was required. The spread sheets had to be perfect for the launch of the new powerhouse magazine being born out this charade. Time to make her rounds.

3

David smirked at seeing how his baby sister had cleaned up her mess. It was vintage Kathy. Maybe she hadn't changed that much. The big groove aside, which he knew was from the plastic foot of the couch which always popped off leaving a big exposed screw behind, there was also a substantial amount of ash, now wet and clogged into the space between the coffee table's glass surface and its metal frame. David pondered whether or not to tell her that he didn't smoke anymore and preferred to keep this a non-smoking apartment. He sighed as he stood up from his haunches and walked over to his kitchen. Then he decided, seeing his old wet dirty ashtray in the sink, that this was in fact a non-smoking apartment.

* * *

David made himself a cup of coffee, had his shower and rolled into work at 12:30. Walking past the rows of desks and navigating his way through the crowds of cops and apprehended robbers, he spotted Bill Dudley's large frame talking to someone who was obscured from view by some kind of large pot plant that was completely out of place in this grimy setting. Eventually David reached his office and went in closing the door behind him. He had about ten seconds of peace before the door swung open and Bill trudged in holding his usual clipboard.

"Afternoon Detective. Hour's a little late, isn't it?"

"Hello Bill. How's your day been?" David slipped off his coat and hung it on the back of his uncomfortable chair.

"Tiring. It's been a long day already. Not all of us can afford the luxury of strolling into work come afternoon time."

"Well it's Sunday. I think we deserve a little slack on a Sunday." David took his seat. "What are you doing here on a Sunday anyway Bill? Surely the world can wait till Monday to get the answers they need."

"I'm here all day, every day Detective. You should know that." Bill did a half paced turn as he flipped through a few pages of his clipboard before making his next comment. "Weren't in yesterday either, as far as I saw."

He was digging and David didn't have the patience for it.

"You got something for me Bill?"

David's desk creaked disapprovingly as Bill seated his left cheek on its edge.

Bill flipped past the first two pages on his clipboard again.

"You seen Andrew yet?"

"Not yet. Why? What've we got?"

"The Cartwright's. Family of four. Fourteen year old daughter, ten year old son. All butchered at their place of residence, which for this one night was Roseberry Homes. Heard of it?

"No. What do you mean, 'this one night'?"

"One night. According to the registrar, they checked in and got done on the same night. The low down is no sign of forced entry, hunting knife was the weapon of choice – unrecovered. Daughter raped, and the big finish – preceding the head of the family's, Mr Cartwright's eleven stab wounds, he was drugged by an exotic agent which was in his mostly empty but largely unconsumed bottle of bedside whiskey."

"What the fuck does that mean?"

"It means that while he was poisoned by what was in the bottle, he didn't drink much of it. There wasn't really any alcohol in his blood so it looks like he had maybe a sip or two before he was out."

David shook his head to try and get rid of Bill's words. "Okay, so he was drugged and that means that he was unconscious when he was killed."

Bill was nodding.

"So it was a hit."

"Could be."

David shook his head again. "So why not just poison him, why drug him?"

"You got me. Don't know that this stuff was meant to be found. Pretty much disappears in the blood stream. Only managed to find it from the last little bit that was in the bottle."

"We got a work up on this guy?"

Bill lifted himself off the desk and started for the door. "Nothing to ID them on sight, so you'll have to check with Dana on that one."

David leaned back in his chair as Bill left his office, pulling the door closed behind him. He was still tired. He'd had enough sleep but it was all just hanging heavily on his mind. Of course it was all going to get more and more complicated. Now that that bastard Garver was gone, he'd have more tools than ever to get him. The only thing left to do now was to wait.

David let his eyes drift around the office which he shared with Andrew. He turned himself in his chair as he followed his eyes as they settled on the window at the rear wall. The heavy light of the day was shafting through the blinds. David stood from the chair, still following his eyes as they drifted closer to the window. He lifted the blinds, letting the light fill the gloomy office. Things were coming apart and he didn't know if he would be able to put them back together again. He wondered what Jane would think about him. Now that her name was Jane Booney she could think what she wanted, but did she leave room to let herself understand him? He hoped so.

The streets and sidewalks were alive. Its people moved to and fro, filling their lives with the things and tasks that afforded them the meaning needed to help press them on. He let the blinds fall closed again.

* * *

Dana was their girl at the keyboard, hidden away down in the basement along with Bill Dudley's unit. Her environment was a series of small cramped maze-like rooms where she and her handful of staff sorted through the behind the scene lives of every name that came across every desk in the building. David wondered how anybody could function down here. Even in the narrow approaching corridor, the walls seemed to be moving in on him. You just couldn't breathe. The air conditioners were audibly working overtime, but still the air seemed thick and stagnant.

Dana had been working at the precinct since before David had started there almost ten years earlier. He wasn't sure how old she was, but he pegged her at about forty-five – four years younger than himself. She had a slight sternness to her and while she was still pretty, she kept her blonde hair short and plainly styled. A lesbian, or at least that's how the rest of the precinct had pegged her. He wasn't sure himself but hell, she probably was. If she was, then she was. David didn't pretend to understand these things, but he knew it didn't make any difference either way. Each to her own, he guessed.

"Hey Dana. How you doing?"

She looked up at him through her frameless glasses. "Afternoon Detective."

She finished typing a few more things into her computer, another one of those things he didn't pretend to understand. After a few more seconds, she swivelled in her seat away from her computer screen to face him.

"You're here for the Cartwright file?" She didn't wait for a response. "There isn't one."

"Nothing come through on their prints?"

"Nothing yet. It might still happen, but then they might just not be in the system. Nothing's come up on that name either, though."

"No ID on them, and nothing in the system. Little strange."

Dana nodded. "I'll keep digging and let you or your partner know if anything pops up."

Dead end from the get go. David decided he could live with that. He had enough excitement in his life as it was.

"Thanks Dana." He turned to leave.

"How's your ex-wife doing, Detective?"

David turned back to her deciding there was no easy out this time. "She's okay. In and out of hospital. Nothing serious."

David could see her eyes reading his own.

"You spoken to her yet?"

"Look Dana, if you don't mind I…"

"You need to. It'll just be more complicated if she finds out from somebody else."

Of course she was right. David didn't know how to say this because he still didn't want to believe it was true.

"I'll see you later." He turned to navigate his way out again.

"Goodbye Detective."

* * *

Now back in amongst the ravel, David was suddenly startled by the small presence of Stacy Keen as she appeared in front of him, blocking his path.

"The boss is looking for you. Now."

As quickly as she had appeared, she was gone. David didn't even see which way she went. A lurking fixture in the place. Time to face the music.

* * *

"Good to finally see you, Detective. You're not an easy man to get hold of these days."

David pulled the door of the spacious office closed. Chief Derrick Groder was sitting at his desk. He was almost sixty years old and although you could see it in his face, he was still a man with whom you did not fuck. Stories had circulated back and forth about an unfortunate mugger who was not privy to this rule. The gist involved a broken wrist and a broken jaw. Some variations included the loss of an eye, but to hear the Chief tell it, none of it was true.

"I'm here now, Chief. Whatever needs to be said can get said now."

"Don't get short with me, Detective. When I call, you pick up. Understand? You fucking go into hiding and I'm left to deal with the mess. I was on the phone for over an hour with Detective Wieze's Captain yesterday, listening to him chew me out about how me and mine fucked up almost a year's worth of work for them." He looked at David waiting for a response. "Nothing to say?"

David didn't have anything.

The Chief indicated to one of the two seats across from his own. "Take a seat."

David pulled out one of the leather-padded chairs and sat down. Here it came.

"Tomorrow you'll be in before twelve. I.A.D. wants to talk to about the Garver Harris shooting. They're gonna want to talk to Andrew as well, so you make sure to tell him." The Chief sought out David's eyes before continuing. "Now nothing has been decided by anyone on this, but it's all just a little too close to home."

"Are you telling me to get a lawyer?"

The Chief paused at this before leaning in across the desk. "David, when I tell you the implications of this are serious, I want you to take it seriously. But I say again, no one has decided anything on this. Just come in tomorrow and tell

38

them what happened." The Chief settled back in his chair. "Of course, if you think you need a lawyer then I can't stop you, but I'm telling you now it would be a mistake."

"Anything else?" David planted his hands on the arms of the chair, preparing for his curt exit.

"No."

"Good." David stood himself up and turned for the door.

"What are you up to now?"

David turned back slowly, hating that the moment was being prolonged. "Ah, new case. The Cartwright business. Family murdered in their home."

David turned his head back to look at the door as the sound of knocking on its glass came through. The door opened and Andrew stuck his head through.

"David, hey. You busy?"

The Chief spoke out waving a dismissive gesture with his hand. "No Detective Bates, we're done here. David."

David turned away from the annoyingly knowing look on Andrew's face to the annoyingly stern one on the Chief's.

"Be in tomorrow on time, and fill in Detective Bates on what's expected of him."

"Will do."

Andrew stepped back out of the way giving the Chief his best smarm as he did. "Boss."

David saw the Chief looking down, ignoring this. Fuck, fuck, fuck. Time to go. David walked out, pulling the door closed behind him.

* * *

"You gonna talk to Jane about this?"

Andrew was driving too fast as usual. They had left David's car at the station.

"Tomorrow." He was still feeling tired, "Tomorrow afternoon, after I.A.D."

"Hmm… Lawyers are asking after you."

David hated these kinds of searching abbreviated talks, though he sure as shit didn't want to talk about it properly.

"I'll talk to them later too."

Andrew let it go.

* * *

David ducked under the police tape, following Andrew into the Cartwright apartment. What a shit hole. He scanned the area and saw bloodstains on the floor by the wall to his left. Andrew continued on to the large window and then threw open the curtains.

"What's up with this?" David gestured to the once green seats of the couch.

39

Andrew strolled over. "That's where the boy was."

"And this?" David eased down onto to his haunches feeling his knees complain, but not too much. He stroked at the bunched up carpet beneath the couch. "Couch turned?"

"Well spotted."

"Why?" David stood back up, using the misplaced couch for support.

"That's the question on everyone's lips."

"The killer."

"Maybe. What are you thinking?"

David stepped off to do a little pacing. Why, how, who, what, when? He looked back at Andrew.

"Did Bill give you a break down?"

"Yeah, boy first."

David stopped pacing. He didn't know. He didn't care. The Cartwrights were dead and they had nothing to go on. He had more important things on his mind, like how good a cigarette would be.

"I don't know. The couch was clearly facing the door so someone turned it away from the door. If it was the killer then he must have been doing a quick hide job from someone who was coming in."

"Could be that Bill got things a little off and maybe Mom came in late. He hears her and turns the couch away so he can... Yeah, something like that. Bill's break down made a lot of sense though. What do you think?"

David thought that he was definitely going to buy himself some smokes as soon as they got out of there.

Andrew continued. "Could be another element to this case. Did you speak to Bill at all?"

David's head was starting to feel tight. He looked briefly at Andrew.

"Huh? Ah, yeah. Sorry. Yeah I saw him earlier."

"What did he say about the poison? The drug in the bottle?"

"Yeah, he said there was something in it. Some drug that seems to have been meant to knock him out. So whatever happened here, it looks like Mr Cartwright was the main target."

David could see by the way Andrew rubbed his chin as he took this in that he was being pulled in by the mystery of it all. Fuck, he needed a cigarette. David wondered if he edged towards the door he could get Andrew to blindly follow him out to the car.

"Okay." It was Andrew's turn to pace. "They drug him to knock him out, but not to kill him. They get their guy to knife him so they know he's dead. The guy makes a mess. Rapes the daughter so it all looks like some random sick shit."

David nodded along without much obvious enthusiasm. It sounded good.

"Dana couldn't pull anything on them. Nothing on any of their prints."

He saw Andrew's eyes light up. He almost wished he hadn't told him.

"Nothing to identify any of the victims. Nothing on the computer. Poison hidden in a bottle. We might have just stumbled onto something big here."

Time to put an end to this excitement. "Well don't get too excited. When I say nothing, think of the word 'nothing' as key." David turned for the door. "I don't know that we should call the government and see if Cartwright is a spy just yet."

David ducked under the tape and then turned back to see Andrew not following. Shit.

"That doesn't sound so crazy." Andrew was finally making to leave with him. David stepped aside as Andrew ducked under the tape and came to stand next to him before finishing his thought. "Maybe he's not a spy but something's going on here. Witness protection maybe."

"You gonna close the door?"

4

"Listen to me you drunk son-of-a-bitch. You'd better be here tomorrow, first fucking thing or else I'm gonna get the lawyers involved and we're gonna sue you ass for breach. I will personally make sure you never work again."

Six o' clock and already three days behind. At least that's how it felt. And now with no functioning Gabe there was little else to do until …

"What did you say? Listen to me you… Gabe, I'm serious. Give Lisa the phone." Jesus, Giovanna was gonna be happy with all the progress when she got back. "Yes, Lisa. Just make sure he's here tomorrow on time or it's your ass too. You got me? Goodbye." Kathy slammed the phone down.

She let herself rest back in her chair and sighed out the tension of the day. What a day. Kathy took in her surroundings. What was this place? Too big to be a closet, but this cramped room would serve as her office until the finish of the first show. After that, if all went well with Giovanna's smooth talking, they'd at least have their temporary office space lined up.

Was that a mop? Kathy stood out of her chair and rounded the small antique, or so she'd been told, desk to investigate. One box, two boxes – yes, a mop. Dry. Thank God for small miracles. It was okay. Once this was done – once the show was underway and the magazine was off the ground – she would be the one scheduled for the office space with actual windows with actual views of actual things worthy of putting windows in front of. Kathy looked back to her chair over which her coat was draped. Time for a smoke. It had been at least two hours. She was quite proud. Of course, the reason it had been two hours was because she had been chain-smoking almost all day and had promised herself to not have another one until her day was done. Still, two hours. Bit of a milestone. She would have a cigarette to celebrate.

Back in her seat she pulled her coat round and took out her lighter and cigarettes. Camel Lights. Not her brand because her brand had not been in stock. She took one out and lit it. As she breathed in the not too bad smoke she remembered that it was her brand of choice back in the day when she bought her first pack. God, that was probably almost fifteen years ago. She'd only started in college, so that would make her … Kathy preferred to cut the thought short before

41

the answer came to her.

She had been stuck in this building for the past too many hours. It was old, run down and not very attractive, but its location was perfect. Pretty damn big too, and once they were done with it it would be a dazzling spot for the first show. Things had slowed down enough for her to pawn off some of the duties, but her day had been filled with pointing, shouting, phone calls, sorting, calming and assuring. At least the catwalk was pretty much finished. Temporary home time.

5

It took some convincing, but Andrew knew that a drink was exactly what David needed. He looked ahead at David's brake lights shining out of the darkness as his car slowed to a stop at a pedestrian crossing. His sister, huh. Andrew had known that she existed but David had never mentioned her in the two plus years they'd been partners. Now suddenly she was staying with him. This was going to be interesting. Why was she back? Why had she left? Why didn't David talk about her? An intriguing little mystery. He was a detective after all. What did she look like?

6

Kathy got out of the lift, having arrived at what she thought she remembered as the right floor. The floor number looked right as she stepped out of the elevator. One, two, three... and there it was. She used the spare key her brother gave her. She unlocked and opened the door. God, what time was it? She ached all over. Late enough. Straight to bed for her. She walked in, turning on the light and closing the door behind her. She walked over to the open plan kitchen and put her bag down on the counter. Slipping off her jacket, Kathy crumpled it down next to her bag before opening the fridge. One beer left. She'd have to risk it. As she reached for the last beer, the sound of David's key hitting the lock made her change her mind.

7

David opened the door and Andrew followed him in. Before Andrew saw her, he heard her voice.

"Hey bro."

Andrew stepped in passed David to see her mildly surprised expression.

"Oh, hello."

"Kathy, this is my partner, Andrew Bates. Andrew, this is my sister."

Andrew stepped forward to shake her hand over the kitchen counter. "Hi. I was surprised to hear you were back in town."

Accepting his hand, Kathy smiled. "Oh really?" She looked at her brother, who Andrew could tell was avoiding eye contact. "Well, I'm here for work mostly. It's good to meet you."

"You too."

She was kind of on the short side. Maybe five four. Andrew liked her hair.

"Ah, me and your brother were gonna go out for a drink. Thought maybe you'd wanna join us."

He could see his partner about to shift down a gear.

"Yeah actually, maybe…"

This would not do. "Come on. I think after today we could all do with a drink. Plus it feels kinda weird us not knowing each other."

Kathy walked out from behind the kitchen counter. "Where to? Some kind of cop bar?"

"No, no. I think we can find some place a little nicer." Andrew could feel David not talking.

"Well you're not wrong about today. I could definitely use a drink." She picked up her bag and coat and walked past him to the door. "You okay Dave?"

"Yeah, yeah, I'm okay. Long day?"

Kathy squeezed David's arm. "You have no idea. Your timing is pretty good though. I only just, just got in. You guys must have been just behind me."

Andrew stepped up, careful not to check out her ass. "I guess it was meant to be then. Should we go? I know just the place."

David was looking at him. He couldn't place the look but figured it was best to tone it down. David reached behind himself and pulled the ajar door back open. He looked down at Kathy, ushering her out past him. He then flashed Andrew the look again.

Quietly. "What?"

David turned and followed Kathy out.

Quieter. "Shit." Andrew followed on after, pulling the door closed behind him.

8

He was a little obvious but kinda cute. Still, she didn't think she'd have time for anything of that sort. He had actually managed to pick quite an interesting place, clearly for her benefit. She could tell her brother didn't know it. Gorgeous women about the place and Andrew would have his work cut for him when the fake breasted, pierced and tattooed barmaid got round to serving them. Here she came. This could be amusing.

David took out his wallet. "I got this one."

Ah, denied. Saved by the unwitting assist. Kathy smiled to herself. Maybe this was exactly what she needed.

"I'll have a vodka and diet coke."

David looked to Andrew as he gave his own order. "I'll have a bottle of Bud I guess. Andrew?"

Andrew nodded. He was looking but not too hard.

"Okay, that's two Buds and a vodka and diet." The tall barmaid aimed her pierced eyebrow down at Kathy. "Would you like ice in that?"

"Yeah, thanks."

She turned and got to work.

Andrew stepped off from the bar to look at her past David, "So Kathy. David told me you're here because of some big fashion thing. Like it's your deal or something."

She had to smile at her big bro and he gave her his slight smile back. He never liked his smile. Or rather allowing himself a big one. Always said it made him look stupid. She couldn't deny this. Maybe it had something to do with him opening his mouth too much. It would probably look alright if he just kept his teeth closed.

"Um, I guess that's true. I don't like to think of it like that too much for fear of being overwhelmed. But yeah, it's mine and my partner's. Giovanna."

"Sounds…" He paused deliberately, being cute, "overwhelming. So where's this friend of yours? Giovanna. What is that, Italian?"

"Hmm," Kathy said nodding. "She's had to shoot off to do some last minute things that always pop up just before any big kick off." Kathy turned to include her brother. "Which is on Tuesday night by the way, so you guys must come if you can. Get to witness the excess up close."

"Yeah, I've never actually been to anything like that before. Sounds like fun."

David didn't say anything.

Andrew carried on with the probing small talk. "So, how long you here for?"

"For good if it all goes well. I'm relying on David's good will for now, for like the next two or three weeks. Just while the shows are on. Then once the madness is over, I'm gonna look to getting a place of my own."

The tall pierced barmaid arrived with their drinks. Andrew took his bottle and without looking away from Kathy, took a sip. Smooth – he'd managed to take his first sip without the bottle frothing over. Kathy never drank Bud for that very annoying reason. Kathy took her own drink from the bar counter and took a sip. She wondered if Andrew's eye contact would be the same if her brother didn't have his back to them as he paid for the drinks. Her answer came as David turned back into the conversation.

"Should we get a table?" He was looking at Andrew whose eyes were now scouting for a location.

"I don't suppose there's a terrace or something where I can have a cigarette?" She wanted one.

Looking at her briefly and flashing an even briefer but solid teeth closed smile, Andrew took her request under advisement. "Yup. Upstairs. There's an open-air section on the roof. Just follow me."

Andrew led the way with her and David following. The place was big and dark. Not too dark. Atmospheric. That was the word. She liked it. Big red light panels tucked away all over the place giving off the feeling of something. She couldn't decide if it was claustrophobia or just warmth. The place seemed to have become crowded all at once. So many different types of people. The pierced versus the controlled. A shoulder bumping. Kathy steadied her drink with her un-bumped hand. God, it was crowded.

Her brother was looking at her. Kathy forced out a natural smile. Calm down, calm down. The fashion floor was just as hectic. Where was Andrew taking them? She let her eyes drift. A table of ladies in black. Kathy looked away because they were looking at her. She looked up ahead. Great. Andrew had just entered the narrowest corridor staircase she had ever seen. Those fucking red lights were giving her a headache. She felt David's hand on her arm as he stepped behind her, giving her way to walk into the crimson corridor. She wanted to snatch her arm away as proof that she was fine. She didn't. She wasn't. Just shut up, shut up, shut up.

Andrew was already out of sight. The narrow corridor staircase had a blind turn in it. She steadied herself on its wall. Her hand was shaky but she didn't think it was noticeable. She would just have to go quickly before David got too worried. Go. One, two, one, two.

9

Cold. Nice and cold. Anthony Whithers took another sip of his beer. He had managed to get a small table in the corner. Just far enough away not to be noticed, but close enough to hear most of what was being said. Kathy, David and Andrew. They had supplied each other's names for him.

Anthony had been on them since the two cops had gone back to check on the scene. He figured she was the sister. The older one's. David's. She had calmed down but she was clearly carrying something. He had their faces now. Good to know who was on your tail, but if all went well it wouldn't matter. Anthony took another sip of his cool beer. It was a nice place. He'd have to come back.

CHAPTER FOUR

1

Andrew stared at the vaguely orange door of Interrogation Room Four. He looked at his watch and then rested his head against the wall behind his chair. He had been sitting there for almost an hour now. He could have strolled about, he supposed, but somehow this seemed like the closest thing to support which he could offer to his partner. Almost an hour. Surely it was gonna be his turn soon. What was he going to say? What did he have to say? There was nothing to say. It was up to David to say what happened and it was his job to back him up. There was nothing to say and that's precisely what he'd tell them. What the fuck was taking so long?

Andrew shifted in his seat to get a better angle at his side arm, which he then eased free from its holster. He turned it in his hands as he examined it. Click. Safety off. Click. Safety on. He sighed loudly and put his gun away. What the fuck was taking so long? Andrew looked at the ugly door again. This was all a waste of everybody's time. Andrew thought about that for a second and then shook it off. They had a new case now that was quickly getting cold with all of this shit weighing them down. Shit. Andrew knew they'd be taken off it if this went much further. If they felt things needed to be looked into, that would be it. Re-assigned. Andrew shifted in his seat. He didn't like that. Fucking IA. Another loud sigh.

Kathy was nice. Sexy. Bad idea. Andrew's head turned to the sound of the door opening. The Chief stood holding it open as David stepped out past him as he looked down at Andrew. Face as impossible to read as ever.

Andrew stood. "All good?" What else was there to say?

"It's fine. Just tell them what you know."

David slapped his shoulder and walked off. Impossible to read.

"Detective Bates." The voice boomed from inside Interrogation Room Four.

Andrew watched David turn and disappear round a corner before going in.

* * *

Andrew took his seat across from the two suits. One was a red head trying to grow what could almost be described as a moustache. He was the first to speak.

"Good afternoon Detective. We just have a few questions for you. Detective Radley has given us pretty much all we need, we just want to confirm a thing or two with you. Were you with Detective Radley on the night in question?"

The red was fluffing about with some papers for some unidentifiable reason. Maybe just to avoid eye contact. Andrew was doing his best to ensure that his own eye contact was making everyone as uncomfortable as possible.

The red looked up, "Detective?"

Number two leaned in. This mean old boy who earned his keep putting cops away, had no problem with staring him down. This little session could be fun.

"You're full co-operation is expected Detective. You realise of course this is being recorded."

The mean old boy leaned back and tapped on the two-way mirror behind him. "If we decide we don't like this stuff with your partner, your little silent act could widen the spot light to shine onto your sorry ass as well."

"This the way it is, Chief? We cool with this?" Andrew gestured briefly at the mean one as he allowed himself to slide down into a nice comfortable slouch.

The Chief, who was standing in the corner simply shrugged and continued with his leaning. The mean old boy spoke out not looking back to the Chief.

"Chief Groder. Would you kindly instruct your officer to give us his full co-operation, or he will be suspended from duty pending a full investigation.

Chief Groder stepped forward to give his words the backing of his imposing mass. "Alright Andrew, cut the shit and answer their questions. And sit up straight."

Andrew couldn't help but smile as he did as he was told. He had to stop himself from responding to the Chief, which would have undoubtedly got him into more shit than these two had at their disposal. He looked back to the suits.

"No. I was not with Detective Radley on the night in question."

"Good." Red was back in play. "So, you went over to Mrs Jane Booney's house. Detective Radley's ex-wife."

"That's right." Andrew could feel just how wrong this line of questioning was going to go.

"Why?"

"She called me. Asked me to come over."

"Why?"

"She was scared. Her husband was out of town and she said that Garver was there. Said he kept coming up to the house, banging on the door." Here it came.

"Damon Harris' older brother. But I mean, why did she call you and not Detective Radley? They're his kids sleeping upstairs in that house. Why not call him?"

Fucking IA. Andrew shifted back down into his slouch.

"Detective?"

Andrew's eyes shifted to the Chief as he stood off from the wall.

"Bates."

"What is it exactly that you need me to fill in? We all know David has a history with this guy. I have a history with him too. David's wife has a history with him. You have the assault charge on file. She didn't want David being drawn out into another set up so that this…"

"Right, the assault charge." The mean old boy was out of his chair and circling round. "That never went anywhere, did it? Fell through after your testimony. Turned out you were there the whole time. Showed just how full of

47

holes Garver Harris' story was."

Andrew was beginning to feel like he was making thing worse.

"What did you find when you went over there?"

Andrew looked back over to the red. "Soon as I got there I saw that the front door had been kicked in." Andrew looked up at the mean old boy now looming at his side. "Do you mind backing off?

After a moment of intensified glaring he took his two steps back. Andrew held his gaze. He could tell with his position of power lost, the mean old boy wanted to retake his seat, but he'd have to wait for a minute or two. Couldn't have it known.

"Why didn't you call in for back up?"

"I was about to. But as I pulled to a stop I saw Jane sitting on the porch steps. She saw me and came rushing over."

The mean old boy took his seat. "What did she have to say?"

"You have her statement. You tell me. My memory's not what it used to be."

Red shuffled through his papers some more till he produced the one in question. "According to Mrs Booney, Garver Harris showed up at her house at about half past eight in the evening and started banging on her door, insisting that she let him in so they could talk. She said he was clearly drunk and behaving violently. When she told him to leave or she'd call the police, he did." Red lowered the paper to look over at Andrew. "She had of course had a run in with him before, correct?"

"Yes." Andrew could see this dib shit's tie was in serious need of tightening.

"Here she claimed that he had threatened her, the result of which was a restraining order. Correct?"

"A claim that seems pretty validated now considering the fact that when I came to her, her lip was bleeding and his prints were on her neck."

"That's true. It does seem interesting to us though that the day after a restraining order is placed on Garver Harris for threatening Detective Radley's ex-wife, he ends up with three broken fingers. And then on the same night he accosts Mrs Booney at her home, he ends up dead. Don't you find that interesting Detective Bates?"

Andrew shifted slightly in his seat, but he managed to maintain a cold disaffected expression.

Red continued. "Did you call Detective Radley to tell him of the situation?"

"No. He called me. He had got wind of where I was."

"And you told him what had happened?"

"I did."

"Would you have called him if he hadn't got wind of where you were?"

"Yes." That was a lie. "It was our case, his ex-wife. Of course I would have called him."

Andrew let his gaze drift towards the Chief. His eyes were low. Who knew what that meant? Probably that he was fucking this up for everyone.

"So Detective Radley went after him. How did he know where he'd be?"

"Garver may not have been under arrest, but he was still a suspect in our case so…"

Red cut him off. "But it wasn't your case was it. No, his brother. That was your case." He was digging through his pages again. "Julia Carroll. You had him on her murder and that was it. Problem was that this clashed with another precinct's major crime case, so yours was folded in with theirs, which in turn brought added complications to your case. Still in court, right? All tied up with their other activities preventing you from getting rid of a simple murder/witness case."

"What the hell is your point?"

"My point is that on top of everything else, this makes things a lot more simple, doesn't it? No reason to let things drag out any more."

Andrew decided it was his time to lean in. "Look, the bottom line is now we had something on him. Something to use for *our* case. Detective Radley went out to find him and arrest him. Garver saw him coming, he knew the score so he tried to take him out. David got there first. And you guys don't have anything that says any different." Andrew sat back but then quickly decided to utilise the moment and stood out of his chair. "We done here?"

No response.

"Good."

"We'll get back to you." The mean old boy grabbing the last word.

The Chief opened the door for Andrew, giving him a small nod as he made his way out.

2

The car eased to a stop. David had slowed right down as he was nearing the house so as not to make any noise. He looked over to his old house just ahead. Three stories with a green roof. Big place – lots of money – his wife's money. A sizable chunk of which she'd used to brush him off when she'd divorced him some three and a half years earlier.

He'd called ahead. She was expecting him. He didn't want to go in there. He'd tried to see her the day after it had happened but she hadn't been home. Then when he tried the hospital he saw that the husband was there. He'd obviously come back and made her go.

The husband was at work just then and the kids were at school. David tilted his head to get a better view of the sky past the surrounding suburban houses and manicured trees. A little overcast. He liked it. Keeps the sun out of your eyes. He looked back at his old house. Their relationship had soured with all this. And she wasn't going to like what he had to tell her, whichever way he decided to spin it. It had to be done. Especially now. They were looking at him hard and it would inevitably lead them to her.

He opened his door and got out. What's the number one reason people go back to smoking? Maybe. He didn't want to start again but they weren't making it easy for him. David swung his door closed. She'd be listening out for the sound.

Green roof, brown door. The lock had already been fixed. Their front door *had* been green like the roof, which David had always liked. The door opened and there she was. Her lip was still slightly swollen and badly bruised from the door smacking her in the face when that bastard kicked it in. It didn't help though, she was still the vision of beauty he had fallen in love with almost fifteen years earlier.

"David."

She knew something was up. Nothing ever got past her. She was younger than him. Twelve years. They met when she was still only twenty-two, but she could always see through his shit. Wise beyond her years. And now that her years were catching up with her, his shit was up with something she just would not put.

"What's going on?"

"Can I come in?"

She stepped aside, pulling the door properly open with her. "Of course."

David stepped in past her, letting his eyes drift down across her body as he went. She wasn't as slim as she used to be, even four years earlier when they were still together. He hoped that back then she hadn't been starving herself for his sake. Was she really that much more content now? It had been an unhappy marriage towards the end. Either way, he thought she looked better now, maybe better than she ever had.

David aimed his eyes forward and continued in. This wasn't why he was here. He'd have to keep himself in check. He heard the door close behind him. He stopped, standing in the foyer of his old house and waited for his ex-wife to walk past him.

"Do you want a drink?"

She looked at him with masked annoyance. She clearly didn't like the obvious deliberation he was putting out there. But she was willing to indulge him, at least for a little while.

"No, thanks."

"Well then, let's have a seat."

She walked off into the well-lit living room just ahead. Big picture windows. She walked through and sat in front of the window, her golden shoulder length hair framed in the soft sunlight. He wasn't here for this. He followed on and took a seat across from her.

"So." Her face was stern. "Tell me."

Her tone gave him pause. She knew.

"What have you heard?"

Jane was out of her chair. "God damn it David, just say it." She was hugging herself in anticipation.

As he tried to speak, his ex-wife turned away from him. He felt his heart swell and sink at the sight of this. He hated being a disappointment to her. He still wasn't answering. He opened his mouth trying to think where he was going with this. No spin would fly. Had he really done anything so awful? Treated her so badly? Did he deserve all this? To have some other man living in his house, sleeping with his wife? He stood.

Her shoulders hunched at the sound. "I'm gonna have that drink. You want one?"

As she walked off David pulled back the hand he had reached out to touch her with. "Sure."

She made her way over to the small liquor cabinet in the corner. When he'd lived here they had kept their booze in the kitchen like normal people. The mobile liquor cabinet was a new addition. Been in his house for over two years now. Jane mixed together the two drinks. Scotch, ice and soda for him. A vodka tonic for her. She turned back to face him and brought over his drink. She held it out for him and he took it. Their fingers touched. She sipped her drink looking up at him, waiting. He wanted to grab her, kiss her. He sipped his drink.

"Garver Harris is dead."

Her eyes closed as she took another sip. "Let's sit." She gently took his hand and led him over to the couch. He sat down with her. Her hand stayed with his. "What now?"

He sighed. He almost felt like he was going to cry. He wasn't.

"Internal Affairs are looking at me. Because of before. They'll probably be coming to talk to you."

She pulled her hand away. "I'm not lying for you David."

"I'm not asking you to. I'm only here to tell you what's going on."

Jane ripped herself free from the couch snatching his drink along with her. "To tell me you killed a man to defend my honour and have now brought down a shit storm onto both our heads. Thanks. I'll tell the kids you stopped by."

David looked up into her eyes briefly but couldn't stand the cold. He eased himself off the couch.

"Jane, I just came to let you know what's happening. So you didn't find out from someone else."

She turned off and walked back over to the liquor cabinet and put the two glasses down onto it. She stood keeping her back to him.

David pushed on. "It's not what you think. They don't have anything on me. I only went there to arrest…" He again felt his heart swell and sink as his ex-wife let out a jagged laugh cutting him short.

It finished with a sniff, which made it sound like she was crying. "You know, David, this is all starting to sound a little bit too familiar. So please, can you just get the fuck out of my house."

Oh God. He stood stunned.

"Now!"

He turned and left.

3

Anthony Whithers sat up and wiped his face trying to force in consciousness. It was late. He reached over for his watch on the bedside table. With a crash, his hand connected with a half empty bottle of whatever had caught his attention the night before. A groan. It wasn't his, despite how much his head was pounding. He opened his eyes and peered through his fingers. Hotter than most. God, how much had he blown for her to spend the whole night? He remembered. At least some of it. It was worth it. She was still asleep. Her body curled up under the thin sheet. He lowered his hand and traced his fingers along the twirling spiking tattoo covering her light brown arm. His fingers traced up along her collarbone. Nice tits. He curled his fingers to snag the sheet between them. He needed a reminder. It slid down effortlessly, easily pulling itself free from underneath her arm. Curving up, over and then down. Nice. One and two. Her nipples were dark brown.

Anthony twisted onto his side. He'd have a better angle with his other hand. He was going to have to move out of the shit hole motel now. He didn't care, it was just an inconvenience. Can't have a whore being able to point him out. He shouldn't drink. He didn't think when he drank. He looked to the stained carpet where his pants were. Yup, there was his gun. Definitely going to have to move. He redirected his attention to his hand as he reached over for her chest.

Another groan as she turned away from him onto her side. "It's a new day, bad boy. No free feels."

Fuck it. He reached back over to his bedside table, again connecting with the bottle and then finding his cigarettes. The lighter was next to it. He slid one out and slipped it between his lips. He looked back down to see the whore stir as he lit the smoke. Her greasy black hair shifted as she turned her head to look back at him.

"Got one of those for me?"

He smirked, sliding out a second one. She twisted over and extended her thin arm to take it. Looking at him teasingly with her big brown eyes, she slipped her cigarette between her big brown lips. As Anthony recalled, the reason he had pulled over in the first place. Flick. The lighter sparked. She raised an annoyed eyebrow at him. Holding the flaming lighter resting up on his chest, his smirk widened. Crawl bitch.

She was a pro. She'd played these kinds of games before. After a pause she threw the tangled sheet aside, letting herself be exposed and slid towards him. Anthony felt his contempt growing as she rest herself on his arm, craning her neck forward to connect the cigarette to the flame. He thought about burning her. With her cigarette lit, she slid back to sit against the wall blowing her smoke out into his face as she went.

"Get the fuck out of here."

"Don't worry, I'm going." She stayed.

Anthony turned to look at her not leaving. She took another drag. Wide hips. She smiled blowing more smoke at him.

"Now!" He deftly scooted back turning himself to face her and then kicked out, his foot slamming into her hip.

She screamed out, in fright more than anything, as the force pushed her lower body off the bed. *Thump.* Her face bounced off the edge of the mattress.

"Aah, God." She squeezed her eyes shut as she brought her fingers up to touch her bleeding lip.

Anthony watched these events slowly unfolding with as much patience as he could maintain. Enough. He sprung up onto his feet immediately seeing her snap to attention and scramble back away from him. He stomped after her along the bed, feeling the charged air on his naked body. He jumped off and stomped down next to her. She let out another scream as he grabbed her by the scruff of her neck. Like a dog. Anthony felt himself getting harder. This kind of thing had stopped surprising him. He wondered what that meant. He yanked her to her feet and propelled her across the room. She managed to keep her balance and got her hands out before she hit the wall.

"Fuck! Okay! I'm going."

Satisfied Anthony sat down on the edge of the bed and watched while he finished his cigarette. She bent down scraping together the few items of clothing closest to her. She slipped quickly into her panties and mini skirt, all the while watching him watching her. She moved over to the bed kicking aside his pants as she went. His gun spun out from underneath. It stared up at the two of them. She froze at the sight of it. She looked at him again.

Anthony continued to smoke his cigarette. She shook off her freeze and simply snatched up her bra and top which were lying there. Quickly into the bra, quickly on with the shirt, back over to the door. There she reached into one of her boots and pulled out a wad of cash. She gave it a brief count before giving Anthony one last look. It was cold but he couldn't tell what was going on behind those big brown eyes. Shame he hoped. Hell, he would settle for fear. He gave her a wave as she disappeared out the door preparing to put her boots on and start walking. The door slammed shut behind her.

Anthony lay back on the bed stretching out for the, as he saw it, upside down bottle that had taken his fancy the night before. This time his connection was a successful one. He locked his fingers around its neck and brought it over to his face, splashing himself as he did. He shouldn't drink. Two burning swigs made all the more harsh by his awkward horizontal drinking position. He coughed out on the second, spluttering more alcohol onto his face. With a sharp movement, the bottle flew from his hand and smashed against the door. What did he care? It was checking out time. He brought his other hand up to his face and wiped away the wetness. From the same hand he then drew in the last bit of smoke the cigarette had to offer. Flick. It sailed towards the door. He didn't look. A soft thud. He smiled. No raging inferno today.

After a defiant pause he sat up and let the momentum carry him into a stand. He walked round the bed to where his pants lay. He picked them up feeling at the pocket. There it was. He pulled his cell phone free and flipped it open. 14:37. Shit. That was a bit ridiculous. He shook it off and dialled in the number. Three rings. He sat back down on the bed. Three more rings and it'd be the answer phone.

"About time you called."

"I got distracted. What you got for me?" Anthony reached back and grabbed his cigarettes. "Do I need to keep my eyes on these two?"

Anthony didn't like him. Didn't like having to ask him if he needed to do this or if he needed to do that. He'd been living in squalor in this shit hole motel room for over a week on his say so. Waiting to do his bidding. Anthony didn't like any of it. He didn't like this guy and he didn't like how quickly Leon had been willing to get in bed with him. Old friends clouded your judgment.

"My eyes are on them Anthony, don't worry. Your two cops shouldn't be a problem. Check *The Times*. Page eight. It's not front page news anymore but it will be again soon."

Anthony lit his cigarette. "What's this?"

"They were the arresting officer's in an ongoing trial. What's not in the papers yet is the fact that one of your cops just killed the defendant's brother. Details are hazy just now, but with the obvious ramifications of this, I don't think they're gonna have much time for the Cartwrights."

"What about the body. You got eyes on that?"

"Still where you left it. Give it another couple of days and it'll be found."

"Okay. You let me know and I'll get Leon on the horn to you."

"Check out *The Times*. Page eight."

* * *

...and with two months behind it already, the defence for the accused, Damon Harris, has clearly begun to wane. The surrounding hoopla of trouble beyond the court house walls with accusations of supposed harassment involving the Police Department have died down and once again the issue seems to be leaning towards the facts of the case. There is a definite sense that the twelve members of the jury are quite simply biding their time until they can strike the accused off their list.

Having plead innocent to the charge of murder in the first, as well the lesser charges of resisting arrest and possession, if found guilty Damon Harris could be facing a life sentence. The trafficking charges levied against Harris never stuck, and did carry the distinct aroma of a Police agenda. Along with Garver Harris, Damon's brother, Damon was suspected of being involved in a mid-level organised crime syndicate. This, of course, has little to do with the case at hand and as a result was recently thrown out, despite repeated attempts by the prosecution to show cause for its inclusion...

* * *

The whole thing was a cut and paste job and stunk of yesterday's news.

Anthony enjoyed the feeling of power that came with knowing that that was about to change. It was good. The Cops wouldn't be any trouble. Anthony folded up the paper and put it down onto the chipped Formica table. He picked up his coffee and looked down in disgust at what was left of the plate full of grease he had just consumed. Coffee wasn't bad, though.

His eyes drifted across the room and settled on a young couple seated over in one of the window booths. They were finished with their grease as well. They looked more satisfied by it though, or at least the guy did. His, maybe younger girlfriend looked a little bit more dissatisfied. Pale, dyed black hair, skinny. Anthony was liking the look of these two. Dirty fingernails. The blond boyfriend, anything from nineteen to twenty-six, was trying to comfort his little girlfriend by stroking the stringy hair out of her face. It wasn't working. She swiped it away and stood out of her chair, clanging the dishes on the Formica table as she did. A few heads turned her way. She kept her eyes low for what should have been outburst time. She headed for the door, again swiping her blond boyfriend's hand away as he reached out for her.

Anthony recognised this scene. Junkie on the mend. The blond boyfriend was after her. Nobody chasing. In a joint like this you make the kids like them pay you upfront. Anthony was definitely liking this. He dropped a couple of notes and then strolled out after them.

4

Andrew slowed down to make a left. The neighbourhood quickly deteriorated the deeper he went. It was already past eight, too late for this kind of thing. No David all day since his emergence from beyond the orange-ish door. Andrew had thought about swinging by that place where Kathy was working, and check out the fashion scene. But he didn't think David would have liked that. He would see her tomorrow night. Was it tomorrow night? He nodded, satisfied that it was.

Andrew slowed to make the next turn and then after two more blocks pulled to a stop. He got out and closed his door. Checked, locked. He waited for a car to pass and then headed for the building. As he went, he caught sight of a cloud of smoke wafting from the shadows of the alley. Andrew could see the young whore there. She'd shrunk away into the darkness to avoid being hassled. God, was it that obviously an unmarked police car? Andrew opened the cracked glass door and walked into Roseberry Homes.

* * *

He pushed the door open and ducked under the tape. There was no longer a flat foot outside the door. All had been dusted and photographed. The place was just a big bucket of dead ends. It stunk of weed. He turned on the lights.

"Hello. Anybody in here? I'm a police officer, so if there's anybody in here I suggest you come out now."

He didn't think there was. The smell was stale. The local kids and what not were just making the most out of the empty space until the management got their shit together and cleaned it back up.

Andrew made his way through the apartment. Front room, bathroom, kitchen, bedroom. No unwanted guests. He found himself standing outside the young girl's bedroom. He reached in and turned on the lights. All of the Cartwrights' meagre belongings had since been boxed up and stored away as evidence. He stared at the exposed mattress, a small bloodstain at its centre. Andrew looked about at the bare walls. They were the same now as they were two days ago when he'd first seen them. No posters, no pictures, no nothing. No real belonging. Checked in to get murdered. This wasn't right.

* * *

Andrew made his way back down the narrow steps towards the torn carpet of the small reception area. He sidestepped as an elderly black man mumbled his way up. The look Andrew didn't get made him feel like a sore thumb. He swung round the banister support at the bottom to come to a leaning stop at the reception counter, staring down at the sleeping beauty behind it.

Andrew had to wonder why this guy bothered with all the product when it seemed all he did was slouch here and not do his job.

Slam! Open hand to counter. The beauty's wheeled chair almost betrayed him.

"Wow." He jerked violently, showing off his steel tipped cowboy boots before settling properly in his chair.

He clenched his words at the sight of Andrew's badge. "Officer. What can I do for you?"

"I'm investigating the murdered family. The Cartwrights. Fifth floor apartment."

"Look, I can't be responsible for the kids going in and out of there. They kick the lock. Your man is no more there to stop them."

Andrew nodded along, allowing him to finish. "Hmm. The Cartwrights. They were only here for a day."

"One night. They come in when it's dark, pay for three days and then they go upstairs with their takeaway food and three suit cases and then that's it."

The nearest appropriate takeaway joint had been checked out on the day. No cameras and no memory of their description. Another dead end.

"No one coming in asking about them or anything like that?"

"No. I tell all this to your people already. I was asleep most the night. I didn't see anybody. Sometimes people come and go. I can't stop everybody. But if you want to get into the rooms you need a key."

A key. No sign of forced entry.

"Who was in the room before the Cartwrights? It was only one day, right?"

"Don't get excited. This place doesn't run at capacity as you say." He

56

reached under his desk and pulled out the ledger before turning it round for Andrew to inspect. "There you go." His finger was tapping the relevant name.

Andrew looked, "Paul... Paul? He was in for two days and checked out the day they checked in." It was a fake name. This was his guy. Andrew had no doubt. Checked in, got a copy of the key, checked them in and – pow! "Do you remember this guy?"

The clerk was nodding. "Sure. He's one the locals... how is it? Vagrants. Just a drunk who wanted a night out of the cold."

Andrew's heart sank. He knew how this went. Paul Paul was given a few bucks and the use of the room for a night in exchange for the use of the key. And unless he was very much mistaken, Paul Paul had also exchanged his life for the privilege.

"You seen him around lately?"

"No. He comes and goes."

"Okay. Do you know anyone who knows him, or do you maybe have a picture?"

"No. I never see him with anyone. No picture. I can describe him for a drawing if you like."

Andrew knew it was a waste of time. "Okay. I'll send somebody down to do a drawing of him."

Slapping the desk Andrew turned to leave. "Thanks."

"No problem."

5

David stared at Harry's full red-brown moustache as it went up and down, up and down. Harry hadn't stopped yapping since he'd sat down next to David some thirty minutes earlier. The two of them had met maybe once before on some jurisdictional mix up. David hadn't liked him or encouraged him then, and he sure as hell hadn't encouraged him this time. He supposed it served him right for coming to a cop bar.

Another shot down. He was starting to feel a little wasted. He wouldn't drive, he wasn't stupid.

"You okay Dave? You're knocking it back pretty steadily."

David was taken aback. That was the first thing Harry had said to him that was intended to illicit a response. He folded his arms onto the bar counter and buried his head into them. Or maybe he just hadn't been listening close enough to his inane babble.

"Huh?" David dragged his face across his arm in order to get it to face towards Harry.

Funny looking old man. Too fat, too bald, too many years past his pension to be of any use to anybody. Nothing worth retiring to, he supposed. Was that going to be him or was it him already?

"You want another smoke?"

David pushed himself upright, conscious of the bar stool beneath him. "Yes I do." David took the partially extended cigarette from the pack on offer and put it in his mouth.

The first one Harry had given him hadn't been as satisfying as he had imagined and had made him feel a little ill. That and that whole disappointment feeling you got at knowing that despite however long without, you'd just fallen right back into it. Harry lit the cigarette for him. They were going down better now. That was the good thing about him coming into a cop bar. He could smoke.

"While you're at it Harry, do you think you could buy me another beer? That last shot was the last of my cash."

Harry stubbed out his cigarette into the overflowing ashtray. He seemed hesitant about fishing out his wallet. David kept his eyes on him. He felt confident he'd get another drink. He may not exactly have been happy to have Harry's company, but the guy had certainly bought him his fair share of drinks.

"You're not gonna drive or nothing are you?"

"I'm gonna get a cab."

"With what?"

"I got my card. Don't worry about me."

Harry was looking at him guiltily, as if he were an accomplice to some misdeed currently underway.

"You gonna tell me what's on your plate that's got you like this?" His wallet was out.

"Nope." The cigarette was very satisfying. He'd have to buy a pack of his own.

Harry seemed insulted by David's brief answer. He stood off his bar stool and signalled to the bartender.

"One more for my friend here." He held up the empty beer glass.

The bartender nodded and walked off. Harry left a note on the counter and then made his way past David with a pat on the back. Could have saved a lot of time and misery if he'd actually taken offence to the actual insults David had been constantly sliding his way. David redirected his attention to the counter in front of him. The note was gone and a fresh beer was in its place. Unfortunately, the cigarette was gone too. David smoked on the last of what there wasn't left to be smoked before stubbing it out. He sipped on his beer.

Long fucking day. They may not have had anything specific on him but David knew he was in for a suspension. Where it went from there he wasn't sure. He didn't think they would really be able to get anything on him. No, nothing specific anyway. David ran his fingers over the dried scab that had formed across the top of his left hand. He'd seen the piece of wire sticking out before it had caught him. David shook his head. He could have gone about it so much better. He was smarter than the way he played it.

There may not have been anything specific to get but soon the papers would have the story and once that happened the pressure would be coming from somewhere a lot harder to wrangle. He stood off his bar stool, making sure not to stumble, slip and smash his face on the tiled floor. Success. He looked at his beer.

Still two-thirds left. He thought about knocking it back but the turning in his stomach caused by all the movement made him decide on just a parting sip. David turned for the door and tried to make a beeline for it. Time to find a cash machine and then a cab. Should have found a place closer to home to drown his sorrows. He hoped his car would be alright. He hoped he'd be able to remember that it was here.

6

She didn't know why she was being so frantic about it. She'd only been back in his world for a few days. She didn't know his habits anymore, but still, her big brother had been worrying her. He seemed so sad and she hated not being able to tell why, or even to know if he was. She opened the second drawer of his bedside table. Nothing – nothing. She thought about calling Jane. She knew her number but no, that was too much. She closed the unhelpful second drawer.

* * *

Kathy stepped off the elevator and walked sharply over to the front desk. The desk clerk was one she hadn't seen before. Young, maybe twenty-one. Cute, if a little stupid looking. He was dealing with an elderly couple in their dressing gowns that were up way past their bed times. They were asking about some noise situation on the second floor. The young clerk spotted her and threw her a subtly spent look. She eased her intensity and issued him an equally subtle look of empathy. After another two agonising minutes of watching this solution-less exchange, Kathy could bear it no longer.

She stomped herself up next to the old man who had been letting his wife do most of the talking. "Excuse me. I'm sorry. I just need to ask him one quick question."

The old man stepped back, happily relinquishing his place in the queue. As he did, his wife's glaring look was revealed. Kathy gave her the briefest of fake smiles before turning her attention to the clerk whose sanity she had just saved. The little old lady, who had resigned herself to defeat, dragged her husband off in a huff. Kathy could hear her quietly berating him for standing for such rudeness.

The young clerk gave her a thankful smile. "Hello. How may I be of service?"

Kathy returned the smile examining his name badge. "Jason, right?"

He checked his name badge. "Right."

"Jason. I need a favour."

"You're Mr Radley's sister, right?"

"Yes." Relief. That would help move things along. "I'm Kathy."

He nodded, satisfied with how much he knew in this world. "Yeah, I heard you were coming."

Kathy felt herself nodding as well. She shook it off. This little knowing interchange was slowing things down.

"Um, Jason, look. I need to get hold of my brother and he's not answering his cell, so I was wondering if you guys had any *call in case of emergency* numbers back there." She was indicating to his general area of employment.

He seemed a little thrown by the question. "Ah, numbers?"

Nope, he had just switched off while staring at her breasts. Kathy didn't want to embarrass him so she chose not to fold her arms up across her chest.

He fumbled on. "Yes, we should do."

He looked down and started fiddling about on his computer. He then stopped and looked back up at her breasts.

"This should be alright – for me to give out these numbers to you?"

"I'm sure it'll be fine."

Kathy folded her arms up onto the counter and rested her head on them. He ducked back down to continue. Tap, tap, tap.

"I got a cell phone number here for a Detective Andrew Bates."

He looked up into her eyes this time. Though in their current position, they were at breast height. She righted herself.

"That's great. Could you write it down for me?"

At this request, Jason the clerk did an excited little half turn to his left, knocking over an unseen object before turning back to the right in search of the appropriate materials. He scraped together the needed items, leaving a trail of destruction in his wake. He gave her a nervous smile. She smiled back. Sweet kid. Virgin.

"There you go."

He handed her the little yellow Post-It page as well as his pen. She handed him back the pen. He grabbed it back with a stupid laugh.

"Thanks Jason. I'll see you later." She turned to leave catching his sharp wave out of the corner of her eye.

Kathy walked over to the elevator and pressed the button. She kept her eyes low. She wasn't looking for any further interaction with young Jason the clerk. She'd give Andrew a call when she got back upstairs. She hoped he'd still be up detecting with David, or at least that he wouldn't mind being woken up by the flaky sister.

The front door opened and Kathy looked up to see her big brother swaying his way in. Jason pointed excitedly over to her.

"Mr Radley, your sister."

At this David stopped in his tracks and peered confusedly in her direction. Clearly trying to unite her two wavering forms. She gave him a small wave. *Ting.* The elevator door opened behind her.

7

Oh God. David straightened himself up as he watched his baby sister step into the elevator. She turned back to face him and put her hand out to hold the doors. David sighed and made for the straightest route possible to the dreaded iron box. What a day, what a day. Wait, it was a new day. This was turning into a week. He shook his head at the obviousness that this week was just the start. He then stopped because the shaking was making him feel dizzy.

"Kathy." He stepped in past her and then found the nearest wall to lean against.

"David."

Her echoed response eased him a bit. It seemed she wasn't going to dive in just yet. He could ride the floors in peace. Maybe she'd even let him slide right on through to bed. She wasn't looking at him. Her eyes were on the elevator door. *Ting.* They opened and out she went. David shouldered himself away from the wall and made the same turn she had. He assumed she knew where they were going. As he turned into the corridor she was nowhere in sight. He then spotted his open door off in the distance. David stumbled on.

* * *

David pushed past his front door, which wasn't quite as open as he needed it to be. It slammed back and hit the wall with far more force than he had intended. He cringed slightly at the sound and held back a laugh at his reaction. He cut out the smile at the sight of his sister, watching him from behind the kitchen counter.

"What?" What exactly was her problem?

She didn't respond. He turned and carefully closed the door. As he turned back to the music he took off his coat. The place was hot.

"David, it's three o'clock in the morning."

David tried to decipher if her tone was sad or angry. He studied her face. Her expression wasn't helping.

"Kathy, what are you talking about? You've been dumping your crap around my home for three days and now I have to call and ask for your permission to stay out late?"

Her expression solidified, angry. "Don't you talk to me like that. I was worried about you."

She made her way out from behind the counter and powered towards him. David almost put his hand out to defend himself against her over sped advance. He instead stumbled half a step back. When she reached him she prodded him right in the ribs. This almost made him fall over. Her hand retracted long before his could come up to swipe it away in defence.

She continued. "I'm worried about you Dave, okay? You seem so sad." Her eyes had changed to sad. He wanted to look away. "I just want to know what's going on with you."

She turned off to sit on of the armrests of one of the couches. She smiled at him.

"Come. Sit down before you fall down."

David had to roll his eyes at this as he pulled himself out of his obvious rigidity. He walked over and sat down across from his sister. As soon as he was down, she was up.

"You want a glass of water?"

He did. "Please."

Kathy bounced off to secure one for him and before he could cup his head in his hands, she was back.

"Here you go."

"Thanks." He took the glass from her and then greedily chugged down his first three sips.

Kathy retook her seat. He hadn't been able to get those cigarettes in the end.

"Can I have one of your cigarettes?"

She shot him an overblown look of disapproval. "And now you're smoking. See what I mean."

He gave her a half-hearted half smile. She didn't hold up the act.

"Sure. They're in my room. Just hold on. I'll go get them." She jetted off again giving David his chance for head in hands satisfaction.

He raised his heavy head at the flick, flick of the lighter. She held out his cigarette. He took it. She lit her own. They looked at each other for a few moments as they each smoked their smokes.

"So." She leaned in, to which he leaned back. "Why are you smoking again?"

He didn't think he'd be able to pull out of this one gracefully. He didn't like it. Bad timing. He was too honest when he was drunk, and he couldn't afford for this one to go too deep. She was waiting.

"You haven't come at a very good time, sis."

Her eyes stayed on his.

David picked up his glass and took another two big sips. "There's a bit of mess we have to clean up." His avoidance was making his words slip.

David shut his eyes tightly as he squeezed at the bridge of his nose. A headache was threatening to come on. He sat up.

"There was a case me and Andrew were on. It's finished now. Well, almost. We arrested the guy. A bad guy. A murderer." The words were coming fast now. He slowed it down a step. "Anyway, we arrested him for the murder of a teacher at this college. An older woman. It wasn't what we wanted him for but... No, no... it's what we had him for but he was part of another case that..." David shook his head. He could tell he was losing her. His words were making his head spin.

"That's not important. Uh, so..." He needed to calm down. He was starting to feel sick. "Um, I'm losing my train of thought here."

He felt his sister's hand on his. It had an immediate calming effect.

"It's okay. Tell me what happened. He killed a woman." She left it for him to continue.

"Yeah, this guy was linked to a lot of deaths involving people working with him or against him. Him and his older brother were running this mix and match outfit. Drugs, guns that sort of thing. It was small time, but these were ruthless creeps. Dead kids used as couriers. That's what happened. The woman was one of the courier's Mom and she started shouting the odds and then he killed her and we got a witness and..." David drifted off as he reached for his water to drink down the last of it.

Kathy was still waiting, watching him. David didn't feel well.

"So the older brother was still out there, making a noise, making threats."

"Against you?"

David nodded. "Me and also against Jane. Trying to force someone to make it all go away. He was trying to hurt me through her, and I couldn't let that happen." His words were getting away from him again and he could feel it. Kathy's expression had changed but he couldn't hold it in focus.

"It's nothing... It was just that we..." He needed to get his words straight. "There was a raid and then the brother was killed and it's just turned it all on its head because..." He trailed off.

David looked at his cigarette. It had gone out. He looked at his sister. She was looking at her own. She looked unsure. She saw him looking at her and took another drag. She spoke.

"Is it Jane? Did he hurt her? Is that why you're so..." She too trailed off unable to hold onto her thoughts.

"No... Yes, but she's fine. She's fine but now she's upset with me. She thinks that it's the same thing again and I..."

"The same thing as what?"

David forced himself up. "Look Kathy, I'm really tired and don't feel so well and..."

"Goodnight David." She wasn't looking at him.

"We'll talk another time and I'm fine, really."

She nodded giving him a brief smile before looking away again and taking another drag. David watched the cherry blaze and then made for his bedroom. Unconsciousness awaited.

CHAPTER FIVE

1

Andrew walked into Bill's claustrophobic environment to find it now teeming with life. White coats everywhere dealing with the minutiae of all the crime scene investigations. Bill was off to the back hunched over one of the metal tables, looking through one of their contraptions. He had the same little black haired helper at his side.

Andrew made his way through the techs and sidled over to where Bill and his little helper were working. Andrew came to stand next to her seat and saw that in the clear light of day she looked quite cute, even in the big goggles that she was now looking at him through.

"Bill."

Bill looked up from his contraption and sighed in exasperation. "What is it, Detective? I'm busy."

He didn't have anything to go on. No leads, just a never ending supply of dead ends.

"I was hoping you'd have more for me on that poison."

"Like what?"

The little helper was still looking at him. Standing too close he imagined. The look was not pleasant. Andrew shifted back half a step and she looked back down at her work. Andrew smirked. Still stewing over that spilled coffee. He looked back up at Bill who did not look impressed.

Andrew flashed him a look of innocent oblivion in return, followed by a slightly guilty smile. Bill stood up from his low stool and snapped off his gloves. He walked past Andrew with an elbow touch, which Andrew took as a *follow me*. He did.

Bill dumped the gloves in a nearby green trash bag and then turned to Andrew. "Just don't, okay?" He was keeping his voice low.

"What?"

"She's an intern. The last thing I need is you fucking one of my students."

Andrew made a brief attempt at feigning shock but dumped it as Bill continued.

"It'll be nothing but headaches for me and then eventually she'll end up leaving because you don't look her in the eyes anymore and I'll be stuck without an assistant."

"What are you talking about? You're the head of the department. All these guys are your assistants." Andrew found himself enjoying how unimpressed Bill was. "Bill, I don't know where you're getting this from, but I assure you I..."

"Yeah, yeah, yeah. Just don't, okay? I like this one. She's a sweet girl and a hard worker and I'd like to keep her around."

Pause for effect. "Okay. You're the man."

Pause at annoyance. "Okay. So, why the fuck are you down here?"

Andrew felt himself deflate. "I need something on this case or else it's just gonna float away. Can you tell me anything else about the drug? Is it common? Can we trace it? Something."

"Thing is, Detective, it's not common but I couldn't actually tell you where it came from or even what it is. Some of it is clear but I'm still trying to break it down. It's a bit of a cocktail. If we had more of it then maybe, but as it stands I can mostly just tell you what it does, and that's knock someone the fuck out. But then you already knew that."

A moment of silence hung between them. Andrew gave Bill a slap on the shoulder.

"Okay, thanks Bill." He turned and made his way back through the techs going towards the exit.

"Oh yeah, Bates?"

Andrew turned back to see Bill standing back next to his dark haired little helper and holding up a folded newspaper.

"I forgot to tell you. Check out the front page."

2

David looked at the picture on the front of the newspaper which he'd just bought from the vendor. They had chosen to print it in black and white. Looked like a mug shot. He was still stinging from his brief meeting with the lawyers. Pissed off about the whole thing, of course, but more so at the fact that they hadn't been able to get hold of him. He was due for the stand soon but now there was a lot of indecision about that. The final decision was to just go with it because if they didn't then the defence sure as hell would. They'd just have to try and sell his side of things. The fact was that he didn't think that he even cared anymore.

There was no direct accusation in the story but they sure had their spin on the back-story.

* * *

Garver Harris, the brother of Damon Harris, was shot and killed two nights previous by Detective David Radley, the arresting officer in the Damon Harris murder trial. The fact that these events have only just come to light leads one to ask the question, 'Was this kept quiet for some particular reason?' It's of course more than a little interesting to note that Detective David Radley had previously, some months ago – soon after Damon Harris's arrest – been charged with an assault, which resulted in the deceased being taken to hospital with three broken fingers.

* * *

It went on to lay more charges at the feet of the police department whilst never making any mention of his ex-wife. There was no mention of the restraining order or any indication of her connection to the events. Irrelevant, he supposed. David crumpled up the paper and chucked it into a trash can as he walked past. He lit one of the cigarettes he had just purchased from the vendor.

Tags were visible on his car's windscreen, making his walk to it at the sidewalk a short one. He'd have to go to the station. Put in an appearance with the Chief, find out if he was suspended.

3

Front page. Cliff had been right on the money. Anthony sipped his black coffee. He was watching the front door of the diner as the people came and went. No sign of the duo as yet. He never expected them to be on time. They would be along, though. No way they were going to pass up the opportunity to make a quick buck.

* * *

Their walk home the day before had been a round about one. First to the corner store to buy what looked like a can of cold soup. Two screw driver holes later and Little Miss Smack Head was chugging away. From there, it was a five-block slog, stopping every half block so the blond boy's little girlfriend could decide whether or not she wanted to throw up. She never did.

Their destination was what looked to be a chop shop. The two of them made to wait out front for some ten minutes before their contact, a bald skinny thug came back out and slapped a small brown parcel in their greedy hands. Just weed, as it turned out. After that the blond dragged his girlfriend back over the five blocks they had just gone down, clearly regretting having brought her along. No stopping this time. Half way she fell to her knees, unable to keep up. He was quick to pull her to her feet and drag her onwards. Anthony hadn't been able to hear what she said, but when the blond boy turned back to her he was sure it had earned her a belt in the mouth. He didn't do anything. Pussy.

Down an alley, through a fence, under a walkway and then down two more alleys before arriving at the derelict building these two had obviously decided to call home. The front left side windows on the top two floors were all broken out. The fire responsible had left its mark on the buildings red brick face. The result, a shit hole hideaway for any degenerate able to find and hold onto a space. The double front doors were still on their hinges, but only just. The two stepped over the broken red tricycle there and went in.

Inside was a long dark narrow corridor, the only light source coming from the opposite end where the double doors had long since come off their hinges. The sunlight streaming through the open doorway reflected off the old linoleum floor. The rooms of the building stretched off along the walls of the narrow corridor. Anthony assumed there was an old broken down elevator somewhere but he hadn't been able to spot it. The two went up the stairs, which were right by the door adjacent to the corridor. The place was littered with strange faces. Some asleep on the stairs, others sitting in groups on the corridor floors. On the third floor a fight had broken out. Two old bums fighting over some missing money. Too drunk to really be effective but with some hard, awkward falls. Enough to loosen a few teeth. How did these two survive in this place?

They made a dark turn. No working lights anywhere in the place. Knock, knock. The two of them stood waiting outside the solid looking door, her sweating and half hunched over.

"Who is it?" A nervous voice called out from the other side of the door.

The blond boy answered. "Chess."

After a moment the sound of something heavy being dragged away from the door could be heard. The door then squeaked inwards. Chess looked back then to see if anyone was about. He hadn't seen Anthony standing squarely ahead, as he was masked by the darkness. He pushed the door open and let his girl go in. As she passed him, he tossed in his newly acquired parcel to an unseen source.

Once in, the door began to close. Not fast enough. Anthony was there to kick it in.

"Oh my fuck!"

Anthony assumed this came from Chess. Anthony saw him fall back to the floor as he came in through the open doorway. Despite the sheets covering the many windows, the room had good natural light. The windows were perfectly placed to catch the sun.

The place was just one big room with a number of mattresses and crates on the old scuffed wooden floor. Chess was on the floor looking up at him. The little girlfriend, curled up on one of the corner mattresses already. Probably hadn't even realised he was there. Then there were the two skinnies. The guy sitting by the wall was the one to whom the parcel had been tossed and number four was standing by the wall shiveringly holding himself. Neither of them were what Anthony was looking for. Too wasted away. It was Chess and his girl that Anthony wanted.

* * *

The two of them came walking into the diner. Chester Stark and his fifteen-year-old girlfriend, one Jamie 'Switch' Nuemyer. Anthony had been told that she earned this nickname by stabbing a social worker in the elbow when she'd tried to stop her from running away. She looked better today. Together. The staying clean had either fallen by the wayside or she was past the worst of it. As they approached his table she was continuously fussing with her hair, which kept slipping out from behind her ears. She was fidgeting. Still off the junk.

Anthony had slipped Chester Stark a hundred as he stood over him in his shit box room and told him to come to their mutual Diner at forty-five minutes ago.

Chester let little Jamie slip in before him. She gave Anthony a nervous smile. Her teeth were bad. Her skin was pasty and pimpled and her long dark brown hair was dirty and brittle. She was too skinny and her eyes told that she'd been through too much in her short life. There was a sweet pretty young girl buried in there somewhere, but Anthony had surmised that it was too late for her and her boyfriend. That was why he had chosen them.

"You guys hungry? My treat."

Chester waved his hand declining. Anthony looked to young Jamie. So tentative, so meek. She smiled her pathetic smile again. How had this creature ever mustered up the will to stab anybody? Clearly this wasn't the same girl. Anthony handed her the table menu.

"Don't be shy Jamie. Whatever you want."

She took the menu and proceeded to examine its many delights. Anthony redirected his attention to Chester. He wondered what this early twenty-something's story was. He didn't think he'd sell himself to pay the bills. He looked just tough enough to take what he needed. Yes, these were the two for him.

4

"I don't know where he is. He's not answering his phone."

The Chief was standing behind his desk with his hands supporting his lean over the back of his chair. Andrew could tell he didn't like his answer.

"Well you're his partner, aren't you? If you don't know then who does?" The Chief pulled out his chair and sat down heavily into it.

"Is he suspended?"

Andrew could tell the Chief liked this response even less.

"Just find out where you partner is, Detective, and tell him to come and see me. Anything else is none of your business."

The door to the office open and they both looked at it to see David entering.

"You wanted to see me, boss."

"The lawyers get hold of you?"

"They did. I saw them a couple of hours ago."

The Chief stood out of his chair and walked round to the front of his large desk. He then sat on its edge and continued.

"David, I'm afraid I'm gonna have to ask you for your gun and badge. This is just until we can sort this mess out."

Andrew watched his partner automatically remove his gun from its holster and hand it over, along with his badge. The Chief took both and then set them down on the desk behind himself.

"I'm sorry David. Now I hate to say this, but you know this doesn't excuse you from your obligations to this trial."

David nodded. There was silence. Andrew wanted to speak but there was nothing to say. The Chief stepped forward and extended his hand.

"We'll get this all cleaned up. There's nothing final about this."

David took his hand and shook it. The moment made it all feel way too final for Andrew's liking. David turned and left. Andrew looked to the Chief unsure. The Chief looked back, not giving anything. Andrew turned and left following David.

* * *

"David. Wait."

Andrew caught up to his partner as he turned to face him. He looked older. David had never looked his age to Andrew, but he was looking it now. These last few days were weighing heavily on him. What did he say? Now that he had his undivided attention, what did he say? Re-hash what the Chief had just said – *Everything's gonna be okay*. His career was on the brink of being flushed down the crapper.

"You still going to your sister's big fashion thing tonight?"

"Yeah." Nothing.

"What time?"

"It kicks off at about seven I think."

"Can I still come?"

David cracked a small smile. "Sure."

5

David pulled out of the precinct parking lot. He was numb. He couldn't figure out what it was that he felt. Twenty-nine years as a cop. Could be all over. The way Jane had looked at him. The way Kathy had looked at him. His hands were whitening on the steering wheel. Was he beyond forgiveness? He missed his wife. He missed his old life. He used to be a better man. He would change. Get to know his kids again. Become someone she could respect again, not just fuck on the side.

CHAPTER SIX

1

Two hours and twenty-two minutes until curtain. The place was a mad house. Kathy had been on the go since seven in the morning. Her feet were killing her, her head was killing her, she was killing her assistant. Cindy Tao had to have been the only person with more to do than her. After all, she was playing helper to Giovanna as well. Things would be better organised for the next show.

Kathy did a 360. Where the hell was she? Damn she was fast. What was it she had spat into her ear? Giovanna wanting her. She'd have to wait.

Models, models everywhere and she needed more than a drop to drink. The make-up and changing room space they had set up was pretty damn impressive she thought, especially considering how quickly they had done it. Her heart almost sank at the idea of doing it twice more. God, whose idea was it to do it in three different locations? She shook it off. Giovanna was here now and she could take some of the heat off.

He was still shouting away at her. Kathy hadn't been paying attention. People were constantly brushing up to her – sign this, where's him, where's her, who's who?

"I 'm sorry Federico, you want me to...?" Kathy watched his small face contort in shocked disbelief.

"Gabriel! I..."

"Oh right. Sorry. The pictures of your dress, for the magazine."

"Yes. He says he will not do them again."

"What's the problem?"

"He hide everything away in the shadows. I don't like. How are people going to see my creation?"

She really didn't have time for this. Where the hell was Cindy when she needed her?

"Federico, trust me. Your dress will be seen. We've got photographers all along the catwalk. The Gabriel shots are just to make it all seem a bit mysterious." He clearly didn't like the sound of mysterious. "But there will be other shots as well."

She was backing away. Someone's hand was on her arm. She gratefully turned to whomever.

"Kathy..." Cindy stopped as Kathy finished the sentence for her.

"Giovanna needs me. There?" Kathy pointed, to which Cindy nodded. Federico was still moving in on her. "Cindy, you know Federico." Kathy pulled her between them, "Federico needs some answers on the whole Gabriel drowning everything in darkness fiasco."

Kathy ducked off leaving it to her faithful assistant. Their conversation would be a short one. Neither would be interested in what the other had to say. Federico would just hunt her down later and corner her. She'd be able to deal with him better when she had less on her plate.

* * *

Giovanna had arrived the previous morning, but this had been the first day Kathy had really had her help in the trenches. She had been dealing with paperwork side of things now that she was back from her quick fix cross-country trip. It was all about ensuring that the magazine would have the jump-start it needed. These shows were only the beginning. They were looking to create a new major rag and that would take money and buzz. Money, buzz and bought and paid for pages of advertisements, which, when all was said and done, was why they were having these shows.

Giovanna was their girl in front of the camera. She was being hounded all day. Kathy didn't know how she did it, but she was always there with a smile and a meaty response for everything. Kathy rounded the fake separating wall they had set up. Make-up and hair. The models were seated and being fussed over. More lift, more shadows. And there Giovanna was, talking to more cameras and… shit… she had spotted her. Kathy did an automatic half step back but there was no escape. Giovanna was already dragging the reporter and cameraman in her direction. Kathy recognised the reporter. Jilly Sanders from *Fashion Daily*. It hit her. They were in the midst of the biggest fashion event of the season. If all went well with this show and the next two, she and Giovanna could be behind the biggest thing in fashion for the last ten years.

"And here is my co-conspirator." Giovanna had her round the waist.

She knew her too well and she wasn't going to let her go anywhere. Time to put on her smile and try not to look like an idiot.

"So this is the illusive Kathy Radley. You are not an easy woman to get hold of."

"Well I'm a busy girl. Lots that needed to be done and still more to come." Kathy was happy with that but once said, for some reason, there was dead air left hanging. Maybe the question was meant to elicit some lengthy self congratulatory response, but …

Giovanna quickly jumped in to save her with her perfectly pitched, slightly throaty, infinitely sexy voice. "All this behind us and out there," Giovanna indicated, and the camera man twirled catching nothing but fake separating wall. He twirled back. "Is all Kathy's doing. She has been doing the work of ten strong German men."

A forced laugh rattled past Jilly Sanders razor lips. "Fabulous venue you've knocked together out there. The dingy harshness of the metal supports and walls baring down on you from the darkness all centred on the stylishly designed and beautifully lit centre stage."

"Yeah, the lights are there to help show off the dresses. That was Giovanna's idea." Kathy smiled, regretting having said that.

She'd had enough. She needed Giovanna to take back the lime light.

"From light to dark. That's the theme of your shows. Tell us about this one. What can we expect to see when the models step out?"

Giovanna jumped in. "Tonight there is *Darkness* and all the things that go with it." Giovanna gave Kathy a quick smile before continuing.

Kathy happily retreated back into the fray. She gave Giovanna's arm a grateful squeeze and left. Still, she had been the one who had pulled her into it, so maybe it should have been a pinch.

* * *

Giovanna was one of those that had it all, one of the ones who just had everything going for them. She was tall, beautiful, and slim, but not all over. Thick long wavy black hair. She was very smart, savvy and when needs be, tough as nails. And to top it all off, she was impossible to hate. That was the thing Kathy had hated most of all about her when they first met. This bitch was all of the above and nice to boot. Who the hell wants to work with someone like that? But, as it happened, they got on really well.

You couldn't help but gravitate to someone like Giovanna, because you knew that if you held on tight enough you'd be in for one hell of a ride. They'd met three years earlier when she'd first moved to France. Both working for the same rag and both of them wanting more. Kathy knew that she'd never be doing any of this if it wasn't for Giovanna. She was the driving force. The inspiration who made things happen.

Kathy watched her sweet talk Jilly, pulling that throaty fake laugh out of her with the ease of a true insider pro. Back to work. Lots to do, lots to do. She turned back and navigated her way through the rows of people, seats and mirrors being careful not to be the cause of some streaked lipstick or separated extensions. She got through without much trauma and exited through a parting in the separated walls. With the building now swarming with contracted professionals and glamorous guests, she had to do her smoking outside. No doubt throngs of those jittery professionals would be desperately looking for her the entire time she'd be gone, but they'd just have to do without her for the next seven minutes. Down the concrete steps and out the blue metal door.

Ah... she had the whole place to herself. As she took out her cigarette she surveyed her mini kingdom. Loose gravel, lots of space and lots of power line. Her cigarette lit, she blew out some of the tension. She looked at her watch. David. He had probably arrived by now. She fished out her phone.

2

David was texting Kathy back. Andrew was amazed that David even knew how to work it, but he seemed pretty adept. What a place. Andrew looked about taking in the surroundings. It was quite the spectacle and the freaks were out in force to enjoy it.

The central catwalk and surrounding seating only took up a small portion of the large empty warehouse. Behind the catwalk was another erected structure covered up by black surfaces, which in the darkness of the warehouse actually made for quite a weird effect. A seemingly black void. That was until the laser hit it, making it gleam, showing that it was coated in some kind of glossy sheen. Andrew was impressed. So, that little Kathy creature was behind all this. It was something.

The Devil slid up to him and David with a tray of drinks. Champagne. Not exactly his drink of choice but it was free. Both him and David took one. As it had been since they had arrived some twenty minutes earlier, Andrew could think of nothing to say to David. Someone who, as these last few days went by, he was beginning to realise he didn't really know that well at all. So Andrew continued to let his eyes wander. The mostly empty floor space was taken up by maybe five hundred people. Most of them strange. Some downright scary and all of them obviously rich enough to buy their way into Heaven , though they were clearly enjoying a little taste of Hell. The novelties kept coming as he kept scanning.

"David. Check it out." Andrew tugged his partner's arm.

David looked to where he was pointing. Cage dancers. Done before, but you can't improve on a classic. Sirens. Nice. Andrew was very tempted to go take a closer look at one of them, but he knew Kathy was coming to get them and he figured he'd just look like a bit of an unsophisticated idiot.

"Cage dancers." David had decided to participate. "Classic."

Andrew smiled. He couldn't agree more.

"Hey guys. What're looking at?"

"Hey sis."

David touched his sister's arm awkwardly. She smiled at him but didn't really make eye contact. It was a strange exchange that was making Andrew feel uncomfortable. He cut in before the atmosphere had time to get too thick.

"This place is something else, Kathy."

She smiled sweetly, the girliest he'd seen her so far. She was looking good. A sleek, stylish black suit with her cleavage being revealed as she leaned into her sweet smile.

"Thank you Andrew. I'm glad you like it."

"I do." Andrew looked about to emphasise his point. "So this is what you do? Organise this kind of thing? Bringing it all together."

Kathy snagged a glass of champagne from a passing demon, "Sort of. This and articles. As I said before it's all really just a prelude to our magazine that we're... I should introduce you guys to Giovanna." She was off. "Come on."

Andrew shook his head at not remembering the magazine bit.

* * *

Andrew followed on after David with Kathy leading the way. She had taken

73

them round the crowd and through a velvet rope barrier guarded by a big black bald bouncer. Then it was up some stairs built into the black void-like structure at its side. Through a black door and then into the overpowering whiteness of the back stage section.

Andrew didn't know where to look. Mean skinny bitches everywhere. He looked at David who was behaving like an adult. Kathy led them on. One of the topless ones flashed him what could have been a sneer, but he'd take it as a smile.

"Giovanna."

The tall goddess turned at the sound of her name. She smiled at seeing her friend.

"Kathy, Jesus. Where have you been hiding?" She walked up to them.

"Thought I'd let you do some of the work for a change."

"Ha-ha, very funny. And who are you're friends."

At hearing her voice, it was everything Andrew could do to stop himself from grabbing hold of Giovanna and doing horrible things to her.

"This is my big brother David."

Giovanna extended her hand which David shook, "So glad to finally meet you. I've heard so much about you. The older policeman brother. It's all very sexy."

David laugh, flattered and probably turned on. "It's nice to meet you, Giovanna."

"It's nice to meet you too, David."

She turned to Andrew. He reached out and took her hand. Kathy was watching.

"Hi. I'm the policeman brother's partner."

Andrew felt the weight of the words as he said them. He could tell they were stinging David.

Giovanna took his hand into the firm softness of her own, "Ah, now *you* I have not heard about." As she shook his hand, she gave Kathy a look.

Andrew wasn't sure exactly what it meant, but either way he was glad it existed.

"I'm new on the scene. Andrew." He backed up from it all. "I was saying to Kathy how impressed I am with what you two have put together here."

"Ah, you know fashion?"

"Not at all, but I know big."

Giovanna laughed about as perfectly sensual a laugh as one could have. After her brief laugh she pulled Kathy to her.

"I'm sorry boys, but I'm afraid I'm going to have to steal this lovely lady away from you. There's still much to be done before the show starts."

Kathy allowed herself to be dragged off. "I'll send Cindy to find you and she'll take you to where you can get the best view of the show."

Giovanna spoke again as they were just about to disappear from sight. "We should all go out to celebrate sometime." She blew a smacker of a kiss.

Andrew and David waved them off. David turned towards him.

"And what do we do now?"

"Well there are worse places we could be."

David smirked at this. Andrew continued.

"Do you want to talk about today?"

David shook his head very slightly. "No, I don't think so. Not now." He looked around, dealing with his surrounding, "Come on. Let's go get another drink."

Andrew wasn't in any hurry to leave. Half naked supermodels everywhere.

"I don't know if that's what your sister meant. I think that this Cindy was going to come find us here."

"I don't give a fuck what she meant." David started for the way they had come in.

Andrew sighed a personal goodbye to them all and followed.

3

It was her day off, which wasn't something she was happy about. Or at least, it wasn't exactly something she was comfortable with. The first show was done but there was a seemingly endless list of things that needed to be done before the next show and then the one after that and then for the magazine and so it went on and on off into… Kathy took a deep breath. It was her day off and she was going to make the best of it.

Giovanna had clearly been feeling guilty about having to pull her in a day early from France and leaving her to pretty much pull the first show up from nearly scratch in only a matter of days. Kathy sighed out another deep breath knowing that just like she'd been able to deal without Giovanna for a couple of days, Giovanna would be able to cope without her for one. Fashion in the park next. Deep breath.

Kathy was reading the paper. She'd stepped out to pick it up to see what was being said in print. As far as the night went it was a *'scintillating success'* as someone had put it. Tadworth Reed's creations were the focus and his dark Gothic stylings were being described as *'bold expressions of inner darkness'* while still being pretty and accessible.

It couldn't have gone better and Kathy was just about willing to believe that they might just be able to pull it all off.

The reviews of the show were on page fourteen but as Kathy continued to walk along the sidewalk she found herself being drawn back to what she'd not bothered reading on page one. *By the book or by any means necessary: A police story.* Kathy read on to find her brother's name connected to the word suspicion. Again and again, and less and less abstractly as the article went on. *The police department so far have been unavailable for comment and as this story seems to be something that they were hoping to keep under wraps, this should come as no surprise.*

There were no facts in the article but that word kept spinning around in Kathy's head. *'Suspicion.'*

* * *

It was her day off so her clothes were simple and comfortable. Tatty jeans, dirty sneakers and an old T-shirt with a picture of Che Guevara on it, who had become fashionable again, so she was a little embarrassed at having chosen to wear it. Her hair done up in a ponytail and no make-up.

All this she regretted as she strode in through the oversized doors of the New York Public Library. Not that she was the only casual in the place, but she felt maybe she looked a little too casual. Like at any minute an old security guard was going to come up behind her and inform her that if she didn't stop loitering she'd be thrown out and directed to the nearest shelter. As it went though, she was just going to have test this theory in order to find the section with the old newspaper slide reels.

Kathy walked over to the counter to ask the grey woman there. "Ah, excuse me."

The librarian looked up and then down at Kathy. "Can I help you?"

Her disguised scowl made Kathy feel like her own assessment of her look must not have been far from wrong.

"Yes, can you point me to the newspaper slides section please."

The librarian gave her a strange look in response. Kathy felt like assuring her that she wasn't going to use them to sleep under. After a few more back and forth exchanges of different looks, Kathy was finally armed with a series of keep left, through the corridor, second door on the right, over the bridge directions, and after getting turned around a few times, she was finally seated at one of the screens. Then, with a little assistance from the young man she had been informed would be there to assist, Kathy was on the right track. The *New York Times* from nearly four years back, starting the day after a date she'd tried all too hard to forget.

She didn't know what it was she was expecting to find. Some major story or just some name in the obituaries. There was something to find though, she was sure of it. She had seen it in David's eyes. What would it mean if she found something?

She still thought about him. Not often anymore, but he was still with her. She had wondered how she'd handle coming back home, seeing her old world again, but she'd handled it fine. She was a stronger person now. A promise she'd made to herself that day was never to let anyone make her feel that weak again. She was rubbing her left hand.

Nothing was coming up and her butt was beginning to hurt. She'd been in the chair for well over an hour and had gone through more than two months' worth of papers from the day after it had happened. Kathy let herself fall against the backrest of the chair, her arms falling away from the desk. Maybe someone like Calvin Hargreaves wasn't news. He wasn't news just like she hadn't been news. She'd escaped any measure of spotlight that day. She'd been found lying in the rain soaked through and had almost died of pneumonia. Nothing came out about it though. Her brother had been there in time for that bit. Nobody knew. And it looked like nobody knew anything about Calvin. He hadn't told her the name but she heard him say it. Whispers into his phone from behind the curtain as he'd stepped away from her bedside.

Then a month later, just after she'd gotten out of hospital, he'd told her that the bastard had been taken away and that he couldn't hurt her anymore. The new job that she'd been about to start had moved on away from her and after six months of looking over her shoulder and crying into her pillow, Kathy had packed her bags and headed for new shores. She was still a catch and the work was waiting for her. For three years she hadn't looked back, and now one little drunken conversation and a stupid headline and she was trying to dig up her pain again. There wasn't anything in the papers.

* * *

Kathy told the cab driver the address. As far as she knew it was still the same. Kathy couldn't remember if the divorce had happened before or after she'd left. At first she had tried to stay in contact but… Her hand was still aching. It was going to be awkward again. She didn't want to rush in there jumping to any conclusions. She'd have to feel it out, find out if their marriage coming to an end had anything to do with Calvin Hargreaves.

Kathy needed a cigarette. The plan had been to try and finish with it after last night. She'd smoked too many. When she woke up her lungs had felt like lead and the chest pain was back. But she hadn't had one all day, so one before she went in to talk to her long lost friend about potentially being the cause of her broken marriage wouldn't hurt.

* * *

The cab pulled to a stop with the green roofed house just down the suburban road. Kathy opened the door and got out stepping onto one of the manicured lawns. As she took her smokes out of her jeans pocket – no purse today – she watched the cab drive off. She lit the cigarette. She didn't even know if Jane knew she was back. It was going to be a little weird. She was definitely home. A trip to Jane's office had told her as much. It had been well over two years since they'd last spoken. How was she going to approach this? Not the easiest subject in the world to broach. Kathy was glad she'd decided on the cigarette.

* * *

"Oh my God, Kathy." Jane's face and arms were open to her.
Kathy accepted the invitation and stepped into the embrace. "Hello Jane."
Jane squeezed at her a little harder before separating and holding her at arm's

length. She was smiling broadly, happy to see her old friend.

"You look amazing. I can't believe it."

"Not my best outfit, I promise."

Jane waved a dismissive hand at this comment as she pulled Kathy inside. "Come in, come in."

The house was almost exactly the same. Whatever differences her new man had brought to the place, Kathy couldn't put her finger on it. Jane walked up behind her and ushered her toward the living room.

"Come and sit down. Talk to me." Jane sat Kathy down in front of her. "How long have you been back?" She was shaking her head. "I'm sorry, I just can't believe it."

Kathy smiled. Pangs of guilt shooting through her. Guilt at having let their friendship just slip away, and now of course at the fact that she had come back essentially only to dig at her past.

"I meant to come see you earlier but I've just been so busy."

Jane had pulled a seat rest forward and was seated staring straight into her eyes.

"I got in about four days ago. Just with seeing David again and…" Kathy could almost see the flinch behind Jane's eyes. "…and my work on the show."

Jane sparked up. "Oh God, that's right. You're here doing a big fashion event. I read something about that months ago. I was going to call you but…" She trailed off briefly but then immediately sparked back up and continued, "…but you should have called me, at least told me you were coming down."

"I know, I know. It's just being back…" Kathy noted Jane's smile soften. "But you're right. Anyway, I'm here now and I wanted to ask you…" She wasn't going to ask, "…if you wanted to come to our next show. It's an outdoor day time show in this lovely little private park and it's happening this Saturday." Kathy almost jerked back as Jane excitedly touched her leg.

"Oh I'd love to. A glamorous fashion show." She paused thinking. "Saturday…"

"It starts at two in the afternoon."

Jane smiled. "Perfect. I couldn't bring the husband and kids to something like that could I? I mean, I imagine that sort of thing, strictly speaking, just wouldn't be allowed."

Kathy laughed. "No, no. Not possible, you go ahead and tell them that I said you couldn't."

Jane shot up. "This counts for a drink."

As she headed to their mobile drinks stand, Kathy piped up. "Why don't we go out for a drink? Have some lunch." She was finding that she was enjoying seeing her old friend again. "My treat."

"How can I resist an offer like that? Let me just go and freshen up. Change." She started off for the stairs but stopped as Kathy grabbed her wrist.

"Please don't." Kathy indicated to herself, pointing out her less than stylish outfit.

4

David pulled to a stop in front of the school. He wasn't sure what he was doing there. He looked over at the large grey building beyond the walls and fences. He wasn't picking them up so why was he there? He hadn't seen either of them in over a month. He wiped his face as a wave of shame flushed through him. Jesse had every right to hate him. David realised that he hadn't even thought about either of them in all that time. The only reason he went over to the house anymore was to sneak around with their mother and he didn't even think that was going to happen anymore.

And there they were. Samuel. A happy little kid. David smiled watching his kids come out of the gates surrounded by all the others. Maybe he was too old to connect with his fourteen-year-old daughter. She was good to her brother. A tough little cookie. She took after her mother who had allowed her to have pink and purple streaks in her hair.

Their mother wasn't there to pick them up yet. The thought came. Was that why he was there? Steal a moment with them before she arrived. Then she'd come and see him with their kids and so it would go, and so on and so forth. It wasn't a good idea and besides, it was too late. A car pulled up in front of them. Not their mother's. The mobile drinks stand was doing his share of the parental duties. Hell, at least he could see that Jesse didn't like him either. They got in and the car drove off. He would make it right.

5

How had it gone? She hadn't really been social or keen to see anyone or be around people nearly at all. But she had been getting financial help from the happily married couple of David and Jane. Kathy was sure there had been cracks before it all but she could remember now that maybe a month or two after it, whenever she saw them together she'd seen that detachment. Not fighting, just this weary distrust.

She could remember it now. Another day to come around. Her brother picking her up from the shrink and coercing her into coming back to the house with him. She'd seen it then and from then on until she'd left. The divorce had happened after that. After she'd left. Kathy had seen it through the doorway. David had reached out to touch Jane and she'd flinched before looking up at him and crying.

Kathy remembered that her first thought had been that David must have been having an affair which Jane had found out about. As she thought about it now, of course it was all lining up. It had been a month. She'd only just gotten out and it was maybe a week, not even, after he'd told her they'd got Hargreaves. Was that it? Had Jane seen that something missing from his eyes and pulled the truth out of him? Was that why she flinched?

Kathy took her seat across from Jane at their small, dark green outdoor table, which was just above street level and overlooking a busy sidewalk. Kathy had never been there before but it was nice. No dress code apparently, but she was constantly being reminded of her appearance by the not so subtle looks of disapproval from those who were serving her. She figured out that she didn't really care and found herself staring directly back at them with her eyes just wide enough to say: *You got a problem?*

The place was Jane's suggestion. She said she'd been past it a thousand times but never went in. The waiter took their drink orders. A beer for both of them. As Kathy remembered it, Jane had never been a beer drinker but it was clear that she was taking her cue from her.

"So what's the story? Are you back down this way for good? You're doing a magazine with this partner of yours, right? You guys must be staying."

"Ah, yes, I think so. Once the shows are done we're gonna launch the magazine. If all goes well it'll come out within two months of the last show. Then we're gonna hope and pray it's well received and sells so we don't fall flat on our faces and bankrupt our investors." Kathy laughed this off and desperately fished out her cigarettes. "No, they'll be fine. It's just me and Giovanna who'll be ruined." She lit her cigarette and smiled.

Jane clearly didn't know how to respond. "Ah – fantastic." She smiled back. "I know you'll make this work and I can't wait to see your next show. What's it about? What's happening?"

Their disapproving waiter arrived with their drinks. Kathy took a sip of her cold beer and then a long drag on her only second cigarette of the day.

He was also holding an ashtray. "I'm afraid we do not permit smoking."

He held the ashtray out dramatically in front of him. Kathy stubbed out her cigarette and avoided his eyes. She was beginning to miss Europe. She turned back to Jane who was rolling her eyes in the direction of the retreating waiter. It made Kathy smile. Was she going to go there? Turn the conversation to her brother. Ask her old friend, who she had lost contact with, if she knew what happened to the man who was causing her left hand to throb. She put her beer glass down.

"Um, the last one, which was last night, was about darkness and all the things associated. So we had this big Demon-themed thing. All the outfits were sort of dark and mysterious. So now, this one is obviously light and all that goes with it…"

"So – angels?"

"I know, I know. It sound hackneyed…"

Jane jumped in. "No, no, I'm sure it's…"

"Don't worry. It is. But trust me. The events work."

"I have no doubt." Jane raised her glass towards Kathy. "To you, Kathy, and to your success."

Kathy lifted her own and clinked it against Jane's. "Why thank you, Jane."

"And then?"

"What?"

"It's three shows, right? What's the theme for the third?"

"Oh, it's the grand finale. Possibilities."

"Mysterious." Jane smiled again and sipped her beer. "Hmm, good idea."

Kathy nodded and sipped her own. After a moment of silence Jane leaned forward and crossed her arms on the table.

"This is nice. I'm so glad to see you again."

Fuck. Was she just the worst person in the world, or was Jane just making this ridiculously hard for her?

"It is." The two drags she'd had from her departed cigarette had not nearly been enough. "You hungry?" Kathy fumbled at the small menu.

"How you doing, Kathy?"

Hello... Kathy raised an obscure eyebrow. Jane touched her hand tenderly. Kathy let her clarify.

"Being back."

Fine actually. "It's been tough."

Jane squeezed her hand, giving Kathy a genuinely caring look of concern. Kathy could feel that she was a bitch, but she was also on a roll.

Kathy pulled. "Yeah. I mean mostly I'm fine with it. But then it hits me and I suddenly feel like I can't breathe." She stopped. That felt true. She shook it off and carried on with the line. "It's okay though. I made a commitment to face all this when we decided to come here for the magazine."

Jane was hooked. "Oh Kathy." She gave her hand one more squeeze and then eased back away. "I'm proud of you. You're obviously doing well."

Or maybe not. That last line Kathy didn't need. It was an end of topic line. She needed to keep it on the go just a bit longer.

"Only, I kind of feel like it's still hanging over me. Not knowing." Truth wrapped up in deceit. "You know."

Kathy looked at Jane searchingly. She could see that Jane was no longer as comfortable with this as she had been. She knew what happened. Which way was she going to go? Let her old friend carry on living in the dark. Or, was this the perfect opportunity for her to unload a heavy secret?

"Uh, Kathy..." The former. "...David told you didn't he? They got the guy, I thought."

The shadow of their disapproving waiter darkened the table. "Can I get you ladies another drink, or perhaps something to eat?"

Kathy felt the words before Jane said them as she grabbed her coat and bag. "You know, I'm not really feeling that hungry just now." She stood out of her chair and eased past the waiter.

"Jane, wait." Kathy reached out for her arm to stop her but Jane's manoeuvring was too fluid.

"Sorry, but I just remembered I'm supposed to pick the kids up from school."

She was almost at the exit of the restaurant's sidewalk courtyard. Kathy thought about getting up and going after her but she could tell that the waiter was prepared for such an obvious check-dodging move. Jane called out her last as she walked past their table, making her way down the sidewalk.

"I'll call you."

Kathy watched her until she was out of sight. She then looked back up to her looming waiter.

"Another drink?"

Kathy fished out and held up her card. "Just the check please."

<h1 style="text-align:center">6</h1>

Andrew made his way through the labyrinth of rooms that made up Dana's dark little corner of the dungeon. She'd had a hit and the message was to get down there as soon as possible.

"Detective Bates."

Andrew had finally found her in their little six by eight grey office kitchen. Almost every inch of its single length of counter was taken up by appliances and half empty cookie wraps. She had a freshly steaming cup of coffee in her hand.

"Dana. You got something for me?"

She walked past him, sipping her coffee as she went. He followed as she made a more logical route through the rooms. Andrew wondered how they worked down here. One of the pairs of glasses looked up at him as they walked through its dark world. With the interruption over they were aimed back down at the fingers slamming away at the keyboard.

Dana rounded a small half-circle counter and sat down at the computer there. Andrew wasn't sure if it was her workstation or some main computer, but he kept to his side of the counter for fear of maybe knocking her and her cup of coffee onto the central main frame. Or maybe it was that he found Dana to be quite intimidating and didn't want to stand behind her, arched over her shoulder without her say so.

"Come round."

He did as he was told. Dana tapped the keyboard and scrolled up an image. There he was – Cartwright a.k.a Don't ask. The entire image was marked in a lot of red writing that screamed trouble at you. There was no information on the deceased other than the picture.

"I haven't told the Chief yet." She looked up at Andrew making him stand up straight and step away from her shoulder. "But I thought since it's your case and you were in the building that you should be the first to know."

Andrew wasn't exactly sure what it all meant but he could feel himself getting excited.

Dana swivelled in her chair to face him. "This was flagged as soon as it came up and was followed by a phone call and a fax." She reached over, picking up a piece of paper, which she then handed to him.

"Flagged by who?"

"The FBI Detective. They're going to be in first thing in the morning. You need to take that piece of paper you're holding up to The Chief and the two of you need to call that number at the top."

Andrew looked at the faxed copy of the Federal Bureau of Investigation headed stationery. There was a name and number at the top left corner: Special Agent Harry Hodgeson.

"Is that why it took so long to go through? Because he belongs to the Feds?"

Dana shrugged. "I don't know. I would've thought the opposite was true."

Andrew nodded, pondering this as he turned to navigate his way out.

7

Things were in order. Cliff had called earlier to inform him that the body had been found. They would be able to tell that it had been moved but it didn't matter. They would have their inside man and all reason to pursue the matter any further would dry up. That was if Special Agent Cliff Wilcott had done his side of the job properly and not given them any reason to. Anthony sure as shit knew that he hadn't.

If all went the way it was supposed to, the whoever who had shot Special Agent Jack Griffin wouldn't matter. A greedy double-crossing partner. No, all that would be brushed aside in favour of making the whole ugly mess go away. All in all, it may not have been his idea and when it came down to it, it wasn't a scene he was glad to be in the middle of, but things were going well and Anthony couldn't help but smile. He began to enjoy himself even more knowing that his broad smile was beginning to creep out his new friends.

Anthony had decided, despite how late it was, to pay them a little visit. See how they were settling into their new home. A five star luxury establishment compared to anything they had ever known before, he imagined. It was, in actual fact, only okay. The kind of place where you paid cash and so long as it was on time, nobody asked questions or did any checking. Safe for him and safe enough for them. Too good to be true? Of course. But kids this down and out, Anthony found easy to convince. Or maybe they were just willing to be used if they knew they could get some comfort out of it.

Little Jamie was not watching the TV and trying not to take notice that his eyes were aimed at her. She was still off the stuff so far as he could tell. Look at this – still off the junk, living in a new place, a new job, getting her life back on track. Good for her. Anthony picked up his preferred bottle of bourbon off the small round yellow table that housed the lamp next to his seat and took a long swig. He dipped down trying to settle into that elusive sweet spot in the uncomfortable armchair. Fully furnished, nice place.

"Chess."

Chester looked over from his position in the kitchen doorway. His leaning was meant to make him look unfazed by Anthony's presence.

"Yeah?"

"How old are you?"

"Twenty-two."

"Ever killed anyone before?"

He was fazed. Little Jamie looked up at her man. He didn't look back.

"Look, I...." He stepped out of the doorway towards Anthony, his hand help up like he was directing a taxiing plane. "I don't know…"

"Don't fucking walk up on me." This froze the blond boy in his tracks.

"I'm sorry."

Little Jamie 'Switch' Nuemyer was shaking now, more than usual. Chester backed it up again. Anthony smiled again. Fully designed to creep his employees out.

"I'm just fucking with you Chess. No, no. I'm just gonna use you guys as couriers. You pick up, drop off, that kind of stuff."

Anthony could see the relief wash over Chester's face. Exactly what he'd hoped for. Couriers, he could handle that. Little Jamie let out a shaky laugh. They both looked at her. She shrunk back into herself.

Anthony raised his bottle in her direction. "That's right Switch. The good life is just up ahead."

She was looking at him, afraid not to make eye contact. Anthony looked back over to Chester who was now back in his doorframe.

"Let's all have a drink. Get some glasses and we'll all have a drink to celebrate our new friendship."

Chester stepped off into the small kitchen and clinked through some glasses as he selected the appropriate three. He returned and placed them on the table next to Anthony. Anthony proceeded to pour out three shots worth.

"Go get your girlfriend."

Jamie looked up to her boyfriend as he stepped over to her. She clearly didn't want to partake but she didn't resist as her boyfriend who was clearly aware of what was good for them, leaned over and pulled her up.

Anthony marked both of their reactions as they turned back to him to see his gun now on the table next to the three glasses. "Was making me uncomfortable. Come on over here, you." Anthony scooched forward and put his hand around Jamie's bare waist, which she'd been trying to hide from him since he'd arrived.

She tried to pull away but when that couldn't be done without making an issue of it, she allowed herself to be reeled in. Soft skin. Anthony didn't want to scare them too much, just a little fun. He guided her down onto his knee. Chester's eyes shifting between him, his girl and the gun. Anthony handed out the drinks.

Jamie tried to deny the offer. "I feel sick."

Anthony pushed the glass into her hand. "Well this is medicine." He gave her a peck on the cheek and could see Chester's own cheeks flush from the corner of his eye. "Come on Switch, nobody likes to drink alone." He looked up at Chester, making him look into his eyes. "To us."

Anthony waited as Chester blankly knocked back his drink. He then looked at Jamie. Her eyes avoided his but when she couldn't find Chester's she straightened herself up and knocked back her own. It hit her hard. Her hand immediately going up to her mouth as her eyes filled up with water and her throat convulsed. She stood up off Anthony's knee, managing to keep her cold soup down. Chester scooped up his girl and lead her back to the couch, back to safety.

Anthony couldn't help but laugh.

"And on that note," Anthony knocked back his shot and stood, "I'll leave you guys to get some rest."

Chester was on the couch with Jamie, holding her in his arms. Maybe trying to reassure her of his protection. Anthony picked up his gun and slipped it into the back of his pants. He then fished out a fifty from his coat and laid it on the table by the empty glasses.

"I'll see you guys again soon."

No goodbyes? Anthony chuckled to himself as he walked to the door and let himself out.

CHAPTER SEVEN

1

David shot up dead straight in his bed. He looked around the darkness of his room searchingly. He brought his hand up to his face and wiped away the sweat. He was covered. A chill ran through him. His sheets were soaked through. God, what had he been dreaming about? He tried to remember. Something about a row boat or – no – there was a rowboat he thought, but... No, it was gone.

He looked at his bedside clock – 03:42. He lay back down. Shit. He swung out of bed and pulled off all the bedding in one continuous movement. Going to be wide-awake by the time he was done. Never going to be able to fall back asleep. He turned on the light. Didn't matter, he supposed. Not like he had to be at work in the morning.

He slipped off his boxers and tossed them onto the wet pile of sheets crumpled up on the floor. After selecting another pair he quietly opened his bedroom door and made for the hallway closet hoping for something usable, thinking that his sister had probably snagged the best of it and left a tea cloth. He felt about at the top of the closet and managed to find two decent blankets. There were sheets too but that could wait for the next night.

He was still dead tired, he'd be able to drop off again. Toilet. David tossed the blankets onto his bed and headed for the toilet. That done it was back to bed. After the blankets were comfortably moved about and the dry pillow moved to the top, out went the lights... Nope. Not going to happen. He was wide-awake. Screw it. David kicked off the blanket and bounced off his bed and over to his chest of drawers. He pulled out his most comfortable sweat suit, pulled it on and headed for the TV. A few beers and a late night movie was what fate apparently had in store for him.

2

She needed caffeine. Kathy dragged her feet towards the kitchen. It was too early and she was tired and her stomach was all tied up in knots. Giovanna's late night call had not made her slumber a pleasant one. The meeting was at ten and it was across town and it was a fucking waste of time. How could they know it was really a problem already? It comes up last night and now suddenly its fucked and there needs to be an immediate money meeting about it. She hadn't even been given the chance to smooth things over and sort it out. This meeting was the problem. It was wasting time, and that was what was going to fuck things up.

Kathy made her turn into the kitchen and grabbed the kettle and stuck it under the now running tap. Full. She put it back onto its base, clicked it on and prepared for the eternal wait. The one she'd left in France practically finished boiling the water before you even clicked it on. Her ingredients mixed in, Kathy turned and propped her butt against the counter. The TV was on. She edged her butt a little to the left and then leaned that same way to see past the outer counter's pole support.

David was sprawled out on the couch, his jaw fully unhinged with a faint wheezy guttural sound coming out of his mouth. Kathy wiped her tired eyes. An empty whiskey bottle was lying on its side on the glass coffee table. About a quarter of its contents spread around it. She didn't want to feel this way about her brother, this sense of distrust. She'd been staying here for too long. She needed to be closer to Giovanna anyway. In the city. The kettle clicked off. At-a-girl, leave him now. Just when he needs someone the most. Walk out without saying goodbye. Maybe leave a note telling him how much you hated him for not protecting you and how much you detest the fact that he thought he could find redemption in killing the man who caused him to fail you.

She walked out of the kitchen. He could have her coffee. He was going to need it more than her. She needed to get going, she had a very important meeting to get to. She needed to get out of there before he woke up.

3

Fucking Feds. Andrew had to admit that this little mystery was more than a little intriguing to him. A family murder suddenly involving the FBI. It was juicy stuff, but now it was going to be taken away. They didn't give him or the Chief anything, just orders. Have all reports on hand. All information at the ready. What the hell were the Cartwrights into? Andrew figured this for a witness relocation thing gone wrong and had asked but they politely suggested that all questions wouldn't be answered the next day when they could all talk in person.

Andrew rolled over and stared at the back of Bill's little helper's head. She'd had her hair cut since he'd seen her the time before. One of those crinkle cuts. He had found it quite striking when he turned into the crime lab looking for Bill. No Bill. For the best, he wouldn't have been happy. Looking at her hair now, Andrew decided he didn't like it. What he did like was her back. So smooth with the lightest of tans. Probably the bottled variety. He traced the knuckle of his finger down her spine and then moved the sheets down to get a fuller view. She stirred slightly but didn't wake. Andrew continued to move the sheets as he spotted and marvelled at a small cluster of moles just above where her panty line would have been. He wondered if they made her self-conscious. Did she not wear midriff tops and low rider jeans because of them? Did she love them, thinking they made the view all the better? Or did she not care? He'd never know. Andrew pulled the sheet back up.

4

David opened his eyes and was immediately slammed into a world of pain and regret. His head felt like it needed to be screwed off and chucked in the garbage. He didn't think he could move from his sprawl. David looked at the bottle lying on its side. There hadn't been any beer, but he wasn't going to be denied. He sat up and immediately began paying for it as his head began to pulsate from inside his skull.

What a mess. The whole getting his life back together thing was going to have to wait. David pushed himself up into a stand. A bath, that was an idea. He tried to take his first steps towards putting his plan into action but he was stuck. At some point during the night he had pulled the glass coffee table closer, wedging in his legs. Groaning, David bent down to move it. The sudden rush of blood to his head was not helping matters. He pushed the table away and watched as the shift caused the bottle to roll away and fall off the table. He supposed he could have stopped it but that whole synapses thing just wasn't happening. It smashed to the floor.

"Ah, good." I'm glad.

Why was he even up? The light in the apartment told him that it was still too early for him to be awake. David stopped moving and tried to focus his hearing. What was that sound? He focused on it. It was his phone alarm coming from his bedroom. It was a reminder alarm as well and he knew what it was for. He had to be in court. David shook his head as he navigated his way past the jagged mess on the floor and headed for the bathroom. What a first day he was having as a civilian.

5

Andrew stepped into Chief Groder's office. Despite the situation he was glad to finally be at work. The ride in had been awkward. Andrew hadn't figured on it being the most convenient and logical choice to drive Denise into work. It was a quiet ride. She had got the message when he'd suggested that it was time for her to leave, it being time for him to go to work and all. She hadn't been upset, just plainly pointed out the more logical option. At least Bill hadn't been around to see her get out of his car. She was too young for him anyway, though he couldn't say he regretted it. What a body.

The Chief was busy with some kind of paper work, his reading glasses perched on the end of his nose. Somehow they seemed to make him even more of a menacing presence than usual, or maybe it was just the obvious tension in his shoulders.

"Morning, boss." Andrew closed the door behind himself. "No sign of the Feds yet?"

"No." The Chief continued to furiously scan through the pages spread out in front of him. "Your reports are a mess."

"Not up to Federal issue standard?" Andrew slipped into one of the two chairs across from the Chief.

The Chief looked up at him and removed his glasses. "I don't want any crap from you, Bates. I want you on your most cordial best fucking behaviour. When they get here I want you out of that seat and pulling it out for one of them to sit in." He had his finger aimed at Andrew.

"You expect any less of me?"

88

The Chief retracted his finger and slipped his reading glasses back on. "Unfortunately, we're only going to be as involved as these bastards see fit to allow, which I doubt will be very much." He looked back down to the offending reports. "Still, with the Harris case being the way it is, it might be for the best that your attention isn't so divided."

Andrew leaned in. "Are we even going to try for a piece of this?"

"Just leave most of the talking to me."

Andrew acknowledged his boss' dominance with a prerequisite moment of silence. Message acknowledged, he pushed on.

"So when they getting here?"

"Soon."

"And I'm not supposed to say anything?"

He'd toned it back half way between question and reiteration. The Chief looked back up. He was clearly tired and not in the mood to indulge this back and forth.

"How's your partner doing?"

Andrew didn't know. "He's doing okay." His seat was uncomfortable. "I mean I think he is. He seems to be handling it okay."

The Chief's studying stillness was making Andrew's chair even more uncomfortable.

"You need to keep an eye on him. He hasn't been fired yet, Detective. The books still have him listed as your partner and you guys are supposed to look out for each other."

"Is that supposed to mean something?" Andrew's tone came out with more intensity than he would usually allow himself with the Chief. He'd seen the results of such an act many times before. The Chief was usually willing to indulge a little banter and anger, but if it pushed further than he was prepared to allow you could find yourself in trouble. This was because the Chief was not above being petty and when it came to utilising the time of the offenders, he could find some pretty wastefully useless and time consuming endeavours for them to wade through. Either that or he was liable to throw his desk at you.

Andrew was spared the opportunity to press his question any further when the tiny presence of Stacy Keen opened the door and stuck her head in.

"Chief, Special Agents Devlin and Webb are here to see you now."

The Chief stood out from behind his desk. "Send them in."

Stacy ducked her head back out and pushed the door open. Before they entered, the Chief forcefully indicated to Andrew to *get his ass out of the chair*, their previous near exchange forgotten. Andrew did as ordered and stepped off to stand in the corner where he could get a look at these guys before they saw him. The first was maybe in his early thirties, younger than him but not better looking. Weak chin.

"Chief Groder." The first extended his hand, at the same time catching sight of Andrew off to his side. He looked back to the Chief. "Sorry to keep you waiting. I'm Special Agent Webb."

Special Agent number two was right behind him. Older but not by much. His look was more defined. From his jaw line to the lines of his suit, this guy was in charge.

"Not a problem. This is Detective Bates. He was handling the case."

Andrew decided to step forward and be recognised. He accepted Webb's hand.

Webb indicated to his partner. "And this is Special Agent Devlin."

Devlin was now standing off in the opposite corner, too far to shake hands with. This made Andrew's teeth clench. This guy was playing the hand that he had just folded. Agent Devlin gave them each a slight nod. The Chief stepped back round to his side of the desk, trying to get back some of the dominance he'd just given away.

"Please, sit down." The Chief sat.

Agent Webb accepted the offer. "Thank you."

Seeing that Special Agent Devlin was making no plans to move in, Andrew decided to step forward and re-take his seat. As he settled in he chose not to make eye contact with the Chief.

"Coffee?" The Chief tried to subtly organise and slip all the pages back into their folders.

Andrew didn't like seeing his boss stepping and fetching this way. Not the man he'd grown to fear and respect.

"No thanks." Webb politely waved off the offer. "So, what can you tell us about the Cartwrights? Any leads, any suspects, anything at all?" Webb was looking at the Chief who directed his gaze to Andrew.

Andrew shifted in his seat to keep both Feds in his sights. "They were discovered on the morning of Saturday just past. All but the mother were stabbed to death with what we think was a large hunting knife. The mother had her head smashed in with a golf club and their fourteen year old daughter was also sexually assaulted." Andrew studied their faces for clues as to whether this stuff surprised them or not. Devlin wasn't giving anything away, but Andrew thought he could see some shifting happening behind Webb's eyes.

Webb spoke, and if Andrew's words had rattled him, his tone didn't reflect it. "Any suspects? Anything pointing you in any specific direction?"

"Mr Cartwright was poisoned." This got both their attention.

"Poisoned?" Webb was still doing the talking, but Devlin was circling in closer. "What kind of poison?"

"We don't know. We found an empty bottle of booze next to Cartwright's bed. Looked to be he'd drunk himself into a stupor and was just too drunk to know he was about to be stabbed. But our lab guy, Bill found that there wasn't much alcohol in his blood so he checked what was left in the bottle and found some stuff in there."

Devlin was standing between the two chairs and speaking over them to the Chief. "How many of your people know about this?"

"Just a handful. It's not public knowledge."

"Good. Make sure it stays that way. We're going to need all the paper work you have on this case and written statements from your handful of privy staff, As well as your assurance that this information will not slip into the hands of the press."

The Chief handed the folders over to Webb. "Don't worry, there aren't going to be any leaks."

Devlin continued. "We'll need to talk to this 'Bill'. We're going to need everything he has on this case and especially on the foreign agent he discovered." Devlin stepped back and Webb stood out of his chair to join him.

Andrew looked from Devlin to Webb, whose silence had taken on a pained quality. "And can we expect any info from your end?"

Webb didn't seem to register the question. Devlin looked down at Andrew as if his words had somehow put a bad taste in his mouth. He spat out his response.

"Detective Bates, We are not required to tell you anything."

"Not even a little bit?" Andrew gestured the desired amount between his thumb and forefinger.

"Bates!"

There was the man he loved and feared.

"No Detective, Not even a little bit." Devlin had turned smug. He looked to The Chief. "We still expect your full co-operation."

"You'll get it."

"Good. Now we'd like to talk to *Bill*." Devlin emphasised the simplicity of the name.

"Chief Groder," Webb stepped up to the desk holding out a card for The Chief to take. "If you remember anything else, here's my number at the office."

The Chief took it. "I'll arrange for someone to show you down to the lab." He picked up the phone and pressed one of the buttons. The sound of Stacy's phone could be heard outside the office. It cut out as she picked it up. "Stacy, could you get Donovan in here for me?"

After her reply The Chief put down the receiver. "Detective Parkett will show you to the forensics lab. I'll inform Mr Dudley that you're coming to see him."

The door opened suddenly bumping Special Agent Devin's arm. Donovan stuck his head in.

"Ooh, 'scuse me." He looked to The Chief. "Sir?"

"Show these two down to the lab for me. Bill will be waiting." To the Feds, "You can tell Mr Dudley how you want to go about transferring the bodies. He'll see to whatever you need."

Donovan backed out the doorway. "If you guys will just follow me."

The two looked to Andrew and The Chief before following Donovan. Andrew gave Webb one of his nods. Devlin stepped aside to allow Webb to pass before giving his last word.

"We'll be in touch." He left pulling the door closed with him.

Andrew let his head fall back towards The Chief. "What do you think?"

"About?"

Andrew straightened in his chair. "About what this is all about."

"I don't know Bates, and neither do you, and you're not going to know either, so the only thing I need you to do is to drop it."

Andrew slumped down. "Yeah, pretty interesting though."

The Chief leaned back in his chair. "Yeah, pretty interesting. What are you up to today?"

"Well, no court appearances and no case so not much."

"Why don't you check on your partner? Make sure he's dealing with all this okay."

Andrew took his cue and pushed himself up. What else was he going to do? It was as good an excuse as any for a little drinking on duty. He gave The Chief a small wave gesture and headed for the door. As he opened it he turned and gave his last word.

"Be sure and let me know if those two need anything, so I can be as helpful as possible."

The Chief didn't react. Andrew took his leave.

6

Kathy's mind snapped back from its elsewhere at the echoed sound of her name. She refocused her attention onto the three faces across the large shining finish of the boardroom table.

"Miss Radley, should we expect more of the same?" Apparently continuing, said the one in the middle with the over-centralised facial features.

This was professional. Yes? What was the question? Kathy could feel Giovanna not helping. I'm sorry Mr Bulls Eye, but what the fuck are you talking about?

"I'm so sorry... sir." Sir? "...I didn't catch that last part."

A specifically audible sigh sounded out from the seat next to hers.

* * *

"What the fuck was that?" Giovanna's lighter was struggling against the funnelled wind shooting up the sidewalk.

Giovanna was a passionate person but Kathy had never really found herself on this side of it before.

"I'm sorry, okay? I got distracted."

The six inches Giovanna had on her was making Kathy feel like a petulant child. There was trouble with the third location. Trouble... It was gone. There was a last minute legal mix up with the paper work and licensing which had been put on Kathy's to do list when she got into town, as Giovanna had had to hot foot it across country. As it went though, wires had gotten crossed and Kathy had somehow just confirmed it in her mind. And thus the Planetarium, with its grand dome ceiling onto which a world of infinite wonders could be projected, had simply pulled out and taken its business elsewhere. What was she going to say – she was overworked? Didn't make any difference. They were still without a hot spot for the grand finale. Or maybe trouble at home. Blame David even though this would have happened without his help. She started to cry, apparently settling on the latter. She hated herself for it. For this weakness.

"Kathy?" Giovanna's previous tone was forgotten and Kathy felt herself hating her for that too.

* * *

Their coffee had arrived. Black, no sugar for the both of them. When it came to becoming the masters of your own universe, no substitute would do. The coffee shop had been just down from where they were standing and Giovanna had been quick to guide them over and in. Ever the image doctor, never would she have allowed this spectacle to be visible to those who mattered.

Now Kathy felt like a bitch. Giovanna had been soothing her right through her unshakable torrent, trying to assure her that yes they'd lost the location, yes the investors weren't willing to shell out any additional funds; yes it was a cold and windy day, despite forecasts of clear and sunny, just like the ones for the day after tomorrow when their day time outdoor show was to take place, but it would all work out okay.

"You okay?"

Kathy nodded. She took a small test sip of her coffee. Still too hot.

"What's this all about?" Giovanna was already drinking hers.

* * *

Cold day then too. Worse. The wind had been harder and not to mention it had been storming rain. Back then she'd been your average one pack a day, if that. She stepped out of the cab. Gridlock. She couldn't wait any longer. She'd have to brave the weather. The subway station was only a couple of blocks down. She regretted it instantly. Rain and wind stinging her face, her clothes already beginning to stick. Had to be done. She was already late. She navigated her way through the labyrinth of stalled cars till she found herself on the sidewalk, which was still bustling with its own traffic.

A shoulder bump. She dropped her expensive handbag and saw it splash down, spilling its contents onto the wet pavement. Fuck. She went down onto her haunches and began scrapping together her belongings. She could feel herself getting wetter by the second. No dry clothes to change into. Quite the impression she was going to make. Up and on her way. Her handbag probably ruined, as well as her make-up, her chequebook for definite. Good start to the day. Great start to the new job.

She turned into the slick narrow concrete steps that led down into the subway station. Empty. She was rushing. Rushing to get where she was going, rushing to get out of the rain. She slipped. Her foot shot out in front of her as she screamed in fright. She panicked for the handrail but her hand merely glanced against it as her other foot's ankle twisted painfully under the unexpected extra weight. Her knee buckled and she went down. Her hip was first to make its sharp connection with the edge of the concrete steps. The pain rattled its way suddenly up her spine. Her elbow was next. The awkward jarring slide of her descent was turned into a roll. The end came with a smack as her face bounced grazingly off the last step.

Silence, all too briefly... The last thump was echoing through her head. Her eyes were shut, she could taste blood. She brought her one hand up to her swollen lips. They parted in a groan and she could feel the warm line that followed and flowed down her chin. She touched her hand gently to her face, afraid of what it might find there. Her cheek was swollen too, raw, scraped, her eye. She opened the other to see the scraped flesh of her shaky palm.

With her head now raised, the pounding wave was echoing louder. She dropped it low allowing her hand to cradle it above the wet floor. This soothed it slightly. The sound of hard soles were suddenly clapping towards her. A man. He was saying something. She looked up despite the wave. Her vision was blurry, tears in her eyes. She wasn't crying. Just her body reacting. He was asking if she was alright. She pulled her other arm out from underneath. She could feel, but took no notice of the blood being drawn as her hand was pulled from its wedge between her and the edge of the last step.

He was above her now. Same question. She planted both palms flat and tried to push herself up. He wasn't helping. Tentative hands on her sides – he was helping. She let out a groan instead of a thank you. More blood escaped. She could feel the loose skin against her teeth. Up. Her wet palms were away from the pavement – her knees. She was standing, his hands still on her, still holding her up. Her consciousness wanted out, wanted that blissful nothingness. She didn't want to give in to its desire... Too embarrassing. She shook her head and railed against the oncoming black. It worked.

She forced out a sluggish reply to his previous question, trying to appease his worried tone. He was asking if she could stand. She put her hand against the grimy dull yellow paint on the wall as a response. He understood and removed his hands from her sides. Her other hand joined the first. She stated the obvious. It made her swollen lips sing. He let out a sympathetic laugh and told her how it was no big deal, how just last week ... That question came again. Her forehead scraping against the rough wall. The black invading. His hands were on her again. She heard the word *Hospital*. Didn't sound like a bad idea. *David*, she heard herself say.

* * *

There were more people now. Quite the anecdote she had turned into. A woman first. The two had helped her along. Next a security guard. People were rushing by, widening their eyes as they past, some just standing off to the side watching. *He* had been there.

The first was on her phone talking to her brother. Said that he was coming. He wasn't far. No big scene with an ambulance, thank God. Too much traffic anyway. Her brother was going to come on the train. Said he was only a few stops away.

* * *

She was in the security guard's booth. He was very young. He had his medical aid kit and was dabbing something on her lip. It burned. Said it wasn't too bad. Just a concussion. The first was gone. Train to catch. The woman too. Her brother was going to get her to the hospital. Another few stops away. She could tell the young security guard was eager for his arrival. This clearly hadn't been a big part of his everyday job description. Her head was killing her. Too painful to think. He'd given her some sugar water. Trying to stop her from drifting off. Just a concussion. The world kept shifting in and out of focus.

Unconsciousness wanted her. She couldn't drink the sugar water. Her swollen jaw wouldn't allow it. She closed her eyes. She heard his chair shift as he bolted out of it to shake her up. She looked at him, told him she was fine. His expression told of a renewed desire to get a better job.

They both jolted at the incredibly loud crashing sound. Her brother had later told her that *he* had thrown something on the tracks. Hit the juiced rail and caused a loud and distracting eruption of sparks. The young and inexperienced security guard was out the booth, making his way over to the distracted crowd. David had made sure that he had gotten into trouble. Repercussions for letting the wounded sister of a cop get kidnapped right from under your nose. She didn't know what had happened to him. She didn't think she cared.

The door to the flimsy security booth erupted inwards barely before it had had a chance to close. She didn't see what he looked like. Couldn't tell you if he was white or black, tall or fat. All she saw were his teeth and his eyes. It happened too quickly. Her world was still in slow motion. He didn't seem to move. Just appeared closer and closer with each flash in her head. First him, then his hand, then a slamming jolt. With it she felt the rising wave thundering its way up. His hands were on her. Pulling her up. She tried to hold onto the light, fight off his dirty wanting hands. He was behind her. She saw her knees give. She was passing out. She needed to stay awake. She needed to scream. She needed help and then... The security guard was back. His words echoed through the engulfing blackness... *'Mr Radley?'*

* * *

She came to, shaking all over. Stones digging into her wet back, rain pelting down on her face. An alley. He wasn't gone. She felt him. No! The word never

95

passed her lips. Her jaw was humming out. His punch. It was broken. No, no, no, no. She couldn't see him. She couldn't make her body work. Couldn't lift herself to see him. She didn't want to see him. Her legs were being opened. No! No!

She tried to roll away from him. He asked her where she thought she was going. She wasn't going anywhere. He was above her, one hand on her shoulder holding her down. His breath was hot on her face. She was going to be sick. She pushed against his chest but he wasn't going to be moved. He was laughing. He told her not to struggle. She was crying. Panic. She wasn't going anywhere. This was happening. He told her if she didn't struggle he wouldn't use the knife. She saw it before she felt its cool blade against her jaw, reminding her of how much it was aching.

All she could see now were his eyes. Hungry. With his hand still bearing down on her shoulder, he pushed himself up. She heard herself squeal as his weight made the uneven concrete dig into her shoulder blade. He dragged the knife pointedly down her body. Down, down. She moved. She couldn't help it. He had her. She was his to take. The promise of his warning was screaming in her head but she couldn't be near that knife. Her skirt was up. She was still moving. He had barely noticed. She wasn't going anywhere. His hand pinning her down, his knees between her legs giving her nowhere to go.

She felt the cold metal slip underneath her panties, lifting them away, and she squealed again. Her hands darted down as his knife hooked into place. He slashed out cutting them away, his blade bloodying up one of her desperate hands as it went. It didn't hurt. She didn't pull back. She was exposed. Both hands went to cover herself. No!!

His other hand was quickly in between her legs trying to pry hers away. Bloodied hand, now aching, was not to be moved. No longer held down she felt herself rolling – her only route of escape. Rolling away from him, tucking her legs in, making it safe.

He didn't warn her again. Her spine jolted her head back as the knife went in.

CHAPTER EIGHT

1

David had found him. Went to one of his shit hole hang outs and asked the right people the right questions and got the right answers, or at least, the kind of lies that he could see right through. He'd been doing this job too long to not know how to find an arrogant shit heel punk who didn't know how to hide.

He had run. Bolted off into the night the second the door had been kicked in. David didn't think he'd seen who had done it, but he must have known what was coming because he was out the window in a flash. Friends downstairs must have tipped him off in the precious seconds prior, as he'd managed to get his shoes and pants on. His girl was looking at him from behind her protectively hiked up sheet. He probably had time to get his gun too. Good. It just meant David wouldn't be able to follow him out the window. He turned back for the door. He'd get him outside. He quickened his pace. David knew he'd take the obvious route. The house backed onto a high fence, beyond which was a railway yard. Once out back the house would corner him into running left and from there he'd stick to the road. He was panicked and not a thinker. He was just a thug that had gone too far. David made his way back down through the dilapidated house. None of them got in his way. They knew he was a cop.

Outside David could see him hot footing it down the sidewalk. The street lamps catching the glistening flesh of his back as he passed beneath them. David climbed into his car and tore it off the lawn after him. Hearing the car was slowing his pace as he turned his head to see it coming. David waited for him to turn off. His gun was digging uncomfortably in his side, begging for release. Garver jumped the gate and made the turn. He had him. David slammed on the brakes, the car screeching to a halt just past the gate leading to the turn in the high fence that Garver Harris had just ducked down. David was instantly out the car with his gun in hand.

The high fence formed a make shift alley with the closed hardware store. After an adrenaline-fuelled vault over the chest high gate, David slowed his pace as he neared the end of the building's sidewall. The fence continued on, appearing to round the back, forming a small open storage yard. David could hear him. Not on the move, scuffing, trying to figure out his next move. Break into the store? Try and climb the fence? He didn't have a gun or he would have taken a shot by now. The sound of shattering glass came through. David stepped past the end of the wall and aimed into the open area towards the back of the closed hardware store. There he was standing on a crate with his hand through a broken windowpane, desperately searching for the latch.

"Freeze Garver! Police!" David had his gun trained on the back of his head, the trigger already almost fully pulled in.

Garver slowly retracted his hand and brought it up to be with his other one.

"Get down from there!"

Garver did as he was told. He hopped down, causing a swell of dust to plume around his feet.

"Detective Radley." He took a step forward. "I didn't realise it was you. I wouldn't have run if I'd have known..."

"Stay where you are and don't fucking move!"

"What are you going to do?" He was still coming, "Arrest me for breaking and entering? I told you, I thought you were one of the bad guys."

David was backing away now. "You know God damn well why I'm here, you piece of shit. You're under arrest for assault. Now stay where you fucking are."

Garver's raised hands were less ridged now... still approaching. "Oh, I get it. What did she tell you? I just dropped by to get her to give you a message. If I'd had your number, I would have just called."

It happened so fast. David had backed into the fence. The unexpected stop had thrown him and before he knew it Garver had dropped his hand and pulled out his gun, which had been obscured to David by the darkness, from the back of his pants. David fired off a round which hit Garver in the left side of his neck as he fired one off at David. David fell to the side as the bullet hit the fence next to him. He hit the ground and took aim at Garver again.

Garver was hunched over and staggering wildly as pumping blood forced its way past his clamping hand. His back was to David as he ambled his way back towards the gate he had come over. His gun was still hanging loosely at his side. David could tell that he was trying to hold onto the strength that was ebbing away so that he could turn and face him.

"Drop the gun Garver!"

Then the gun swung out as Garver began to fire wildly behind himself. David shifted back as the dust began to kick up around him and fired off a second shot which tore into Garver's lower back. The erratic firing stopped and the gun hit the dirt. Garver sunk to his knees then, and after a brief sway on his haunches, fell flat on his back and died.

* * *

David leaned back, having finished retelling the story for about the one-hundredth time. The scabs across the top of his left hand were itching. It had happened when Garver pushed him aside as he rushed past. David had seen the piece of upturned wire sticking out before it snagged his hand as he fell against the fence.

Mr Colbit, for the defence, didn't believe his story and was keen to make the jury feel the same way. It shouldn't have mattered, to this case at least. The facts of that night weren't the facts of this case. But that was the way it worked. It was all about distraction. They make you focus on another thing until you forget that it actually has nothing to do with the first. Distraction and confusion.

The questions continued. They didn't really have anything particular to take from it. Colbit was just forcing it into focus and then seeing if he could get him to trip up on any of the points. Get him flustered. He wouldn't.

"I'm done with this one." Colbit turned off in a self-righteous disgust that had been practiced to perfection.

"The witness may step down."

David stood himself awkwardly out of the cubicle seat just as Colbit turned in for one last assault.

"Um, Detective Radley. You're currently under suspension pending an investigation over this, is that…"

"Objection, Your Honour." The prosecution finally stepped in.

"Sustained. Careful counsellor, you're on thin ice as it is."

"Your Honour, how long are we going to let this smoke and mirrors act go on for?"

"Mr Steegan, I will not have you tell me how to run my courtroom. Your objection was sustained, now sit down!"

Red faced, the prosecution sat down. Rookie move. Laura Stanwick was next to him whispering something in his ear which he was resistantly nodding to. David knew that he wasn't in Stanwick's good book either. What did he care? Colbit's fat face was smug. Another small victory. If he piled together enough of them, he could maybe end up taking the whole lot.

"The witness is excused!"

David snapped to at this teacher-like reprimand, realising that he had frozen himself into his mid-rise stance when everything had started up. He took the hint and completed his journey. He was done for the day. Both sides had their turn with him so he was going home. Maybe. Damon Harris' eyes caught his as he made his way between the two tables. He didn't look anything like his older brother, without whom he was nothing. Certainly couldn't rely on his good looks. Short, stocky and kind of strange looking with his slightly unbalanced blond goatee. David felt himself hating the brother of the man that he had killed.

* * *

"One more." David held up his empty glass.

The fat bartender nodded and went about fixing David's third whiskey sour. He checked his watch. Just past two o'clock in the afternoon. Better make this the last. He hadn't eaten and the first two were already trying to have their way with him.

Another person who didn't like him had been at the Court House. Detective Jenny Wieze. The way she'd looked at him as she turned out the lobby and left. I.A. would be getting to her soon enough. David shuddered at the thought. He looked around deciding that he liked the place. Quiet. He could drink in peace. David reached back awkwardly and fished his phone from his coat, which was hanging over the back of his bar stool. To call or not to call? The last time he'd done it he was drunk. He could tell it upset her. Call now while he was still sober, show her he could change. Or just leave it to chance and end up making the same mistake once he was drunk. His thumb was poised, ready to select her number. The whiskey sour arrived.

"There you go, pal."

"Thanks."

The bartender was already waddling away. David tapped the phone against the rim of his short glass. Sounded like a high-pitched alarm bell. David smiled to himself. Two roads... Ah, fuck it. He wasn't much for choosing. He picked up the glass, slammed back its contents and pressed in the call button. With his mistake made he held the phone up to his ear and waited.

...Four rings, five rings... for the best... he missed her... did she miss...

"Hello?"

"..."

"David?" Her voice was everything at once: Nurturing, caring, careful, sad...

"Yeah... Hi Jane, I..."

"David," ...disappointed, angry, resentful. "Why are you calling? You know..."

"I want to see you." ...desperate, pathetic.

"Have you been drinking?"

"No. I told you. Not like that."

"I know what you can get like, David. You just head down that road and you can't drag yourself back..."

He took a deeper breath than he intended. "I just want to see you Jane, please."

Silence. "I can't. I can't do it anymore. I don't know why I did but I can't keep doing this. David, please don't call me again."

"Don't say that, it doesn't have to be..."

"If you want to see me so bad then maybe you should want to see your kids too!"

David's hand tightened around his phone as the line went dead. He resisted the overwhelming urge to cry out as he hurled it over the counter at the mirrored image of himself. David uncurled his fingers and watched as his unwinding phone rolled onto the bar counter. Every ungraceful bounce thundering into his ears.

The bartender was standing across from him. David looked up as he spoke.

"One more?"

2

Andrew turned into the small empty parking lot behind the bar. Public service time. Part of the job description. David hadn't answered his phone. The thick accent had told him that his partner had left his phone on the bar counter before staggering off into the mid-afternoon light. Andrew walked into the dark blue surroundings of the fairly spacious hot spot. There was room for a lot more

100

tables and chairs, but this was one of those standing room only kind of nightspots. Drug dealings in the corners and whores in the bathroom. What was David doing coming to a place like this? Quiet in the day time but come the evening Andrew was sure the regulars would enjoy taking advantage of a drunk off duty cop, and David was about as incognito as his unmarked car.

"You Derrick?" Andrew made his way over to the tub of lard wearing the once upon a time white shirt.

"Yeah, you the guy who called? Andrew?"

"That's me."

The bartender bent over to retrieve the phone from the lost and stolen and came back up with surprising ease. How much was this gonna cost? Andrew knew he could flash his badge and get it back with little fuss, but he didn't want to single his partner out unnecessarily, just in case he had managed to blend.

The phone was on the counter. No mess, no fuss.

"Thanks." Andrew picked up the phone, stuck it in his pocket and turned to leave. "Be seeing ya."

"You know you should look out for your friend." The Bartender was wiping his dirty hands on an even dirtier rag when Andrew turned back to him. "He was in a pretty bad way."

"Thanks. I'll do that." Andrew started to turn but was again pulled back.

"I don't know him from nothing but he was in a pretty bad way. You should look out for him."

Andrew nodded, not as quick to turn this time. "I will."

The bartender nodded back and started smearing the bar counter with his trusty rag. Andrew turned and left.

* * *

Was he letting his partner slip off the edge? It hadn't been the way Andrew had seen it. Just giving him some room to breathe, to sort it out. You didn't crowd someone like David. He was old school. He wouldn't take to being coddled. Was that the way he had seen it? He didn't know what to say to him. Andrew didn't know what had gone down that night, and if it hadn't kicked up the shit storm that it did, he wasn't so sure that he would've cared. Just one less for him to have to tag and bag. Andrew wasn't so sure that was true either. He was hard line but he'd never broken the law to get the job done. Just bent it in the right places from time to time. Was it just that he didn't care enough?

Andrew shook his head in disgust as he pulled off when the light turned green. Apathy rules the world. He turned off, headed for David's place. Drink induced coma or not, Andrew was going to get him up and knock some sense into him. He didn't want to be that guy.

Andrew felt the vibration before he heard the ring. He fished his phone out, keeping his eyes ahead. He pressed the green button to answer, just bending the law.

"Detective Bates here."

"Detective Bates, this is Laura Stanwick from the district attorney's office."

"Yes Laura, hi." Laura Stanwick was too old for Andrew, late fifties going on early sixties. "What can I do for you? I wasn't supposed to be in today was I?"

"No, no. You're up tomorrow. It's just…"

Andrew cut her off excitedly. "It's David. Did he not go in today?"

"Detective Bates – no, it's not that. We need to see you before you go on the stand. Can you come in today?"

Andrew let the next turn pass him by.

* * *

Andrew double-parked his car in front of the plain but ominous grey of the office building. There hadn't been any direct comments or questions, but Andrew could hear that things were bad. He took the three steps that led to the front door all at once and almost bumped straight into what looked like a young blonde college student. She was wearing some kind of red woollen hat. Andrew smiled and she smiled back a little embarrassed as she tried to navigate her way past their near collision. Andrew thought about asking her for her name. Undoubtedly she was impressed by how nimbly he'd overcome those steps, but he decided to let this one go. Andrew got out of her way and caught the front door before it closed.

The inside was as plainly decorated as state funding would allow. The hustle and bustle of what was essentially the foyer was overwhelming. Desk upon desk with all manner of suits, flat foots and jump suits surrounding them. Andrew had been before and knew where he was going, but whenever he was here he always felt like this place wasn't going to let him leave. It was a feeling he could never quite put his finger on. He stepped out of the way of the jacketless suit belonging to an overwhelmed young man and made for the lifts. He flashed his badge to the security guard there and pressed the button. Too many additional seconds in this hellhole before. The doors opened and he stepped in. Andrew didn't understand how anybody could work in a place like this. He wondered what the blonde college girl had been doing here. Should have asked for her name.

* * *

Andrew stepped out of the lift and into the narrow corridor on the fifth floor. White walls and a dirty grey carpet. The whole building was bustling but it was more tolerable up here. Andrew let two legal aids frantic their way past him before heading down to the end of the corridor where Miss Stanwick's office was.

Knock, knock.

"Come in."

Andrew opened the door to the over-stacked office and was greeted by the weary sight of Laura Stanwick and one of her endless lackeys. This one was a man, early thirties and balding prematurely. He stood up.

From behind her mighty desk Laura indicated, introducing them. "Detective Andrew Bates, this is Cal Rove. He's assisting on the Harris case."

They both nodded and shook hands. Andrew sat down in the empty seat next to Cal's as he retook his own.

"What's this about?" Andrew was looking at Laura.

Cal spoke. "We took a blow today. David's credibility is starting to come into question."

Andrew felt himself flush. He knew what this was about but he stated the obvious anyway, "Our case against that little prick is solid. The facts are there. Prints, witness. Fucking what do you people need?"

Laura let the air hang for a couple of seconds before she calmly clarified what he already knew. "When it comes to Damon Harris and his arrest, your partner was the lead Detective – the arresting officer and…"

Andrew cut her off, "That's right, my partner. I was there every step of the way. All of this…" Andrew flicked at some of the undoubtedly unrelated papers that were stacked on top of Laura's desk. "All of it was gathered by the both of us."

Cal pointedly stepped in. "But you weren't with him on the night Garver Harris was killed."

The surprises kept not coming, "That doesn't have anything to do with the case." Andrew could feel himself indulging in this play.

Laura stepped in to cut the production short. "Yes Detective. It's just not fair. We all know that. And if you think it doesn't boil my blood as much as yours then you're very much mistaken."

She stood out of her chair and gracefully slalomed her way through the boxes of files to come and sit on the edge of her desk in front of and over Andrew.

"Damon's lawyers are expensive enough to know that their best bet at winning this thing is to chip away at the weakest link, and right now that's your partner's character. This is an ugly mess that he's dragged us into and I need to know if you're going to be able to keep us from getting buried in it."

"I…"

"None of it matters Detective." She was on her feet again and circling her way back to her chair. "The facts may be there but if the jury starts to believe that this man, who now is inextricably linked to the defendant, had a vendetta against him before his arrest, which is what they're going for, then none of these facts and statements and witnesses will matter. Hell, I'm even surprised the judge hasn't already called a mistrial."

She eased her way back down into her seat. She had played to his type of crowd before and she knew when she'd sold her point.

Andrew asked the question she wanted. "And what am I supposed to do about it?"

Cal was back in play. "We're going to need you to sell to the jury that neither of you knew the defendant or had any significant contact with him before you were put on the case. We need them to understand that his arrest, which we'll stress over and over, was by the books, based on indisputable facts and evidence. That there was no personal connection."

Laura chipped in. "We can't disguise the fact that things got personal after the arrest, but we're sure going to hammer home that that's not what this is about." She gave a little smile. "Which in the end I guess, means that we are on the same page."

"Okay." Andrew found himself re-evaluating his previous assessment of her and their age difference.

"And it starts…"

Andrew felt his heart sink.

"…right now. I'm afraid we're going to need you to stay with us for a while, Detective."

3

David splashed water over his face wiping the remnants of sick from his mouth. He'd made himself throw up and now he was going to have a cold shower. And after that he would fix himself and strong cup of coffee. David looked at his flushed contorted face in the mirror. He did want to see his kids again. It was just past nine and not yet too late to call, but first the shower and then the coffee.

4

Kathy was back late. She and Giovanna had lots to sort out for the second show, not to mention the troubled third. And while they had been at it hard, Kathy was back intentionally later than necessary. She didn't want to see her brother. Not yet. She didn't even know if she was angry with him, but she wasn't sure that she'd be able to look him in the eyes. She unlocked the door and quietly opened it. The lights were out. No noise. Her brother was in bed. She walked in and took off her coat, tossing it and her bag onto where she knew the kitchen counter to be.

Would Jane be at the second show? Could she ask her about it after what happened at the restaurant? She'd give her a call tomorrow to see if she was going to make it. Kathy turned on the light and closed the door behind her. The place was clean – good sign – no thanks to her. Smelled of smoke. Was that a bad sign? She rounded the kitchen counter headed for the fridge and decided that at least for now, it meant that she could stop feeling awkward about smoking here herself. No beers in the fridge. Her heart swelled at the notion that she had done next to nothing as contribution since she'd come to stay. How many days now? A week? Was she really going to move out and leave her brother here by himself?

Giovanna had been weird around her since the coffee shop. She had the connections and was staying in the penthouse apartment of a friend who only used it six months of the year. Kathy closed the fridge and clicked on the kettle deciding that whatever her reasoning, she now had to be near to Giovanna because of all the complications that needed to be sorted out. She needed a cigarette. Kathy stepped over to the dividing counter and searched through her bag. Fuck. She'd forgotten to get another pack. The kettle clicked off. She'd talk to her brother in the morning.

CHAPTER NINE

1

David woke up and raised his head to look at his closed bedroom door. The sun was shining through the split between the curtains. Not too late he hoped. He wanted today to go well. He looked at his bedside clock: 07:45. It had been set for nine so why was he awake?

A timid knocking sounded through the door. "Dave?"

"Come in."

The door opened and his baby sister came sneaking in. She was holding a cup of coffee.

"Morning." She flicked on the lights.

David let his head fall back to his pillow, his eyes blinking in defence against the light. He didn't feel too bad. By the time he'd gone to bed he was stone cold sober. He had even cleaned the apartment, something he used to take pride in.

"Hey sis."

"I got some coffee for you."

"Thanks. What's up?" He pushed himself back into a seated position and aimed his blinking eyes back at her.

She placed the coffee cup on his bedside table. She was smiling softly. She had something to say.

"Sit down." He patted the edge of the bed.

Kathy sat down and re-smiled the smile that she kept dropping. David wanted this day to go well. He wanted to start making those things right that he had let fall by the way side.

"Kathy." This made his heart pound. "You can talk to me. Tell me anything. Ask me anything."

She smiled again. "You're okay, right Dave?"

David couldn't help but feel relieved. He was smiling despite himself. Not the question he'd been expecting. "Yeah, I'm okay."

"This thing with you being off work. That's just temporary, right?"

His smile softened but he made sure to keep it from disappearing. Maybe she didn't know. His relief was now coupled with a shamed sense of disappointment. Maybe it would've been better if she'd sounded out about what she clearly suspected. They could talk, fight and maybe get to know each other again.

He didn't know if it would be better for him more than her, but what he did know, looking at her eyes, was that she didn't want the truth right now.

"Yeah, this is just for now. It's all political and they need to look tough for the papers." He could see her willing on his lies. "Believe me, this will all wash over in a week or so."

"I'm glad."

They sat there, the space between them more obvious now than ever. She stood up off the bed.

"Thanks for the coffee." David raised it up, indicating before taking a small sip. She had no idea how he took it.

Already backing away. "My pleasure." There was that smile again, "I've gotta go. Big day number two is tomorrow. You must come if you can."

"I'll try."

With a small wave she left his room, pulling the door closed with her.

2

Kathy leaned her head against the hallway wall across from her brother's bedroom door as soon as it closed behind her. Her heart was pounding. This wasn't supposed to be this hard. She let her forehead roll against the wall as she gritted her teeth. She'd been an idiot to think that after all this time, after all that had changed, she could just waltz back home and have it be like nothing had ever happened.

She couldn't bring herself to say the words. Her bags were already packed and waiting. None of it was her fault. She hadn't done anything. What was happening now with David, that had nothing to do with her. Just bad timing.

Kathy realised that she was repeatedly bumping her forehead against the wall. She turned for the living room. Her bags were there. She'd leave the key at the front desk.

* * *

The weather was as promised – hot, sunny, windless. The question was whether or not it would hold out for tomorrow. The location again was fantastic. While the set up was not as complicated on the ground as their previous show, it promised to be every bit as sensational. The runway, which had been re-assembled from before, and altered of course, ran over a small walkway bridge, which spanned the width of a small creek in the centre of a small private memorial park. The park was the property of a little upper-class gated community who, after a series of meetings had decided to rent it out for the two days required, at an eventually agreeable price, as well as the addition of appropriate seating for certain select residents.

It was a stunning location which provided plenty of space but without being so large as to dwarf the proceedings. The fence and high trees also provided the privacy required from the outside world as well as from the balconies of the residents, who would also be kept at bay by a quickly erected chain link fence, a number of security personnel and a signed contract. The second location had been one of Kathy's suggestions. It was one which she'd remembered seeing when she used to live in New York, but it had been Giovanna who had secured it. Like the first and like the third, which Kathy had lost.

The not unlovely burly figure smiled at Kathy as he opened the gate after seeing her laminate. She smiled back. He was so tall and his dark black skin caught the light of the beautiful day to such immaculate effect that it made the arm which he ushered her through with look like it had been assembled one muscle at a time. She found herself sashaying a bit as she walked. There was still time to sort out the third location. She was feeling better. Still time.

Her bags were at Giovanna's temporary pad. She hadn't had time to see it, but the driver who dropped her off before dropping her bags off had sent her a message saying that the job was done. She'd see it come night time and hopefully she would have enough good news under her belt to be able to enjoy it.

Kathy spotted Giovanna by the low to the ground stadium style seating which was being assembled over the creek to either side of the bridge and runway. As they were only able to settle on the two days according to the agreeable price, all the pre-show work had to be done today. Tomorrow it would be models, today it was construction workers.

Giovanna was drinking a grande coffee from... the name of which Kathy couldn't make out. She smiled down at Kathy as she came to stand next to her. It was awkward. There were no cameras today but they were both spruced up, though that was Giovanna's general way of looking and it was of course just that much more stylish than her own. A dark blue-grey jacket over a free flowing knee-length charcoal dress. Looking at her, Kathy resigned herself to the possibility that it was the way she wore it.

"Love the suit." Giovanna nodded at her outfit before taking another sip from her giant black coffee.

"Thanks. Love the dress."

Giovanna made a sound of acknowledgment through her sip while her eyebrows raised briefly, as though it were nothing. When it came to Giovanna, this of course was no false modesty. Just another fabulous outfit in a seemingly never-ending line. Kathy's, though, was for a specific reason. The money men were coming in to see how the second show was shaping up and based on that and a little arm twisting, they were going to decide whether or not they would rethink their position on the additional funds front. The third spot for the grand finale had to be a spectacle that would dwarf the preceding two, and as it was going to be last minute, the costs were going to be exponentially higher than at first agreed upon. But as Kathy fully intended to remind them, the magazine couldn't be launched with an embarrassingly and obviously underwhelming send off. They had to be willing to spend a little more to protect what they had already put in. Kathy had her whole point-by-point attack planned.

It had been Kathy's hope that Giovanna would have still trusted her to deal with the suits on her own, as Giovanna was meant to be overseeing the chaos in their ever-expanding office department. There was a lot of catch up to be done and they should have been spreading themselves out a bit more. But one major fuck-up, a break down and a past life revelation later and suddenly you couldn't be trusted on your own.

Cindy Tao was there. "They're here."

3

David wasn't suffering but he was feeling a bit used. He flicked the cigarette butt out of the window only just then realising how smoking in the confined space of his car would make him smell. Jane had hated his smoking and it was because of her that he had first quit. He got out of the car hoping that maybe what little wind there was would clear him of the smell. David looked at his watch. School was almost out. He was a little early. Another ten minutes and the kids would come pouring out of the large building which David mused was nowhere near as monolithically depressing as his had been a hundred years before. He doubted the kids would feel the same way.

Jane hadn't arrived yet. She had not called him on his motives. Hadn't remarked; how lo and behold, she mentions his interest in her not involving the kids and now he wants a big old school family reunion. She had simply said that she was picking them up today, told him the time and that if he wanted to make an appearance then he should.

Her red five door came pulling to a stop behind his car. She gave him what could only be described as a tolerant smile as she undid her seat belt. He was grateful for it nonetheless.

David walked over to her car and assisted with the opening of her door as she stepped out. She was wearing an old summer dress that he had always loved. He couldn't hope that somehow this had been done for his benefit because he couldn't remember if he'd ever told her how much he loved her in it.

"You look beautiful Jane." These things had to be said.

"David." Her expression was tired as she swung the car door closed before re-securing her handbag's position on her shoulder.

"I'm not..." he sighed. "I just always loved that dress on you."

She smiled sadly. "I know."

A thundering silence wedged itself between them. David didn't know how to follow on from what she had just said. He wanted her more than he could bear. Wanted to take her in his arms and force that first kiss on her the way he had done some eight or nine months earlier when their affair had started. He had still been a part of Jesse and Samuel's lives back then, but less and less from that day on. Was it because of the guilt that they had both felt at being around them, her new husband, their new life? Or had he just got what he came for? The thought made the hairs on the back of his neck stand on end.

"How do you want to handle this?" said Jane breaking the silence. She continued before he could reply. "I mean, why you're here."

"I don't know. Do I need a reason?" He purposely anchored his shifting feet. "I'm their father, I'm here to see my kids." He could feel his tone.

"David..." She stroked his arm the way she had always done when his insecurities had turned to agitation. "If you want to be part of their lives, then I want it for you. But I don't want to confuse them. Are you just here today, or will you be around tomorrow as well?"

"How would Jerry feel about me being around tomorrow?" David couldn't help but become defensive.

"He has no reason to be unhappy with that, and you have no right to give him one."

Her handbag slipped off her tensed shoulder. David stepped back as she bent over to retrieve it. When she came back up to look at him, her face was red and her eyes were wet.

"David, I can't have you coming back like this. I won't let you ruin my new life." She held onto her breaking voice, "We shouldn't have done what we did, but it's done and now it's over."

She looked at him, giving him a chance to respond. He didn't know what to say. He wasn't even sure what it was he wanted. Jane opened her handbag and got out a tissue. She dabbed it to her eyes, being careful not to smudge her minimal make up.

"The kids are going to be here any minute." She sniffed back the last remaining threat of tears. "I want you to be a part of their lives again David, but not part of mine. Not like that. Not anymore."

4

Andrew loosened his tie as he stepped out back through the door of the courtroom. He was exhausted. He hadn't gotten to bed until well past one and he had been in court since nine. His work was done. For now, at least, it looked like they'd brought things back around. Another few days, maybe a week, and it would all be over. Maybe after Damon went down and it all blew over, David would be reinstated. Why not? It was ninety percent image after all and with no newsworthy story to boot strap his incident to, they might just decide that there was no incident.

Andrew was feeling good. His plate was starting to feel a lot less full. He made a dash for the elevator doors, which he spotted were closing.

"Hold the door."

The old man did as asked, allowing Andrew to turn his rush into an easy pace.

"Going down?" The old man asked as Andrew entered.

"Ground floor please."

The old man smiled, pleased to be helpful, and pushed the button.

* * *

Now back at the station, the fact that Andrew's plate was as empty as it was, was starting to annoy him. There was no word on the Cartwright case since the Feds had shown up and sucked up all their information and evidence. Andrew knew that come tomorrow, now that the Harris case wasn't an overriding issue, if the Feds hadn't come back to them then the Chief would pull him off the case completely and stick him onto a fucking drive-by or convenience store job. He didn't want to let that happen. The Cartwrights was a career gig – he could feel it – and it was his.

"Nice suit." It was Bill.

"Bill."

Bill turned back to face Andrew, having expected his comment to only be in passing. "Andrew."

Andrew stepped up to Bill almost feeling like he needed to whisper. Bill, clearly not feeling the same, backed his head away from Andrew's approach. Realising this, Andrew backed off.

"Can I help you Detective?"

There was something about the case that had been bothering Andrew for a little while now. He leaned in again. "Yeah, you know that stuff that knocked Cartwright out?"

"Yes."

"Is there any way you can find out if it was maybe… meant to be found by us?"

Bill paused, clearly not quite sure he had grasped the question. "As I said, the stuff disappears in the blood stream making it almost undetectable. We were just lucky with the bottle."

"I know, I just mean…"

Stacy Keen appeared out of nowhere to stand almost directly between them. "The Chief told you to report to him as soon as you got in, and you just got in."

* * *

Andrew closed the door to the Chief's office behind him. The Chief didn't look up from his paper work. Andrew waited. He was used to this. After a couple of seconds the Chief sighed and removed his glasses. He looked up at Andrew who was now leaning against the door and finally spoke.

"How did it go?"

"It went well… I think." He walked over to the Chief's desk and pulled out one of the chairs and sat down. "The lawyers seemed happy enough, so I think it went well."

"Good." The Chief folded his glasses and slipped them into his shirt pocket. "Good. Maybe if things keep going well and quickly, maybe David can come back."

The end of the Chief's sentence drifted off as he seemed to be pondering his words. Andrew shifted in his seat. He'd see his partner today.

The Chief continued. "How is David doing? Tried to get hold of him earlier but his phone was off."

David's phone had run out of battery. "He seems okay."

"Good. Get hold of him for me. Tell him he needs to come in and see me – and do it in person. Monday at twelve.

"Good news?"

"Just give him the message, Bates." Another long pause. "You're not on anything at the moment, are you?"

Here it came. "No."

"You haven't been off for a while. Take Sunday off, but I want you in tomorrow to…"

Andrew jumped in. "Have you called the Feds back? Is there even some semblance of a loop that they're gonna keep us in?"

"As far as I'm concerned Bates, for now at least you're back in rotation. The Harris fiasco is dying down. The Cartwright case is no longer yours, not even as it would seem in an assisting capacity. They don't want to have to deal with us. And you're without a partner, for now."

"What are you getting at?" Andrew knew.

"I'm teaming you up with Wilks."

"Who?" Andrew didn't know the name, and if he didn't know it then it wasn't worth knowing.

The Chief sighed out having expected his usual resistance but clearly not having any time for it. "Mark Wilks. He got made Detective two months ago…"

"Willick's partner?" Jason Willick was a forty-year veteran of no more real use to anybody.

"No, he's your partner. Willick is being forced to retire. He's got two months left, but seeing as you've got nothing to do and how between the two of them they're getting nowhere in a hurry, I figured you could step in and help Wilks actually solve his case."

"And what's Willick supposed to do?"

"Take long lunch breaks."

Andrew sighed, resigning himself to his fate. "What's the case?"

"Liquor store double."

* * *

There was no answer at David's house. Andrew made the turn he had passed by yesterday. He'd left him a message telling him that he had picked up his phone and was going to leave it with the front desk. Along with the message that the Chief had suggested he deliver in person. Andrew was still burning. He wasn't going to have to deal with Wilks until tomorrow but the idea of chaperoning a rookie was already eating away at his insides. A fucking liquor store robbery gone wrong. The fact that they hadn't solved it already meant that it was probably unsolvable. These things were won and lost on surveillance cameras and eyewitness and obviously neither were giving up the answers. Waste of his time. The Cartwrights, now that was…

Something was fluttering behind Andrew's eyes. What was it? Smoking… He squeezed his eyes shut for as long as the quiet road would allow and tried to summon up the image. On the corner. There was a girl there. A whore. What time had she been there? Had she been there? Had she been there all night? It was worth a look.

The prospect excited Andrew and he pushed the accelerator in a little further. He'd drop the phone off and then turn right back around. Should have had her in already.

<h1 style="text-align:center">5</h1>

Kathy marvelled at the nearly complete transformation of their little outdoor slice of heaven. The suits had left to follow Giovanna to the newly rented office space. Small for now, housing less than twenty on the books employees with something of a minimalist look to it. But it was about showing them the work and how thrifty they were being with their money, along with the additional sums that Giovanna was still trying to twist out of them. It was looking promising, though.

She took a sip of the coffee she'd sent Cindy out to buy for her. The suits had seemed happy. Kathy nodded to herself. She'd gotten her point-by-point attack out well and felt like she'd redeemed herself from her behaviour at their last meeting. Remembering, Kathy's hand suddenly shot down searching for her phone. Her handbag was resting at the base of the tree she was under. She knelt down and rummaged through its contents finding her phone. Standing back up she dialled the number. She waited.

"Hello?"

"Hi Jane, it's Kathy." Kathy wondered if Jane had bothered to program in her number after she'd given it to her. She let it pass.

"Oh, hi Kathy. How you doing?"

"I'm fine, great. You okay?"

"Yes, of course. What are you up to?" Jane cut herself off answering her own question. "Oh wait. Your big fashion show is on soon isn't it? You must be right in the thick of things."

"Well you know, keeping busy." Kathy hated this stilted small talk. "The show's on tomorrow at noon, and I was just calling to see if you were still keen on coming."

The line went quiet. Kathy continued. "Free champagne, beautiful clothes, not a single available man except for the security staff. I could introduce you." Kathy let out a small playful but unmistakably nervous laugh.

"Yeah, I'll be there. You're not going to be too busy for me, are you?"

"Well, I am going to be busy, but I'm the boss so I can re-arrange all sorts of things, as well as order people to cater to your every desire." Her next laugh, she felt, was far more natural.

Kathy wasn't even sure she cared to know what Jane might be able to tell her anymore. Maybe she just wanted her friend back.

"What am I going to wear?"

<h1 style="text-align:center">6</h1>

It was nine in the evening and Andrew had been sitting in his car across from the Roseberry Homes building for coming on two hours, only having realised an hour in that he was still wearing his court suit. The tie had come off but he still felt like a sore thumb. There was no sign of the girl. Too early, too late, too desperate? He didn't know. No promise that she would ever be back. Andrew rubbed his face before tightly shutting and opening his eyes several times. He was tired. It wasn't that he couldn't handle his dance card being so full, it was that he couldn't handle just going round in circles.

What time was it? He checked his watch. It was two minutes later than when he'd last checked. What time had he seen her before? It hadn't been late but it had been dark, he remembered that much. It had been dark for a while now and still no sign of her. Not that it was definitely a particular her. After that first frustrating hour of waiting – Andrew hated stakeouts – he had decided to go and grill his old friend behind the desk. It had been then that the obviousness of his outfit had caught his attention and the tie had been removed.

The way the receptionist, Kristoff – as Andrew had felt compelled to find out – told it, there was usually somebody there, but not always, and usually not the same girl for very long. The sketch artist apparently hadn't made her way round yet either. That was something Andrew was going to have to chase up so that he could get another dead end going.

Andrew sighed, wiping his face again. He wasn't sure how much this girl could help him, but if she'd been there on the night then Andrew felt pretty confident that she'd have something worth saying. He had learned a long time ago that on the street there weren't many who saw as much as the whores did. Their eyes were always wide open. Gotta be aware, keep an eye out for the next trick, for the cops, for that potential beat down from some fucking smack head looking to steal your roll.

Yeah, if you could get one to talk they usually had a lot to say. If you could get them to talk… Hauling them in was always an option, but it was time consuming and more often than not it was counter-productive. Andrew had witnessed too many thugs with a badge try to strong arm the information from the girls. Quickest way to find yourself talking to the wall. Andrew himself had never really had any trouble. The girls tended to like him. He never made any bones about the fact that he was a cop and that what he wanted was information. But Andrew found that there was no need to be unpleasant about it.

Kathy had popped into his mind. Her next show was coming up. He hadn't really thought about her lately, dance card being so full and all. He let his eyes drift along the sidewalk in front of Roseberry Homes. When had he last spoken to David? 'Be in at twelve on Monday' had been left with the desk clerk. Partners for over two years and it had taken time, but they were never really friends. He didn't really know David. The more it went on the less Andrew knew… the less he wanted to know. The Harris thing was ugly.

Andrew squeezed his eyes shut again. He was tired. Ten more minutes and he'd call it a night. Tomorrow was a new day with a whole new and exciting case to look forward to…

"Ah fuck it." Andrew turned over the ignition and shifted the car into first.

CHAPTER TEN

1

"So… do you get along with him, or…?" David let yet another sentence trail off as he watched his wilfully – he had no doubt – distracted daughter empty her seventh sugar packet onto the red tabletop. They were in some burger joint he couldn't remember the name of. He'd never heard of it before and he'd never come back. His stomach did a half turn as he looked down at the other half of his burger. Since giving up on it, it had seemingly excreted a puddle's worth of grease in which it now sat.

The kids had simply inhaled theirs. Samuel had beamed his thanks, emanating it from his entire being. Jesse hadn't even said the word. His stomach completed the turn, forcing a surprise burp on him. Jesse sneered up from her growing sugar pile.

"Pardon."

She gave a half-hearted shake of the head and then looked back to her masterpiece, which she was now disrupting with a ketchup packet. If she started adding ketchup to the pile David was going to step in.

"Can I have another quarter?" Samuel was beaming at his side.

David reached into his pocket and handed him a dollar bill. He immediately darted off, headed for the checkout till where he had already twice gone through the process of exchanging notes for coins. Once that was done he'd be back to the solitary arcade machine eager to pay to have the older boys play with him.

"Did you enjoy the burger?"

Jesse shrugged her response as she slumped back in her chair. Her eyes were now searchingly looking to the outside world for something nominally entertaining. Anything to save her from having to talk to her old man. He was an old man. Too old to have a fourteen year old daughter. Too old to relate to one. Too late?

"Jesse, listen."

She was looking at him. The look threw David off his game making him shift his elbows off the table. Now what? She was listening.

"So… Do you and Jerry get along?"

Jesse rolled her eyes and looked back out the window. God… he knew why that was the wrong thing to say.

She spoke. "So, what else are we supposed to be doing today?" Her eyes stayed with the outside world.

It was a good question. He had them for another three hours. The time frame determined by the length of his sister's fashion show which Jane was attending. Three more hours.

"Movie?"

Andrew didn't like him. Too young and too eager to please. How the hell him and Willick had ended up as partners Andrew did not know. Nor did he care to know, or to know this kid. Eyes on the road, hands at ten and two. Andrew didn't like this. This baby-faced-twenty-five? year old was making him feel old. At least with David, he was the kid. Andrew had even seen that flash in his eyes when The Chief introduced them. That, 'Finally, a mentor I can look up to' flash. Andrew had suppressed the urge to pistol whip the blond right off of him. See how long that lasted.

"What are you thinking?" The hairlessness of the face that had just taken its eyes off the road to look at him really disturbed Andrew.

"About what?"

"The tapes."

Before climbing into his new partner's annoyingly clean car, Andrew had been subjected to twenty plus minutes worth of security tapes showing the same two, head-to-toed-in-black, kill the same two people from some four different angles. First a young couple leave; statement secured from both: 'We didn't see nothing.' Then the glass front double doors open. Two individuals enter, their heads kept low. They are most likely male, considering their size and body language. They separate – the store is empty save for one customer, a middle-aged black woman and the owner operator, a Korean man in his mid-fifties. Perp number one circles behind the woman while perp number two surreptitiously rounds his way over to the counter. The woman screams as she's grabbed from behind, gun to head. The owner turns to the sound to find he's looking down the barrel of a gun. Some unheard instructions are given and the till is opened with the money quickly being brown bagged. Some unheard screams of anger – 'Where's the safe, Pops?' – the owner hesitates – the woman is thrown to the floor – kicked – twice – gun then aimed at the back of her head. The owner ducks behind the counter – perp number two scrambles over frantically (worried about a silent alarm). He pulls the owner up who's pointing at the safe, which is under the counter. Perp number two pushes him back down out of sight to continue – one... two... three... (click) – BANG, BANG – owner dead with one in the back the head and one at the base of the neck. No hesitation from perp number one – BANG, BANG, BANG... BANG. Number one joins number two. They fill up some bags and are out the door within four minutes.

Not exactly the model for the perfect crime, but from what Andrew could gather, it was good enough. No witnesses and no prints, and considering that it had taken place over two weeks ago, Andrew couldn't see this leading to anything other than another unsolved liquor store double. Waste of fucking time.

Was that a smile? Andrew felt his twitching hand edge for his gun.

"Well?"

"What?" Smack! Head through the driver's side window. Andrew felt a small smile of his own.

"The tapes."

"Look Wilks, like I said – let's just get there and then we'll see."

* * *

It was a hot day. As the car pulled to a stop in front of the liquor store, Andrew found that his thoughts were on Kathy again. Her second show was happening in a park or something. He'd been flicking through the channels last night and had turned onto the fashion channel for any little titbits, and low and behold, there they were. Little Miss Kathy Radley and the strikingly tall Giovanna Brazzi.

It wasn't the kind of thing he'd ever normally watch and the show that he caught would certainly have been enough to ensure that remained true, but there she was and his interest in her was officially renewed. The visual focus of the piece had been of Giovanna. Long hair, longer legs, dusky skin, smouldering lips and the list just kept on going. She was something else but Andrew just found there to be something irresistibly sexy about Kathy. She was petite-ish, some baby fat but that only served to make her face cuter and her body sexier.

Amongst the brief sound bites of: 'Who can we expect in show number two?' and musings over the third show minefield, there was a brief snippet of Kathy being stopped by a reporter before she went into some swanky do in Paris wearing this fitted green shiny number with a plummeting neck line. She had just looked so soft and grabbable. Kathy Bates...? That sounded weird for some reason. Well, he didn't want to marry her. He just wanted to fuck her. She was nice though. Good to talk to. He'd see her again.

"After you, Detective." Wilks was holding the door open.

Wilks was wearing blue jeans and a brown leather jacket, the same as he was. Andrew shook his head as he walked in past Wilks. Now they were going to look like a gay couple all day. Did gay couples dress alike? The store was open for business. It was a family place and life had to go on. Andrew looked over to the counter at the young Korean girl serving. He wasn't sure but she looked like she couldn't be more than sixteen years old. Her eyes caught sight of them, recognising Detective Wilks her sweet angelic face twisted into that of a moody little teenager as she backed away from them, instantly becoming a foot shorter.

"Miss Jung." Wilks spoke out from behind him.

She didn't reply as she turned away and disappeared behind a mock-up wall. As they reached the counter Andrew spotted the stool that she'd been sitting on. Tiny little thing. Sixteen years old and working in a liquor store. Andrew wasn't too sure what it was that he thought he could ask them that hadn't been asked before. Just putting his time in, he guessed.

"Miss Jung." He wasn't happy with his pronunciation. "It's the police. I'd just like to ask you a couple of questions." Andrew turned to Mark Wilks, who was still behind him. "Can she speak English?"

Wilks nodded. "I think she's gone to get her mother."

117

Leaning in, Andrew found that he could hear the girl's voice as she spoke, presumably to her mother. The sound of her mother's fast paced response then came through much louder.

Wilks piped up again. "I think she's officially tired of us."

Andrew didn't respond. He rapped his knuckles on the counter as their Korean back and forth continued from somewhere behind the mock-up wall. Turning his back to the counter Andrew surveyed the scene. Apart from them, the place was empty. The blood had long since been mopped up and bleached out, and considering the sheen of the place, Andrew figured that any holes made by the bullets had probably been plugged up and painted over.

Andrew couldn't figure how they carried on working. Just kept on keeping on right where their husband or father had just been killed. Too much. He caught Mark's eyes as they widened in indication. Andrew turned back to see the sternest expression he had ever come across.

"Mrs Jung?"

"Yes. You are more police?"

She was even smaller than her daughter with the counter edge catching her mid-chest. This must have been almost exclusively Mr Jung's spot in the store, because Andrew was having a hard time picturing Mrs Jung working the till without fear of the drawer hitting her in the face every time there was a transaction.

She looked older than her husband had been, maybe close to sixty. He wondered how she'd cope. Have to put in some kind of step platform for one thing.

"Yes, I'd like to ask you a few questions if that's okay."

"I answer and I answer." Her head bobbed viciously, making her tight helmet of hair shake unnaturally. It didn't look like a wig but it did move like one. She continued. "You will not find the men. I know this." She had raised up her tiny fists and was shaking them awkwardly. "I want only to be in peace and be left alone."

"Mrs Jung." Andrew had his own hands up in a gesture of peace, hoping that it would alleviate the tension that had seemingly sprung out of nowhere. "Just a couple of questions, that's all."

Her face was growing red.

Andrew decided to go for broke. "And maybe ask your daughter one or two as well."

Mrs Jung's hand then sharply dropped to her sides and her complexion suddenly reverted back to normal.

"She is not my daughter." Her tone was plain and her eyes were focused. "She is daughter of friend and she comes to help me in store. She has only been here for one week and she does not know anything. You are not allowed to talk to her."

Andrew turned and raised an eyebrow at Wilks who shrugged sheepishly in response.

"He try to talk to her last week but he not listen when I say she not know anything."

"You didn't tell me she wasn't your daughter." Wilks' tone was defensive at having being made to look incompetent.

"Maybe I tell you and you not listen." Mr Jung was pointing. "If I no tell you then I tell old man."

Wilks was making eye contact with Andrew. "Well, she didn't tell me."

"I not like that old man." She paused for effect and then looked back up at Andrew. "And I not like you. Get out of my store!"

In a flash she was gone from Andrew sight having disappeared behind a giant magazine rack, then she was at their side with a broom in hand.

"Get out of my store! You waste time."

This was his new case. And his new partner actually had his hand on his gun, ready to drop the old bitch if she went from ineffectual poking to intent to kill. After deflecting the end of the broom handle twice, Andrew threw his hands up in the air and turned to leave. He noted that Wilks was following him, his gun thankfully still in its holster.

She was right to kick them out. They were wasting her time. It wasn't Wilks' fault they hadn't got anywhere. He was clearly enthusiastic enough and from what Andrew had gathered from the reports, he had checked all the corners. It was just a dead-end case. Shit work you threw at the rookie and the has-been. Andrew sighed at the waste of time that lay ahead. What did the Chief expect? Andrew shuddered at the thought of re-interviewing witnesses who hadn't seen anything.

"What do you think?"

Andrew could feel how tired of that question he was going to become.

"What do I think?"

Wilks was twirling his car keys awaiting Andrew's wisdom.

"I think we should go and get some lunch." An idea was forming and Andrew was starting to think that maybe their relationship should be more harmonious. "My treat."

* * *

"Do you think she's protecting the daughter? Stopping her from having to tell us something that might put her in danger?"

It wasn't that ridiculous a thought, but no, Andrew didn't think that was it. Mrs Jung was just tired of going round in circles.

"Had the girl been around from the get go, or did she only arrive on the scene a week later?"

Wilks' eyes dropped ponderously as he reached for his glass of diet Pepsi and took a sip, the straw making that slurping sound again.

"No, I don't think so." His voice was laced with the disappointment of realising that things had just reverted boringly back to square one.

"More coffee?"

Andrew didn't look at her as he indicated a yes response. He was punishing her for clearly being more attracted to his new partner than him. The one with ketchup on his face. Wilks sunk his teeth into his burger again as he gave her a beefy smile.

"Nothing else for you?" she said to Wilks, apparently having finished with Andrew. "Another glass of diet Pepsi?"

"Nah." Wilks said through a mouth full of masticated beef.

She smiled again and sashayed off. Jesus. He wasn't that good looking. Effeminate if anything.

"So... Wilks."

"Wha –?" Some beef escaping.

"Jesus, swallow your fucking food."

"So-ey..." His eyes betrayed his embarrassment.

Andrew hadn't meant to flare up like that. He needed this kid to accommodate him and shouting wasn't going to help smooth out that process.

"So..."

"Wha –?" Bits of beef.

Sigh. "Take your time, Wilks."

Wilks, clearly sensing the growing tension, crunchingly swallowed down the compacted cheek-to-cheek mass that he'd quickly built up. Andrew winced at the strained action and then looked around to see if anyone else had seen it.

"You done?"

"Sorry Detective. Just hungry I guess." He took another slurping sip of his diet Pepsi and then wiped most of the ketchup from his face, his eyes remaining transfixed on Andrew's the entire time. Pressure.

"How long have you been a cop?"

"Since I was twenty-one."

"And you're..."

"Twenty-Eight."

Seven years – Detective – not bad.

"Why'd you become a cop?"

"To shoot people." Wilks smiled.

Andrew laughed. "Like there's any other reason."

Wilks continued, clearly pleased that he'd shared a moment with his stern partner. "No, no, I've just always wanted to be a cop. Went to college when I got out of school to appease the folks, but soon as I got out I joined up."

"What did you study?" Andrew didn't care.

"Just business studies. Generic, I know, but it has always been about being a cop for me. Never had any other interests."

Andrew couldn't decide if that made him like him more or less. "You graduate?"

Wilks looked up at him sheepishly from behind the rest of his burger, which he had just picked up. Andrew sighed and to Wilks' clear relief, signalled for him to carry on. Andrew resigned himself to saving the sweet talk for later.

3

It was a beautiful day as promised. Kathy had been watching it all safely, hidden behind one of the trees for about forty minutes now. Everything was going smoothly and there was no need for her to be backstage. She watched as the photographers snapped away at the glamorous creations that were carried by long legs down the shiny catwalk. The potential for glare on the lenses was removed by the huge expanse of synthetic fabric that had been hoisted, with great difficulty, over the bridge-cum-catwalk and its surrounding low stadium seating. The covering tarpaulin-like fabric was also capable of doubling as a shield against any unforecast down pours, but thankfully Kathy could not have asked for a better day. Not a breath of wind and not even a hint of a cloud.

Giovanna was talking to Jilly Sanders again with the dazzling spectacle going on behind them. This time, Kathy made sure that she was safely out of range. She couldn't hear what was being said but despite the confidence of Giovanna's radiant smile, Kathy knew what questions she was being asked, questions she was skilfully deflecting.

Word seemed to have got out that there was trouble with the third location, and this in turn had started making advertisers nervous. Most of her morning prior to the show had been filled with the more and more fidgety Cindy Tao fielding calls with the big fish being passed over to her.

Mostly things were contained and between the two of them, her and Giovanna had managed to alleviate any major concerns, as well as getting the money men to bow to the fact that more money was needed. However, what Giovanna was not telling Jilly Sanders was that they simply didn't have a suitable spot for the final show. What their cobbled team of researchers were quickly finding out was that anything that fell into the range of appropriate was either too far out of their newly expanded price range, or was simply already booked out.

The show had to happen next Saturday and that was that. Flights had been booked and hotel rooms had been reserved. The date had been marked off on the social calendar, and any deviation from that would disrupt the natural flow of this spiteful world and would forever blight the sheen of their new rag before it was even launched.

An attractive but odd-looking waiter slowed to a stop next to her and held out his silver tray, upon which were four glasses of champagne. Kathy put her empty glass on the tray and took a fresh one before thanking the struggling model. Kathy took a long sip. She felt very much like getting drunk and just forgetting about all this shit. She could have stayed in Paris working as a writer, earning a good living and not being responsible for countless sums of other people's money, not to mention their future happiness and well-being and...

She took another sip. Finished. Where was that skinny waiter? Gone. Kathy raked through her bag. She needed a cigarette. Giovanna had suddenly quit

121

smoking and was enforcing a no smoking rule in her friend's apartment. This meant that at possibly the most stressful point in Kathy's life, she had to continually leave the penthouse and go to the roof to smoke. There was a balcony but as it happened it was only accessible through the room Giovanna was using. Kathy knew that this cack-handed system wouldn't last. Once the tension between them had subsided a bit and she felt more comfortable in her new surroundings, she would simply buy an electric fan and smoke in her room.

Despite the obscure fact that the place had no communal balcony, it was quite something. The roof terrace was exclusive, but taking a flight of stairs every time one needed a smoke seemed somehow counter-productive to Kathy.

She hadn't been in much of a state to appreciate it all when she'd got in the previous night, as once the set-up was complete it was off to their hopefully temporary office to make an endless stream of calls and riffle through endless reference sights in the hope of pulling number three out the bag. But what she had been able to fully absorb was how comfortable her queen-sized bed was. The place was beautifully decorated with its professional colour schemes and eclectic furniture selection, which complemented the open plan of the central room. But all that paled in comparison to the infinite hug that was the world's single most comfortable bed.

When she had woken too early, and pulled herself free of her new lover, she had been able to appreciate where she was. And after trudging up the cold wooden steps and out into the colder morning air to have her first cigarette of the day, Kathy had been overwhelmed by the view and by the promises of it all. The place was a preview to the life that Giovanna had first convinced her they could have. Or it was a cruel joke and if she didn't fix things then it was as close as she was ever going to get. She had caught herself leaning to look over the low concrete wall. On top of the world and it was a long way down.

"Kathy." It was Cindy Tao. "Your friend's just arrived."

"Thanks Cindy."

Cindy turned and walked off expecting Kathy to follow. Lighting her cigarette, Kathy followed on.

* * *

When Jane hadn't been there from the start, Kathy had figured that she had probably changed her mind having got anxious at the idea of having her ex-husband's little sister prying into her past. That being the case was enough for Kathy to just drop it, but she told Cindy to liaise with security and have them let her know if Jane did in fact come and…

But Kathy was in no mood to try and underhandedly elicit information from her old friend. She'd been in that mood a few days ago but today with her world the way it was, she just wanted to see a friendly face. As they navigated through the crowd Kathy couldn't help but smile to herself as she followed Cindy on her roundabout route. She was the most efficient creature Kathy had ever come across and just then she was earning her money by ensuring that her boss, who was a little out of sorts, would not have to come across any press or influentials who might want to invade her space.

Kathy had first met Cindy in New York some five years earlier. Then she had been the PA to some awful media mogul who Kathy constantly had forced dealings with and as a result, had constant dealings with Cindy. While Cindy's boss was a maniacal, demanding and insufferable pig, Cindy had always managed to make their dealings run as efficiently and smooth as possible. Then, about three years later, when Kathy had been in a position to need an assistant of her own, she tracked down and sweet-talked Cindy into emigrating to France. Being the little slice of momentum that she was, she jumped on a plane and learned the language in just over half a year. And now here she was, back in the States and really the cement that was keeping their 'Under construction Empire' together.

"I told her to wait by the security guards while I found you." Cindy didn't look back as she huffed on. "I instructed some waiters to make some passes round her way so she could have food or drink if she wanted it."

"Thanks Cindy. That's great."

"No problem."

Kathy could tell Cindy was disappointed in her. Really, she should have been backstage. Her presence wasn't urgently required, but there were still things that needed to be done, situations that needed to be dealt with and egos that needed to be smoothed out. Things were backing up and she knew it. Kathy felt her heart rise and fall at the thought of it all.

"There she is."

And there she was. Jane was standing talking to Kathy's tall, dark and handsome security guard. She was laughing at something he said and her fingertips were sliding down his muscular forearm.

"Do you need me for anything else?"

"No thanks Cindy."

Cindy stood for a second not leaving and looking at her.

"Cindy?"

"Giovanna was looking for you earlier. I said I hadn't seen you but she knew I was lying."

Jane had spotted them and after another lingering touch of the security guard's forearm, she made her way over.

"I'll talk to her."

Cindy turned and left. Kathy called out after her, feeling the guilt that Cindy had decided she needed to acknowledge.

"I'll be along soon."

Jane touched Kathy's arm as she came to stand next to her. Kathy turned to her friend and put her arms around her.

"Hey... Oh..." Jane tentatively hugged back. "Kathy?"

Kathy let go, realising the awkwardness of it. She wasn't crying. Jane's hand squeezed her arm, less restrained now as she leaned in to look at Kathy's face.

"Hi."

"Hey Jane." Kathy said stepping back and back into character as she held Jane out at arm's length, examining her dress. "You look so beautiful. I love the dress."

"Thank you. It's new." Jane played along. "It's been too long since I've had the opportunity to doll up and strut my stuff. Do you think it's appropriate? I thought since it was outside, something a bit more summery would work rather than too glamorous."

Kathy was nodding along, watching Jane as she swished her dress from side to side. She did look lovely. Her hair was done up tightly with just a wispy trail of a ponytail.

"Do you like my hair? It's the reason I'm so late."

Jane walked up to Kathy and skilfully linked their arms together before leading them towards the action. Kathy knew that Jane could sense her disillusionment and was trying to hold the moment together for the both of them. She wasn't saying anything. Jane was smiling.

"You look lovely too, Kathy. Never shy of letting that ample cleavage do your talking for you." Her smile was cheeky.

Kathy laughed, but not for long. She had to speak before she cried.

"Thank you for coming, Jane."

"I wouldn't have missed it."

Kathy knew that wasn't entirely true, but in their moment as it was, it did feel true and it was nice to hear.

"I can't believe that you're at the centre of all this." Jane made a dramatic sweeping gesture, which Kathy followed. "It's amazing. It's so big. Since I saw you last I've been reading up on all this and following the fashion shows a bit, and it's pretty clear that in this world, you and your partner are hot shit."

Kathy snorted out another brief laugh at this.

"Really... phrases like 'New Blood' and – and other ones that sounded equally if not more impressive."

They were getting closer to it all. The crowd was getting thicker. The voices were growing louder. The persistent flash of cameras became brighter, louder, faster...

"Kathy?"

Kathy's eyes snapped focus back into place to find Jane looking directly into them.

"Are you okay?"

Kathy squeezed her eyes shut and bowed her head, trying to catch the breath that had somehow slipped away from her. Jane was holding her and Kathy was glad for the support. Her knees felt week.

"Come on." Jane's hand was around her waist, guiding, pressuring her to turn.

Kathy didn't resist and allowed herself to be moved back away from the crowds.

"I just need some water." Kathy heard herself saying from behind her forearm, which was wiping the sweat from her brow as her feet stomped beneath her. "I'm fine really, it's just the heat."

"Do you want me to call that… Your assistant?"

"No don't, I'm fine." Her eyes were still closed. "I just need to sit."

"Kathy!"

Jane's voice rattled up sharply as Kathy felt her arm being pulled up. Kathy opened her eyes sharply, steadying her feet as she realised that she'd been in the process of sitting down on the ground in the midst of people, guests, professionals and, most likely, cameras.

She looked up at Jane who was still recovering from her surprise. "Somewhere less public."

Jane smiled her way past it. "Good idea."

Kathy steadied herself as she continued to allow Jane to supportively lead the way. Kathy kept her face hidden behind her red hair, which she hoped wouldn't single her out to anyone in the know.

"Kathy Radley!"

Shit! Cringing, Kathy looked up to see a tuft of bleached blond hair above a pair of stylised Buddy Holly glasses, still a way off but skipping in fast.

"Who's that?"

"Jason Teaple. He works for a gossip show."

"You're kidding."

"Nope."

"How you doing?"

"I've been less sweaty."

He was close enough now for his expression to expose his suddenly peaked interests.

"Kathy Radley. My goodness. What a find." He took her accessible hand in his and kissed it.

"Hello Jason."

"You are a hard woman to get hold of, and me without my cameraman."

"I thought you'd be in amongst the crowds getting everybody's on the spot reviews." Kathy could see him examining the glossy sheen of sweat that was covering her body.

"I was taking a little boy's room break when I saw that magnificent head of hair and I just had to catch you. Don't suppose I could tear you away from your *friend* and convince you to come find my cameraman with me?"

Kathy suddenly realised what he was looking at as he continued to screech on while his eyes traced their way along her body.

"Or you could bring her along if you want." He held out his hand. "Jason Teaple."

Accepting, Jane replied, "Jane Booney."

With this movement it became all the more obvious. Kathy felt Jane's fingers protectively pressing into her side and as she shifted to accept Jason's hand, she felt her own breast shift against Jane's. She wanted to laugh.

"I don't think so Jason. I'll be heading back in a second anyway. If you manage to sneak in backstage we can talk then."

"Yes, surprising to see you on this side of the stage."

"Just a short break. Nice talking to you."

"You too. Bye bye ladies."

Kathy, feeling revitalised by the distraction, took the lead and turned Jane away to walk on. Once they had some distance on him, Kathy spoke.

"Well, that will give him an angle."

Jane looked at her surprised. "Do you think he saw you?"

"No." Kathy couldn't help but laugh.

Jane was smiling, confused but keen to be let in on the joke. "What?"

"I think…" Kathy licked her lips suppressing another laugh, "I think he thinks you're my lover."

"What!" Jane's face eked at her own loudness. "What?" she whispered almost as loudly. Her smile was still present but laced with guilt.

"Don't worry, unless you think I'm not good enough for you?"

Kathy resisted the urge to give her friend's bum a playful squeeze. Better for the gossip to be conjecture rather than an eye witness report.

* * *

"That's not gonna make trouble for you is it?"

They had found a rustic barrier-style wooden fence to lean against. It blocked off a bit of the creek, which fell below them to a sharp six-foot drop. They were safely away from the crowded centre of the show and Kathy found that she could breathe again. Jane handed her one of the bottles of water she had just procured and leaned herself against the waist high length of wood that ran along the top of the fence.

"No, no." Kathy laughed again. "God, it'll probably give them a reason to like me. Make me a bit more interesting."

Jane raised an inquisitive eyebrow.

"I'm the behind the scenes girl. Not much to write about. Giovanna is the interesting one." Kathy didn't like how that last comment came out. Sounded like she was looking for a pity reply. She jumped back in, overcompensating. "Yeah, better they write about me being a lesbian rather than about me looking like a nervous wreck about to have a breakdown."

Kathy felt her awkward smile slip from her face when she looked at Jane and saw that she wasn't looking back. Kathy took a long sip of her water. Her moment of reprieve had past and now reality was coming back.

"How you feeling now? Better?"

"Um, yeah." Kathy found herself standing away from the support of the wooden barrier. "God, we should get back. I invite you to my show and you haven't even got to see it yet."

Jane pushed herself off to join Kathy in a slow walk back towards the fray. "Well, we don't want you getting in trouble either, so…"

"I am still the boss."

She forced a smile and Jane forced one back. They walked in silence. Kathy felt better – fine. Her panic had subsided but she didn't want to go back. She didn't know how to fix things. How to…

"Are you okay?"

They were drawing closer to the centre and the crowds, but they were still essentially alone for the moment.

"I'm better. I just…"

Jane cut her off, her tone more astute. "When you first came round to mine, I couldn't believe how great you looked. You had that light back in your eyes."

Kathy's heart was going again. She felt Jane look at her but she didn't look back.

Jane continued. "It wasn't there when you left and it hadn't been there for as long as…" She allowed the sentence to drift away before picking it up again. "Then when we got to the restaurant… I can't remember what you said, but you wanted to know about David and…"

Kathy grabbed her friend's arm stopping her and turning her to face her., "Jane, I know I came looking for something from you but…"

"I don't care about that Kathy." She paused. "I did, but I also didn't want to see you looking for something that might take that light out of your eyes again."

The moment hung in the air between them. A gust of wind pushed its way past them and Kathy felt her hair kick up around her face. She saw Jane's hands go up to protect her own. With the wind gone both opened their mouths to speak before stopping to let the other continue.

Kathy spoke after another brief moment. "I was looking for something. I'm sorry. I'm so glad to see you again really. It's just that…"

Jane reached out and tenderly stroked Kathy's arm, assuring her that she understood. Kathy was glad of it and steadied her accelerated rate because of it.

"I don't even know what I was looking for. Closure."

"I don't think digging into what happened is what's best for you. I don't like the idea of you losing what you've got back."

Kathy tried to speak but Jane raised her hand stopping her.

"But seeing you today…" She shook her head. Kathy could tell her heart and her head were fighting for dominance.

Jane sighed loudly, committing herself to what she would say next. "If you need to know what happened…" She tilted forward asserting her position. "I'm not sure how much you think I know, but I'll answer whatever questions you ask me."

Kathy froze. She didn't know what to say, how to follow on from this openness that she would have jumped at only a couple of days before.

"Jane… I don't even know if I – I can't thank you enough for still being my friend…" Her eyes were reddening, she could feel it. Her cheeks flushed. Jane's troubled, concerned face confirming it still more. "But I don't know if I want to know anymore."

Jane's brow furrowed. "But... closure?"

Kathy felt like such a fool. Her hand came up and swiped away the gathering tears before they could fall. "I know... It's just... I've got other troubles now." She forced a resignedly pathetic smile.

"What do you mean?"

"This..." Kathy twirled dramatically, "...is the second grand show in an extravaganza of grand shows designed to showcase the newest talents and hail the coming of a new power house magazine."

"Okay?"

"I fucked up and now we don't have a spot for the big final show."

Jane's eyes turned up and to the left. "When is it?"

"Saturday."

"I can probably help you with that."

4

David slowed down as he entered the manicure of the residential area. Jesse was in the passenger seat staring out her window. She hadn't been happy with the choice of movie and had been expressing her distaste for it in this way since they left the cinema, the same way she seemed to express her distaste for everything. For all David knew, this was how she expressed herself and it was as simple as that. She hadn't been this way when she was ten or eleven. He tried to think. No, she had been a happy kid.

"We're almost home." Samuel had enjoyed the movie as it was animated and geared specifically towards his tastes. Would all their outings be like this? Watching shit kid's films and eating greasy kid's food? He made the next turn.

"Is Mom gonna be home?" Samuel was bouncing up and down in his seat.

"I don't think so. She'll probably be back soon, though."

Jane had called earlier and now instead of meeting her for an exchange and a chat, he was to take them home where Jerry would be waiting. David made the last turn and slowed the car to a roll as they neared the brown front door of his old house.

"So... Dad."

David turned in surprise to see his daughter looking at him. The assuredness in her eyes perfectly complimented the tone in which she had expelled the word Dad.

She continued. "You gonna walk us to the front door? Have a chat with Jerry? You can ask him all those questions you've been asking me all day."

David pulled to a stop in front of the house.

"Thanks for a great day Dad." His daughter turned her twisted smile away and climbed out before closing the door just hard enough to let him know that she meant it.

"Thanks Dad. Awesome day."

David felt what could have been a hug from the back seat before the back door opened and closed. David turned his head back to try and trace the line of where his son had gone before his seemingly endless energy transported him into the house and out of sight. He was already just about at the front door where his big sister had started knocking.

"Bye-bye champ."

Samuel turned back and waved while his sister dropped him a perfect eye-roll. The door opened and the mobile drinks cabinet appeared. Every time David saw him, that belly of his got just a little bit bigger. Jesse breezed past him without saying a word. It was nice to see. Samuel was all smiles and indulged his stepdad in a staged high five. David felt his grip on the steering wheel tighten. Jerry looked up and over after Samuel had gone in. He raised his hand in an acknowledging wave. David tore one of his hands free from his steering wheel and did the same. His day and duty now done, David started the car back up.

"David."

David looked back over to see Jerry's chinos scissoring their way over. This could be interesting. David made sure to let Jerry see him turning his ignition back off.

Jerry reached the car and leaned in. "David."

"Jerry."

"Just wanted to thank you for taking the kids out today. I know Samuel was really looking forward to it."

"No need to thank me, Jerry. They're my kids. I wanted to see them so I did."

Jerry smirked at this. "Well I'm glad and so is Jane. She was really happy that you were taking them out today."

David saw the shift behind Jerry's eyes. He wasn't sure how to play this.

"Really." Underwhelmed.

"You guys been talking a lot lately?"

Did he know? "Well Jerry, we've kept in touch."

"Uh-huh." David saw Jerry's fingers whiten as they gripped the door. "And now you're coming back… into the kids' lives?"

David knew it wasn't a good idea to play with this situation. "That's right Jerry. The kids."

David kept his looks to himself. If what he wanted was his old life back, then this wouldn't be the way to play it. Jerry kept his eyes on him, barely able to conceal his own looks.

"Okay." He patted the door and stepped back. "See you around."

David nodded but Jerry had already turned away. David restarted the car and pulled out.

CHAPTER ELEVEN

1

Anthony sat up as his alarm started to scream for him to *Wake up wake up!* He wiped his face and opened his mouth for a big long gaping yawn. He was still tired. His weekend had been a full one and the five hours' worth of sleep that he'd just had was not enough. He yawned again and grabbed the bedside clock, shutting it off. 07:01. Way too early to be up on a Sunday. Anthony threw the covers aside and instantly shivered as the cold morning air hit his naked skin. He swung his legs over the side and stood up. Time for a quick shower and then it was off to the airport.

* * *

Anthony lowered his awkwardly small cup of coffee and yawned again. He covered his mouth this time as the cute blonde behind the counter had laughed at his previous gape. He looked over to see if she was looking. She wasn't. She was dealing with some middle-aged couple.

Anthony looked about the place. The little airport coffee shop was pretty much empty, but with the general foot traffic increasing, Anthony could see it filling up pretty quickly. He checked his watch. 09:45. The plane was delayed and Anthony had been sitting in the coffee shop for coming on an hour. He'd held off talking to the blonde, who was now looking, because come Leon's arrival he didn't want anyone seeing them together. This was more for his boss than it was for him, but when Leon came through the departure gate, which was just across from where he was sitting, Anthony didn't want him to spot any following eyes. Leon Olls was a paranoid man, and now that he was going to be out of his home city comfort zone, he was going to be twitchier than ever.

The decision to move had come as a complete shock to Anthony. He'd never known Leon to stand for change of any kind unless it was checked from every angle. But then he tells him about Cliff, who just because he knew him from back in the day, was suddenly willing to just pack up shop and chase a vague and risky game right across country. There was money to be made but Anthony could feel the weight of the baggage that came with it.

Anthony's ears perked up as an announcement sounded out. Thirty more minutes until the plane would land. Fuck it. He'd chat with the blonde – he would just have to leave her world before Leon showed. Anthony knocked back the last little bit of his coffee and then smoothly slid free of his seat and away from his booth table. He knew her eyes were on him and not on the old lady who was querying about the difference in price between a coffee and a cappuccino. He was happy with the start of his approach.

She smiled at seeing that his eyes were now on her. She was trying to rush the old lady's decision-making process. Twenty-five, maybe. Part-time work for a student or full-time work for a graduate who couldn't quite take the next step. At thirty-eight Anthony could still draw them in. A whore for the nasty but a sweet blonde twenty-five year old made even sweeter when bent to his will. It was something that he'd only just recently developed a taste for.

When you're insane do you know that you're insane? Anthony smiled a smile that he made sure she didn't see. The old lady got her coffee and change and turned and left. The blonde's chest rose and fell in relief. Her uniform looked good on her. The image of it being torn away to expose her large breasts flashed its way through Anthony's mind.

"Another cup?"

"Please. Takeaway this time."

She smiled and stepped over to the espresso machine to do him a double shot with water as he'd requested last time. He wasn't a fan of filter coffee. Never hot enough. She blushed and smiled again when she looked and saw that he wasn't taking his eyes off her. God. The things he could do to her. A flash of her naked, writhing body, covered in sweat, moaning – Flash – Not moving.

"Are you waiting for someone?"

"That's right."

"Your wife?"

He held up his left hand exposing his bare wedding ring finger.

"Girlfriend?" She let out a brief nervous laugh.

"Why you so interested in who I'm meeting?" He put on a sly smile.

"Just making small talk."

"Is that what they teach you? Smile big, be nice, act interested?"

"Maybe." She placed his freshly prepared coffee in front of him.

Anthony pulled out his wallet and then passed her a note. Her eyes were dark brown and she had a smattering of light freckles to either side of her nose. He saw those eyes widen as his hands squeezed tighter.

"And here I thought that maybe you liked me."

She put his change into his waiting hand and allowed for her fingers to tracingly connect with his. "And what made you think that?"

He didn't reply, letting her wait as he added sugar to his coffee while he simply looked at her. She was looking back from her elbows on counter position.

"What's your name?" he finally said.

She straightened herself up and pointed to her nametag: Patricia.

"And what's yours?"

"Mark."

"Well, Mark." She went back into her elbows on counter position in a manner that seemed predatory to Anthony.

She'd do nicely. She continued, now practically batting her eyelids. Anthony felt himself begin to hate her.

"If you're not here meeting you wife or your girlfriend, then who are you

131

meeting?"

He leaned in, just enough to fuel the tension. He could sense her desire to back up, but she was holding on, looking up at him. "What about you?"

"What about me, what?"

"Seeing anyone? Living with anyone?"

She smiled coyly. "No, single."

"Not even a roommate looking out for you in this big bad city?"

"I'm a big girl. I can take care of myself."

"I bet you can. Why don't you give me your number and then we could continue this another time over something with a little more kick in it?"

"Okay." Her tongue was visible as she slid back. Now that it was permissible and found a pen and a piece of card on the back counter. She scribbled down her number and then turned back.

"There you go, Mark." She held out the piece of card.

"Thank you Patricia." He took it from her, ensuring that their fingers touched again. "I'll call you."

Anthony picked up his coffee, turned and didn't look back. He'd do a round before swinging back to the departure gate. He didn't think it'd matter. More and more people were filling up the place by the second, so he doubted either Leon or Patricia would spot each other.

The old man was paranoid, but Anthony knew that was how he'd managed to stay out of jail. Hell, Anthony didn't think Leon's name was even known by a single law enforcement agency. What time was it? Fifteen minutes. He wouldn't stray too far, just out of Patricia's line of sight.

Anthony had had his fair number of run-ins with the law, on and off now for some twenty-plus years. In and out of jail until he was almost thirty. Then he'd met Leon Olls, and while he'd been in their cross hairs more than a few times, he'd never been back to jail since.

Five minutes. Back on the west, Leon would never have been seen in public with him, but over here Anthony's face wasn't a familiar one, so it would pass for the moment. Plus, being so far out of his comfort zone was enough for the old man to take some risks. Anthony checked his watch again. Still five minutes. He was getting tired of waiting. He needed sleep.

Some people were coming out, the young and energetic first. Leon was pushing seventy but he was still a spry, mean old fucker when he needed to be. Taught him everything he knew, everything worth knowing. And there he was. Mean-looking old fuck with a head basher of a cane. Six foot with grey hair, leather for skin and all his own teeth. Those around Leon were giving him a wide berth, like they could sense something off.

* * *

"You call Cliff." Leon's voice had long since surpassed being deep. It now sounded like it was broken, cracked.

"He knows it's today." Anthony slowed the car to a stop at the red light.

"So you didn't call him." Leon cleared the loose gravel that seemed to permanently reside in his throat.

"I left him a message. He hasn't called back. He knows it's today and I left a message saying how the flight was delayed." Anthony pulled off as the light went green.

Leon cleared his throat again and let his eyes wander through the windscreen. They were approaching the city. They weren't planning on playing nice. No gifts to the locals. As it happened the game they were going to play was essentially a smash and grab job. It also meant that Anthony had had to spend the last few days greasing more than a few palms to get the information that they needed to make their game work. It was sloppy to play it this way. Anthony knew some of the relevant names but they were playing it too fast and loose and relying too heavily on Cliff to be able to give them the goods.

Things had been running fine with their game on the west; a game Cliff knew Leon was into, which was what had brought him knocking when his opportunity came. And Leon had just gone for it – the promise of easy money. Easy money always came at a price and Anthony didn't like seeing his rock-like mentor being sucked in so easily. This was underhanded dirty work, which had to be a smash and grab job because if they hung around they would get found out and then they would get caught. And if it didn't cost them their lives it would certainly cost them their livelihood. All bridges would be burned.

"Mind if I smoke?"

Leon didn't answer. He'd quit a year earlier on the doctor's say so. His heart had been giving him trouble, the result of a lifetime of heavy smoking, heavy drinking and lots of fucking. Leon had always enjoyed living the good life and while he wasn't afraid of much, he was afraid of dying. No more smoking, very little drinking and only very careful fucking.

Anthony knew that their moving on and shifting up had a lot to do with his health scare. If he couldn't enjoy the simple pleasures that his success enabled him, then he'd have to make success his pleasure, even if it came at a price.

Anthony started to reconsider the cigarette. No, he needed one. Leon had been off them for a year and this was his car. He rolled down his window and then pressed in the car's cigarette lighter.

* * *

As the car turned into the driveway through the opened electric gate, Anthony spotted Cliff's car – or the car that he was using – parked off in the distance where the road was no longer walled in by Amazon-like hedges. Before being cut from sight, Anthony saw him get out of the car. Anthony checked to see if his boss's face changed expression at seeing the place. It didn't, it never did.

"What do you think?"

It wasn't exactly a penthouse in the city, but as temporary accommodations went, it was pretty damn good. They were likely to be in town for at least a month and there was no way Leon would spend it in the kind of shit hole motels that Anthony had to endure. Once they'd cleaned house they'd go back and start with fresh funds and start a new game. A bigger game. Anthony hated the east coast. Maybe a new country, get out of America.

The place was a single-storey two bedroom overlooking the ocean through glass sliding doors. Fully furnished and practically the same as the one Leon had left behind, only smaller and not cheap. Leon refused to be without his comfort. No names were attached as the place was being paid for through one of Leon's front companies.

"It'll do." Leon opened his door and stepped out onto the bricked courtyard-cum-driveway. "Cliff."

Anthony got out to see Cliff strolling up through the open gate. Seeing that he was clear Anthony pressed the remote and closed them in. The way he'd been told it, Leon had known Cliff from the old days before Anthony had come along. Fingers in all the pies kind of guy. They embraced like old friends do. Cliff was wearing what looked like the same outfit he'd worn when he and Anthony had first met on his arrival in New York. Sent by Leon at Cliff's bidding. No discussion, just do it. He had on his grey suit under a light brown raincoat topped off by sunglasses and a dark brown hat. He looked like a gumshoe in an old movie. The outfit was obviously meant to be a disguise of sorts. The guy was clever but clearly not what you'd call a field agent. Their 'hello's complete, they went inside.

* * *

The furnishings that took up the tiled floor of the open plan living room area were nice but standard. Good enough for the time that Leon would spend there.

"Nice place."

Cliff took off his hat and glasses exposing his narrow features and thinning blonde hair. Fifty plus, the way Anthony had calculated it from his talks with Leon. The other thing that Anthony took from their conversations was that they hadn't seen each other in ten years, meaning that they probably didn't even really know each other anymore. Cliff would be the only one allowed to see Leon's new pad. Any other outside help required would only deal with Anthony.

"Sit." Leon pulled out one of the chairs round the small round table that was off to the side of the living room and sat down, his cane leaning against the table. It was always with him.

Anthony had seen him beat a drug dealer named Santiago near enough to death with it once. The only reason Anthony knew that Santiago hadn't died that night, head split open, teeth in the gutter, was because he saw him a year later in a shiny new wheelchair, gift from the Goodwill, coming out of some church service that didn't mind the stench of the decrepit in their holy house. Anthony always found it amusing that when the filth truly hit bottom, they always found God. Still stayed at the bottom, though.

Anthony and Cliff each took a seat.

"No snags?" Leon was looking at Anthony.

"The cops were just banging their heads against a brick wall. They didn't have anything."

Leon turned to Cliff when he joined in.

"The body was found in a junk yard just that side of the Canadian border about a mile away from his car. They'll draw their own conclusions about the money and double crosses, etc. But now that they have him the Cartwright case will be buried, written off. The whole thing no longer exists."

Leon smiled slyly. "You must be pleased."

"Yes, it all went smoothly. Just like we planned."

It had gone smoothly, just like Cliff said it would. Anthony had to give that to him. All the ducks were lined up and ready for him to knock them down. Even Daddy Cartwright being knocked out from that bottle they'd left for him in his room. He knew his game and that was the only reason Anthony was willing to put up with this whole slap-up organisation of theirs. He'd also done his job calmly and professionally on the night. Anthony just didn't like being called in to do somebody else's vague dirty work.

"So there are no rumblings on your end? No alarms?"

"They just want this never to have happened. The embarrassment of it is something they don't want to face. As far as they're concerned, I don't even know about it. The wife's being fed a cover story..." Cliff paused as a smile crept across his face. "It's beautiful."

Leon turned to Anthony. "And how's our little army coming?"

Anthony pulled out his pack of cigarettes and began shifting it through his hand in a rolling motion against the table, "I've got an in. Shouldn't have any trouble finding what we need." Anthony looked to Cliff who seemed to be hypnotised by what he was doing with his cigarette pack. "So long as you can tell me what it is they like and where they like to get it from, then we shouldn't have a problem. Mind if I smoke?" Anthony slipped the cigarette between his lips.

"Not in the house Anthony." To Cliff, "So what have you got for us?"

* * *

Anthony lit his cigarette and started his car. The game had started. Cliff had the first name for them and soon things would start rolling. Despite his reservations, now that things looked to be getting underway Anthony was starting to feel good. He pulled out the piece of card he'd got earlier. Too call or not to call? He'd call her a little later but he'd take her out tonight. He slipped the card back into his pocket and then shifted the car into reverse. Shit. The gate remote was on the table.

* * *

"Patricia."

"Yes?" Her voice tinged with recognition, but she hadn't been expecting his call.

"It's Mark."

"Oh, hi." Surprised but pleased. "I didn't expect to hear from you so soon."

"Well, I figured why wait and risk letting a good thing pass me by?" Anthony lit his cigarette and watched as his small motel room suddenly filled up with smoke. "I took a chance that you'd finished work. Seemed like that would be about now."

"Yeah." He could hear her smile. "Twenty minutes ago. I'm just about to leave and head home."

"So, what about that drink we agreed on having together?"

"Now?"

"I was thinking in a few hours' time. We could have it over a meal."

"Um." She was a little thrown by the immediacy of it all and starting to realise that she actually didn't have the slightest idea who this guy was, but she'd say yes. "Yeah, okay. That would be great. Where are you taking me?"

"It's a surprise, but wear something nice. I'll pick you up at eight. Where do you live?"

* * *

He hadn't been able to find out for certain, without pushing, if she lived alone. She hadn't actually said the words, but Anthony was pretty confident that it was the case. If not then that would just be something that he'd have to deal with.

"Can I come up for just a second?" The road by her building was quiet and what people there were had no reason to look at him. "I just need to use the toilet." Anthony put on a smile as he said this hoping it would inflict a sense of embarrassment in his voice.

"Of course, come up."

The buzzer sounded and Anthony shouldered the heavy front door inwards. No one in the foyer. He peered past the stairs down the first floor corridor. The lift was stationary. Third floor. He stepped over to it and pressed the button with the knuckle of his index finger. Unnecessary risk. Reckless. As the lift door open he casually turned away and prepared to simply keep walking. It was empty. He stepped in. Third floor.

* * *

The process of stepping out was similar. Anthony was prepared, with his eyes kept low, to stumble embarrassingly into whoever might be about to enter the elevator. After some embarrassed half-turned quick to keep moving apologies, he'd be gone. The awkwardness of such a moment prevented eye contact all

136

round. Unnecessary risk. Reckless. Just a little fun. There wasn't anyone waiting.

Keeping his posture easy and natural, Anthony stepped out onto the corridor. Once confident that no one was going to suddenly step out of one of the apartments, he stepped up to Patricia's door and knocked twice.

"Coming."

After some frantic rushing sounds and the clip-clip of heels on hard wood floors, the door was opened. She smiled, leaning against the open door.

"How do I look?"

She looked good. Her black dress seemed to wrap around her with its pleated hem ending just above her knees. Her hair had been straightened and her make-up was immaculate.

"You look amazing." Anthony stepped forward slipping his arm around her waist and kissed her before she could resist. He was quick and the kiss was brief. He backed off as he turned them into the apartment.

Patricia suppressed a nervous laugh as Anthony stepped back. "Thank you."

"For the kiss?"

"I meant for the compliment. But the kiss was nice too." She laughed her little nervous laugh again as she watched Anthony back further into her apartment. "Oh, the bathroom's over there. First door."

Anthony turned to the dark little corridor that she was pointing to. Her place was small and she definitely lived alone. Small living room attached to a small kitchen filled with small furniture, small appliances and decorated with small trinkets.

"You got anything to drink?" His back was to her now as he headed for the small dark corridor.

"Oh, I'm not sure. I thought that was why we were going out."

Anthony didn't answer as he pulled the bathroom door closed behind him.

"What do you want?" There was a huff in her raised voice.

"Whatever," Anthony replied closing the lock on the bathroom door.

Clicking on the light, Anthony found himself looking at his reflection in the cabinet mirror above the sink. He smiled at himself. He looked good. Clean-shaven, nice clothes. He examined his environment. Small and clean, like the rest of the apartment. One – two – three – four – five… He quietly unlocked the door… six – seven – he opened the door.

Her back was towards him as she prepared their drinks in the small kitchen. Anthony admired the way the cut of her dress curved in to hint at the shape of her behind. She turned to see him looking at her. She paused and then smiled as she walked up to him and extended her arm, offering him one of the glasses she was holding.

"I'm afraid it's just cheap brandy and coke. Left over from some get together I had here like three months ago."

Anthony took the drink without a word and walked over to the two seater with a green blanket tucked over it like upholstery. He sat down and then scooched over so that the side she was nearest to was free. She was uncomfortable, her one hip jutting out as a finger circled the rim of her glass. Anthony watched her as he sipped his own drink. It was cheap brandy.

"What time's our reservation for?" She took a sip, a casual question.

"Sit down for a second. There's no need to rush."

Anthony kept his smile to himself as he saw her tongue pushing up against her teeth. She was getting annoyed, anxious, who was this guy? This was the last time she was going to go on a date with someone she meets at the airport. Anthony kept his smile to himself again. She bent over and put her drink down on her coffee table before flattening her dress against the back of her thighs and sitting down next to him. After a moment of looking forward, she looked to Anthony to see him simply looking back as he continued to drink his drink.

Patricia let out a barely disguised sigh of exasperation and reached over for her drink, "So, Mark. What do you do for a living?" With her drink now in hand, she angled herself to face him and settled back against the arm of the couch. She wasn't afraid.

Anthony didn't reply, he just stared. He allowed his eyes to explore her body, slipping down to the misplaced hem of her dress and her slightly exposed thigh. He made no attempt to shield his eyeline from her. Patricia's hand darted down to cover herself.

"Look Mark... um, I don't want you to get the wrong idea here. Nothing's going to happen tonight. Okay?" Her tone was assertive and honest, her eyes searching for a connection. "I like you, I think, and I'd like to go out but that's all. Okay?"

Other than the glass in his hand and the bathroom door lock and handle, he hadn't touched anything inside the apartment. Her searching eye contact was still in place and Anthony wanted to hold onto it as long as he could. He wanted to see the switch. That moment when...

She stood. "Maybe we shouldn't do this. I..."

There it was. She wasn't looking at him and half-turned away, about to head to the door, about to make an excuse, about to ask him to leave.

Anthony put his glass down and stood. His tone tried and tested. "Patricia, I'm sorry." His expression was embarrassed. "I come over a little intense. I..." His gestures neutral, awkward.

She'd stopped. The tension in her shoulders slipping away. He continued. His thumb and forefinger squeezed at the bridge of his nose.

"I've just come out of a long relationship and..." He squinted at her past his hand. "I guess I don't know how to play this game anymore." He dropped his hands down to his side in a gesture of defeat as he let out a sigh of futility, his eyes looking down. "Maybe I'm just not ready."

He held the moment, kept his eyes low. After a count he looked up at her, her hand touching her lips with her other across her chest, her head tilted and her eyes smiling. She'd switched back. She stepped towards him with her hand outstretched.

"Come on." She took his hand in hers. "Let's go."

Patricia turned again and led the way to her front door. Her bounce was back. He'd given her something to nurture. Her hold on his hand was firm and reassuring. As she walked, she turned her head and flashed him the sweetest smile. She was lovely. At the door she grabbed her handbag, which was on a side table there and swung it over her shoulder. She then took hold of the door handle and as she began to turn it Anthony yanked her back and, with his free hand, stifled her scream.

* * *

Not being fully aware of one's own true potential was a problem that most people had, eking their way through life until that day when someone finally brought the hammer down. This had been Anthony. Throughout his entire life, he'd simply done what needed to be done in order to fix whatever problem was right in front of him. This of course meant that in his teens, when that problem was not having enough money, he'd simply taken to mugging people. Fourteen years old, no more school, no more family – since his Mom had died a year earlier and no more rules since he'd run away, Anthony mugged his first. Since he was only fourteen and not particularly big for his age, he had decided on mugging a drunk person.

He'd been on the run from the care home for just over two days and had quickly found that begging was not for him. Too much time and too little money. He was hungry and he was sick of being cold.

He waited. The place he'd chosen was just on the edge of the beaten track with two of the roads to walk home on, being quiet and dark. He waited. Nothing before midnight. Anybody leaving before then was either part of a group or not drunk enough. After midnight, Anthony had let several stragglers pass him by. The reasons were numerous. Not drunk enough, too big, too fast, too something. He was nervous. He discarded the brick he had brought with him in favour of a twelve-inch iron rod that he'd spotted stuck in the dirt. He smacked it against the low brick wall that he was sitting on which bordered the steep slope leading to the quarry behind him. The bar was across the street. He didn't think he could be seen from the across the street as he was obscured from any lamplights by the overgrown tree which reached out from the slope behind him.

It was a smallish place, probably a local to most who frequented it. The guy had been wearing a loud shirt. His skinny neck arched forward as though it alone was being pulled by an unseen force, guiding him home. No more waiting. Anthony followed him down one of the pre-selected roads. The one the guy had chosen meant that Anthony had to act quickly. There was really only half a block's worth of decent cover before it crossed paths with another road that had more than a few Asian takeaway stall around it, this guy's obvious destination. Anthony hopped off the wall and quickly crossed the road, sure to keep his twelve inches of iron pressed against his forearm and out of sight.

The guy had had more than his fair share. Anthony doubted he would be able to hear it over his own mumbling and stumbling, but as he neared him Anthony slowed his pace and softened his footsteps. This was definitely the one for him. Stumbling drunk, skinny, not much taller than he was and on his way to spend money. Anthony let his twelve-inch iron rod slip down into the position of a baton. He squeezed it as tightly as he could until it felt as though his own knuckles were separating from his fingers. His clamped teeth felt about ready to crack and burst free from his mouth. All his muscles were tense, his whole body squeezing at the metal in his hand.

Ten feet – it was now or never. Five feet – Anthony raised his hand above his head. The bustle from the beyond the upcoming turn was screaming in his ears. Anthony swung.

"And I'll take you…"

The off key note stopped in an instant as that sound echoed through, like a wet towel hitting the sidewalk. Anthony had his eyes closed. He hadn't even felt any impact, any resistance against his chosen tool. He could feel wetness on his hand. He hadn't thought about how to hit the guy or where or how hard – just to hit him, stop him.

Anthony opened his eyes. His vision was blurry. His eyes had been as tightly squeezed as his hand and jaw. He could see the guy's loud shirt screaming up at him. He could see the fresh red streak down the middle of it. His vision cleared. The guy had been transformed into a crumpled mass. He had simply stopped working and fallen in on himself. The wound at the base of his head was unbelievable; a matted mess of hair, blood, bone and flesh denting into a yawning black hole. He looked at his hand, still tightly clenching the iron rod. It and his hand were wet with blood. He could feel it running down his elbow. He was shaking. He could feel it on his face. He looked down at himself. He was covered – his shirt, his trousers.

He had to move. He tilted on his heels, his body wanting to take him as far away from this nightmare as it could, but he stuttered on them and stood fast. He had something he needed to do. He looked at the body and then he looked at his reddened hand. He was going to have to get new clothes. He went down on his knees and placed the rod on the road. He took hold of the body's arm and pulled. With the piled onto itself position the body had ended up in, it simply popped up and over before flopping down onto its back. Anthony let out a scream of fright as he bounced up and skidded back. He looked around. The world had suddenly sprung into crystal clear focus. He could see everything, he could hear all the voices chattering away just beyond that corner. He could hear footsteps.

Shit! Where were they coming from? Just beyond that corner. He looked at the body – its eyes staring up at nothing – the iron rod, blood soaked on the road next to it. Louder. Voices. Laughing. Money. He darted forward and stumbled going down onto his knees with a painful bounce. He didn't take any notice. He saw the bulge of the wallet and he tore at the pocket ripping it free.

"Hey!"

Anthony looked up and froze. A young couple. They weren't moving. The man's hand blocking his girlfriend's path. She saw.

"Oh my God!"

They didn't move. Anthony rose to his feet bringing the iron rod with him. They saw it. The girl was holding onto her boyfriend, making sure he didn't get any ideas. Anthony began to walk backwards. He took several steps, keeping them in his sights. They didn't move – they didn't speak. He turned and ran back the way he came. It wasn't until he was over the wall and heading down into the quarry that he heard them crying out for help.

* * *

At fourteen, Anthony had killed his first man for less than twelve dollars.

* * *

He had gotten over it and mugging quickly started to turn a reasonable profit. No more killing, get a big enough knife and people will generally give you what you want. After a while Anthony had even managed to get a small crew together. Strength in numbers. Then at fifteen, after living on the streets and in squats for just over a year, Anthony got taken down. His game had been working like a charm, but really he had been pushing his luck with his hits being restricted to one part of town. A completely different part than his first attempt over a year before, so no connection was made.

And so Anthony went into the system, only to have the process repeated over and over until he finally hooked up with Leon, by which time Anthony was a career criminal who'd spent over a third of his life in jail. When he met Leon, Anthony had been working for a small time boss in downtown L.A. who had managed to carve himself out a small piece of the city. The part that Anthony played in this was to keep the blacks from taking it back and the Mexicans from moving in. It was tiring, dirty and thankless work.

Leon had shown up to strike a deal with his boss to work out of his neighbourhood, close enough to the Hills but also deep enough downtown so as to get lost in the mix. Basically, Leon liked to move around within the city limits. The cops couldn't raid you if they didn't know where you were. Not that they even knew who he was. Dealing with people like the one Anthony had been working for was simply part of the game. You had to pay to play in somebody else's sandbox. Of course, the time came that the deal was no longer enough for Anthony's then boss, so Leon had simply set him up to be killed. Competition on both sides was trying to slip in, and when you let someone like Leon in through your front door, you essentially open up your whole life. All this had been perfectly laid out to Anthony as they spent more and more time together.

"You're wasted here."

Anthony knew who the main players were on both sides of the fence and when the time came, he was able to point Leon in the right direction and, of course, open the back door. All this Leon naturally did for a price. No stakes in the business, just a healthy friendship and a taste of those first fresh profits. Though despite any such newly formed friendship and the promises of protection and autonomy, Leon never stayed in that kind of situation for long. The world of gangs and drugs was dangerous and tempestuous, and far too magnetic to the cops. Leon always left a scene with a profit and a favour owed, and that time, with Anthony in tow.

* * *

Coming out of the front door of the building, Anthony stepped aside to hold it open for a young woman of about twenty. She looked up at him to say thanks, by which time Anthony was already edging past her. Their eyes never met and his face would slip from her memory. She caught the door and went in. He'd parked his car two blocks down. Anthony took out his cigarettes. He pulled one free and then slipped it into his mouth. He felt for his lighter. He checked both breast pockets. His hand darted down to his pants pocket. It was there. Anthony slapped his hand to his heart as he laughed and sighed in relief. An unnecessary risk. He removed his lighter and lit his cigarette. Anthony breathed and exhaled. The air was crisp. It was a nice night, and still early.

CHAPTER TWELVE

1

"Glad to see Andrew gave you the message." The Chief put down his coffee and indicated for David to sit.

David shifted his coat into place and sat down. Despite himself, he'd put on his cop clothes before coming in. He hadn't realised it until he'd started the car, but there he was, in his shirt, tie and jacket.

The Chief continued in his usual tone of parental disappointment. "Which was more than I was able to do. You're on suspension David, but that's something I've been trying to fix. So when I call, you answer. Understand?"

"My phone got misplaced and I guess I haven't been home much, sir."

Andrew gave him the message. He hadn't seen his partner in nearly a week and his sister had left his place a few days ago. Both had left notes. He smiled to himself, hoping the Chief hadn't seen. He didn't know if he cared about this place anymore, but he didn't want the boss to think he was being disrespectful. David wasn't sure how well the Saturday with his kids had gone, but it had made some things clear to him. And one of those things was that he just didn't care about scum like Damon or Garver anymore. Part of him still wanted to be a cop, but he knew that to be a good cop you had to care, and if there was one thing he knew he never wanted to be was a bad cop. Or more to the point, a worthless cop. But that power, that purpose, that right it gave you, that would be hard to let go of. He didn't know.

The Chief wasn't impressed by his answer. "Well then, get a new one and look after it."

"I got it back." David held up his phone.

He could see the Chief resisting the urge to hurl the phone on his desk at his head.

He took a breath. "David. The I.A.D. boys were going to have a talk with you, but the message has been passed onto me to give to you."

David didn't know what that meant. Too busy, not important enough, minor information – or maybe they just didn't feel the need to be there in person to give him the message to Fuck off.

The Chief continued after consulting a small scrap of paper and taking a sip of his coffee. "After speaking to Detective Wieze…"

"I knew it."

The Chief looked at him over the glasses he put on to read from the scrap of paper. "That's right, Detective. This case was every bit hers as it was yours. If not more so."

"What did she say?" He didn't want to hear this.

Chief Groder took off his glasses and leaned forward across his desk.

"Detective Wieze went to the mat for you. She was compiling a career-making case against the Harris brothers and their organisation, which you essentially wiped out in one foul swoop."

David opened his mouth but didn't know what he was going to say. The Chief saved him from his stutter as he stood up from his chair and waved away whatever David might have been about to say.

"I don't want to hear it. I don't want to know anything about that fucking night." With his hands strangely placed on his hips, he walked round to the front of his desk. He sat down on its corner looming over David. "And now because Wieze didn't spit fire when your name was mentioned, the I.A.D. boys have decided they don't want to know either. If not for her Detective, your coming in today would have probably had a very different outcome."

David didn't know what he was hearing. He shifted forward in his seat, feeling the need for momentum to get his words out. "Wait... What does that mean? Does that... Am I..."

The Chief cut back in. "It means, Detective," he stood back up, "that once this court case is over and done with and that piece of shit Damon Harris gets sent down – which luckily for your sake, looks to be an imminent reality – that your suspension will be lifted and you'll be back on the job."

* * *

It was a good thing, back on the job. It wasn't what he'd been expecting. It was a good thing. He didn't know what to think. David was sitting in his parked car and had been looking at his phone for well over a minute. After some resistance, the Chief had given him the number. David didn't think it was because he thought it a mistake. More likely the Chief thought that he would just end up alienating and pissing off the person who'd saved his ass. And not to mention the fact that she most likely hated his guts.

He dialled the number. He had to say something to her. They hadn't exactly been friends, or really even on the same page during the case. Different priorities on who or why they should go down. Andrew of course had got on with her and had constantly acted as a go between. That was why David didn't have her number already. Still, she was a good cop and he owed her at least...

"Hello. Jenny Wieze here."

He paused. "Uh, Jenny?" Dumb question.

"Yeah, hello. Who's this?"

"It's David Radley. I'm just calling because I heard that I.A.D. spoke to you and that..."

"And that what, Radley? Why I didn't rat you out? Were those the words you were going to use? Sound right, don't they? Well unfortunately I didn't have anything to tell, so don't be too quick to thank me 'cause who knows... Had I actually been there, seen something, knew something to tell them, I might have."

David let her finish and then after a pause opened his mouth to say something. Something brief and maybe humble, but she saved him when the line went dead. There wasn't really anything he could have said, but having made the call and taken his medicine, David did feel better.

2

"I can probably help you with that." Kathy couldn't believe what had come free flowing out of Jane's mouth after that. It didn't take Jane long to convince her that she could save their bacon, and at a discounted price. She knew people.

After dragging Jane backstage, Kathy quickly found Cindy, who then quickly located Giovanna. A brief glare later, Giovanna was introduced to Jane and after being guided away from any angling ears, Kathy had prompted Jane to tell Giovanna what she'd just told her. A boat, or rather, a yacht, a luxury yacht. The kind that was big, private and way out of their price range.

Jane was an executive in a firm that insured the toys of the very rich. They paid big premiums and thus had to be dealt with on a personal face-to-face basis, meaning that Jane knew, and was friendly with, a lot of very rich people. Her husband in turn was one of the firm's main tax lawyers, which was how they met. This Kathy found out on meeting him at their house on Sunday. Jane had called her husband at the show and asked him to figure out what the benefits of holding such a function would be for the owner. Jerry was a nice enough guy who got on well with his stepson, who Kathy found to be a little too *Village of the Damned*. Jesse had been away which Kathy was sad to see. The two of them had got on really well when she was younger.

The Sunday was spent going over the numbers with Jane hashing out the potentials. Giovanna was happy with her partner again and it made Kathy feel like the weight of the entire fashion world had been lifted off her shoulders. Above all else, the fear of ruining it for the one person who believed in her and what they were doing was what Kathy couldn't handle.

The second show had been every bit as successful as the first, but the rumblings over the third had very much started to shake the foundation of what they'd achieved so far. Jilly Sanders had not so subtly spent hers and Giovanna's last encounter asking about little else. Kathy had watched the interview online that night, and while Giovanna was never less than poised as she skilfully pushed the questions aside in the guise of maintaining the suspense and mystery, Kathy could tell that she was on the brink of snatching Jilly's mike away and shoving it down her throat.

But now all that was forgotten. Jane, herself and Giovanna were all currently in a taxi and on their way to the city's most exclusive harbour where only the richest and most powerful people parked their big-ass boats. Jane had secured them a meeting with a Harold Dulpard, who, despite having a slightly stupid name, was one of the richest players on Wall Street. The way Jane told it, the meeting was little more than a formality since Harold had two yachts – one which was 700 and something feet, that he used regularly and the other, over 900 feet which he used for God only knew. Business events maybe, or just as proof that he was insanely rich. And also the fact that the two of them had always got on really well and he was sure to just do it as a favour for her. And while it all sounded very convincing, all three of them had independently decided that for this meeting, they all had to look their absolute best.

Jane's thick blonde hair had become even blonder and now included a luscious waviness. Her pink, white and brown print dress with its wide shoulder-exposing neckline was fitted and flared. The dress alone might have been a bit much, but it was perfectly offset by the straight cut of her above-the-hips brown leather jacket. Giovanna had on her black *fuck-me-boots* and a purple below-the-knee skirt, exposing just a hint of her perfectly toned skin between. Hair straightened. A black tight sleeveless shirt, a diamante buckled belt, a chiffon scarf and a pair of big black sunglasses to complete the look. Clearly the thinking was that while they were successful, independently made and strongly wilful businesswomen, when it came to dealing with something this important, last minute and in the hands of one man, as this, a little cleavage never hurt anyone.

This was very much the model that Kathy too had decided to adhere to. She'd also opted for a haircut, which she wasn't too sure about, although both of her companions had insisted that it looked *gorgeous*. It was the shortest she'd had it since her college days at just under an inch below her jaw line. She thought it made her face look a little too on the round side – i.e. fat – but then maybe this Dulpard was a chubby chaser.

With the haircut playing on her mind, Kathy had realised that she didn't own a single item of clothing that didn't make her look fat. Then, whilst looking through her various outfits and looking at herself in the mirror, Kathy had realised something else. Things were going well – and there she was trying to find something to be miserable about. She'd become too used to the misery that had accompanied it all. Too used to the burden she'd been carrying and now she was trying to get it back. After that she'd selected her brown string strapped dress that was a straight up and down, but which she knew hung nicely off her boobs. She'd realised something else – she needed to get laid.

"Jane, did you ever meet Andrew?"

"Who?" Jane turned to look over her shoulder from the front passenger seat.

"He's David's partner."

"Don't think so." She turned forward again as she continued. "Must be his new partner, I guess. The only one I knew was called Carter."

Giovanna sparked up and nudged Kathy's thigh. "Oh yes, I remember this Andrew." Her smile had its light back. "He was the one your brother brought with him to the first show."

"Oh yeah?" Jane had turned back at hearing the implication in Giovanna's tone. "What about him?"

Kathy felt herself beginning to flush. "No, I was just…"

Giovanna cut her short as she leaned over to make eye contact with Jane. "You should have seen the two of them. It was disgusting."

"What?"

146

Giovanna laughed at Kathy's reaction. Jane repeated the question, eager for more info.

"No, no. It was just these looks they were giving each other and not giving each other."

"What does he look like?"

"He's cute. Tall, dark, etc. I liked his crow's feet. Like Clint Eastwood."

Kathy thought this description was dissolving into one of Giovanna's own personal fantasies, but she did like how strongly it was being suggested that Andrew had been into her.

"Sounds nice, Kathy."

"What happened there? Have you seen him again?"

"No. Our paths haven't had a reason to cross since."

"Your paths haven't had a reason to cross." Giovanna practically spat the words out in disgust. She wasn't the type to wait for things to happen, and although she usually didn't have to, she would never shy away from shoving a hot poker into the ass of any situation.

"Well..." Kathy said in defence.

Giovanna was unimpressed. "You should call him. Ask him out."

"Are you afraid it's going to be weird because he's your brother's partner?"

Thanks Jane. "Well, yeah. That's a big part of it."

"Bullshit." Giovanna didn't feel the need to qualify.

"Well..." Kathy argued again.

Giovanna leaned across to catch Jane's eyes again. "You should have seen the two of them. You could cut the sexual tension with a knife."

Kathy and Jane laughed. Giovanna just wanted her friend to live and have fun, Kathy knew that.

"Well," Kathy continued, "I do have his number."

"Jesus Christ. And you haven't called? You'd better just give it to me." Giovanna began to grab at Kathy searchingly.

"No." Kathy could feel her stomach muscles weakening as she began to try and resist Giovanna's hands and her own laughter.

* * *

They were led on board the 700 plus foot monster, which was far and gone the largest one there. But as Harry Topler, who had met them at the gate and golf carted them over told it, it was often dwarfed when the oil men were in town. The 900 plus yacht was apparently parked somewhere up in Canada. It was being rented out at an insane price to some company with a lot of money to burn.

As they followed Harry up the walkway which had been rolled over and connected just for them, Kathy couldn't imagine how any one person could own anything as big as this, let alone bigger, that moved. The boat or ship or whatever was magnificent. It was, from dock to top, almost three storeys high, as Harry continued to inform them from below his relatively comedic captain's hat.

He wasn't the captain, he was the steward and he was fifty-seven years old with greying hair that made him look just that little bit older, but with a smile that lit him up and dropped maybe ten years off. He was sweet and clearly enjoying having the rapt attention of 'three lovely young ladies' as he put it.

"Mr Dulpard is waiting for you in the main bar," Harry said, stepping aside to wait for them to reach the top.

Jane looked at them with a sly smile. "This what you guys had in mind?"

Kathy couldn't help but to let her smile broaden. The kind of parties that were held on boats like this were the kind of parties you dreamed about when you were dreaming about what it meant to be a success.

"You ain't seen nothing yet." Harry turned and led them along the wide walkway of the lowest deck towards the rear of the boat. Giovanna, who was next him, graciously accepted the arm that was offered to her. Kathy looked over the edge and then turned her head sharply forward again. It was higher than she thought.

Rounding the turn and stepping down onto the lower deck at the back of the ship – (submarines were boats and boats were ships, Kathy was almost certain) – Kathy became fully aware of the world they were trying to step into. God only knew that in her business she dealt with the super-rich, at least peripherally, but she'd never been allowed behind the curtain before. It was truly magnificent.

Harry led the way stepping down onto lower level of the boat's rear which housed an – as Kathy estimated – 7, 8, 9 or 10 metres across round swimming pool, half of which was surrounded by a crescent shaped leather and stone bench. As they stepped down and turned past the wall, the open plan luxury bar, as Harry had referred to it, was revealed. The width and depth of it easily rivalled the so called luxury penthouse that her and Giovanna were staying in with sunlight seeming to light it up from a thousand unseen windows. A bar counter stretched halfway down one wall, and as far as Kathy could tell, this Dulpard wanted for no booze of any kind imaginable. Along with the bar stools, there were at least half a dozen separate groupings of couches, chairs and poofs smattered about. All this, and still plenty of room for the two pool tables Kathy could see in the back.

"Well, it looks like Mr Dulpard is off freshening up just now." Harry stepped out of Giovanna's arm and circled round to behind the bar. "Why don't you all take a seat and I'll fix us all a drink? What can I get you lovely ladies?" He looked to Giovanna first, who had her one hip jutted out and her opposite hand resting on one of the bar stools.

"Hmm…" she said, pondering her choices and not the time of day. "How about a beer?"

"Nice." Kathy agreed.

Jane was looking a little miffed at her client's lack of respect and courtesy, but clearly the idea of a cold drink agreed with her too. Opting for a white wine instead, she stepped up to the bar counter and all three of them took a seat.

* * *

Halfway into their second beer, Kathy could tell that Harry was starting to get a little embarrassed. He had run out of fascinating facts about the ship and could clearly tell that his not so captivated audience was growing tired of his youthful smile. Giovanna was holding her temper in check, as this was an opportunity they could not afford to blow. But her finger drumming on the glossy finish off the bar counter was starting to feel like the count down to a missile launch.

Jane had only indulged in the first drink as she was still a representative of her firm, even if this was not exactly on the books. She stirred her diet Coke furiously as poor Harry the steward tried to force out some more not so interesting facts.

"… and the actor, Paul Taylor. You know?"

Kathy saw Giovanna shaking her head.

Harry pushed on. "He was in this show call Boulevard Beat. It was a cop show – anyway…"

"Jane, there you are. I've been looking all over for you." All of them turned at once to the sound of the voice as it boomed out from further inside the ship's bar. "This boat is just too big."

Harold Dulpard was exceedingly tanned, which he was showing off to full effect, wearing only a pair of metallic blue Speedos. They were of course the only thing metallic about this pudgy and suspiciously top to toe, hairless man. To Jane's credit, she didn't bat an eyelid as she scooched herself off her bar stool and walked over to him, scoldingly indicating to her wrist as she went.

"Is this how you treat all your potential clients, Harold?"

She reached him and they exchanged their double cheek kisses. Holding onto her arms, he then held her out to get a look at her, whilst also marking both herself and Giovanna.

"Is that what you gorgeous girls are – my clients?"

Kathy and Giovanna both stood off the stools and stepped forward to be recognised. Kathy was starting to feel exposed in her thin material spaghetti strapped dress.

Jane slapped Harold's hands away. "Ah, so only the gorgeous ones, i.e. the women, are made to wait."

"Forgive me, Jane. I would hate to offend you. You know I only deal with you." He kissed her hand and then Kathy found that Harold was suddenly upon them. "And you must be the fashionistas that Jane mentioned."

Managing to keep her skin from crawling away, Kathy allowed him the pleasure of her hand. He stunk. "Kathy Radley, and this is my business partner, Giovanna Brazzi.

"Chow."

Dulpard perked up at the sound of Giovanna's name and grabbed her hand, *"Ah, Italia - Una terra di passione in cui è divorato tutto, dal l'ultima goccia di vino fino all'ultima goccia del piacere di una donna."*

Kathy didn't understand the words and from the way Giovanna's smile had turned into a twitching sneer, she was glad of it.

Dulpard continued as Giovanna pulled her hand free, denying him the pleasure of kissing it. "Now that is a world I can respect."

"Isn't that lovely, but I'll thank you to keep all references to *my pleasure* to yourself." She gave him a light but sharp double slap to the cheek.

Dulpard immediately let out a wheezy teeth-exposing laugh as his eyes darted between the three of them. Giovanna knew her dogs.

"I love it." He turned back to the safety of Jane and took hold of her around the waist.

Kathy couldn't decide whether or not to pull Jane aside and tear her a new one for not warning them, or give her a big sloppy kiss of gratitude and sympathy. She'd decide later.

* * *

They were led on a tour of the ship and, while it was all beyond spectacular with room upon room of new wonders and an open air top deck with infinitely more room than they needed, the whole experience was marred by the fact that Kathy couldn't stop her eyes from being drawn back to the slushing up and down movement that was Dulpard's tightly covered ass.

Dulpard turned to her and Giovanna, relinquishing his hold on Jane as he did, "So there you have it. Beautiful isn't it?"

"It surely is." Kathy felt Giovanna squeezing her arm. It was perfect.

They were on the spacious top deck and Kathy could see it all. The catwalk, the crowds, the cheers, the adoration.

"Well…" He was eyeing them out in anticipation. "What do you think?"

Kathy wasn't sure how to answer. "I love it." She pulled Giovanna in close. "We love it."

"Great, so you'll use it then?"

Kathy looked over to Jane who nodded subtly.

"Yes." She couldn't help but clap her hands together and laugh. "We'll take it."

Harry Dulpard stepped in for a contractually binding hug. Kathy didn't care and opened her arms to accept him.

* * *

As it turned out, it *was* simply a meet and greet and little more than a formality. Jane knew Dulpard as a bit of a sleaze and a social hound who had almost yelped at the idea of having a boatload of models at a calendar marking social function that he could co-host. While this meant that some concessions would need to be made to include him in the proceedings, it also meant that using his boat as a venue wasn't going to cost them a thing.

"I can't believe you didn't tell us about him," Kathy said.

With Harry the Steward now back on his cart after having dropped his three lovely ladies off at an even lovelier little pier restaurant, they were free to scream and express their delight. Kathy had already covered the big sloppy wet kisses and was now taking her time digging it to Jane for tossing them in with Dulpard. The hug she'd received at the end had included the transference of sweat.

Jane waved her off as she pulled up a seat at their fixed umbrellaed table which overlooked the harbour. "I didn't know he was going to be wearing a banana hammock."

Giovanna laughed, apparently having never heard that expression.

"Thing is, Dulpard's a simple man and while I had him on the phone it was pretty obvious that he wanted to feel as though he'd enticed you into choosing him." She paused as she picked up her menu and started to peruse. "So I told you girls to glam it up and the rest of it slid into place."

"Shit, you did say that, didn't you? I thought I'd chosen to play the pretty card." Kathy picked up her own menu. "You're a dangerous woman Jane Booney."

3

His Sunday off had done Andrew some real good. He hadn't realised just how tired he was until he didn't need to be up, and then just went back to sleep for three more hours. Up and out of bed at twelve and after a late breakfast he went to the cinema to watch the latest one that everyone was talking about. Going to watch a movie during the daytime, that was something that Andrew couldn't remember the last time he had done. The movie was shit.

Andrew didn't see anybody he knew all day, which was very pleasant. And then when the evening rolled around, he'd found himself parked across from Roseberry Homes. Three hours later and not a God damn thing.

* * *

"What are we doing here, Detective Bates?"

It was Monday night and Andrew had yet again found himself staring at the same empty sidewalk in front of Roseberry Homes. Only this time he was in the passenger seat of his new partner's car.

Andrew was getting tired of this kid's incessant questions. "Look, Wilks, this is the one, okay. This is the case. Don't you want to make a name for yourself?"

Mark Wilks, looking slightly perplexed as always, rubbed his mouth whilst trying to think of what he meant to say. "I don't want to piss off the Chief though. I'm new and I can tell he doesn't like me and if I'm doing this instead of...."

"Look Wilks, the Chief doesn't need to know. Whether we try and solve the liquor store one or not, it's still gonna have the same outcome."

Wilks was staring out of the windscreen looking unconvinced and slightly nervous. Andrew was regretting bringing him, and especially not bringing his own car. The point of course was to get Wilks involved from the get go. Get him on board so that he could get on with solving this thing. Andrew pressed on.

"We come back with something on this, take it to the Feds, trade info, and get them to bring us in."

Wilks turned sharply to look at him. "That's just it, though. We get something and we show it to the Chief and then he's gonna be like; 'Why didn't you do the case I told you to?' It's fine for you – he likes you."

"Jesus fucking Christ Wilks! Whose dick did you suck to get your Detective Shield?"

The words had exploded out of Andrew. Their eyes were locked. Wilks' seemed to spontaneously dilate, turning them into two black holes in the darkness of the car. Andrew hadn't noticed it before, but Wilks actually had quite big arms. Still facing Mark and with his words still echoing in the air, Andrew reached behind himself and quietly took hold of the door latch.

"Mark…"

There it was. Electricity flashed through Mark Wilks' eyes as his fists shot out with blinding speed. With his fingers hooked into the door latch, Andrew quickly opened the door and pushed himself back as he fended off the oncoming fists – only partially as one made a glancing connection with his lips as he fell backwards out of the car. The taste of iron sprayed into Andrew's mouth from between his teeth as his back connected with the sidewalk.

Andrew was quick to pull his legs from the car before rolling over onto his knees. The dizzying speed of the incident made Andrew sway but he quickly found focus and saw Wilks clambering over headfirst towards him. Andrew found that his hand was on the open door and by God if he had wanted him, Andrew could have slammed the door closed onto Wilks' oncoming head. Instead, Andrew used it as leverage and pulled himself up to stand.

"Wilks!" Andrew moved behind the open door as Wilks came spilling out onto the pavement. "Wilks!"

"What?" Wilks screamed as he shot to his feet, spinning to find Andrew.

His arms were straight down at his sides with his fingers parted and tense. With his veins bulging, Andrew could see the power in those arms behind that gormless exterior.

"You want a cup of coffee?" Andrew spat out the gathering blood.

Wilks didn't reply.

"I think our cover's blown for tonight. Come on, there's a diner just round the corner. I'll buy you a cup of coffee."

Andrew rounded the car door and walked past Mark Wilks who was still flared and breathing intensely through his nose.

"Come on." Andrew resisted the urge to pat him on the shoulder.

Andrew walked off with nothing but silence behind him. Then, as he began crossing the adjacent street, he heard the sound of the car door slam closed.

"Coffee, hun?"

The once upon a time beauty placed the cup she'd brought over to Andrew's window table in front of him and poured out a cup of black coffee from her pot.

"Thanks." Snatching serviettes from the dispenser he noticed Sue, as her name badge informed him, not moving on.

"Rough night?"

Andrew dabbed at his split lip, immediately feeling the serviette paper separating and sticking to it. He grimaced as he yanked it away.

"You could say that. Uh, Sue." Andrew politely widened his eyes at calling her by her name, which she seemed to silently acknowledge. "Do you think you could bring me a bowl of hot water and a cloth?"

"Hmm… You're lucky I feel sorry for you and that I think you're cute, 'cause we usually don't give out clean cloths for customers to bleed on." She turned and walked off into the dim lighting of the quiet diner.

"Thanks, Sue."

The tingle of the bell above the front sounded as Wilks came walking in. He had calmed down but his posture was still rigid and his eyes still seemed to have a distinct lack of blink to them. Mark spotted him and made his way over. The tension that he'd brought with him made a head or two turn as he walked past. Mark sat down across from Andrew. Sue arrived with the bowl and cloth, which she then placed in front of Andrew.

"Careful hun, that's hot."

Andrew nodded as he went about wetting the folded end of the cloth.

"Coffee, hun?"

"Please."

As Sue turned off to retrieve her trusty pot, Mark called out after her, "and some cream please."

Andrew couldn't help but smile audibly at this.

"What?"

Andrew looked up from his bowl of discoloured water. "I'm sorry, man. I was out of line."

Sue put a cup in front of Mark and placed a tiny jug of cream next to it. She poured his coffee.

"I see you boys are doing some bonding tonight." Seeing Mark's shoulders tense at this, Sue continued reassuringly. "Don't worry love, I don't doubt that this one had it coming." She smiled at Andrew. "I can see it in those eyes that he's trouble."

"Thanks Sue." Andrew watched her go.

"My pleasure," she said as she took her coffee pot elsewhere.

Turning back, Andrew watched as Mark put all his concentration into pouring about four teaspoons worth of sugar into his coffee and, all the cream he had.

"Look, Wilks. I hear what you're saying. Technically you ignore your caseload and spend your time and resources on something else, you risk suspension and all the rest. Fuck, even your shield if it goes far enough."

Wilks finished stirring his coffee and picked it up to take a sip. He looked at Andrew, waiting for him to make his point.

"So I get why you're unsure. But if we play this right, we could be part of one hell of a bust. Plus, this was my fucking case to begin with before the Feds came and took it away from me. And I was never officially taken off it, so..." Andrew had a better point to make but had lost it as his rant went on. He was about to back it up when Wilks finally spoke.

"You trying to become a Fed or something?"

The question paused Andrew as he thought about whether or not that was something he wanted. He shook it off.

"Look, Wilks, I just want to solve my case. My point is that there's no reason the Chief needs to think that we've been doing anything untoward. If we get something, I'll take it to him and if he chooses to be pissed off I'll take the heat and tell him I was doing it on my own time. If he likes what we have then we both take the credit." Andrew held his hands up. He couldn't make it better than that.

Wilks sipped his coffee again, not saying anything. All his previous tension had subsided and Andrew could now see that there was more going on behind those eyes than he previously thought.

After a thoughtful pause, Wilks leaned in and replied, "Okay Detective. I'll work with you on this and if we get something on it I'll go with you to the Chief, but I'm not dropping the liquor store. If it's a dead end case then it's a dead-end case, but I still want to wrap it up properly. Okay?"

Andrew leaned back in his seat looking at his new partner. "Okay." He was starting to like him.

* * *

Coming out of the diner Andrew felt Wilks' hand on his shoulder. Andrew turned to him to see him looking off in the distance. Andrew turned to where he was looking and there across the street at the end of the block was a girl in a black S&M wig.

* * *

It was a couple of blocks away from Roseberry Homes, but it was still in the neighbourhood. She'd seen them coming from a mile off and was twirling on her four-inch heels as she waited for them to reach her. Along with the black heels and black wig, she had on a pair of bright red tights that stopped just below the knees and showed off the amplitude of her behind, which was obviously her main calling card. The outfit was completed by a very 80s denim jacket and an even more so dog collar.

154

"Evening, officers."

"Evening."

The two of them came sidling up to her with Wilks letting him take the lead, which Andrew was pleased to see. She was certainly bottom heavy and pretty sexily packaged on that front, but she was not pretty and looked like she'd probably been in this game for far more years than she'd originally imagined.

"You out for a stroll tonight?" Andrew asked.

"Just having a little break." She'd played the game before and she knew to let Andrew keep the lead. "You boys caught me just as I stopped to have a smoke."

A pack of cigarettes seemed to materialise in her hand. She offered it to both of them before taking one out and lighting it.

"What's your name?"

She smiled, she wasn't going to say it. "Clarice. What's yours?"

"Andrew." He offered his hand, which she accepted. "And him behind, that's Mark."

She flashed Wilks a smile and a small wave before looking back at Andrew. "So… what, does this mean we're friends now?"

"Maybe just friendly." Andrew held up a ten.

"Ten bucks? What do you expect to get for that?"

"I'm not looking for much."

"Okay, tell me what you're after." She took the note.

"There's a building back around the corner, Roseberry Homes. It's a couple of blocks away. You know it?"

"Yeah I know it." She was smiling. "That you whose been hanging around out there?"

Andrew smiled back. "Yeah, you been seeing me?"

"It's known that you're there."

It was becoming clear, first a murder with cops swarming around and then with him watching the place. It was no wonder she hadn't come back.

"So the girl, the one who stood on the corner, I take it she knew that too."

Clarice flicked her cigarette at a passer-by who side stepped it but didn't say anything, "She knew."

"Do you know her?"

"I know her."

"Do you know where she moved to?"

"We've gone past the ten bucks territory."

Andrew figured as much, but the fact was that he didn't have any more money apart from four or five singles, but he didn't think that was going to cut it.

"You haven't given me much for my ten, Clarice."

"I told you I knew the girl and why she wasn't where she was supposed to be."

"That's not much."

"'Bout ten bucks worth."

Money had changed hands. Andrew could have hauled her in on soliciting charges and made it work, but really it would have just been a waste of time. Clarice wasn't going to give him any more than what he paid for. A true pro.

This was going to put Wilks' commitment to the test. "Mark, pay the lady."

"All I got are twenties."

After not getting a response, Andrew heard Wilks behind him as he pulled out his wallet and fished through his notes. There was a tap on his shoulder. Andrew reached back and took the note that was being held there. He held it out for Clarice to take, and when she did Andrew didn't let go.

"You'd better give me something for my money this time Clarice." He let go.

Clarice slipped the note into her bra before appearing another cigarette. "I'm not sure what she's up to but she's not turning round here anymore."

"You said you knew where she'd moved on to."

"I might know. Depends on whether she's selling or not."

"Why isn't she around here anymore?"

"She took a beating a few days ago." Clarice shook her head at the thought of it before stilling herself to light her cigarette. "Stupid kid. She tried to hide some of her money from Jasper and he gave her a kicking so she ran."

"Where to?"

Clarice held on to Andrew's gaze for a moment as she took another drag on her cigarette.

"Clarice?"

"What do you want with her anyway?"

"I think she might have seen something?"

"That family thing?"

"She say something to you?"

"If she saw something I'd be surprised 'cause she would have told me."

"You take her under your wing or something? Giving her some guidance?"

"She just didn't know any better. I was friendly with her, that's all."

Clarice was starting to get defensive and Andrew wasn't going to pay any more money. He backed it up.

"Maybe she saw something that she didn't recognise, that maybe I might. I just want to talk to her. Where do you think she might have gone?"

"There was this boy that she'd babble on about. They came over together from some fucking place up north. He's the one who got her turning when his band didn't happen or some such shit."

It was starting to turn into a sob story which Andrew didn't care to hear, but he'd got Clarice talking so he let her run with it. He had a feeling that she was looking to soften their hearts with this tale of woe, last ditch attempt to do right by this young girl whose life she'd just watched get sucked up. Maybe they'd save her.

"…then of course Jasper comes along and tells him to beat it off his turf but to leave the girl." Clarice stomped out her cigarette. "So he does, and that's it. That was like six months ago."

"Where is he?"

"In Jersey somewhere. I don't know where."

"Did she know?"

Clarice nodded. "He had a brother there. I don't know the brother's first name, but the boyfriend was Bobby Staffridge."

"How come she didn't run before?"

"Jasper keeps a pretty close eye on his new girls. But mostly I think she was just too scared, not motivated enough. Guess a good kick in the ass was all she needed."

"And what if she's still turning tricks?"

Clarice smiled a big smile, which actually made her quite appealing. "I tell you what, Officer Andrew. You go check on her boy in Jersey and if that doesn't pan out then you come back and find me."

As she turned to show off her bountiful tail, Mark spoke up. "What's her name?"

"Frankie. That's all I got." She strutted off.

CHAPTER THIRTEEN

1

Kathy looked at herself in her en suite bathroom mirror and then immediately slapped her hand against it to shield her eyes from the horror of what was on the other side. She had gone to bed with her make-up on and while it was the expensive kind, most of it was now smeared onto her pillow and across her face. Her head was pounding and there was no aspirin behind the mirror. Kathy turned on the sink's cold water tap and ducked her head down and began to slurp away. She needed hydration to plump up her brain again and get it to stop from banging against the inside of her skull. Kathy was having a hard time remembering what they'd got up to.

Somehow their celebratory drink at lunch had extended right on into the night. Or at least there had been night. How much of it Kathy could not say. With her belly now overloaded with water, Kathy shot up and looked at herself again. She'd made out with some guy in the club. She squeezed her eyes shut in pain and painful remembrance. He couldn't have been older than twenty-two with really, really styled hair. Kathy remembered that, after a while, she even let him grab her boobs. She opened her eyes again and saw herself staring back with her hands over her mouth and her eyes wide. Her hands then went up and she grabbed her hair and pulled. She hated her hair cut.

* * *

The big windows of the living room were attacking Kathy with the excessive amount of light they were letting through. She shielded her face while ensuring that she moved in a steady but controlled manner so as to keep the brain rattle factor down. Somehow she'd managed to change into a T-shirt and sweats before bed which she was glad of, as she didn't think the straps of her dress would've been able to stand her tossing and turning.

Kathy knocked on the door. No answer. She knocked again. Still nothing. Kathy was about to knock again when she realised that her knocking was designed more to protect her from the noise of it rather than to attract attention. Kathy knocked again and recoiled from the sound.

"Morning."

The voice on the other end of the door sounded pleasant and refreshed.

"Giovanna?" Kathy turned the handle and pushed the door open.

Kathy recognised the faint smell in the air. It was one she hadn't smelt for herself in a good long while.

"Morning." This voice was deeper and belonged to the body of the young, bald, black and gorgeous college boy that Giovanna had brought home with her.

158

Kathy was getting flashes of them in the cab with him. Another flash told her why she didn't have her one, and it wasn't pretty. Kathy felt compelled to clear her raw throat.

"Giovanna's in the bathroom," said the very pretty college boy from his seated position beneath Giovanna's sheets.

He didn't seem to know what else to say and Kathy didn't want to have to say anything back.

"Where's Giovanna?"

"Here I am, Kathy." Giovanna appeared from her en suite looking as naturally make-up free and beautiful as was possible for a mere mortal to be. She handed Kathy a small box and then kissed her on the cheek before pushing her gently backwards and re-closing the door.

* * *

With a cup of strong coffee in her hand, slippers on her feet and a blanket over her shoulders, Kathy opened the door to the roof terrace. The morning air was chilly but refreshing. Kathy didn't know what time she'd got to bed the night before but she wasn't surprised to be up as early as she was. Their days started early, and while she had called Cindy before all her reasoning had left her, telling her they'd be in late, they were still going to have to get a move on. But for the moment Kathy was going to relax, drink her coffee, smoke a couple of cigarettes and let the four aspirin she'd just knocked back take effect.

Putting her cup on the elegantly designed metal table, Kathy pulled out one of the chairs and sat down, being careful to get as much of her blanket tucked underneath her as possible. Kathy took out a cigarette, lit it and breathed deeply. Her chest felt heavy and her throat felt rough from having too many throughout their impromptu celebrations, but this one was going down well. Kathy felt a smile creep across her face as she looked out over the city in the clear morning light. It was all coming together. It was all going to happen for them, for her.

2

His boy Chester had cleaned up nicely the past week or so. Access to a hot shower every night and enough money to keep a working fridge relatively stocked certainly agreed with him. Anthony, seated in his car, watched him from across the street as Chester spoke to the group of boys he'd assembled.

Anthony had been keeping Chester busy, giving him a sense that he'd been earning the fifties that Anthony had been slipping him. For the most part the work was bogus, except for the occasional package Anthony needed dropped, it was just empty boxes being left at nowhere locations. Anthony had told Chester that he had a lot more work that needed doing and to gather some of his friends so that he could get a look at them.

He was still feeling Chester out. If all went well and the boy could be trusted, he'd have a player to keep his boys and girls cool and calm. Keep them in line. As it went, Anthony wasn't yet sure that Chester had the stomach for this game. But if that was the road they ended up on, then having little Jamie 'Switch' Nuemyer around would prove very useful.

There were three of them but only two were what Anthony was looking for. The third was too far gone. His greasy skin was a mess of acne and their reminiscent scars, and his arms were lined with infected tracks. The other two were good. Anthony pegged them anywhere from sixteen to twenty-one. Better if they were under eighteen but it wasn't serious. One of them had his shirt off and while he was thin, his Latino skin complimented his sleek muscles. He was short at maybe five foot six. Not pretty but close enough. If he was on the junk it didn't show.

The third was a classic rent boy junkie. Skinny, twitchy, dirty and pretty. His hair was short and his skin was pale, but his blue eyes and sharp cheekbones could have landed him a modelling gig if his life didn't revolve around the junk. The two would do for now. He'd also need some girls soon enough but the name they were starting with called for a boy. Chester indicated for them to wait and then made his way diagonally across the road towards Anthony's car. The car was as much as they were allowed to see. It wasn't his anyway. Chester arrived at his window and squatted down to be at eye level with Anthony.

"They're keen enough and I think they'll do the work if it means they'll have the opportunity to keep getting money."

"That's called a job." He held out two twenty dollar notes, which Chester took. "Give these to the two of them and tell pizza boy to get lost. Tell them to hang tight and not to go too far. I'll get back to them."

"Okay." Chester stood back up and turned to head back.

"Chester."

"Yeah?" he said turning back.

"I'm gonna need some girls too. Do you think you can hook that up?"

Chester took a slow step back towards the car. "What do you need girls for?"

Anthony found himself looking up at Chester. He didn't like it. "Same thing I need the boys for." He waved him off. "Give them the money."

Chester did as he was told and trotted back over to the three boys who were peering over at Anthony's car. Anthony knew he was far away enough for them not to be able to see him properly. Chester reached them and after a brief scuffing of the feet, the pizza boy shrunk away. Anthony liked it; clearly Chester hadn't wasted time on polite niceties when telling him to fuck off. The other two held up their notes and waved to Anthony's car. They ran off, most likely to score.

Chester rounded the car and opened the passenger door. He climbed in not looking at Anthony.

"Can you get me girls?"

Chester closed the door and put his foot onto the dashboard slouching into his seat. "What do you want girls for?"

Anthony started the car and slipped it into gear. "Tell me Chester. Do you like our little arrangement?"

"Yeah." His voice was soft. He knew he was being set up.

"Easy, isn't it?"

Chester didn't reply. Anthony drove the car out of its parking spot and joined the flow of traffic. He continued.

"I give you a package and you drop it off and in exchange you have a place to live, food in your fridge and money in your pocket. Now when you think about it, that's a hell of a lot like getting money for nothing, isn't it?"

"You got a smoke?"

"Glove compartment."

Anthony watched as Chester fished out the cigarettes and lit one for himself. The boy was trying to maintain an air of aloof dignity in the face of being treated like a child. He was also doing it carefully. It was this combination of strength and brains that Anthony had originally chosen him for.

"Give me one."

Chester did, along with the lighter. Anthony lit his cigarette and the two of them smoked in silence for a moment. Chester knew what was coming and Anthony thought that he was ready for it, despite how quickly he was smoking away at his cigarette.

"It's time for you to start earning your money, Chester. More money. No more packages. If I have anything that I need moved, you'll get somebody else to move it." Anthony paused and looked at Chester. He didn't react. He just smoked on his already almost finished cigarette and kept on looking ahead.

"But that's not what this is about. I think you know that."

"You want girls for hookers, right?"

"Close. We're not talking street corners here. And it's not just gonna be the girls."

Chester tossed his cigarette and then immediately sent his shaky hands after another one.

"What we're getting into is a little bit bigger picture and bigger money. You do what I say and you'll be able to get your hands on a lot of it. Our game runs fast and hard. And then you can take your Jamie and go make a life for yourselves. You hearing me?"

Chester nodded blowing out the smoke from his just lit cigarette.

"Can you bring me girls?"

"I know some and I know where to look."

"They need to be decent looking and young." Anthony didn't look but he saw Chester's eyes snap towards him. "Not too young, but they must be under seventeen."

Chester's shoulders loosened as he turned his eyes front again and took another drag from his shaky cigarette.

3

Things were back on and in full swing. The show was on Saturday night and meant they had around three days to get things happening. The lawyers were currently across town sorting out the final details and come the evening time the hope was that papers would be ready to sign and preparation could get underway bright and early in the morning.

Kathy walked up alongside the cubicles that had been set up on the open plan floor of their cheap and definitely temporary office space. Their staff of twenty were working away at a frenzied pace, playing catch up now that they had a confirmed spot for the third show. There was lots to be done. Certain things were ready and waiting. Workers to re-assemble and vastly expand their catwalk had been booked as well as the catering company. Drivers and cars to ferry certain high profile guests to and from the event were on standby and all the other little things that had been in place for the original planetarium gig.

But now notices needed to be sent out informing the sayers and the players of where the spot for the third show was going to be. Insurance needed to be taken out to cover having an event out on open water. Licensing fees. New staff needed to be hired to ensure the safety of the guests and to insure that the insurance would not need to be paid out.

Most of this would make up for the fact that the use of the boat itself wasn't going to cost them anything.

The theme would have to be tweaked but at least the open ocean did lend itself to the idea of possibilities, which was now leaning towards infinity. Decorations, of course, had to be totally overhauled and so on and so on.

Kathy looked over to Giovanna's office, as it was known. It was more of a room with a chair, a desk and a filling cabinet. Her own was much the same. Giovanna was on the phone getting the good news to the right people. 'It's on a giant yacht – that was the big surprise all along... and y'all doubted us.' Giovanna was all smiles and her confidence was back on form with their new location essentially locked down and better than they ever could have hoped for. That, and what Giovanna said was one of the most 'eager to please' lovers that she'd ever had.

Kathy was on her way down stairs to talk to Gabriel who was setting up for the photo shoots for the third shows dresses. She had another strong cup of coffee in her hand and an additional two aspirins working their way through her system. She was still feeling a little used from what her memory flashes kept telling her was a wild night. But she was feeling good, feeling that drive again.

* * *

The floor below was set up strictly to accommodate Gabriel and his shoots. Clothes were stored and rooms were set aside to house, spruce and paint the models for said shoots. Kathy walked through the open door from the stairway and into Gabriel's domain. He was expensive and one of the costlier investments for their first issue, but he was also one of the best and, in order for their financing to hold its course, the first issue would have to prove its worth. His pictures would help make that happen, as would their attachment to their extravagant and upcoming show.

It was the issue at hand that she had come down to deal with. Kathy made her way down the walkway, which ran along the edge of the room. She watched the lack of spectacle below on the open concrete floor where Gabriel sat on a stool behind his camera sitting atop its tripod. A bored, glammed up model sat impatiently in front of him with a team of half a dozen blue jeans waiting in the wings to bring whatever inspiration Gabriel had instantly to life.

Gabriel was having a problem shifting his thematically charged pictures into this new aquatic direction. The shoots for the previous two shows had to be put on hold. As for the outdoor shots, the only chance Gabriel would get to shoot on Dulpard's boat would be limited windows on Wednesday, Thursday and Friday, as work to set up the boat would need to be done and once the show was over Dulpard wanted his boat and his privacy back. This was, of course, also fuelling Gabriel's creative hissy fit.

So this day was about models waiting around under some very hot indoor lighting while the artist tried to figure it all out before lugging it all outside. Thing was, models were expensive and they couldn't afford to have them sitting around getting even thinner.

"What's the problem, Gabe?"

He didn't turn to look at her. "There's a reason you people hired me – isn't that right, Miss Radley?"

"On the money, Mr Hutton."

He turned slowly on his stool to face her. His white shirt was undone, showing off the fine blond hairs that covered his not quite so firm as it once was chest.

"And what would that reason be?"

Kathy didn't want to play this game. If she indulged Gabriel in his antics then her cloud nine position could very well slip out from under her.

"Just take some pictures, Gabriel, like we hired you to."

He shot his eyes at her and bounced off his stool before grabbing it and violently shoving it aside in a moment of uncontrolled rage, all the while being careful to avoid knocking his very expensive camera over.

"Just take some pictures!"

Giovanna refused to deal with Gabriel. She had no patience for him. On the rare occasions they had been forced to interact, it had almost always ended with one of them storming out. Giovanna could usually charm just about anyone, especially men, but when it came to Gabriel it was all she could do to stop herself from twitching in revulsion.

Kathy figured this was to do with just how ridiculously childish this sleazy alcoholic could be. Kathy could take him. Their relationship had just about turned into that of a mother and child. Well, if that's what it took to keep one of the most high profile photographers in line, then that's the way she'd play it.

He was looking at her expectantly. Those who hadn't worked with him before had backed off in shock at his outburst.

"Yes. Just take some pictures. Get the blood pumping. Get a feel for the clothes." She walked over to him and put her hand on his shoulder. "What do you need, Gabe?"

He looked at her like a confused child. The violence of his rage was now gone. "I don't know. You people can't just pull my work away and tell me to re-work a new theme and to do it now. I can't work like that."

"I know Gabe." Kathy guided them into a walk and talk. "It sucks. It does, I know it does. Everybody upstairs is dealing with the same thing that you are." Kathy wanted to swallow that last sentence for fear that Gabriel would take it to mean that his work wasn't unique and special and that it could just be lumped in with everybody else's. She looked at him. He was still hers. She continued.

"It's a struggle, I know, but sometimes we have to struggle. Most of your best stuff has that kind of fight flowing through it like electricity." He looked at her. She knew what she was doing. "If you could bring that kind of power to these pictures, maybe this is the best thing that could have happened."

He brought their walk to an end by turning to face her. He was nodding. He knew he was being handled but also liked what he was hearing. Kathy threw him a bone so he could manoeuvre himself out of the situation with his dignity intact.

"Now tell me what you need from me and I'll make sure you get it."

"Anything?"

Here it came. "Anything."

"I wouldn't mind if you'd uncross those legs and let me fuck you." There it was, attached to a leering smile.

"Nice." She turned and went back the way she came. "Now get back to work."

From behind her, Kathy heard Gabriel's preparatory double clap before he shouted out, "All right people! Let's try something. Bring me that other model. I'm sick of looking at this one's face. Oh, Kathy." She didn't turn. "Nice haircut."

Dick! She kept going.

4

"Hay Dana. You got something for me?"

"Detective Bates." Dana moved a glass paperweight aside and handed Andrew a paper folder, pausing to not say anything about his bruise and split upper lip. "The home address of one Alex Staf-bridge, located in New Jersey."

Andrew opened it and looked at the first sheet. "*Bridge* – you sure?"

"I'm sure. No Staffridge and Alex Stafbridge there fits, so logic dictates."

"Thanks Dana." Andrew started to leave.

"Jersey, huh?"

He turned back. "Yeah."

"Seems like a way away from your liquor store."

Andrew smiled and Dana smiled back. "Yeah, every avenue. You know how it goes."

"Hitmen being brought in from off the island. Something like that."

"Something like that."

He turned to leave but then again turned back to listen to Dana.

"Chief's not going to take it too well if you're ignoring your caseload, Detective."

"You're just the social conscience around here aren't you, Dana?"

"Just like to ensure the place keeps running smoothly – and I won't be doing any more of your under-the-radar bitch work either. Anything else you need gets properly logged." She smiled again.

"Thanks again Dana." Andrew waved the folder in indication and left.

* * *

"We got something?"

Wilks was sitting on the corner of David's desk. He had spent a good half an hour going back and forth, moving his stuff into Andrew and David's office before Andrew found himself snapping that their partnership was only temporary and that this office was for senior detectives. To which Wilks replied that his desk had been reassigned to somebody else. The conversation had begun to make Andrew's head hurt, so he let Wilks carry on, though he told him not to move any of David's stuff out the drawers. His own stuff would have to stay in boxes for the time being. Wilks had obediently obliged and now there he sat looking content with his place in the world.

Andrew grabbed his coat from his chair and slipped it on, transferring the paper folder from hand to hand as he did. "We got an address. Come on."

* * *

They took Andrew's car. He didn't like being held at the whim of his new partner.

Wilks was reading the sheet. "Alex Stafbridge, forty-nine years old. Busted twice for possession, once for drink driving and he's been pulled up about a dozen times on assault charges – mostly domestic. He's spent two years behind bars for breaking some poor guy's legs."

"Sounds like he did a little work as a debt collector."

"Yeah, he's still on parole so this address should be good." Wilks reshuffled the papers and slipped them back into the folder. He looked at Andrew. "Do you think we should call this guy's parole officer? Get him to organise a meet?"

"No."

"Why not? If we just show up he may tell us to take a hike. He doesn't have to talk to us if he doesn't want to. We get in with his P.O." Wilks un-shuffled the papers. "Simon Riker – then he can call him and tell him to co-operate with us."

"Look Wilks, I don't want to get mixed up with this guy's parole officer who's then gonna want to know what we want before he goes and checks with his boss, all so he can organise for me to talk to someone I haven't even come here to talk to. Besides, if his P.O. starts calling out of the blue and either him or his brother are doing something off colour then they're going to get spooked and the brother will probably high tail it outta there. I don't want to bust anybody, I just want to talk to them and that's something I'll be able to make clear face to face."

Mark contemplated all this as he nodded for what seemed close to a minute. "Do you think our girl will be there?"

"If she's not there now then she will have been at some point."

"What is it you think this chick saw anyway?"

More questions. "Something."

"What makes you so sure?"

"Just something off about the whole thing that's all. Nothing about that scene fits together and that means there was more going on and if there's something going on that's more than you want people to see, then that means there's something to see – and if there's something to see then somebody's likely to see something. Fair enough?" The look he gave Wilks was enough.

"Fair enough."

* * *

The address led round the back of an old factory that, according to its faded sign, produced extra-large sheets of glass. There didn't seem to be much activity inside or around it. No cars out front and all the doors and windows shut. Closed down, Andrew guessed. The old wooden tiered condo style housings that were built up against its back were faded and rough. They probably had a landlord but to Andrew's mind this was only a couple of steps up from squatting in derelict buildings.

Andrew pulled the car to a stop at the edge of the large section of open plot which stretched out in front of the building. It was littered with everything from Coke cans to abandoned cars, and where the grass and weeds weren't overgrown the ground was filled with rubble. Beyond that, the area twisted into a maze of spaces in between factory after factory. Andrew had selected his spot carefully and as they got out, they were mostly out of sight to those that were hanging about on the wooden walkways and stairs that were built along the front of the building. He didn't need anyone announcing their arrival.

The ground was littered with the remnants of more than one night's gathering and the blackened ground was still warm from the fire that had been sparked off there, only a few metres away from the wooden structures where they lived. Must have been one hell of a party. A girl of about thirteen or fourteen turned off her stairs and stepped towards them. Her movements were sly but Andrew had seen her coming.

"Hey!" she said as if it would startle them.

"Hey yourself." Andrew hated kids and this one looked worthy of his hate.

Her clothes were layered, tight and multi-coloured and her face seemed to be more developed on one side, thanks to her seemingly permanent sneer. Her hair was pulled back tightly and she had giant hoops for earrings. She also stunk of booze.

"You cops?"

"We're looking for a girl named Frankie – couple of years older than you – blonde hair."

"She skinny?"

"Maybe."

"Never seen her." She barely got the words out before exploding with laughter at the hilarity of her own joke.

"Alright, alright. Get out of here before I shoot you." Andrew took her shoulder and pushed her behind them as they walked past.

Regaining her equilibrium, she shouted after them, "Hey you can't touch me. I could have you fired for that."

They didn't turn back and after a couple more unintelligible threats she got bored and ran back up the stairs from which she came.

* * *

Andrew checked the number again. It was the right door. He knocked on its cracked blue paint again. He didn't want to use the police word until he had to. They were on the second tier of the three tiered structure and Andrew was wondering if his couple could have snuck out and climbed down without being seen, having heard them coming.

"Probably at work."

Shut up Wilks. "What time is it?"

"Just after five."

Andrew knocked again, harder and longer.

"Shit." He turned to Wilks. "Did it say what his job was in his file?"

"Said he worked in that glass factory." Wilks pointed up, indicating over to the large, suspiciously quiet factory behind the residence.

"What the fuck do you want?" boomed from behind Andrew.

Andrew turned back towards the open door stumbling against Wilks, who hadn't even seen the door he'd been facing open, before they were nearly stormed upon. The owner of the voice was grey all over, but still solid as a rock. He was in his indoor wear – blue dressing gown, boxers and a wife beater.

"Mr Stafbridge?" Andrew said removing himself from his position against Wilks.

"That's right. What do you want?" His voice seemed to be laced with an excess of saliva.

"We just want to talk." Andrew said, trying to subtly take half a step back.

"Cops, huh?"

"That's right. We just…"

"I ain't done shit since I got outta the joint."

"That's between you and your P.O." Who he probably paid off with whatever he was into to keep up the pretence of working in a closed factory. "We just want to come in and ask you a few questions."

"This is Detective Mark Wilks," Andrew indicated behind himself, "and I'm Detective Andrew Bates. Do you mind if we come inside for a second?" Andrew held up his badge.

Stafbridge's thought process flashed across his face as he contemplated his options. Send them away and risk them coming back with a warrant after going through his P.O. End up messing up his gig and possibly getting him sent up by his P.O. for violation to cover his own ass. Or answer some questions and hope they went away.

"What's this about?"

"Can we take a seat inside?" Andrew indicated past him and started moving forward.

Stafbridge threw his arms up in exasperation and went back inside leaving the door open for them to follow. Andrew looked to Wilks. He looked steely, but Andrew wasn't yet confident about having this guy guarding his six on entering the dark apartment of a known felon. He went in anyway. The place was dark, cramped and as grey as its owner.

"Take a seat." Stafbridge pointed to the small fold-out kitchen table with three chairs around it. He was over by his cluttered sink making coffee. "Coffee?"

"Thanks."

Andrew took a seat and shook his head at Wilks, stopping him from taking one of his own. He nodded and then stepped back to lean against the wall next the doorway, which Andrew was happy to see still open. If not for the light from the outside world, Andrew couldn't imagine the dim lamps and lights about the place providing much illumination.

Stafbridge seemed more relaxed now that he was in his home. "What's this about?" He turned holding two cups of black coffee, which he handed to each of them.

"Thanks." Andrew took a sip and then put the cup down so as not to repeat the process.

"Well Mr Stafbridge, we're looking for someone. A young girl named Frankie." Andrew saw Stafbridge's shoulders tighten slightly at the mention of *a young girl.* Should he deny or just confirm? That possibly ran the risk of making him an accomplice to something.

Andrew didn't want to give him reason to lie – he did just want to talk to the girl. "Mr Stafbridge, I have absolutely no interest in you or your brother. We're looking for Frankie and your brother's name came up, and then this address. We just want to ask her a few questions about something we think she may have seen in the city. Again, nothing to do with your brother." Andrew almost picked up his cup of coffee.

Andrew knew they were there or at least had been there recently. Mrs Stafbridge was obviously long gone. A man like Stafbridge kept his woman in her place, making sure that such a woman kept his place in working order, which this place was not. This being a certainty, there were, however, a few feminine sprinkles about the place. A gossip rag on the counter which was far too youthful for Stafbridge's taste, a clearly new and delicate cactus on the windowsill above the kitchen sink, some lip balm sitting on the coffee table next to an empty packet of Marlboro Lights. Stafbridge had his own brand of Chesterfields in front of him.

Andrew could feel Stafbridge about to deny it all as he leaned into his impending 'I don't know where they are and I think you should get the fuck out of my house.'

Andrew cut him off. "So, what time are they due back?"

Stafbridge didn't say anything. His shoulders were again tense. His eyes were darting between the two cops who he'd let walk into his house. Again his face told Andrew what was about to be said. Andrew stopped him.

"Listen Mr Stafbridge, as I said before, I just want to talk to this girl. If the girl's not here then I just want to talk to your brother and ask him to tell me where the girl is. But if you tell me that neither of them are here then I'm gonna want to talk to you again, because I will suddenly find you very interesting." Andrew leaned back in his chair enjoying the frozen look on Stafbridge's 'how did it come to this face.' "I mean, already, after having looked at your file, you seem like a very interesting guy."

"Very interesting," echoed Wilks, leaning into his words before leaning back against the wall again.

Stafbridge looked back to Andrew who was no longer looking at Wilks. Andrew let him speak.

"If this hasn't got anything to do with my brother then what's it about?"

Andrew slammed himself out of his chair, which went rocketing back. "None of your fucking business! I'm getting sick of all the run around. It's obvious the girl was here. Either you tell me where she is or you tell me where your brother is. I know you don't care about the girl and I don't care about your brother, so just tell me!"

"I'll have to call him." Stafbridge stood to find the phone.

This wasn't working. Stafbridge either didn't trust them or he didn't trust his brother. The girl didn't matter to him but if she mattered to the cops then maybe that was connected to his brother who was connected to him, and so on until everything was brought down. Andrew didn't know how to play this, how to dissuade him of these thoughts. He didn't want him calling his brother. Tell him to put the phone down and step away. All of it was starting to border on illegal. Andrew could see it in Wilks' shifting eyes and shifting feet. He'd had enough. Stafbridge was over by the small cabinet that sat by one of the closed doors. He had the phone.

"Put it down Stafbridge."

With the receiver almost at his ear, Stafbridge turned his slightly hunched over frame towards Andrew. He was smiling. "Put it down? What are you going to do, cop? Shoot me for making a phone call?" He started dialling. "I'm just going to call my brother and tell him you want to see him. I'm sure he'll be right over."

Stafbridge knew what he was doing – forcing Andrew to make a move. Get in there and manhandle the phone out of his hands. This kind of territory could cost a cop his job. He wasn't meant to be here. How did it come to this?

"Look Stafbridge, I don't want to have to get into this with your P.O. over the scam you've got going on with the glass factory."

Stafbridge was smiling. Had he been reading him at all?

"It's ringing." He pointed at the phone.

Andrew's ears perked up. There was ringing. Andrew turned to the open front door. There was a cell phone ringing out there and the ringing was growing louder. Andrew turned to Stafbridge. The phone wasn't being answered by his brother who'd obviously recognised the number and was about to arrive home anyway. What should he do? Call out a warning and make his brother run, forcing the cops to chase him? What if they did just want to talk? Andrew gave him a smile. Stafbridge sneered in return and hung up the phone. Andrew backed himself further into the apartment, keeping both Stafbridge and the open front door in his sight. Wilks, too, backed up remaining parallel to the doorway.

Andrew looked out into the dull afternoon sky beyond the open doorway. The air in the place didn't feel right anymore. He felt his gun against his hip. He saw Wilks' hand lingering by his own. They had no cause to draw their guns. There was a confused tension in the air. Stafbridge was tense. He didn't know what to do. There could be a gun hidden away somewhere. There almost certainly was. Andrew didn't want to draw his gun. Turn the moment into a self-fulfilling prophecy.

"Bobby, run!" Stafbridge screamed, just as the doorway was darkened by two figures.

Andrew wrenched his gun free from its holster and ducked down to the side in anticipation of a hail of gunfire. Instead a young girl of about seventeen or eighteen came stumbling in, screaming as she went down. Her boyfriend was already gone and Wilks was off after him.

Andrew's eyes were on Stafbridge who was not doing much of anything. Andrew had desperately wanted to see a big Dirty Harry magnum 44 in his hands so he could blow him the fuck away for being so irritating. Not exactly just cause, but the guy had been really irritating.

Andrew wasn't too sure how much trouble all of this was going to get him in and he didn't have time to ponder over how much more there was waiting in the wings. He took out his handcuffs and beckoned for Stafbridge to give him his wrist. The fire in Andrew's eyes and his tightly gripped gun made him comply. Andrew slapped one end onto his wrist, and then, pulling Stafbridge to follow, he fed the other end behind a pipe in the radiator, which was towards the kitchen area.

"You. Come here now." Time was of the essence.

Frankie was all eyes at this point. Her world was fucked. Pushed by her boyfriend who then just split and left her, again...

"Now!"

She pushed herself up and quick-stepped her way over to Andrew, holding her wrist out as if it were an offering. He took it and twisted it into the other end of the cuffs.

"Now, don't go anywhere."

CHAPTER FOURTEEN

1

"...the suspect's name who then fled. Seeing that my partner, Detective Andrew Bates had the situation in hand – his gun drawn covering both suspects (Alex Stafbridge and Frankie 'The Girl') I pursued Robert Stafbridge out the apartment and down the stairs. I, Detective Mark Wilks, called out: "Police, freeze!""

Andrew snapped the paper away from his eyes and put it on top of the other two that he'd just read. He couldn't read anymore. He looked over at the Chief who was looking back over his desk at him.

"Is that about the sum of it?"

"In *so* many words, yes."

The Chief smiled. It looked like the pleasant kind but Andrew knew better. Wilks hadn't run into any problems with Bobby Stafbridge, but the two of them had done some running and by the time Andrew had found them, Bobby was in cuffs and back-up was already on its way, called by Wilks. Everything from then on in had just slipped further and further from Andrew's grasp. As it happened, a patrol car had been close by and was already there when they got back. The girl and Stafbridge were already loaded into the back. Stafbridge had been instantly recognised and so his parole officer had been called.

Words were then had as to whose prisoners these two were. In this, Andrew came up short. No shots fired but they did have suspicious behaviour and resisted arrest. Didn't really explain the girl and Stafbridge being cuffed together. At the parole officer's insistence, Stafbridge was not to be taken across the bridge, and, as the girl was cuffed to him, she was to stay as well. Bobby was theirs – resisting arrest – but there would be no holding onto him once Simon Riker got through with his procedure checklist. It was all beyond ridiculous. On getting back late, Andrew had called the Chief hoping for some forgiveness and some string-pulling magic. There had been none. Simon Riker had already made the call and would be seeing them in the morning.

The Chief had told Andrew that both he and Wilks were to write out reports and be waiting with them by his desk when he arrived in the morning. The Chief, when he arrived, had elected to read Wilks'. Wilks had been instructed to wait outside. Breaking his smile, the Chief spoke again.

"I wish I could say this surprises me Bates."

"But it doesn't?"

"No, it doesn't." His demeanour was unusually calm. "However, you're now dragging others down with you."

"Thing is, Chief, I was never officially taken off the case so I was just following up on a potential witness and..."

"Be very careful, Bates." His voice was even but the words were vibrating

172

against a clenched jaw. "You had no business being down that way and with the side stepping you did… If this Simon Riker prick doesn't take to you, you could lose your badge over this."

"What about the girl?"

The Chief lost his momentum at hearing the question. After a moment he looked down at his paper-covered desk and did a brief shift through them. Finding the appropriate one, he traced his finger down.

"Frances Fey Bradley." He looked back up. "She's sixteen, Bates. There was no actual arrest and no guardians to speak of, so social services were called and she went straight into the system."

"Shit. We got a line on her?"

"Bates. Did you hear me? You're in real trouble on this one. What the fuck did you think you were doing?"

"Boss, I'm sorry. I just had a lead on…"

"Sorry? I don't give a fuck if you're sorry, Detective. And it's not my ass you should be kissing…"

"Don't worry about this P.O. Just let me talk to him alone and all of it goes away. The kid hasn't even been processed."

The Chief was leaning back in his chair. "You got something on this P.O.?"

"Let's just say I know he won't want to be looked at, so I think we'll be able to come to an understanding."

The Chief was nodding, his feet now on his desk. "Okay… You take care of this mess. I'll make sure Riker is sent to your office. And then, once it's out of my misery, you come back here and you tell me why you think this girl can help on the Cartwright case. Then, if I like what I hear, I'll get you your little chat with this girl."

Andrew stood out of his chair. "That's all I wanted, Chief." He made for the door.

"Make sure you're in your office when he gets here. I don't want to have to see him."

"I'm headed there now." Andrew opened the door.

"And send Wilks in."

* * *

Simon Riker was such a sleazy, short sleeved, button up shirt with a brown tie and evil looking glasses that the little twitchy bastard just plain had to be on the take. He came rushing into Andrew's office after two fast and un-answered knocks. He was looking to make an impression.

"Who the fuck do you think you are?" His spindly fingers were aimed at Andrew who was only two metres away from him sitting adjacent to his desk.

"Would you like to take a seat?" Andrew indicated to the chair in front of David's desk, which sat against the wall.

Riker looked at the chair and then back at Andrew.

173

"No I don't want to sit. I want you to answer my question. I want to talk to your boss. Where's Chief Groder?"

Andrew stood up and Riker immediately shrank back. Andrew had a good foot on him.

"Chief Groder is busy. Look Simon…"

"No you look Detective Bates," his finger was out again, "Alex Stafbridge is on parole and that means, as his parole officer I'm in charge of any action taken against him. Had your actions been legal, they would have come through me first. As it stands, you stormed into his house and hand cuffed him without reading his rights. Not to mention the fact that you had no legitimate reason to be there." He had an open mouthed smile going. "I mean, talk about abuse of power and a violation of my client's civil rights. I'm sorry, Detective Bates, but I take my role at helping these men reintegrate their way into society seriously. And rehabilitation is made next to impossible by cops like you who think they can use these men as punching bags. I'm afraid I'm going to have to see to it that you never have the chance to do this kind of thing again."

Andrew gave a nod. "Right. Look, you ridiculous little pretend man."

Riker's highly expressive face turned into a blank canvas.

Andrew continued, stepping into his words. "I have no interest in your parolee or his little brother. The brother is here and when you sleaze off, you're more than welcome to take him with you. Now, I'm hoping that this means we can put this behind us and just forget the whole thing. No hard feelings." Andrew held out his hand for Simon Riker to shake.

His expressions were back. "You just fucked yourself now." He turned back to the door. "I'm going to press for jail time now. Good day Detective."

"So… the glass factory is where Stafbridge works?"

Simon Riker stopped and didn't turn.

"As I said, I'm not interested in your boy – or you – but you are both very interesting and because of that I could be tempted to take a look. Now I don't really want to or even care, but I think we both know that if I did …" Andrew let the last word drift off and hang in the air.

Simon Riker turned slowly.

Andrew re-extended his hand. "No hard feelings?"

Simon Riker shook it and left.

* * *

"Too neat, huh?" The Chief stroked his chin.

Andrew had laid out his vague ins-and-outs for the Chief and basically that was it. The sloppy crime scene was just too obviously not that sloppy, and that meant something. The Chief was happy enough to buy all of this, and even that if the girl had been outside, being a whore – especially a nervous one – her eyes might pick up something that shouldn't have been there. The 'what?' of course was the big question. But also 'so what?' was being raised. And of course that was what Andrew had finally convinced him that he'd find out. First the 'what?' which was where he was headed, followed by the 'so what?' when he took it to the Feds.

* * *

Andrew turned his car through the gate which was being held open for him, and drove into the parking allotment which was round the back of the four building compound, which was now young Frances Fey Bradley's new home. It was a hell of a long way from small town Massachusetts and looking at the dead white of the surrounding walls, Andrew figured the looming threat of a place just like it was probably the very reason she'd run in the first place.

Something about a single parent dying when she was thirteen, shipped between foster homes, nothing sticks, troublemaker, bad friends, bad boyfriend, skips town to hit the big city and the rest is history.

* * *

No Wilks on his tail as Andrew walked along the green linoleum tiles of Building B's second floor corridor. It was a relief, but as it went Andrew was starting to get used to him. There were streaks within Wilks' personality that Andrew was growing to like. Still, it was a relief to be away from his incessant questions, give him a chance to think.

Andrew's guide through this maze was a little Korean man named Akoni, who was dressed all in white and had the tiniest hands Andrew had ever seen on a grown man. Andrew pegged him for about sixty based on the wrinkles and weathered skin, but Akoni had the kick and spirit of a fifty year old with very bad knees. The pace was slow but the smiles were plentiful. Akoni didn't speak much English, but he did a lot of smiling and pointing. Andrew, investing hope in hope itself that he knew where he was going, simply nodded and grunted in agreement.

Then, after a staggered wide-armed turn, Akoni took Andrew by the wrist and pushed him towards a green door, which they had just passed. That done, Akoni continued back on his long journey from whence he came.

"Thank you, Akoni."

Andrew immediately felt guilty as this caused Akoni to stop in his tracks to do another wide-armed turn to deliver a parting wave and smile. Andrew did the same and then turned away from Akoni's slow-mo about face. Andrew knocked on the green door.

"Mmm, come in," came the muffled response.

Andrew opened the door which then banged against the back of one of the guest chairs in front of Jennifer Clarkson's impossibly cluttered desk. She waved Andrew in as she chewed down her mouth full of some greasy looking sandwich that she had in front of her. The office was ridiculously small and cartoonishly overloaded. There were boxes full of papers on the filing cabinet and boxes on the floor stacked against the filing cabinet. Andrew squeezed himself the rest of the way in before trying to speak.

"Jennifer Clarkson? I'm Detective Bates. I believe my boss Derrick Groder called ahead." Andrew extended his hand. "Thanks for seeing me at such short notice."

Jennifer Clarkson was nodding as she sucked her stubby fingers clean in preparation for their greeting. Andrew held his hand fast in hope that a serviette would be included in this task. It was and she stood to reach across her desk and shook his hand.

"Hmm, Detective Bates. That's no problem. I know your boss very well. He's done lots of favours for me in the past."

Moving her dumpy frame round the desk, she waved him off. "Can you get out please, Detective Bates?"

"I'm sorry?"

"It's part of my system which makes this office work. I can't get out until you get out."

"Oh." Andrew backed out the way he had just come in.

After a few seconds of the sound of shifting chairs and some bumps against the door, Jennifer Clarkson came backing out as well. Once free, she turned and smiled at Andrew without even the slightest hint of embarrassment. This woman dealt with the real world and its leftovers every day and if you didn't like it then you could fuck off. Andrew smiled back. She was actually kind of cute. A little older and a little rounder than his usual type, but all the same, cute.

"You know Chief Groder?"

She waved off the question as she locked her office door. "Yeah, we're old friends. Both just trying to keep this city from tearing itself apart at the seams. Follow me." And she was off.

Andrew paced his speed to keep up with her without making it look like an effort. "How's the girl faring?"

"She's alright. I think she was just tired." She favoured Andrew with brief, sharp up-turns of her head as she spoke. "She's been on her feet for a long time now. Only just woke her up about an hour ago after Derrick called."

"What's gonna happen to her?"

A tut was added to her up-turn. "God only knows." She pushed the swinging door violently away as she lead Andrew into a turn and down a flight of steps. "She's our problem for now but that's another mouth the state can't afford to house, clothe and feed, so she'll probably end up being shipped back to Massachusetts for them to deal with."

"Bum deal."

"Same difference." She made another turn.

* * *

Their journey had come to an end after a quick walk across the courtyard and up onto the third floor of Building C. Here the floors were blue.

"Frankie. This is the Detective I told you about."

Sitting on one of five metal-framed beds in a small one windowed room, Frances Bradley didn't look a day over fifteen. No make-up with her hair clean and in a ponytail, wearing a simple red cardigan that was obviously too big for her.

She looked at Andrew nervously as though nobody had told her anything and as if all her sins were about to be tallied up. Jennifer sat down on the bed next to her.

"Don't worry, Frankie. You're not in trouble. The Detective just wants to ask you about this one night. Something happened on the corner where you used to stand, and he just wants to ask you a couple of questions."

"But I don't know anything." She drew her knees up against herself.

"That's okay, just listen to what he has to say." Jennifer stood up off the bed. "I've been assured that this has nothing to do with you and that you cannot get into any trouble over whatever it is." She turned her eye sharply onto Andrew. "Isn't that right, Detective Bates?"

"Absolutely." Andrew stepped past the strangely intimidating presence of Jennifer Clarkson and sat down on one of the beds across from Frankie. "I just want to ask you a few questions about this one night. It was a Friday night about two weeks ago, okay?"

After looking at her latest parent figure and getting a nod of encouragement, Frankie looked back at Andrew with her wide moist eyes and nodded.

"Great." Andrew was finding it more than a little annoying that the whore he was meant to grill looked and was behaving like a little girl who'd lost her teddy bear. "Do you know the night I'm talking about?"

"I think so."

Andrew ears almost started burning. "You do? Excellent."

Andrew eagerly edged himself forward and then shifted back as he saw Frankie shrink away and felt Mrs Clarkson's one eyebrow raise.

Andrew continued. "You know what happened that night?"

Frankie cradled her imaginary teddy bear for safety and then revealed her missing front tooth beneath a fading bruise on her upper lip. "A family was murdered."

Andrew felt his annoyance fading and sympathy sliding into its place. How did she lose the tooth? Did Jasper punch her or maybe kick her when she was down? Or had she fallen after the former and knocked it out? Too much. The girl was damaged.

"That's right. A family was murdered there and the murderer was a nasty piece of work who enjoyed what he did."

Frankie shrunk further away and Andrew saw some agitated shifting from Mrs Clarkson.

"Now the thing is Frankie," he needed to draw her out, "you don't mind if I call you Frankie, do you?"

She shook her head.

"Good. The thing is that as violent and ugly as it all was, it was also very carefully done. Do you know what I mean?" She didn't.

"There were no fingerprints or anything like that. It wasn't random and it wasn't casual. They were killed…" Andrew paused searching, "…efficiently. Like it was done by a professional."

A light seemed to turn on behind Frankie's eyes as she shifted in her seat and let her legs drop away from their cradled position against her body.

Andrew leaned in, "Did you see somebody like that, Frankie? Somebody who didn't belong – out of place?"

She was nodding. "There was somebody. He was parked in his car watching the place – like you, only better. He was more hidden away. I didn't see him until he got out of the car and started walking towards me."

"He came over to you?" Andrew sighed.

"Yes. He was asking me all these questions like…"

"That's not what I'm talking about Frankie. I mean…"

"No, no, not like that." She was eager to make her point. "He was like you."

Andrew was listening again. "What do you mean *like me*?"

"The way he talked, the questions he asked."

It didn't fit. "Like what?"

Frankie seemed to shrink back down again, embarrassed. "Just about me. What I was… Why I was there and…"

"Did he go inside?"

"He did but he didn't… I never saw him come back out."

"Are you sure?"

"Yes, because about an hour after he went in another man came and he got into the first man's car and drove it off. I think he took it round the back."

"And you're sure it wasn't the same guy?" He was egging her on and she was feeding off his reactions.

"Positive. This guy was dressed all dark and the first one had on this grey suit."

It was starting to fit. "Did you get a look at the second guy, the one in the dark clothes? The one who took the car?"

She was silent for a moment. "I don't know… Like I said the first guy parked the car in like this dark spot and he had his head low and…"

"You saw him as he went to the car, didn't you? The car was on your radar so when you saw someone headed for it, you looked and you saw him."

She was nodding slowly, the wheels turning.

"Did he come from round the back of Roseberry Homes?"

"I think so… When I saw him he was coming to the car from up the road."

This was his guy. Andrew had no doubt. He had come from round the back where he'd followed the first guy out the window. The grey suit. The first guy was a Fed. Andrew had no doubt. He'd then distanced himself from the building before going for the car. The car that he obviously knew was there. They weren't together. Frankie wouldn't have seen the second guy if the Fed hadn't put himself in her line of sight. The turned couch. No, the first guy was a Fed and he was dead and missing from the scene. What the hell was this?

"He didn't see you did he?" The answer was clear because otherwise she'd be dead.

"No, I didn't like the look of him so I hid behind a wall when I saw he was headed for the car and…." She trailed off as her thoughts caught up with her. She looked to Mrs Clarkson, her voice now drained of its enthusiasm.

"I – I didn't know he did anything… If I'd known that he'd…"

Jennifer Clarkson stepped forward and waved off Frankie's defence. "Don't worry about that, Frankie, you're not going to get in trouble. Just tell him what you know."

Frankie nodded and let her shoulders drop back down. "Okay."

"Mrs Clarkson is right, Frankie. You won't get into any legal trouble, so long as you tell me everything you saw now."

Jennifer Clarkson sat down next to Frankie again and made sure that Andrew took note of her eyeline. He pulled back.

"The first man – the one who first got out of the car – do you remember what he looked like?"

Frankie thought about it for a minute before nodding. "I think so."

"Okay, good," Andrew shifted his eyeline to include Jennifer Clarkson. "Now what I'm going to do is send someone over, and then I want you to describe to them what they look like so they can draw them. Both of them, because I think you saw that second man and if you think about it, I think you're going to remember what he looks like."

* * *

"How much longer is she likely to stay here?"

Andrew and Jennifer Clarkson were walking across the courtyard, headed for his car.

"I can't really say. It depends on how much red tape there is. Maybe Massachusetts is resistant to take her back and it gets buried for six months, or she gets fast tracked and she's gone in less than a week."

"You think sooner rather than later."

She gave a resistant nod.

"Look, Mrs Clarkson, I don't know what's going to come of this but I'm probably going to need to talk to her again, and that won't exactly be easy if she's suddenly shipped out of the state."

They stopped. "Detective Bates, I don't control these things, I…"

"I know that, I just need you to keep a tab on her situation. Let me know if she's going to be sent off – give me a heads up. At least until I can get a sketch artist in there. After that, if I need to, I might be able to keep her here."

"What does that mean?"

179

"I'm not going to get her in trouble, but if she's a witness to something then she'll have to stay."

"Isn't that already the case?"

Andrew sighed. "It's complicated."

2

Little Jamie 'Switch' Nuemyer was watching him from her usual spot in front of the TV. Like Chester, she was looking better. Less greasy with a little more meat on those young bones. Still off the junk. Anthony cracked the ice tray and then turned his 'I can see you eyes' on Jamie. She put hers back onto the TV.

Chester was in the kitchen with him waiting on the drink that he had insisted he join him in. Anthony dropped two ice cubes into each of the glasses and then poured in the Bourbon. With the cap back on, Anthony put the bottle back into the lower cabinet at his knees, which was where he kept it. They had known he was coming around this time. Anthony had called ahead on the cell phone he'd gotten for Chester, but they still weren't prepared for having him round. Anthony handed one of the glasses to Chester. They each sipped their drink, looking at each other.

"How's the girl hunt going?"

Chester swallowed. "I got a few. Just let me know and I can round them up for you to look at."

"How many?"

"Five, maybe a couple more."

"Okay. Tomorrow."

"What time?"

"Make it ten. We have stuff to do tomorrow so I want to get this over with. And not out in the open like with the boys. A guy talking to a bunch of young scrappy looking girls out the open will turn too many heads. Find a more secluded spot and let me know. Remember – I see them, they don't see me."

Chester's ice was rattling. "I can try for ten but I gotta find 'em and get 'em all together, so I don't know if…"

"Okay, make it twelve." Anthony was becoming disgusted at Chester's up and down behaviour. He needed to shake those emotions out of him. "You can drive, right?"

Chester nodded.

"Okay. I'll get you a car and a license. You sort out the girls for tomorrow at twelve, and then we'll see about getting you a car."

Jamie's voice sang out. "I'm going to bed Chess."

"Okay."

Anthony threw Chester a look of disappointment. "No, no, no. That's not how it works." He raised his voice in the direction of the living room. "No, no. Jamie. Why don't you come in here and say goodnight to your man and his guest like a proper little lady."

The sound of her little footsteps had halted at the call of her name. As he and

Chester waited, Anthony could sense her gritted teeth and tensed neck as she forced herself to turn back towards the kitchen. And there she was. No belly button revealing top this time, but she now had a complexion that Anthony found equally enjoyable.

She kept her eyes low as she passed Anthony, her shoulders tensing and curving her route. She had her arms folded across her body. She reached Chester and raised her head to which he stooped down and kissed her.

"Goodnight Chess."

She turned to face Anthony and looked him in the eyes. There was a fire there that Anthony hadn't seen before. Then she turned and stomped her way out. Very nice. Anthony was liking her more and more.

"You taking good care of her?" Anthony sipped his Bourbon.

"Trying to."

"That's good." He stepped up towards Chester, making sure to crowd him a little. Chester tried to take it in his stride, sipping the Bourbon as Anthony leaned in and based his voice down to just above a whisper.

"You've gotta realise though, that also means keeping her in line. You let her get comfortable, let her sass you, disrespect you, then you're not doing her any favours. You understand?"

Chester nodded. Anthony let a smile spread slowly. He stayed close.

"I don't think you do." He pulled back and let his voice slip back into its natural rhythm, "and that's part of your problem."

Chester was still. Anthony backed up further and raised his glass and smiled a more natural smile.

"But I guess it's your own problem and none of my business." Anthony saw Chester's tension slip. "A man should never have to answer questions in his own house. Cheers."

Chester raised his own glass and hesitantly chinked it against Anthony's, which was extended out towards him. They sipped their drinks.

"Uh, so who's this guy who's coming round?"

"He's helping us."

"What's his name?" Chester sipped his drink. He was trying to act cool and regain his composure.

"That's none of your fucking business." Anthony kept his tone plain. He gave a sweeping indication of the apartment with his drink still in his hand, the ice chinking against the glass as it went.

"I'm going to be using your place for these kinds of meetings from time to time. I know you don't mind."

Chester shook his head.

Anthony sneered. "Of course not. So I want you to be here when I tell you to be here, but I also want you to leave when I tell you to leave. I decide I don't like what you're hearing or if your pretty face starts to become too distracting for me, then you leave. No questions, you got it?"

He got it. "I got it."

There was a knock at the front door. Anthony headed into the living room and then wandered over to the armchair and sat down, his back to the front door. Chester stood awkwardly at the kitchen doorway. The knock came again.

"Answer it."

Chester left his eye line and opened the front door. A speechless silence followed, which Anthony allowed to linger for a few seconds before breaking it.

"Come on in."

"Anthony?" Cliff stomped in and rounded his way into Anthony's view.

Cliff was in his usual hat and raincoat, which he slipped off while looking at Chester.

"Who's this?"

"That's Chester. He's helping me with the day to days of my work. Sit down."

"Right."

Anthony looked at Chester who looked like he wanted to be told to leave. "Fix…" Anthony saw Cliff's expression as he sat down on the couch across from his chair, "…our guest a drink."

Cliff had put his raincoat on the seat next to himself and was now holding an A4 manila envelope. He tossed it to Anthony who caught it with ease.

"I thought we were meeting in private."

Ice was chinking in the background.

"It's private enough." Anthony opened the envelope and began to slide out its contents.

"And this one," Cliff tilted his head in the unseen Chester's direction, "is he your line into our little players?"

"I know what I'm doing. It's why I'm here after all."

The game they were about to play wasn't quite as established as the one they'd walked away from, but it was in a similar line. And it was why Cliff, who had known Leon and what he was into from back in the day, had thought that they'd be the ones to help him get it off the ground.

Chester arrived with Cliff's drink and didn't look him in the eyes when he passed it to him.

"Chester, beat it."

Keeping his eyes low, the grateful Chester turned and did as he was told.

Over the years Anthony got to know all the relevant players across the country. If you dealt in sex trafficking then you made contacts. And now those contacts, or at least the knowledge of them, was what they were going to play with. Anthony looked at the large black and white picture of their second mark, Senator Daniel Westerman. The first was being played tomorrow night but this was a smash and grab and they had to get as many names in the bag as possible before calling in the big collection. Tomorrow it would be a boy, but for Senator Westerman it would need to be a girl. The Senator liked them youthful if not young and Anthony would make sure that she'd be just young enough to serve both their purposes.

Playing with marks this big was dangerous, but it was also something that once done, if they walked away from it, they could walk away with some real money.

The pictures of the somewhat large Senator Daniel Westerman that Anthony was looking at were taken two years earlier when the Senator was under investigation and surveillance for something that in the end led to nothing. This was what Cliff had to bring to the table. A high enough clearance level and very light fingers gave Cliff access to what he knew how to find.

The files were there and the secrets were dark. If the profile fit then they could be squeezed. The trick was to make them think someone else was asking for the money.

Anthony looked over to Cliff who had finished the last of his drink, "I'll get started on it. Do you want another drink?"

Cliff stood and picked up his raincoat. "No. Make sure tomorrow goes smoothly."

Cliff left and Anthony got up and fixed himself another drink.

CHAPTER FIFTEEN

1

Getting back to the station from his talk with the young ex-whore Frankie, Andrew had laid it out for the Chief who liked what he heard and gave him the card left by Special Agent Webb. The thing was that when it came down to it, Chief Derrick Groder hadn't liked the Feds snatching up their case either, and without even giving them so much as a whiff of what it was about, or even the slightest hint of professional courtesy. Truth was he liked the high profile smell of it just as much as Andrew did, and if there was a piece to be had then he was all for grabbing hold.

No Special Agent Webb to answer the call. Andrew wasn't sure how it worked, but he left his message with what he assumed was a secretary. The message was vague but the name Cartwright as well as the word witness were left hanging. The call from Special Agent Webb came through maybe an hour later.

"What is it you think you have, Detective?"

"Just confirmation that things aren't quite right with the Cartwright scene."

"What do you mean – you have a witness? A witness to what?"

On hearing the voice, Andrew remembered which one it was who had left their card. It was the younger one, the less angry one. This one he could work with.

"That's what I want you to tell me, Agent Webb. I don't like being shrugged aside. We already gave you guys all our information with the understanding that it was a two way street. Share and share alike. And now that you think I have more you expect me to just tell you. That about the sum of it?"

The responding voice was threatening, but there was no heart in it. "Detective, if you don't tell me what I want to know, I can bust you for obstructing a Federal case. Do you know what that means?"

"For what? Are you recording my phone calls for training purposes? Did you actually listen to what I said to your secretary or whoever that was? There's nothing there. I just want to talk, that's all."

The line went silent.

"Agent Webb?"

"I'm not recording you." The line went silent again.

Andrew resisted the temptation to call out his name again.

"I'll meet with you tomorrow."

* * *

And that was where they were headed. The meeting spot and the time were dictated by Agent Webb. Breakfast at 11 am at some little restaurant that Andrew had never heard of. Taking Wilks along for the ride was dictated by the Chief.

"You've got your wits about you Bates, I know that, but I don't trust this guy not to set you up."

"I don't mind Wilks, Chief, I don't. It's just that he's a bit of a..." searching and then settling, "a Goof. And if I show up with him to what can only be described as a secret meeting, this guy Webb is going to get spooked. Or pissed."

"I don't care. He's an extra pair of eyes that will be there to see what's happening."

"But..."

* * *

Of course the argument hadn't worked, and there he sat. Wilks was stuffing his third doughnut into his face, even though they were going for a breakfast – though the thought of Wilks clanging away with a knife and fork while he and Webb spoke in hushed tones gave Andrew an idea.

"Don't order any food when we get to the restaurant."

Wilks looked at him, stalling before he swallowed. Andrew continued.

"Your job is to just sit there, look, listen and look pretty. No talking."

"What if I have something to say?"

"You don't have anything to say. You can have coffee."

"Hey, I was the one who pointed out that whore on the corner. If it wasn't for me you'd probably still be sitting in this car, parked across from that shit hole building."

Andrew's response stopped just as it reached his lips. That couldn't be right. His grip tightened on the steering wheel. Andrew didn't like being up staged.

"Coffee. That's it."

"Whatever you say, boss."

* * *

Andrew spotted Special Agent Webb's sharp suit and weak chin sitting at a corner table. The large windows making up the one wall filled the place with morning sunlight and made its brown wood interior shine out quite extremely. Andrew noticed that while Agent Webb was obscured from this blinding light, the rest of his table was bathed in it.

Andrew took the lead and was recognised by Webb who then spotted Wilks and stood out of his chair. Reaching him, Andrew extended his hand.

"Who the hell is this?" Webb bypassed Andrew's hand and pointed at Wilks.

"Agent Webb, this is Detective Mark Wilks." Andrew lowered his unshaken hand.

Wilks stepped up and held out his own. "Nice to meet you."

Webb stood looking at them. "Stop calling me Agent. Just call me Ian." The sharp off blue suit he was wearing did the job anyway.

185

They all took a seat, which immediately made Andrew feel overwhelmed.

"Good table." He stood up and went over to the large window and began trying to pull down the appropriate individual shade.

"Can I help you?"

Andrew turned his head and peered past his still raised arm to see the sly smile above the white blouse and black apron. Her blonde hair was pulled back with an angled parting running through it.

"Uh, yeah." Andrew lowered his arm and turned to face her. "Sun's a little bright."

With the smile still in place she angled her body and then pointed past Andrew, indicating that he was standing where she needed to be.

"Oh, yeah." Andrew backed up and let her pass. She smelled as good as she looked.

Pulling at a now obvious string, she lowered the blind and then turned back to Andrew. They were close.

"Anything else?"

"Just coffee for now." Andrew sensed his blond, good looking, younger partner about to speak and put a hand on his shoulder to silence his presence. "All round, thanks."

"Coming right up."

She left Andrew with a view of the up down that was tightly covered by her black pencil skirt.

"You finished?"

Andrew re-took his seat. "So, Ian… why the clandestine meeting?"

"What is it you think you have, Detective Bates?"

"Is this how it's going to go again? I tell you and then you leave and leave me with nothing?"

"Look. I'm not supposed to be here and if you don't give me a reason to stay then I am going to go. Understand?" He looked at Wilks again, whose presence he wasn't happy with. "Who is this?"

Andrew answered. "He's just here to back me up. He's… my partner. You don't have to worry about him."

Wilks smiled, proving that he indeed wasn't worth worrying about.

She was back. Two more cups and a refill for the nervous looking one in the sharp blue suit. Wilks was looking but she was still looking at Andrew. She left them to it. Webb did look nervous.

"Alright." He was looking back at Andrew. "What do you know?"

"There was someone else there. An agent."

Webb was in. "How do you know that?"

"We have someone who saw him. A whore. He spoke to her. Way she told it, it was pretty clear."

Webb leaned back in his chair, processing what he'd just heard. His face betrayed him. He wasn't liking it. Wilks looked from him back to Andrew as he added more sugar to his coffee. Then something clicked for Webb and he leaned back in.

"What do you mean there was someone else? Who else did your girl see?"

"The Fed went in but never came out. Later, somebody dressed in dark clothes comes around from the back and drives off in the Fed's car. The scene itself. The couch with the dead boy on it – it was turned away from facing the front door. As though to hide the body from someone walking in." Andrew paused, "Is this making sense to you *Agent* Webb?"

Webb, who seemed lost in Andrew's words looked up at being referred to as *Agent*. He shifted in his seat and then moved his coffee away from himself as though it were offending him.

"Off the record, the case has been buried and I'm not supposed to be here. The whole thing is an embarrassment to the Bureau, and if it got out there would be repercussions. A Federal Agent killing a family for money. It would be a giant black eye for the Bureau and to stop that from happening it's all been swept under the carpet."

"And so you guys pulled it away from us before we could get anywhere."

Webb acknowledged this with a tilt of his head. "An Agent raping a fourteen year old girl and murdering a family to get them to talk and give up the money they supposedly had access to. It would have been a nightmare."

It didn't fit. "But you don't buy it."

"Nobody believed the Cartwrights. He had low-level connections to organised crime and was using his supposed knowledge of some missing load of cash as a bargaining chip to manipulate us into keeping him safe. He was just stringing us along. It was supposedly on the other side of the Canadian border – a nice little piece of red tape."

"So then why is everyone else buying it? Why are you here alone? Why aren't you here with a dozen other agents and some kind of Federal say so to make me give up my witness so you guys can clear this whole thing up? What is it you have on your boy?"

"More coffee, boys?"

Webb favoured her with a forced smile as she began to refill his cup even though it didn't need it. Wilks thrust his own up and out towards her, which she then also filled.

"Anything else for you?" She was looking at Andrew.

His hands were guarding his cup. "I'll get back to you on that."

Okay." She trotted on her turn and left.

Andrew looked back at Webb who was looking at his coffee. "Why does everyone think this guy, this agent did it?"

Webb looked up from his coffee. "Nobody even noticed that he or even the Cartwrights were missing until Jack's body was found in a small town junkyard just the other side of the Canadian border. When we found him we looked into his backlog and that's when it all started to fall into place. He was working as part of a team looking to bring down a major international pharmaceutical company. It was a big spread-out team, so no one noticed that he wasn't there and no one raised an eyebrow when he handed the transfer papers over to those who were only too glad to be taken off the bullshit detail of watching the Cartwrights. It's all good enough so no one cares or even notices when he quietly slips them out the back door.

"Now we know they're missing and we check and find that he's put a block on their prints. The block is removed and voila – their prints come through and we find you and we find them dead. And then just as a final solution you tell us that Cartwright's been poisoned with something that, supposedly, Jack had unique access to. A compound collected from his work on the pharmaceutical company. It's in the process of F.D.A. approval and in all likelihood will be, but it's totally unattainable elsewhere so all roads point to Jack. Fact is that anyone in the Bureau with a little access and a nose to get it could have swiped the stuff."

Mark chimed in. "Did this pharmaceutical company have anything to do with the Cartwrights?"

Webb seemed annoyed by the question. "It's not about the Cartwrights. The Cartwrights don't have anything to do with this. It's about Jack. Somebody wanted Jack dead and they didn't want anybody asking any questions, and that's exactly what they got."

Andrew couldn't believe it. The Cartwrights were nothing more than a smokescreen. All the things that didn't make sense were starting to make perfect sense. He couldn't contain himself.

"There was nothing about that scene that I liked. Your man goes in there and makes it messy, makes it violent, makes it look maybe random to us and then what… like punishment to you. But it stunk of a scene that was made to look like something it wasn't, and too obviously so – like whoever it was wanted us, or I guess *you* to see through it. That stuff in the bottle. The bottle's empty and he's passed out like a drunk, only there's not enough alcohol in his system but then there's just enough left in the bottle for us to analyse and identify the poison. Too neat."

Webb was nodding. "This wasn't about raping some kid and killing a family to get at a pile of money that didn't exist. This was about shutting Jack up. The compound doesn't point to the pharmaceutical company because it points too obviously at Jack – but I know Jack was onto something with them. The case had been going stale for a long time and Jack even said to me that these guys were always ahead of them. He was convinced that they had someone on the inside feeding them information. I know he hadn't done anything official with it yet – he didn't have anything solid, but whoever it was must have felt the heat and organised this mess to cover it all up. All of this stuff was way above Jack's pay grade, so I know there had to be someone else pulling the strings."

Andrew loved it – this was real. "And now we have a witness who…"

Webb shook his head. "Your witness doesn't prove anything. And this was done by a pro, so I'm betting that she didn't even see this guy's face."

"It was dark so it's touch and go but she saw him. I think the face is there waiting to be remembered."

Webb didn't look impressed but then, "Well I guess that's something. The problem is, Jack's body was found on the other side of the border where Cartwright had always claimed the money was hidden. He'd taken two in the chest and one in the head. His car was found about a mile away. So what? He had a partner who turned on him when they got the money and then split. So all your girl saw was his partner. Simple as that."

Andrew wanted this so bad he could taste it. Expose a Federal cover up. Bring a murderer to justice – vindicate the reputation of an innocent man. There was glory to be had here.

"So what are we going to do about this?"

Webb was silent again. He looked down to the cup of coffee that he was slowly turning around and around in his hands. He looked back up.

"I can back door you some files."

2

Once again Kathy was surveying the progress of one of her up and coming shows – this time with Giovanna at her side. Giovanna gave her arm a squeeze. Kathy looked at her friend to see her smiling at her. A breeze had Giovanna's hair dancing behind her. It was another beautiful day with the promise of more to come.

"This is it, Kathy. It's all working out just like we planned."

Kathy smiled back softly. The sting of her near miss was still a little fresh, but Giovanna was right and she was starting to let herself believe in the truth of their success, or at least its promise. They were the hosts of the hottest ticket in town, and not just in the fashion world. Once the word got out where the third location was, all of the rich and social wanted to be seen to be at the splashiest event in town.

Things also seemed to be moving along without them now. Thanks largely to the man approaching them from beyond the slowly evolving runway. Along with his wife, they were crossing all the t's and dotting all the i's, leaving herself and Giovanna with very little to fret about. It was a novel sensation.

"Jerry, our knight in shining armour." Giovanna stepped up to Jerry and gave him a hug, which Kathy notice he made sure to turn his crotch away from.

He blushed and smiled goofily as they separated. The trademark of any man who'd felt the warm promise of one of Giovanna's platonic embraces. Giovanna liked Jerry – she found him endearing. Kathy wasn't so sure what she thought and she couldn't quite see what would've drawn Jane to him. He wasn't attractive in any way that Kathy could see. Just a somewhat overweight middle-aged man.

Kathy sighed and tutted at herself for thinking that way. Too long in the world of the beautiful and vacuous. She didn't know him and if her friend loved him then that should be enough. Kathy felt anxious as her mind flitted past an image of her brother before settling on one of his partner.

"Well I don't know about that." He was still blushing. "I just came over to let you both know that Mr Dulpard has invited all of us out for a meal tonight at

Eve's Temptations."

Jerry's delivery was excited but the rustling sound of the sea became deafening in the seconds that followed.

"What? Eve's Temptations. Did I mention that it's his treat? I should have mentioned that, because it's his treat."

"No, it's great." It was all too awkward for Kathy, "We'll be there."

She could feel Giovanna not concurring that it was indeed great news. Dulpard's larger than life presence at their finest hour show-stopping show of a show was one thing, but the other thing was that he had taken a particular fancy to Kathy's tall olive skinned friend with the sensuous voice, and was not afraid to have it be known.

"Okay great, I'll get Jane to call you later with the details." Jane's husband turned and faded into the background.

"Fucking wonderful. Have to see this guy enough during the day with him always hanging around, and now I have to spend my evenings with him."

"Evening – one."

The truth was that it didn't matter. Giovanna would spin him around until their time was done and he'd be left smiling and thinking that he'd actually got somewhere.

"What about the show on Saturday? That's in the evening."

Giovanna had her arms folded and her bottom lip jutted out. Kathy stroked her head, which required a bit of slightly awkward reaching.

"Okay you're right. The mean old man who saved our asses from the fire is punishing us by taking us out for a nice meal at an exceedingly expensive restaurant."

"Yeah, it's alright for you. You're not the one he's trying to get into bed."

"Hey, I'm not out of the running. I think he's got a ménage a trois planned."

Giovanna threw her head back in a throaty laugh, which quickly had Kathy joining in. A few hard hats turned their way, which prompted them to move it along. Giovanna regained her voice.

"But if he buys me any jewellery, I'm going to shove it down his throat."

3

Three again. Anthony was looking them over from within the burned-out crust of an abandoned building. He was standing in a heavily shadowed ground floor doorway looking out onto the small open plot of dead-grass covered land that essentially served as a courtyard to the three low buildings that surrounded it.

Chester was talking to three little white girls as Anthony had specified. They were all three alright. Two blonde, one brown. Two skinny, one plump – but all were definitely under seventeen and youthful looking without being too obviously so. Chester came over and it went as before. Twenty for each of them with the promise of more to come.

4

Andrew's head was swimming. It was everything he could have imagined, but as it stood he wasn't sure how much of it the Chief would want to hear. Back doored files. Federal files. Dangerous career defining and destroying lines. Webb was going to get him some pictures and files on some of the likely, or at least possible, button men who might have been able to pull the Cartwright job off. See if anything jogged Little Miss ex-whore's memory. Webb's wheels were greased again and he was going to be doing some more internal digging. If they did turn up anything real then they'd bring their little understanding to light, but only with something concrete.

The murder and framing of a respected FBI Agent uncovered and revealed. A name cleared and a killer brought to justice. The boys upstairs, of course, wouldn't be happy that the investigation had happened, but bringing down the man who orchestrated it all, to Webb's mind, undoubtedly from the inside, would be huge.

"What are you going to tell the Chief?"

They were on their way back to face this very question. Andrew eased the car to a stop at a red light. Tapping his fingers on the steering wheel, he came to a decision.

"I'm going to tell him exactly what Webb just told us." After all, the Chief had been with him up until now.

* * *

"No." The Chief was standing.

Andrew's head turned briefly to Wilks who was standing by the closed office door and not making eye contact with anybody. Andrew stepped up to the desk on which the Chief then planted his hands and leaned forward, awaiting Andrew's response.

"No? Sir, how has anything changed? Break the case, take the glory. This guy Webb is going to feed it to us and then..."

"Back doored files. Are you fucking kidding me, Bates? You found the girl who confirmed your doubts about the case, great. But that's as much as I was willing to let you get away with. You take the girl to them, they take her in and we get folded back into the investigation. That's it. They don't want to know, then it's over."

"Just like that."

"Just like that, Detective." The Chief pulled his chair back out and sat down. He looked back up at Andrew. "And don't think I don't know about what you said to Jenny about keeping you informed on your girl's situation."

The Chief reached across his large desk to pull his ill-placed phone closer before lifting the receiver and dialling.

"As far as I'm concerned, this ship has sailed and I'm going to inform Mrs Clarkson that our business with the girl has officially concluded."

Andrew knew better than to argue when his boss was this deep into his rant.

191

There was never going to be a turn around. He backed off and turned for the door. As expected, Andrew turned back for the Chief's inevitable last word.

"You're both back on your old assignment from which I expect to see results." He was pointing now. "And Bates. We're done with this now, you hear? If I find you're still on this I won't be as understanding as I have been. You understand?"

Andrew didn't answer. There was nothing to say.

The finger shifted. "And that goes for you too Detective Wilks."

Wilks almost jumped out of his skin, but at least resisted his obvious temptation to point to himself.

The Chief continued. "If I hear you've gone off case again because of Detective Bates, or if I hear Detective Bates has gone off case and I don't get a knock on my door from you to tell me just that, I'll have your Detective Shield. Understood?"

Wilks swallowed his first attempt to speak but then forced the second out. "Understood sir."

"Good. Now get the fuck out of my office." The Chief looked at his unanswered phone and then replaced the receiver.

Andrew turned and opened the door, ushering Wilks out before him. Fuck!

<h1 style="text-align:center">5</h1>

The place was a grand spectacle, with that obviously being as big a part of the appeal as the high priced meals. The incredibly high ceilings were made up of vaulted arches from which over a dozen chandeliers were hanging. The entire place was blanketed in a golden hue of light.

The four of them followed the maître d' past the unending bar counter on their left, with a sea of tables to their right. They were on the top floor of a building with many, many floors and the almost 360 degree view on the other side of the huge sheet windows was extraordinary. Manhattan at night from up high was something that never failed to take Kathy's breath away.

Their journey had taken them past a small velvet rope, leading to a wide swirling staircase which took them up to the balcony seating away from all the riff-raff. Jerry was wearing his best going out suit and he didn't look too bad. He was the only one who had truly been looking forward to the evening, but now that they had arrived Kathy was pretty excited herself. More previews of her life to come. Jane too seemed to be in awe of the place as she squeezed her husband's hand and they exchanged a look. Giovanna remained a little stone-faced.

Between the three of them there was far less cleavage this time around, but coming to a place like this, the desire to look good was overwhelming. So as it went, they all still looked pretty sleek. It didn't matter. Dulpard was a dog, and if he wanted to look then he would.

The tables up on high were larger and fewer, each slightly sectioned off from the rest by individual raised platforms, which allowed for better views of the city and of the tables below.

"Ladies and gentleman!"

There he was, standing out of his chair and ensuring that all eyes were on him. His suit was of course tailor made and looked amazing, but his smile made up for all the improvements.

"Harold." Jane stepped up the two large half circle steps, graciously accepting Dulpard's hand as assistance.

"This is Juliet," said Dulpard pointing to the ample cleavage that sat in the chair next to his.

"Hi." She put a brief hand up.

Juliet was young, blonde, pretty, overly tanned and had very big fake boobs. How she'd ended up at Dulpard's side was anybody's guess. The possible explanations were too numerous to count but the reasons narrowed pretty quickly to a sharp point. Kathy stepped up to the table where the maître d' was holding a chair out for her. It was unfortunately next to Dulpard's chair, which Giovanna had been clever enough to circumvent her way away from.

"Thank you," Kathy said as she sat down.

Dulpard was helping Giovanna with her chair as the various Hellos continued. Kathy leaned in to get Juliet's attention.

"Hello. I'm Kathy." Kathy held out her hand, which Juliet accepted.

"Hi." Her hand back, she gave another sharp wave and a nervous giggle. "Juliet, like the book."

Kathy smiled. "It's a lovely name. So, how do you know Harold?"

Juliet's chest puffed out in preparation for her lengthy response, but then deflated as Dulpard sat down between them and answered for her.

"I'm helping the lovely Juliet Riviera get into acting. I have contacts."

For the first time Kathy noticed the chunky gold that adorned his wrists and fingers. He pointed to Juliet's breasts and waggled his finger to indicate to each of them.

"Gonna have to do something about these first." He laughed loudly and Juliet blushed. "Seems wrong, somehow, but big tits don't really fly when you're trying to be a real actress."

Jerry offered a polite laugh which went unnoticed as Dulpard's attention turned to their waiter who was waiting patiently in the wings.

"What do you..." Jane juddered back in her seat as Dulpard slapped his hands together.

"Drinks," he said ensuring that all eyes were once again on him. "Bring us two bottles of Cristal. You all like Cristal. Fantastic. I was going to have some waiting but I just wanted to be sure."

The waiter nodded and left.

"So what do you do at the moment Juliet?" asked Jane, this time in entirety.

Dulpard again deflated Juliet's attempted response. "She's in porn."

"Wow!" said Jerry.

Jane looked at him to which he gave a non-committal shrug.

"Harold, you promised."

She was blushing furiously, which Kathy thought was very strange for someone who swallowed cum on camera. Out of her depth, Kathy supposed – or at least being made to feel so.

"What? They don't care." He had his palms up as he looked to all around the table.

He settled on Giovanna, whose disgust Kathy – hopefully alone – could see as clear as day.

"Do you care, Giovanna?"

"No, Mr Dulpard, I don't care. But you obviously care a great deal that we should know. Don't you?"

Dulpard shrugged. "I've got nothing to hide."

"I'm not in porn anymore."

"Nobody cares, sweetheart." Dulpard patted Juliet lightly on the shoulder, deflating her even further.

Kathy could practically feel the heat emanating from Giovanna's side of the table as the image flashed through her mind of Giovanna on all fours scrambling across the table before she smashed Dulpard's half empty beer glass into his fat neck. Then the Cristal arrived.

6

"So what are you going to do?"

"Don't ask me questions like that, Wilks. Just drink your drink."

Wilks opened his mouth to say something else but then thought better of it. He turned his attention back to the glass of beer that was on the counter in front of him. Andrew hated cop bars . No women. He turned on his stool to survey the depressing crowds crowding around small tables and telling racist jokes. There was Connie in the corner. She was all right – tall, wide hips giving her a sort of hourglass thing. Bad idea. He swivelled back to the counter and slapped his hand down onto it making the bowl of bar nuts there do a little jump.

"Jackson!"

Jackson was tall. That was what you could say about him above all else. He also had big hands. When you owned and ran a cop bar you needed big hands to man handle the big egos that frequented your establishment. Jackson removed his hulking upper body and forearms from the far end of the counter where he was chatting to some of the older regulars.

"What can I get for you, Bates?"

"Another couple of beers and shots for me and my partner." Andrew was starting to feel a little drunk. It was a start.

Wilks waved his hand. "No shot for me. Just a beer."

"Ah Jesus, Wilks, if you don't want to drink with me then why don't you just fuck off home?"

Those who were nearby grew silent and with that, Andrew could suddenly feel his blood warming up his veins. He kept his eyes on his nearly empty beer, which was in front of him. He took a sip. The silence coming from the bar stool next to his was drowning out the shit music that was blaring from the old style jukebox that was by the front entrance. He had Wilks in his peripherals and he wasn't moving.

Jackson's head was out of Andrew's low field of vision, but Andrew could tell he was waiting, ready to shoot those long arms of his out and grab hold of whoever needed to be ushered out. Wilks stood off his stool leaving only a half-meter between them. Andrew sipped the last of his beer.

Wilks asked the question, "What the hell is your problem with me, Bates? Huh!" The last part rose above the music and brought everyone's attention to the inevitability of their moment.

"Okay, calm down boys. I don't want you breaking anything…"

"No! I just want an answer to my question. Well?"

Andrew turned on his stool to face the flexed version of Wilks that he'd seen before. The one he could have taken then and the one he could take now.

Andrew lifted his voice for all to hear. "My problem, Wilks… is the incessant stream of stupid fucking questions that keep coming out of that pretty mouth."

Jackson saw it but wasn't fast enough. Neither was Andrew. He saw Wilks' right hand blur at his side and then felt it connect with his left cheekbone. Andrew's hands shot up as if in afterthought as his body sailed back, angling his bar stool out from under him. Andrew crashed to the floor feeling the back of his head connect with the leg of one of the other bar stools.

There was shouting and commotion all around Andrew, which he tried to get a hold on as he shook his vision back into place. The blurry surrounding was closing in but then Andrew found focus at the centre of it as Wilks' exposed teeth came bearing down on him. Wilks' hands were on him, grabbing his shirt and Andrew could see that the blurry surroundings had their hands on Wilks who was then suddenly ripped up and away from him.

Andrew pushed his toppled bar stool away from its awkward position beneath him and then rolled over onto his knees. His head was pounding. Andrew touched his fiery cheekbone and then saw the blood that was there. Looking over to the still struggling image of Wilks, Andrew pushed himself up and darted towards him but instantly found that hands were all over him too.

"You fucking son of a bitch!" Andrew pulled, feeling himself slip a little closer to his target, only to then feel shifting hands reeling him back in.

Jackson was between them. "Enough!" He stepped up to Andrew, blocking his view of Wilks. "Enough."

Andrew's eyes found themselves angling up and meeting Jackson's, whose hand he then realised was holding his jaw.

"Take your hand off me."

Jackson let go. After a pause, he then turned to Wilks.

"Okay. Get him outta here."

The crowd shifted and from behind Jackson, Andrew could see Wilks allowing himself to be shifted. Andrew relaxed and felt the surrounding hands tentatively loosen. The bar's entrance opened and then closed. The crowd parted and Andrew saw that Wilks was gone. He shook off the last remaining hands that were still holding him.

Jackson turned back to Andrew. "The kid's fast."

Andrew smirked. "That's the second time I've let him hit me."

"Maybe you should get your hands up faster next time. Or maybe just play nice." Jackson patted Andrew's arm before turning back, heading for his position behind the bar.

"Yeah, all good advice."

Andrew slapped at his pockets as he heard his ring tone sound out. No phone. Andrew spun around to see it being picked up off the floor and then held out for him to take.

"Thanks." Andrew took the phone and pressed the receive button as he looked at the displayed number that he didn't recognise. "Andrew here."

"Andrew?" He recognised the woman's voice. "Hi, it's Kathy. Um, Kathy Radley – David's sister. Do you remember me?" She sounded nervous.

"Yeah, of course. How are you?" Andrew put his finger to his other ear as he moved towards the restrooms, which were further away from the crowds and music. David flashed through his mind. "Is everything okay?"

"No, yes, everything's fine." A pause. "Uh, you remember the fashion shows that I'm doing?"

"I remember. That first one was pretty impressive. You're doing three, right?"

"That's right." It was said a little over excitedly. "We've done the second one already but the big finale show is happening on Saturday night and I was wondering if you wanted to come and see the spectacle. It's on a seven hundred foot yacht."

"Wow." He was impressed. "That's something else. Saturday night?"

"Yeah, it all kicks off at seven and it's going to be this whole big thing with the show and then a party. So..." She sped it up. "If you want to come, I'll put your name on the list and I can put you down for a plus one if want to bring a date or..."

"I'd love to come. My social scene has been pretty stale of late." Andrew looked at the worn faces about. "Just me. Will I see you there?"

"Yeah, you'll see me."

"Okay. Till then."

"Okay. I'll text you the details. Bye."

"Bye."

7

Kathy slapped her flip phone closed and let out a heavy sigh. That was *not* cool and casual. Kathy looked at herself in the expansive rest room mirror. She smiled. Andrew had seemed pretty receptive to the idea of seeing her again, so Kathy was satisfied that it had been the right move. She flicked her hair. It didn't look that bad.

* * *

Kathy retook her seat next to Dulpard who had been letching over her the whole evening due to her more accessible proximity. Giovanna had held her tongue thanks to Kathy's own ability to casually bat away smug advances.

"Dessert?" Dulpard indicated to their waiter.

The evening was thankfully almost over. Still, it had been quite the experience and the food had been too good to be true. She did want dessert.

"Is everybody else having?"

Kathy looked to see that Jane and Juliet were also planning on indulging. Kathy reached for the menu and felt a hand on her thigh. Her flinch went by unnoticed as she began to peruse the menu.

"Um," Kathy slid her hand back off the table taking a fork with it. "Chocolate cake."

"Shit." Dulpard's hand instantly retreated from the sharp jab to his knuckles.

"You okay?" Jane leaned in to see if she could spot what was wrong with Dulpard's hand, which he was rubbing.

"Oh, I'm fine." He shook his hand dramatically. "Just banged it."

Kathy saw Giovanna's smile and gave her a conspiratorial wink.

CHAPTER SIXTEEN

1

The evening was steadily approaching and the time for their first job was close at hand. Having seen the first lot of girls around noon, Anthony was feeling like things were coming together a bit more. Things were a little bit more solid. He liked the plump brunette for Senator Westerman.

Tonight, though, it was all about the classic, dirty, skinny, twitchy, could have been a model, rent boy named Freddy. Chester found him and, on Anthony's say so, took him back to his place where a shower, a shave, some new clothes and when the time came, a nice juicy hit of heroin to curb his twitching, were waiting for him.

Anthony had Chester, who was still too full of weary emotional conflict, do the sweet-talking. Tell the nineteen-year-old Freddy that he was going to get fucked tonight. Chester hadn't relished the idea but Anthony knew it wouldn't be an issue for Freddy. Even if he hadn't taken a dick in the name of a hit before, the amount of money they were dangling in front of him would quickly wash away any dilemma he might have felt.

The real issue of course was relying on Chester to relay Anthony's instructions to the little smack head. On this instance it wasn't a problem for Anthony to step up and take over, but he needed to know that Chester would be able to do it in the future when he had to do it alone.

The conversation played out in the living room while Anthony watched from the darkness of the hallway. Partially obscured from view, Anthony wanted, for the time being at least, to just be a presence in the back of young Freddy's mind. They'd meet each other properly later. As it happened, Chester laid it out quite successfully and, as expected, Freddy was very much game.

Music came from behind the closed bedroom door where little Jamie was waiting for it to all be over and out of her house. Anthony wondered if she knew there was heroin in the house. If she'd seen Freddy, she would have instantly pegged him for a junkie. Had Chester told her what was going on? If he was smart then he'd told her it was business and that she should stay in the fucking bedroom until it was over and they were out of the house, which was where she was. Chester was a smart kid so it probably had gone something like that.

Five hundred was slid across the coffee table with another folded wad staying put in front of Chester. Freddy's eyes sparkled as he nodded furiously whilst he listened to the half now, half later portion of the prepared speech that Chester was laying down.

It was half past six and time was fast approaching.

* * *

198

Anthony sat in the back and watched it all play out. The place was nice, a jazz lounge – and with it being a Thursday night and not too busy, Freddy didn't have to work too hard to get noticed. This was apparently the spot where District Court Judge Henry Freeman liked to look over all his boys and maybe have a quick chat and a drink. The low lighting of the quiet spot and the fact that his plain clothed entourage got the drinks meant that his presence would go by unnoticed.

In most of Anthony and Leon's games, it was best not to have any outside help or involvement. With their new game, unfortunately, that wasn't possible. The kind of information they needed had to be acquired from those on the inside. Cliff had access to the; where they got their goods from, and Anthony knew people in those houses, people in the know. The trick was knowing which ones could be bought, and then getting them to sell you the information without knowing who they were selling it to. It was expensive, but so long as they knew that it would be worth their while, then generally it could be done.

Anthony had been in the process of setting up mostly this first one, but also the next lot of communication lines since he got into town. And anybody who one of these inside men got to see would always be twice removed. After tonight, if all went well, Anthony would get Chester to get himself a lackey to be their second removed man and from then on all further contacts would go through the two of them. There were still contacts they needed to make.

It all worked because, in this world, money talks. But playing it fast and loose like this there was always the chance that he might be found out. He didn't like it.

The Judge's approach was casual as he sidled up to the sleek-in-black Freddy who was leaning against a wall. This wouldn't take long. Freddy had been the right choice and from where Anthony was sitting he could tell that the very respectable and good looking middle-aged judge was having to stop himself from reaching out and touching this beautiful boy.

Anthony finished his drink and made for the exit. The judge would be the first to leave, with Freddy being chauffeured along maybe five minutes later.

* * *

The door had been left open earlier in the day by the man Cliff had orchestrated a similar inside man connection with. Anthony suspected that this man would be once removed from his own man who would be inside Judge Freeman's detail. Plausible deniability. As expected it was an out of the way motel. One pinhole camera in the corner of the room was all that was needed. Once the job was done it would simply be a case of swinging round back and yanking the narrow tube that housed the camera through the small hole which Anthony had made in the wall at the top corner of the room.

Anthony watched them as they pulled into the parking area outside the front of the two-story building, which was in the form of a square U. The road Anthony was on extended up and around with the motel parking area below. He was leaning against his car, which was parked on the shoulder of the road. No hazard lights, but the road was quiet enough. Through the long lens of his camera, Anthony saw the Judge get out of the back seat of his black four door Lincoln. He walked up one of the stairs that lead to the second floor walkway with one of his men at his side. Anthony's angle on their door was perfect. He snapped a couple of shots of the Judge waiting outside as his man went in to check out the room. After less than a minute his man was back. The Judge gave him a few instructions and then went inside to wait for his prize. His man waited outside.

* * *

The second car arrived and Anthony managed to get a few decent shots of Freddy being ushered out the car and being made to walk a meter out in front of man number two as directions were fed to him. Anthony settled his lens on Freddy as he knocked on the door. The door opened and there was the judge in an all but open robe. Anthony began snapping away as the judge's hand shot forward, grabbing and cupping at Freddy's crotch. Anthony had it all; his face, his hand. Judge Freeman reeled Freddy in practically by his crotch before grabbing the back of his head and shoving his tongue down his throat. Once they were far enough into the room, the judge's man pulled the door closed and waited to chauffeur the used goods back to the city.

Andrew couldn't believe the stuff he got. With the shots he had he barely needed what the camera was about to pick up inside the room. And so long as the camera wasn't discovered, which would of course be followed by Chester's address being forced out of young Freddy, then, along with the last two things that Anthony needed to take care of, this night would be a complete success. Their future boys and girls would not be allowed to see Chester's apartment.

Anthony took out his phone and called Chester's, telling him to get a cab and wait for him outside the Jazz Lounge where Freddy would be dropped off.

And that was the game. The trick was, once they ordered their boy, for Cliff to get his man to call back in and cancel it. Then they simply slot their new one in his place. The money got paid in cash to the boy so no one's the wiser. Then when you have enough names and pictures taken down, you call in for a mass collection. Everyone gets done at once so no one has a chance to get any the wiser. Then when it comes to them figuring out who set them up, their usual suppliers take the blame, by which time Anthony and Leon have skipped town. That was the idea at least.

* * *

"Give the man his money, Chester."
As expected, Freddy was dropped back off outside the Jazz Lounge where

Chester was already waiting. Once Judge Henry Freeman's men were gone, the two of them had climbed into his waiting car, which then promptly drove off.

Chester pulled the wad of notes from his breast pocket and reached over himself to hand the cash to Freddy who was bouncing around in the back seat. A combination of excitement at receiving another five hundred and the fact that his last moderate hit was wearing off, making him return to his usual jittery self.

"So, Freddy," Anthony watched Freddy though the rear view mirror, his body language instantly changing at hearing his voice for the first time, "how much did he pay you?"

Freddy squeezed protectively at the wad he'd just been given. "Um, like a hundred and fifty bucks."

He was lying; it was more like three hundred and fifty. "Hundred and fifty. So that means you've scored one thousand, one hundred and fifty bucks for one night's work. One hour really."

Anthony could feel Chester's growing tension in the seat next to him.

Freddy was keen to please. "Yeah, it's incredible. I can't thank you guys enough. Anytime you need me…"

"Any time. So you don't mind letting some guy fuck you for money? Means nothing to you?"

Anthony watched Freddy as he awkwardly shifted in his seat, knowing that he had to answer.

"Uh, I guess… I don't know, man. I mean, I've never even seen that much money before. I mean… thank you again."

"That's right. If it was just a suck and a fuck for fifty bucks to get your next hit, that you could have done on your own." Anthony did a little turn of his head to catch Freddy's eyes as he friendlied up his voice. "Which you probably have done in the past. Am I right?"

Anthony toned his question to sound rhetorical so Freddy could get away with not answering it. But Anthony wanted his next question answered.

"So, tell me, Freddy. What makes you think that what you did tonight was worth a grand?"

There was no answer from the back seat. Anthony couldn't see his eyes, which were now low, his heart pounding, that cold sweat coming on, eyes darting about examining their immediate cage-like surrounding. Anthony still wanted an answer.

"…"

Chester stole his moment, "Where are we going?"

Anthony began to feel his own heartbeat quicken as he turned his eyes on Chester, who then immediately shrunk into himself.

Freddy's voice quivered from the back. "You can just let me out here, I don't mind. I can walk… or get a cab back."

There were tears waiting behind that voice. Anthony put his eyes back on the emptying road again.

"Don't worry, Freddy. We're just going to go find another one of our boys who did some work for us. Pay him the rest of his thousand as well." Anthony let out a chuckle and smiled at Chester who wasn't looking back.

That voice sounded out again. "Do you want the money back?"

* * *

As the car slowly rolled to a stop, Anthony could hear Freddy trying to open the child lock secured back doors. He wasn't going anywhere.

"We're here." Anthony opened his door and stepped out onto the cracked and buckled concrete of the deserted section of pavement they were pulled up on. Dark and desolate looking buildings loomed all around. There was no one else here.

Chester got out and looked at Anthony who spoke to him from over the roof of the car.

"Get him out."

Chester was looking at him with his usual worried eyes. He opened and closed his mouth a number of times before forcing out the question that he didn't really want an answer to.

"You're not going to kill him, are you?"

"No."

"No?"

Anthony didn't think Chester really believed that answer, but just hearing the word had brought instant relief to his voice. It wasn't a lie.

"Just open the door, get him out and don't let him run off."

Chester's eyes were searching for the answers in Anthony's. He wasn't going to get any. Realising this, Chester then did the only thing his weak will would let him and did as he was told.

"Don't try and run, Freddy, or I'll shoot you in the back." Anthony made his way round to see Chester holding open the back seat door, from which a hunched over Freddy was emerging. "And I don't want to have to kill you."

He was shaking. "I don't want to die."

"Good. Then you'll do as you're told, won't you?"

He was nodding, tears now running, nose sniffing. His shaky hand reached into his back pocket and pulled out his three folds of cash. He held it out to Anthony who was looming over him. Chester was just standing there, still holding the door, his mouth slightly open.

"That's good, Freddy. I'm glad you appreciate that you don't really deserve that much money."

"I don't want it."

"Give it to Chester."

Chester threw Anthony a look. He didn't want to take it. He didn't want to be part of this, any of it.

Freddy moved his hand over to Chester, his teary eyes still low. Anthony looked at Chester who knew he had to take it. He did, maybe still hoping that he

202

didn't know what was coming next. He didn't.

"Good. Now we can all just be friends again."

Anthony reached out and put his hand on Freddy's shoulder, who seemed so small to him now. Freddy flinched at his touch. He was vibrating beneath Anthony's hand. His crying had become audible, softly but... Anthony angled his ear closer. Praying. Another bottom feeder finding God. Anthony smiled to himself and pulled Freddy in close. His arm over his shoulder, walking like two pals drunk at the end of a long night.

"You religious, Freddy?"

Freddy wasn't looking at him, his feet were dragging, his crying getting louder. Anthony gave him a sharp shake, letting him know that an answer was expected.

"Please let me go." The words were little more than a wheeze.

"Do you believe in God and all that? The idea that all the good little boys and girls go to heaven. Do you believe in all that?"

Still no answer. Chester was still standing by the car behind them in their slow walk. Undoubtedly shaking himself.

Anthony pulled Freddy in tight against himself. "Thing is though, you haven't been a good boy, have you? Probably not really ever in your whole life, and certainly not tonight. So if there is a God and a Heaven and a Hell and you were to die tonight," Anthony felt Freddy's weakening weight sag as panic gripped him, "do you really think some last minute 'I'm sorry' is going to stop you from going to Hell?"

"Anthony, just let him go. He did the job, it's done. Just let him go. Please."

Anthony heard Chester take a couple of steps towards them, but certainly not enough to put him in the danger zone. Not enough so that he could do something if he had to. They had reached a wall in their walk, which Anthony turned Freddy's back to and leaned him against it.

"Can you stand, Freddy?"

Anthony still had him by the shoulder and with his other hand he had him by the chin, holding his head up. Freddy nodded through the loll of his weakly supported head. His eyes were glazed and fighting to not roll back. He couldn't stand on his own. Anthony held fast.

"Anthony, please just let him go."

Chester wasn't far from tears himself now. Anthony could hear it in his voice.

"Chester, tell me. The stuff you do for me." There was silence behind Anthony now. "Do you really think it's worth what I give you? The apartment, the pocket money... Do you think that you've earned it all?"

Anthony waited. Freddy was limp, all but catatonic with fear.

Chester spoke, his voice measured. "Anthony, just let him go."

Anthony didn't look back. "And what if I don't? What are you going to do?"

Anthony saw it before it happened.

"Pl-please..." Frankie's head lolled again and his mouth opened, releasing a splutter of semi-transparent yellow liquid.

Anthony stepped aside out of the line of fire. Without Anthony's support, Freddy fell forward onto his hands and knees as he continued to retch out his fear. Anthony kicked him, ribs cracking audibly. Freddy fell onto his side, now choking on his own sick as air refused to go in or out.

"No!"

Anthony looked up, impressed to see Chester running head first towards him. Anthony let him connect and push him back, but then Anthony quickly used his momentum against Chester and grabbed, pulled and then slammed him against the wall.

Chester was winded. Anthony pulled out his gun and held it up to Chester's face, which was only an inch away from his own. Chester saw the gun.

"I'm impressed. At least a little."

Chester sucked in a little air, his face bulging in his attempt to speak. "Don't…"

Anthony grabbed a handful of Chester's blond locks and then gave the back of his head a sharp crack against the wall.

"Don't what? Don't kill him?" Anthony looked over to the writhing image of Freddy. His cheek pressed into the concrete as he gasped for air. "Maybe you shouldn't be so worried about the whore. Maybe you should be worried about yourself. If you aren't any use to me, Chester, then maybe I should just kill you as well. I kill you and then go over to that nice apartment that I let you live in." He had Chester's attention.

"Don't you touch her."

Anthony let his demeanour soften. He lowered his gun but stayed close, holding Chester in place.

"I don't want to kill you Chester and I don't want to hurt little Jamie. But I will… If I have to.

"Why?"

Chester's eyes were intense. The rage was there. Good. Anthony stepped away from him and produced a second gun, a 38 sub-nose revolver which he held out, palm up to Chester. Chester looked at him and the gun, confused. He reached his hand out slowly and when it touched the gun he froze as Anthony aimed his own gun at Chester's head.

"Take it."

Chester was still touching the 38. He took it and held it awkwardly with both hands. With his gun still trained on Chester's head, Anthony swivelled his position until he was side on to Chester. It all finally dawned on Chester as he turned his head away from Anthony to look at Freddy, who had now found equilibrium in his shallow breathing and was on his one hand and knees crawling away.

Chester caressed his gun and spoke without looking away from Freddy, "Please…"

"He's getting away."

Anthony waited, watching as Chester continued to caress his gun. Then it happened. His grip tightened and his jaw clenched with resolve as he marched over the slowly escaping Freddy. Freddy heard the footsteps as he looked up to see Chester arriving at his side and aiming his gun down at him. The two boys were frozen, looking at each other before a loud crack sent a bullet tearing into Freddy's forehead above his right eye. His body slammed down as his upturned head twisted awkwardly, bobbing back before slapping face first against the concrete. Another loud crack put a second bullet into the back of Fred's dead head.

Anthony smiled, "Well done Chester."

The gun was hanging limply at Chester's side as he stared down at what he'd done. Anthony stepped over to him. Chester didn't look up and didn't look away from the boy he had just killed. He didn't resist when Anthony took the gun from his hand.

"Good, good. Okay, get in the car."

Chester did as he was told.

CHAPTER SEVENTEEN

1

"Detective Wilks came storming into my office this morning requesting, though very nearly demanding, that either you or he be reassigned because he doesn't think he can work with you anymore."

They were both seated across from each other with that big desk between them.

The Chief smiled. "And now that I see you, I can tell that he may be right."

Andrew felt his welted cheek throb out at its mention. He didn't respond.

"Goes nicely with that just healed lip of yours, which I now take it was born out of a similar incident."

Andrew knew the Chief was enjoying the idea of it all – Detective Bates pushing that smart mouth of his a little too far and finally getting it smacked back into place. Andrew let him enjoy it. He was still in the Chief's bad books so Andrew knew better than to start something that didn't need to be started. He was a big boy, he could take it.

The Chief's expression hardened again. "I'm not going to do it."

Despite himself, Andrew let out an exasperated sigh. It did not escape the Chief's attention.

"Oh, are you not happy with that decision, Detective?"

Andrew straightened his position in his seat. "I'm sorry sir, but maybe Detective Wilks is right." Andrew pointed to his inflamed cheekbone. "I mean, clearly we can't work together."

The Chief leaned back in his chair, seemingly pondering Andrew's point. "You plan on pressing charges?"

The question threw Andrew. "No."

The Chief snapped forward again. "Then *clearly* you guys are fine. No, Detective, I want you two to work this out because truth be told I like how short a leash it keeps you on."

Andrew stood out of his chair and turned for the door.

"Where are you going?

"I don't know… to work."

"I'll tell you exactly where you're going. You're going to find your partner and you're going to go back to that liquor store…"

"Sir, that case is dead weight. If we have to work together then…"

"Bates, so far as I can tell, you haven't actually done a single piece of actual work on that case since you were assigned to it. Now get out there and solve it or you fucking show me that it's a dead case. Till then, get to work." His nose was back between the various papers and folders that littered his desk.

Andrew left.

2

"As we can see behind you, there's still a lot of activity on the *Jessica Bell*."

Jilly Sanders' cameraman panned up past Kathy to get a view of Dulpard's ship, which was still buzzing with activity. Lots to do, lots to do, and just over a day to do it all. There was an array of helping hands of every description coming and going from the several walkways that had been added to the side of the boat. From workmen to caterers, from designers to assistants, to a handful of models who were part of Gabriel's continued shoot, which was going at a wilfully artistic pace, and, as a result, was slowing everything else down. On this, Kathy had decided to bite her tongue and just let him boil everyone else's blood for a change. The shots needed to get done and if they rushed him anymore, another bout of gone for days could erupt and that they could not afford.

The camera was back on Kathy and that microphone was again waiting on her to say something interesting. Had there been a question?

Jilly pulled the microphone back. "Any chance we can maybe get on board and sneak a peek at the whole work in progress side of things?"

This was the kind of thing that Kathy always avoided like the plague, and usually that was fine because she had Giovanna on her side who always shone in the spotlight. But by this stage, Giovanna had been interviewed by just about everyone who cared, especially Jilly Sanders, who'd spoken to her at least five times over this current run. So now it was her turn. There had been a question.

"Ah... no." Smile. "No, sorry, Jilly, but you're just going to have to wait until tomorrow night like everybody else. But don't worry, it'll be worth it." Kathy cringed, her forced smile making her sound like an over enthusiastic stewardess.

"I can't wait. Now tell me..."

3

"I don't know what else to tell you, officer..."

Andrew didn't know how much more of this he could take. The long hair was the fourth person they had re-interviewed and the answers were all the same. Long hair flicked his hair back as he continued, trying to keep his eyes from constantly darting over to the small wooden box at the corner of his cramped, magazine strewn living room.

"Like I said. It was about a block away and I sees two guys come running out and then before I know it they've just like totally melted away into the night."

"Just disappeared?"

Wilks was by the front door not leaning on the sticky chest of drawers that was there. He'd already been through these interviews and he no longer had a burning desire to do right by this case. They were both now stuck with it, and each other.

"Yeah, they were both in black so that's probably why."

Andrew was nodding. It made sense. They hadn't disappeared. There was a street camera down the line that caught them but these boys were smart enough and kept their heads low and their hoods up when passing it. The witnesses from that thread of the case had, of course, been even less help than this one, having not even been aware that there was anything to witness.

"Yeah..." Andrew stood up, slowly stretching as he did and prolonged his first word. "So, Izzy... What's in the wooden box?"

Andrew made a move towards it and allowed himself a smile as Izzy, the long hair, scrambled out of his seat, instantly catching his foot on a carelessly placed bean bag chair, and tumbled down onto his precious wooden box – hard. The word *No* echoing as he went down.

Izzy looked up at them with his hair in his face and his hands now cradling the box. "It's nothing." He grimaced – he'd hurt himself. "Hey, don't you guys need a..."

"Stay out of trouble Izzy." Andrew turned and walked out the door which Wilks was holding open for him.

Now out in the hallway with the door closed behind them, Wilks spoke his first words to Andrew since the start of their day.

"What was that for?" His words and tone were solemn, unlike the Mark Wilks that Andrew knew.

"A smile. I guess I needed one." Andrew led them towards the stairs leaving it to Wilks to keep it going if that was what he wanted.

Andrew didn't want any grudges, but he sure as shit wasn't going to apologise again for being punched in the face.

Wilks was clomping his way down behind Andrew. "Bates, you're not going to get me in trouble, are you?"

Reaching the bottom of the single flight of stairs, Andrew headed for the exit. The question sounded so childish. The door opened with a buzz and a group of teens came in. Their laughing chatter stopped instantly at the sight of him and Wilks. The long hair's friends who'd obviously been informed of the police presence that had been expected today, but supposedly much earlier. Ducking their heads and saying their 'excuse me's', they all rushed for the stairs. Andrew could only guess what treats they were carrying. He caught the door as the last one scuttled past and then stepped out into the sun.

"Bates."

Andrew turned to face him. "I'm finished with it, Wilks. It's done. This... this is our case now." His hands slapped down to his sides, emphasising the futility of it all.

"I'm not going to cover for you. I won't lose my Shield over whatever this obsession you have with this case is."

Obsession? It was *his* case – nothing could be simpler. Andrew was searching for the words as he looked at Wilks and nodded. The only ones that were coming were the ones that caused trouble, and Andrew was getting tired of trouble.

He slapped out the back of his hand against Wilks' chest and then turned in the direction of his parked car. "Come on, let's go talk to Mrs Jung."

* * *

It had, of course, not gone well. Mrs Jung was more annoyed than ever to see them back and curiously guarded about her young helper who, as before, she was adamant that no one should talk to. Her protectiveness of the girl did make Andrew wonder if maybe she was being a bit too protective, but this was something he shook off when he saw the girl behind the counter chewing and snapping on her gum as she poured over her celebrity rag.

A few words were exchanged between them, which sounded heated and resulted in the magazine being slapped down onto the counter before the girl came round to the front and headed for the side storeroom door. She gave Wilks a look as she went by that was somewhere between contempt and playful teasing. She didn't know anything.

Enough was enough and Andrew had had plenty. Back to the station where the two of them typed out their final reports and then waiting until the Chief finally left before putting them on his desk. This case was done.

4

Anthony was tired. Too much driving for one day. Too much back and forth. Too many last minute quick fixes. This relationship they had with Cliff was, as Leon told him earlier in the day, definitely worth all the trouble. Anthony opened the door to his little helper's dark apartment. He walked in and turned on the lights. There was a bottle of Bourbon in the kitchen that he planned on polishing off.

Anthony closed the door just loud enough to let Chester and little Jamie know they had a houseguest. He headed for the kitchen, leaving the thick stack of bound and blood splattered files on the side table next to the armchair where he planned to do his relaxing. Anthony turned on the kitchen light and then hunted out his bottle. It was there – glass, ice, go. He took his coat off and settled into the armchair. The remote was out of reach, over on the couch where he always saw little Jamie squatting.

"What are you doing here?"

Anthony looked up to see the little devil staring at him from the entrance of the darkened hallway. She was in her sweats, sweater on top. She was looking healthier every day.

Anthony settled back into the comfort of his armchair. "Ah, Jamie. Can you be an angel and pass me the remote control for the TV?" He pointed.

She didn't move. "Why don't you just leave us alone?"

Anthony sighed and then stood up to get the remote himself. She didn't move. Maybe he'd picked the wrong member of the couple. Anthony turned away from her to eye out the TV as he turned it on and then began selecting a channel.

"Are you sure that's what you want – *Switch*? You want me to just leave you alone?" He gave her a brief look over his shoulder.

"What did you do to Chess?"

"I didn't do anything to *Chess*." Anthony spat out the name. "And if Chess were to stop doing things for me – which is what you're actually suggesting – then do you think you'd be living this nice warm little life you've got going on here?" Anthony settled on a show that he didn't know but that looked colourful and vacuous enough to painlessly hypnotise his mind for a while. He retook his seat.

"Chess doesn't need you and I don't need your stuff, and after whatever it was that you did or made him do, he's gonna realise that too."

Anthony felt his fingers tighten around his glass. This little bitch was starting to get in the way of his relaxation.

"You know *Switch*, I think I liked you better when you were on the junk." He gave her a look. "How's that going by the way? How long do you think you would have lasted if I hadn't come along, huh?"

She was still just looking at him. Not moving. Ungrateful little bitch. Anthony's hand tightened. He stood. She flinched.

"Do you think you'd still be clean if it wasn't for me? You might not want to see it, but I fucking saved your life."

"I'm not scared of you."

The muscles in Anthony's arm contorted and his whiskey glass flew across the room and smashed against the wall not two feet from where Jamie was standing. The bitch screamed and Anthony found that his feet were moving, pulling him towards that magical sound. She saw him coming. She turned for the hallway but then stopped. Anthony stopped. Chester was there aiming the gun that Anthony had made him use – made him keep.

"What are you doing, Anthony?"

"Ah, give a boy a gun and suddenly he thinks he's a man." Anthony turned back and collected his smokes from his coat. "Or maybe it's what you did last night that's given you a fresh perspective." Anthony lit his cigarette.

"That's not going to happen again."

Little Jamie's eyes were darting back and forth between the two men in her life. Chester looked at her, his aim still on Anthony.

"You told her about it yet?"

His jaw tightened and his voice cracked. "You leave her alone, Anthony."

Little Jamie's arms were around her man.

"I told you I would."

She spoke up, pawing at him now. "Please Chess, let's just go. Let's just forget about all this… please."

He ignored her. "What were you going to do before I showed up."

"Look Chester, last night…"

"I won't do that again."

"You won't have to." Anthony was getting tired of looking into the now trembling gun. "That was special. Just for you. Now I know that you can do the job."

It was the truth. In all likelihood, no more killings would be necessary. The kids would be paid two hundred in two halves and could keep whatever the johns gave them. Used once, then they could run off having never seen his face, only Chester's, and simply kill themselves.

Jamie was still pawing. "What did he make you do, Chess? Talk to me." Her voice was cracking too. "Please, Chess, please talk to me."

Ignoring her. "What were you going to do before I showed up with the gun Anthony?"

Anthony took another drag from the cigarette it turned out he didn't feel like, and then stubbed it out in the now empty ashtray. The whole place had a strangely renewed air of cleanliness to it.

"Now that I know what you're capable of Chess, now that I know you can earn your keep, now you'll start to get paid. And I know what I told you, but I also told you to keep her in check."

Her eyes flashed fire at Anthony. She turned up to her man who wasn't saying anything. He looked at her.

"Go to bed, Jamie. I'll take care of things, okay."

She lowered her eyes and then turned without resistance and did as she was told, like a good girl.

Chester lowered his gun. "Just leave her alone Anthony."

"I wasn't going to touch her. Just wanted to scare her back a bit."

"Just…!" Chester's jaw clenched itself shut again before he could get the rest out.

Anthony raised his hands in compliance. Chester had earned his little moment. He turned and disappeared into the darkness of the hallway.

Anthony went to the kitchen and fixed himself another drink. Back in the living room he re-took his seat to relax with a little TV. His eyes caught the bound stack of blood-splattered files.

5

The idea had been to wait. Andrew looked at his un-rung phone at the corner of his narrow living room. Everything about the place was beige and narrow. It was depressing. Obsession? Andrew didn't like that idea. He took off his jacket and threw it onto the lonely two-seater couch that made up a third of the living room furniture. Couch, big TV and a coffee table. What more could a life need?

Andrew took off his gun belt and placed it on the coffee table. He picked up the remote that was there and flicked on the big TV. Sports – Old movie – Sports – News – Chat show – Game show – Reality show – Sports – Sitcom – Drama series – Reality show – Restaurant show – click – click – click – Andrew's eyes drifted back over to the phone. What time was it? Ten. Too late? The idea had been to wait. Wait and see. Wait for a call. He calls fine, then he'd see, decide whether or not to carry on with it all. If he didn't then that would be it – over. He would just leave it alone. Andrew had his number.

211

"Agent Webb?"

The voice on the other end sounded different.

"Who is this?"

This felt wrong. Andrew wanted to hang up.

"I'm trying to get hold of Ian Webb."

"Agent Webb is dead. Now, I ask again – who is this?"

Dead. What the fuck? Andrew wanted to hang up. His thumb was shifting up to the red button. He couldn't hang up. He stilled his thumb. Phone records – the works – it would be a mess.

He had been quiet for too long. He had to answer. "My name is Detective Andrew Bates. I was on the Cartwright case which brought Agent Webb down our way. I was just calling to see if he had any information on that case."

There was silence on the other end. Andrew began pacing. Dead.

"What interest do you have in that case, Detective?"

Shit. "It was my case and basically it was hijacked by you guys with the suggestion that we'd be kept informed, so I was…"

"Were you in contact with Agent Webb, Detective Bates?"

Shit. Andrew's pacing quickened but he managed to keep a hold on his voice. "I was trying to get in contact with him, yes. How did he die?"

Silence again. Andrew killed the pacing for fear that his creaking floor might give him away. Andrew waited.

"I'm going to need to confirm your identity. Where are you calling from, Detective?" He didn't wait for an answer. "Give me your badge number and your precinct."

Andrew gave up the goods knowing that it would result in a call to the Chief. Shit. Dead. Fuck. Andrew couldn't believe it. What had he gotten himself into?

6

A problem. Anthony was in another car on his way to Leon's house. Cliff was also on his way there and apparently there was a problem. If there was then it wasn't on him. He had done his side of it. Quick, easy and clean. Leon hadn't been specific but the word was that someone had called the dead Fed's phone.

'He's alone on this – Just a friend grasping at straws. He doesn't have anyone to tell'. Those had been Cliff's words – Alone. Anthony had known that Leon was being too quick off the mark on this. The idea had been to fix this little hiccup as fast as possible. The revelation that somebody was secretly digging into the files, which the meticulously paranoid Cliff was keeping a firm eye on, had obviously really scared him. The name had popped up on his computer in the morning and in his babbling phone call to Leon he'd made it reluctantly clear that there was still a link there if someone cared to find it.

None of this had anything to do with Leon or himself – this baggage, these killings, these loose ends. It was the price Leon had been willing to burden them with to get in on this from the hip gig. The unknown people Cliff was working for wanted Jack dead without bringing attention to them. This they had done, but now it was obviously snow balling and trying to get out of control. What you don't know can kill you, and Anthony didn't know Cliff or the people he'd roped them in to do the hit for. It was bad business.

The decision had been made to kill the Fed.

* * *

The action was a simple one. Be there before the Fed got back and then just surprise him in his car. Cliff had the details, his beady eyes on all the potential players from the get go. Nice quiet street, gets home round eight, dark by then, probably won't be anyone about. Cliff had been right.

At eight twenty, the silver sedan had pulled up in front of the nice white two-storey house with the green lawn. Anthony had waited across the suburban road in the darkness of his freshly stolen, and later quickly dumped car. Out the car and across the street, gun in hand. The Fed never saw him. Files strung together on the passenger seat, the driver's side window shattered as the first of the two silenced bullets found their mark in the Fed's head. A neighbourhood dog started barking. No rush. Pushing the slumped body back into place, Anthony reached past it and grabbed the bound stack of files. Back across the street and into the stolen car. The job was done.

* * *

Leon was standing in his now reasonably stocked kitchen wearing a dressing gown when Anthony arrived. Cliff was pacing. He looked shaken. To Anthony's mind, this was the real Cliff and it was the side of himself that he'd never really been able to hide. Things went south you didn't want to have to rely on his type.

Anthony tossed the bound files onto the central work surface and with its slap all eyes were on him. "So, what's the problem?"

Cliff immediately snatched up the files, tore free the bind and started to frantically sift through them.

"You want a drink?"

Leon raised his own now empty glass up at Anthony. Drinking the hard stuff. Leon didn't show it but all this was definitely getting to him.

"Sure." Anthony walked over to Leon's corner where the bottle was. Cliff was still sifting. More Bourbon. No ice this time. Leon was adamant on that point.

"What's the problem? The question was directed specifically to Leon this time.

"One of the cops. The ones first on the case. One of them called our very recently deceased friend's phone."

The words smacked into Anthony. He instantly knew which one it was.

213

Detective Andrew Bates. He'd seen a fire in him, but until now he'd thought it had burned out. Anthony looked at Cliff to see that he was looking at him.

"Tell him, Cliff."

"From what I heard, the cop claimed to just be requesting a belated update on the Cartwright case and nothing more, but it's already too much."

Whatever Cliff had gleaned, it was already making too much sense for Anthony. He knocked back his drink and waited as Leon poured him another. This was a toxic case and even if the Fed hadn't bought the set up, he wouldn't have been dealing with the cop unless he had something. One word was turning its way through Anthony's mind. The obvious one – witness. That was on him.

Flashing open files at Anthony, Cliff confirmed it. "There's more here than I thought. He's got files here on hit men. Look. Local button men. Pictures. They're looking for you."

Anthony knew his face wouldn't be in any of those files but if they kept digging then maybe…

"It's another simple issue. We kill him. The cop lied about his involvement. If he has anything he hasn't told them. Another little hiccup quickly stifled."

"No, we can't just kill him. Cartwright's name has been mentioned and now it's connected to Webb. To his death."

Not worth it. "So, what are you saying?"

"Look, nobody will want this to be about the Cartwright case, and if they don't have any real reason to then they will just go back to thinking the more obvious choice, which is that Agent Webb's death was related to his work in Union Racketeering."

Leon jumped back in impatiently. "So what's the problem? You got the files. Nobody knows he had them. We kill the cop and the whole thing goes away."

Anthony looked at his boss. "What if there's a witness?"

Leon looked at Anthony. "Did you leave any witnesses?"

"I don't know. Nobody saw me inside but outside… maybe. I don't think so, but if they've got pictures of button men to show…"

"But they don't, do they? We have the pictures and if this cop does have a witness, then he's not doing anything with her, but the longer we wait, the more chance he has to shoot his mouth off."

"It's not about the witness."

They turned their eyes back to Cliff.

"It's not just the witness. If the cop who called Agent Webb's phone talking about the Cartwright's suddenly turns up dead, then all the doors will suddenly re-open and they'll check it all. There will be too many bodies, and then it won't be long before the Cartwright thing stops making sense." Cliff was sweating badly. He held up the files. "They'll start to go through everything Jack was into and the people who hired me to get Jack out the way will be looked at for his death. It'll all start coming apart at the seams."

Anthony could only hope for the heart attack that Cliff's reddening face promised. Free them from his promise of endless riches that was tied to their necks like a dead weight.

Leon stepped forward causing Cliff to back off. "You tell me, Cliff – you tell me you have more for me than just a list of reasons why we can't fix this problem. Because if you don't…"

"I can fix it, I can fix it." The words were said rapidly before Leon could get any closer or say something that might put a strain on their relationship. "I have something that we can use. The cop needs to die but his death needs a reason. I have something that can help us."

CHAPTER EIGHTEEN

1

It was the big day which Kathy could hardly believe had finally arrived. It was still early so the not quite yet finished top deck was quiet. Kathy sipped her warm coffee which tasted very good. A shiver ran through her as the morning chill was suddenly amped up by a passing breeze. It would warm up quickly though and all reports promised a pleasantly mild night.

Kathy stood at the front edge of the nearly completed catwalk and put her coffee cup onto the white sheen of its surface. She then hiked herself onto it, despite the lack of give in her jeans. There were short sets of steps to either side of the catwalk's end, but Kathy didn't want to risk it in case the glossy paint was not yet dry. Getting up off her knees, Kathy picked up her coffee cup and immediately saw the brown ring that it left behind. Her foot went about trying to make it go away but was quickly stopped at seeing the now sizable brown smear that had replaced it.

Kathy sighed at her own stupidity as she tenderly touched her sneaker to a fresh spot of catwalk and then raised and moved it aside to see the brown shoe print that she knew would be there. Ah, fuck it. Kathy planted her foot back down and then did a 360, surveying her kingdom. The lonely pin drop audibility of the two splashes to the catwalk surface that accompanied this spin, quickly prompted Kathy to get back down.

* **

The place was busying up again. Kathy was making her way down the spiral staircase that ended in the middle of what was originally a small dining hall, which was currently being cleared out and transformed into a sort of getaway grotto. This had been Dulpard's idea, which Kathy feared was meant to promote the possibility of having the party on his boat turn into a free for all orgy. Giovanna and herself had decided to shrug this off. So long as he kept his hands away from them they didn't care if he managed to lure someone into dark corner with promises of all his world's earthly delights. Hell, a little scandal could work for them, so long as it wasn't at the cost of the show itself.

Andrew was coming. It bothered Kathy a little just how much that idea pleased her. He was good looking and charming and all that but he was obviously a bit of a player. Did she really need that kind of drama at this point in her life? This would mark the end of their big fashion spectacular, but really it was only the beginning for her and Giovanna. Their lives would be owned by the magazine for at least the first year while they got it off the ground. Did she really want to risk her own peace of mind with some cop who was probably just looking to have some fun? Kathy smiled. She wasn't so sure that she really wanted much more than that, either.

Yeah. Why not? This didn't have to equal longing, turmoil and heartache. Maybe she just wanted someone to sidle up against, someone who wanted to sidle up against her. But someone with the ability to make her toes curl. Kathy sighed and found that she was becoming quite flustered. She cut her roving images short, knowing that they'd be making her red, and that was something that Giovanna was always able to pick up on.

2

"I thought I made myself clear, Wilks."

Wilks stepped forward from the safety of the corner he'd been standing in since Andrew had first stepped into the Chief's office to get his medicine. He hadn't slept, not really. Andrew knew that he could spin it if the Chief let him, but that was the big question. Maybe this would be the final excuse needed, that last straw. All these thoughts had been echoing through his mind since last night right up to the point when Stacy Keen had opened The Chief's office door and the shouting had begun.

Wilks was trying to speak but he was being shouted down.

"I don't want to hear some fucking excuse! I told you to tell me if anything like this happened again."

"I didn't know, Chief. I swear."

Andrew's previous attempt to speak had been halted by a raised hand and an ever-raising voice as the Chief continued to lay into Wilks. Andrew tried again.

"Chief."

The Chief snapped his head back onto Andrew. "Dead detective." He stood and began slowly coming out from behind his desk. "Two bullets in the side of his head as he pulls up in front of his own suburban neighbourhood white picket fenced house. No noise – nobody hears a thing. Wife discovers him maybe an hour later when she looks outside and sees that his car is there. No idea who killed him. No suspects, no reason, and, from the conversation I had, which included both your name," the Chief was speaking directly at Andrew's face now, "and the Cartwright family name, it's been made pretty clear to me that whatever it's about they don't want it to be about the Cartwrights. So, tell me Detective. Why were you still in contact with the now deceased Agent Webb when I expressly told you that we were done with that case?"

Andrew opened his dry mouth to speak but lost his words when the Chief suddenly turned away headed back round his desk and continued to speak.

"I know you're fascinated with all this, Bates. It's in your nature and it's what makes you good at your job. And I'm not unconvinced that whatever happened to Agent Webb was, in fact, related to the Cartwright family. But I also know that if the Feds don't want it touched then it's trouble. Trouble for you and more importantly, trouble for me."

The Chief sat down. "Now tell me, Bates. Why did you disobey a direct order from me?"

Andrew could spin this. Simple was the best. Uncomplicated. Too much bullshit and he could trip up and...

"Sir, I was just calling Agent Webb to tell him that I couldn't work with him on the case anymore. That's all, sir."

The Chief was just looking at him with a stone cold poker face. He turned his head to Wilks who all but flinched at the unexpected attention.

"I see you put your final report on my desk regarding the liquor store double case."

Wilks' eyes were darting nervously as he plucked up the courage to speak. "Uh, yes sir."

"Nothing else for it? You've checked and double-checked? Re-interviewed all the witnesses – nothing new?"

"No, nothing sir."

The Chief nodded thoughtfully. "Okay. Unsolved. We'll put you on something else. Dismissed, Detective."

Wilks' darting eyes searched for confirmation for a few seconds for fear of having misheard, but he eventually managed to get the message to his brain and then his feet, which he turned on and left.

"I'm suspending you for two weeks without pay..."

"What? Sir, you can't be serious, I..."

The Chief continued talking over Andrew's objection, steadily raising his voice until Andrew was drowned out. "And then after that, I want you on vacation for at least another two weeks. Consider yourself lucky, Detective, because I could have made it a lot worse – and I will make it a lot worse – fired worse if I have to, if you pursue this any further. But whatever happens, I don't want your name attached to this precinct until this Cartwright business has well and truly blown away. Am I making myself clear, Detective Bates?"

One month. Andrew couldn't believe it. "Yes, sir." There was nothing to say.

"Your gun and your badge."

Andrew stepped forward removing both and then placing them on the oversized desk.

"You can get them back when you come back from your vacation. Until then I don't want to see you." The Chief began shifting through his papers. "Dismissed, Detective."

Andrew looked at his gun and badge sitting side by side on the desk. He didn't know what he'd do if he lost them... Really lost them. He turned and left.

3

Giovanna squeezed her hand as it held the railing. Kathy looked up at her tall statuesque friend framed by the twilight sky. Giovanna sipped her champagne. This was their little quiet moment while the boat got busier and busier by the second. A glass of champagne each overlooking the dock as lines of guest continued to arrive. Cameras flashing from those who'd been allowed beyond the gate, security checking names, people shouting, everyone dying to get on board the biggest party in town.

So far, they were being left alone to drink their drinks and enjoy their quiet moment together. It couldn't last long as their bout of organised chaos was about to ensue and they had to hold it all together, out front and back stage.

"We've done alright so far, haven't we?" Giovanna was looking at her now.

Kathy marvelled at how singularly beautiful her friend looked. A white dress which hugged her every curve and shimmered as it turned into each one, off-set by her deep black and now curly hair. Kathy was jealous of her friend's endless endowments; from her every inch to her graceful prowess to her unending desire to make it all ever better, whatever it may be. She was jealous of her but never resented her, not really. She loved her.

"We have, Giovanna. Not too bad at all."

They turned to each other and chinked their glass and then downed their champagne.

"Now." Giovanna took Kathy's empty glass and placed it along with her own on the railing, where it would later be sure to either fall to the sea or to the deck. Giovanna took her hands. The crowds were getting bigger and while they had not yet reached them, they would soon be pulled into it all.

Giovanna smiled again. She seemed sad. "Uh, I hope you..."

Kathy had never seen her friend lost for words before. Kathy waited as her friend's smile rose and fell. Giovanna leaned forward and kissed Kathy on her cheek and when she pulled away again she was back.

"So, how do I look?" Giovanna took her hands back and touched at the corners of her eyes.

"You look amazing. You always do."

"You look beautiful tonight, Kathy. It's your colour."

Kathy did a small faux-curtsey as a way to wave off the comment. Her friend knew not to push but the truth was that Kathy did feel like she looked good. Her hair was successfully up and her backless dress was a deep red.

"Cindy."

Kathy turned at Giovanna's exclamation to see the small figure of Cindy Tao standing there in a slinky cream coloured dress that was emblazoned with lots of tiny sparkles. Her hair too was up and she was without her clipboard.

"Oh my God, Cindy. I don't think I've ever actually seen you in a dress before. You look amazing." Cindy was model thin and it was a model's dress. She smiled shyly but she seemed confident. She was wearing her dress. No clipboard and no jitter. Kathy couldn't believe it. Giovanna came to stand next to Kathy.

"This night belongs to all three of us."

Kathy took Cindy's hand, "We would have been lost without you, Cindy, and I don't think any of this could have happened."

"Just remember that when we actually start to make money." This was the Cindy she knew. "We've still got work to do and at least one of you is needed back stage."

Cindy squeezed tighter on the hand of Kathy's that she already had, and then turned and pulled Kathy back with her along the route she came.

"Bye." Kathy gave a small wave to her friend who would once again be in front of the cameras, rapidly firing out the witty insightful remarks.

4

Andrew's day had been a long one and it was steadily getting even longer. First, the guy at the gate had raised his eyebrows at Andrew's smart-casual look and now this no neck was giving him that 'You don't belong' look as he begrudgingly checked the list for his name. Ah, he found it. The red rope was unhooked and pulled aside. Andrew just walked past and started up the steps. He was just too tired to be annoyed.

* * *

It was a full house – boat – ship. Every corner turned seemed to reveal a new host of either strange or beautiful faces, more than a few of which Andrew recognised. No sign of Kathy, though. What was he doing here? Andrew had been asking himself that same question since he'd arrived and some five minutes ago was when he'd made the choice to stay rather than leave. There was no longer an option, at least not the staying dry kind. Andrew traded his empty glass for a full one as one of the black and whites sauntered past.

It was again quite the impressive spectacle. Mostly low lighting everywhere except for those that shone on the narrow white pathway that Andrew kept running into. It was about a foot off the ground and so far as Andrew could tell, no one was daring to set foot on it. He was quite tempted.

* * *

After about another half hour of aimless wondering, Andrew had found a bar counter to sit at. Getting to it though had required him to step onto and over the walkway, which had turned a few disapproving, heads his way, but the beer which came with the counter was free, so it was worth it.

Shortly after taking up his lonely spot at the long bar counter – which Andrew thought was because most didn't know how to find the route round – the atmosphere changed noticeably. The music, the lighting, a quiet hush through the crowd. Then, after a few minutes, an insane looking spectacle on top of a very long pair of legs came walking along the raised white path. She was then joined by a thunderstorm of clicking buttons and flashing lights. Andrew could only imagine how many of the shots his surprised expression must have ruined. Then the model was gone and so were the photographers. He hadn't seen them arrive and he hadn't seen them leave. Andrew was starting to feel a little cornered but dared not cross the white pathway again, just in case.

"Just follow it around that turn." The bartender pointed in the direction the model had gone.

Andrew collected another beer for the journey and then made his way towards the blind turn which took him further into the boat when what he really wanted was some fresh air. A larger room with the walkway only to one side of it. The room was full of people, some standing and others sitting on what looked to be oversized poofs.

The storm was again approaching and Andrew suddenly found himself surrounded by more poised cameras. There was a spiral staircase in the middle of the room. Up meant air. Andrew shouldered his way towards it. The room exploded into light as another pair of legs came into sight. Andrew went up.

* * *

Up and out. After a couple of additional turns, Andrew found himself on the top deck at the outskirts of centre stage. Some fifty people sat to either side of the main catwalk, which then continued on down to the next deck via some white, and so far as Andrew could tell, pasted on steps. Another model, more flashes. Andrew was more content to experience it all now that he wasn't in the middle of it. His position against the outer railing was just right. Good view, lots of space.

"Detective... Bates?"

Andrew turned his head to the sound of that ridiculously sexy, rough and recognisable voice. There she was. Gee... something Italian. Deep black hair, tight dress, erect nipples. She came to stand next to him. Her scent was intoxicating.

She extended her hand. "Giovanna."

Andrew found himself smiling as he accepted it sheepishly. "Andrew, please."

"I didn't know you were going to be here tonight."

"Kathy invited me."

"Did she?" She smiled.

He wanted to be here for Kathy but the way the wind was kissing Giovanna's dress against her body, Andrew knew that he could be very easily turned. There was no way this one would betray her friend, though. That smile she had on was speaking volumes and Andrew had learned long ago that hedging your bets didn't get you anywhere. An image of their three naked, entwined, writhing bodies twisted its way through Andrew's mind. No... too much to hope for.

"Again, this is all something else." Andrew did an all-encompassing gesture while being careful not to spill his beer.

"Yes, we're both very happy with the way it's all gone. Would you like me to help you find Kathy?"

Andrew didn't know how to answer that question without exposing his position and revealing all his intentions. Always good to have a little mystery in your corner.

"Sure."

Giovanna's smile became ever more knowing, which, rather than annoying Andrew, simply turned him on more.

"Follow me."

Giovanna lead the way which took them down to the next deck via the more permanent steps which were parallel to the ones two more sets of long legs were currently descending.

* * *

After a brief Segway through the steaming hot bustle of the ship's kitchen, Andrew found that he'd been successfully guided to the nose of the ship. It was far quieter on this front deck, suggesting that it was perhaps less accessible – VIP. Andrew felt very privileged.

"There she is." Giovanna stepped aside to reveal Kathy looking very sexy in a clingy red dress.

She looked different. Her hair – it was shorter, or just up. She was next to a stretched out but well cut suit that was snuggling in just that little too closely. Lights, camera, reporter. Andrew couldn't make out what was being said but it was mostly being said by the suit.

Giovanna's smile was a cruel one. "Looks like she's still busy."

She took Andrew's hand and guided him in a short walk past the action. "Ah, there they are. You go on and I'll see about extracting our girl from those greasy paws."

Giovanna stepped off leaving Andrew with the sight of his old partner standing talking to a small skinny Asian woman. He looked relaxed, casual – suit, no tie. His hair looked longer. Andrew walked over. A beard! Andrew had never seen David with even a five o'clock shadow, now he had a beard. The small Asian woman was laughing at what his old partner was saying to her. Andrew felt as though he was about to be interrupting a couple of strangers. He wanted to peel off, catch him later.

"David."

5

Dulpard's palm was starting to feel slick against Kathy's bare arm. She hoped her disgust wasn't being revealed to the camera via the ever-spreading grimace across her face. He was still babbling on. After stepping on several questions directed her way, Kathy had just decided to let him rattle on. What did she care anyway? She hated these on the spot interviews. Now if she could just slip free of his grip without making it an awkward spectacle, then all would be right with the world.

There was of course more awkwardness waiting for her once she did. Kathy angled her head over to where she'd seen Cindy guide her brother. Andrew. She turned her head back before one of them saw her looking. Was this better? Would having both of them there ease that tension she'd been anticipating since sending an invite to her brother? She was glad he had come. Somehow she'd let their relationship slip again and she didn't want that to be the end of it. Andrew being there would, of course, draw some of her brother's attention away from her, which would make things that much easier. But it also meant that she wouldn't be able to flirt outrageously with his partner, which she had very much been looking forward to.

The microphone was aiming at her again.

Fuck it, "Yes... all that and more." Kathy stooped as she unhanded herself from Dulpard. "It's been great talking to you. We're very happy with the reception the shows have been getting and we're ever grateful to Mr Harold Dulpard for hosting this, our big finish. Now if you'll excuse me, I must go and..."

Kathy had run out of words. She walked off leaving a lot of dead air in her wake. One... two... The interview started up again behind her.

Her crowd was to the other side and Kathy had every intention of joining it, but first she needed a drink. Where was one of those lovely champagne trays when you needed one? There was Giovanna, standing by the railing and smiling at her broadly. Kathy advanced on her with purpose but then veered off at spotting one of those lovely trays. She got her champagne.

Giovanna was smoking. What a fantastic idea. A glass of booze and a smoke before dealing with life and all that other annoying shit. Giovanna held out her flaming lighter and lit Kathy's cigarette.

6

"You do, man, you look good."

David smiled at this. He did look good. Better than Andrew had ever seen him. That guarded reserve of his seemed to have lifted, or at least faded.

"I feel good. This time has done me well. Made me look at things a little differently."

Andrew nodded, not understanding. "What do you mean?"

The small Asian whose name Andrew had already forgotten was now standing sort of between them with a somewhat knowing smile on her face. It seemed he was asking questions that had already been delved into. This was a new David, charming the ladies with philosophy.

"Just that maybe I've been trying too hard."

Andrew wasn't nodding anymore. "You mean, as a cop?"

"Well, yeah. I mean..."

"Because the whole things pretty much cleared up though. You should be back in like a month." The last word came with a sting as Andrew contemplated his own time ahead.

"I don't think so."

Andrew shook his head, "Don't say that, it's all..."

"No, I don't think I want to come back. I don't want to be a cop anymore."

The words stopped Andrew. He looked to the small Asian girl as though she might have an explanation. She didn't. Andrew looked back up at his ex-partner.

"Just like that. You've been a cop for what, almost thirty years?"

"I don't need it anymore."

What the fuck did that mean?

7

"He tells me you invited him."

They were on their second cigarette. "Don't start."

Giovanna laughed and then planted a kiss on Kathy's cheek. "You go for it you dirty, dirty girl. Let's go."

Giovanna had her wrist and they were off.

* * *

"Hi."

"Hi."

The moment was already beyond awkward. Kathy looked past Andrew to her brother. He was smiling as he stepped up to her. It was a good smile. Oh God. Kathy didn't think she could handle a hug without crying. Why had everything got so strange?

David took her hands. "Kathy, this is all so amazing. I can't believe how big your life has become."

Kathy squeezed her brother's hands. "Well... becoming." She laughed.

"And you're happy?"

"...I am."

Her brother pulled her in for a hug. She hugged him back. She wanted him back in her life.

When their hug broke, Giovanna stepped in to save her from the breakdown that Kathy knew was trying to come on.

"I think that we all need some more drinks. Who's sick of champagne?"

There was a general murmur of agreement amongst the group.

"Me too. Cindy. Take everyone's drink orders and get it done."

"Oh..." Cindy began doing a half turn to put her drink down.

"I'm just kidding."

Cindy laughed and with that permission the rest joined in. Giovanna turned and stepped into the path of a passing waiter. After a few sharp words he darted off. Giovanna stepped back into their roughly formed circle.

"He says he needs a pen and pad to write it all down."

Andrew's eyes flitted over Kathy's as he looked to the group as a whole before speaking. "So, if you three are here drinking with us, then who's running this thing?"

Kathy leapt at her chance to speak to Andrew, but then immediately found that her words were too big for her mouth. "Well, we are. I mean there's... We

224

have some…"

Cindy took the spotlight, for which Kathy was instantly grateful. "My team is running things. If something needs to be coordinated they call me and if there's a problem, I call them." She nodded in Kathy and Giovanna's direction.

Andrew smiled. "Where do you keep your phones?"

Kathy laughed, Cindy sneered.

"Jane. Jerry."

All eyes turned to Giovanna as she stepped into a hug with Jane before grabbing Jerry to give him a kiss on the cheek. Kathy's eyes flitted over Andrew as their little crowd did its awkward mingling and congratulating. Andrew's eyes were on his empty champagne glass. She wanted to talk to him, but only, only she wanted to do it casually, no pressure. Kathy sighed out her malcontent spotting Andrew's eyes trace up her body at the same time. He didn't see her watching. Her eyes roamed casually away giving him a chance to look.

Kathy's eyes stopped. She saw her brother's hand touch his ex-wife's. She saw Jane's hand linger a second too long before moving it away in a casual gesture as she spoke to Giovanna. She saw Jerry at Jane's other side not seeing anything.

Where was that waiter? Kathy needed another drink. They also all needed to get back to work. The show could run without them for a little while, but really shouldn't be left in the hands of Cindy's subordinates for too long.

8

Anthony watched. This little VIP section hadn't been any harder getting into than it was getting onto the boat in the first place. He just made his way along with the rest of the coming and going workers who had brought this little event to life. And as expected, all the players were present at this talk of the town party that 'little sis' was at the centre of.

It seemed the crowd had grown quite a bit. The sister, Kathy, seemed nervous. Anthony knew it was the troublemaker who was making her fidget and flit her eyes back and forth. They weren't together, not yet. Too much sexual tension for anything to have happened. This was good. It was good to have something to play with. She could come in handy. Anthony even knew what her story was now. That thing he'd seen her carrying. Yes, it was all very handy. More drinks now. Good.

9

"We should probably get back out there." Kathy sipped her vodka tonic, which she didn't want now that she had it. "Make sure it doesn't all fall apart."

Giovanna was smiling at her. "Yes, we really should get back into the swing of things. Cindy, let's get our ducks in a row and make sure things are still timing out for the big finish. You go back stage and just do a check up and get back to me."

Cindy nodded and transformed into the working machine version of herself as she headed off powering through the crowds towards her goal. Giovanna then slid in next to David and slipped her arm into his. "Right, let's get back out there so we can find you guys a good spot for the big climax to this thing."

She set off. Jane was the next to flash Kathy a smile as she hooked her arm into her husband's and led him to follow on behind Giovanna and David. That just left her and Andrew. Another sip of her drink. Now she needed it.

"Thanks for inviting me to this thing, again." He wasn't making a move to follow the others.

"Oh, you know. It's not a problem." A bigger sip.

"Well, thanks. I'm *again* very impressed by all this."

Kathy was nodding. "Hm-hm."

She didn't want to look at him. What to do? She didn't know how to do this anymore. It was one thing to flirt when you didn't think anything would come of it. Harmless fun. But it was another thing entirely when what you were really hoping for was a toe-curling fuck with a man who you weren't actually one hundred percent sure was looking for one with you.

She made a move to dart off and follow the safety of their now disappearing crowd. His hand was around her arm, not letting her leave. She turned to him.

"You don't have to rush off do you? Giovanna and that other one... they can cope without you for a little."

10

"Um, I..." She smiled, relaxing. "They can manage without me for a little while I guess."

"Good. It'll be nice to have the chance to talk to you. We haven't really had that chance. At least not just the two of us."

Andrew was beginning to remember why he'd come to this thing, why he'd stayed. There was something lovely about this Kathy creature that he couldn't quite put his finger on. She wasn't his usual type, but whenever he was around her he couldn't keep his eyes off her, or that shapely body of hers. He wasn't too sure about the hair anymore but he was a big enough man to look past that.

He still had his hand on her arm. Her skin was so soft. He wanted her, and, from the look in those open eyes of hers, she wanted him to take her.

"No, you're right. I was going to call you before to see if you wanted to come to our second show but I just figured you're a cop and you'd be busy and that you probably didn't really care about fashion, at least not enough to come to two shows in a..."

"I would've made the time."

She smiled. The hold he had on her arm was going to start to be weird if he didn't make his move soon. He ducked in for a kiss and she flinched. He went in anyway and kissed her. She kissed him back. Her lips were softer still. He pushed in, deepening the kiss, her lips parting in acceptance. He wanted her. She pulled away, smiling coyly. He let go of her arm.

"I'm sorry." She traced her fingers over her lips, "I just..." She looked over

226

her shoulder.

Andrew looked to where she was looking. There was a camera there, still stuck on the suit she'd been stuck to before.

"Don't wanna be seen with me?" He smiled too, keeping it light.

Her hand was on his chest. "No... Well, at least not like this. I have to retain an air of respectability at my own event."

Her hand was still on his chest, subtly exploring its contours beneath his shirt. She bit her lip.

"Come on."

She grabbed a handful of his coat and they were off.

11

They found their dark little corner. It was at the back of one of the rooms hiding them in plain sight. The party was happening all over the ship and unless you had a key to one of the rooms then you'd have to keep it relatively clean.

Anthony kept them in the corner of his eye as the party rose in the low lighting of this smallish room filled with people gravitating towards the beauty of the nearest coked up model. Nobody was bothering the two of them as they battled to keep their hands off each other. The show was over and the ship was returning to the dock. They would be planning to leave together. Anthony could smell their desire for each other. It made him want her.

12

"I've gotta find Giovanna." Kathy's lips were humming from their non-stop twenty-minute kissing session. She felt like a kid. "We have to wrap this thing up and I need to fix my make-up."

"Should I come and find you when you're done?"

"Yes." She planted a quick kiss on his lips and then whipped herself away.

* * *

Kathy by-passed the fractured love triangle that was standing to the side of the main catwalk. Jerry was making a show of holding onto Jane and David had positioned himself a good meter and a half away from them. The models were doing a beeline walkthrough. She just had to be there with the designers as they took the stage for a little face time.

Kathy found the right door that was manned by her favourite tall black and beautiful who gave her a remembered wink as she went past.

"There you are." Giovanna was rushing down the narrow corridor towards her. "You and the Detective have a chance to talk?" Giovanna had her hand and was leading her towards the light that was bouncing off the catwalk.

"Wait, my lipstick."

Giovanna laughed. "So no then." She changed course, leading them through another door into one of the makeshift styling rooms.

"We talked a little." Kathy couldn't suppress her smile.

"You dirty cow."

Wipes, lipstick, mirror. Kathy straightened herself out.

"We ready?" It was Cindy Tao. She had the door open and was tapping a pen on her trusty clipboard, which was with her once again.

"Ready."

Cindy stepped aside. "Let's get going then."

Giovanna went first. She peeked back at Kathy over her shoulder.

"Should I expect you to turn into a cloud of dust as soon as we hit the dock?"

"Leave me alone."

"Just don't do anything in the communal area, that's all I ask."

"Shut up. Eyes forward."

Up the stairs and out into the bright lights at centre stage.

* * *

Applause, cheers, flashes, smiles, kisses, and it was done. They had done it. Now the real work would begin. Kathy suddenly felt tired, but not *too* tired. The congratulations were subsiding and she was able to push through and make a break for it. Where was he?

"Oh God, I'm sorry." Kathy was blushing at the man who'd collected her up from her almost crashing tumble into him.

"Think nothing of it." He was holding onto her upper arms, making sure of her capacity for balance.

He must have thought she was just another hammered socialite.

"I think I must have caught something with my foot."

"You should be careful. Party at sea. Dangerous combination."

There it was. Did she look drunk? She hadn't had that much to drink. A flash of slack jawed images of herself, frozen on some fashion programmed looped through her mind. He still had one hand on her to make sure she didn't end up waddling over the edge.

"I'm fine, really." She gently took hold of the patronising grip that he had on her arm and turned it into what she hoped was a dismissive handshake.

Kathy had decided that she very much didn't like this guy. Good looking, sure, but obviously aware of it. And the way he was looking down at her with his knowing smile spoke volumes of what he thought about her – about women. Kathy felt him let go of her hand after what she realised was a long shake. He was too close.

She began to side step him. "Thank you for the catch but…"

He was again in front of her. "Karl."

"Karl. Thank you Karl. It was nice *bumping* into you, but I've got to go."

It was getting awkward. The crowd around was still thick enough so that if Karl didn't move she'd have to push past. Kathy didn't want to force a scene.

"That's very clever. I like that."

228

"I try. Now Karl, I'm actually in a bit of a rush."

He wasn't going to make this easy. Clever. Kathy was quickly finding herself despising that cheeky grin.

"I would very much like it if you'd have a drink with me."

Kathy looked at the hand he'd again put on her arm. She hated guys who used touch to break the ice, forcing that familiarity on you. She wanted off this boat. She was starting to feel tired again.

"I'm with someone."

"A man?"

Oh, wasn't that classic. "Yes Karl, I'm here with a man and he's waiting for me, so if you would excuse me."

Kathy took hold of his hand again to remove it from her arm. The hand stayed fast. Kathy renewed her grip and this time pulled his hand away. He was ignoring her look.

"Just one drink."

He was closer.

"No Karl, please." Kathy swallowed trying to help strengthen her voice.

His hand was on her side. "Just one."

There were people all around. He was closer. She took his hand again. It slipped away from hers and she felt his fingers digging into her behind.

Her eyes were closed. "NO!"

His hand was gone. Kathy opened her eyes. He was gone. Some were looking at her, most just passing.

"Are you alright?"

It was one of the retired models and her older gentleman partner. Just what she needed. Kathy shook it off and wiped away the rogue tear that had gotten away from her.

"I'm fine. I'm fine."

"What happened?"

"Just this guy. He got a little insistent, that's all."

The pair looked about aimlessly and then looked back at her questioningly.

"He left."

They nodded, pretending to understand.

"I'm fine." Kathy raised a hand to wave them off but then pulled it back when she saw that it was shaking.

The older gentleman set them walking again. The boat was about to dock and half of the party guests were filing up making ready to leave. Kathy nodded at the small goodbye wave the ex-model gave her. Kathy raised her shaky hand again to catch another rogue tear. Son of a bitch. She found herself starting to sit down. Her knees shaky now. She caught herself with a grab to a nearby handrail.

She was okay. Deep breaths. Nothing happened. Deep breaths. She was fine. Kathy looked about. No one was looking at her. No cameras, no reporters.

Andrew. The idea of it all made her feel ill. No, she wanted her friend to take her home. Her hand came back up, going to her forehead this time. She was sweating. She needed to sit down. She had her phone – dialling Giovanna's number. She didn't want to tell her why. Not now. She just wanted to get home.

"Kathy?" It was noisy.

"Yeah… um, listen I…"

"I can't hear you. Are you with the cop –?".

"No G…".

Kathy dropped the phone away from her ear as she headed for the door that was to her left. Her hand was up to her mouth keeping it all at bay. The door opened and there was welcome silence beyond. She didn't look where she was but she felt alone. She slid down, her back against the door. She clenched her teeth, hating herself. Hating that she could be reduced to this, for breaking that promise to herself. Nothing had happened. Deep breaths, deep breaths…

CHAPTER NINETEEN

1

David took a deep breath, pulling the air in through his nose and then exhaling it from his mouth. The curtains were open and the sun was streaming in through the second storey bedroom window. White crisp sheets surrounded him. His skin was sheened in sweat. He looked over to the figure that lay next to him in the bed – his old bed. Her eyes were closed but she was smiling. She knew she was being looked at.

The twisted sheets only partially covered her. Her skin, like his own was glistening as the rays of sunlight bounced off their naked bodies.

"What are you looking at?"

She didn't open her eyes and the smile remained. David didn't answer. He turned over onto his side and then began tracing his fingers along her exposed ribs. Goose bumps immediately sprung up around his fingertips. She let out a small giggle. David flattened his hand against her and ran it over the smooth flesh of her stomach, moving the twisted sheet away as he did. She was biting her lip. David felt himself getting hard again. He wanted her. He wanted all of her. He wanted all of it back.

His flattened hand glided up to the subtle spread of her settled breasts. He palmed the one and elbowed himself towards her to meet the other one with his mouth. He sucked on her nipple and felt it harden in his mouth. She moaned. He looked to her and saw that her eyes were still closed. He moved himself closer, pressing himself against her side. He was hard now.

He felt her hand slip away from its hold at the back of his head and make its way down along her side. Her fingertips found him and he eased himself away from her side to allow them access. Jane wrapped her fingers around and gave it a pull.

"I think I like this new you."

David let her breast slip from his mouth as he looked to see his ex-wife smiling at him. Her eyes open and inviting. David shifted his weight and moved himself above her. She still had him in her hand, tugging smoothly. He kissed her. There was no condom this time. He'd had one and it had been used. Her tongue and lips clashed against his own as she continued to tug as he grew ever harder. He felt her thighs against his sides as Jane drew her knees up. Her free hand was then on his hip, pushing him back. David complied as he felt her angling him down towards her. Then, feeling her, David pushed himself forward. All at once he felt his ex-wife's whole body tighten against him.

"David," She tore herself away from his kiss and continued. "David. Oh God."

She had his face in her hands and pulled his eyes onto her own. She stared at him, forcing his pace to quicken as her body tightened before her eyes pulled her own head back and her spine pushed her body up against his to meet him in their mutual explosion.

The world blurred in the fluid mix of everything around him. Their bodies were crushed against each other, soaking up the electricity that seemed to be transferring between every inch of them.

David took a breath and heard his own groan. It had been a very long time since it had been like that. Jane kissed his neck. He didn't want to let go. The electricity was still charging through him. He loosened himself from her slightly and she quickly found his eyes again.

Jane laughed. "Wow."

David smiled. They kissed. He didn't want to let her go.

* * *

She was downstairs in the kitchen as David lingered in the shower. She hadn't said anything else afterwards. Just held him for a few minutes until both their heartbeats settled back down. Then, another kiss and she slipped out from under him and slowly made her way across the bedroom floor to the en suite bathroom to have a shower.

When she came out she had a robe on. "Coffee?" was all she said. He'd nodded and off she went.

The high-pressure water felt good on his warm muscles. He wanted back in this house. This was his home, his life. He wanted it back. He wanted the chance to do better at it. No more being a cop. No more obsessing about work. He wanted to get to know his family again.

The past some days had been amazing. Everyday he'd picked the kids up from school and driven them home – talked, listened, argued. A little of everything. His daughter was looking him in the eye now. No smiles, but still, definitely progress. And Samuel was soaking up all the worldly and manly advice his Dad was keen to give him. "Don't smile so much" may have been a little harsh, but the kid was weird. Thing was, David really felt like he was becoming a part of their lives again.

Every day he saw Jane. Working from home for no good reason and there to say hello every day when he dropped the kids off. A chat at the door turning into a cup of coffee in the kitchen. Jerry had been told about the lifts. No place to say no. He'd become a late worker recently and was away on business today, kids away at play. This information had been dropped seemingly as small talk on the Friday as David had stood across from her in the kitchen. He'd grabbed her and kissed her then, the same way he did when they'd first begun their affair. Then as now she'd kissed him back.

It wasn't mentioned again. Their hands had touched on the ship and David knew that she was his to have again. Come the morning he was parked around the corner from his old house, waiting. Then after her husband drove off he was at the

232

door. She'd answered it in her robe and now it all felt like it was all over.

David turned off the shower.

* * *

"You were in there a long time."

Jane was sitting with her elbows on the kitchen table holding her cup of coffee. Her hair was still wet and her robe hung slightly open, revealing the inner curves of her breasts.

David walked past her to the coffee pot and poured himself a cup. "I was just in there thinking."

"About what?" She turned to look at him over her shoulder.

"Just thinking."

"Come sit down. Talk to me."

She turned back waiting on him to take his seat across from her. David walked back round but chose a section of counter to lean against instead. She didn't say anything. He sipped his coffee and kept his eyes on anything but her. She didn't say anything.

David didn't want to do or say anything. It felt like whatever he did would steamroll things on towards the inevitable.

"I don't think this is going to be enough for me anymore." He looked to her.

She was nodding. "I know that." She smiled. "You've changed so much that I barely recognise you."

He didn't know what she meant. Her words weren't telling him anything. He needed the real ones, the definitive ones…

"Do you love him?"

Her smile dropped. "Yes."

"Do you love me?"

"Yes."

She still loved him and she still loved her new husband. So… What? What did it come down to? What could make her decide? Had she decided? Was there even anything *to* decide? David sipped his coffee.

"So what does that mean?"

"I don't know."

"I'm not going to be a cop anymore. You know that, right?"

"You told me and I think that's great."

"I'm not drinking anymore. Not really anyway. Not like…"

"I know David, I know. I've seen it in you, but…" She stood away from the kitchen table to walk up to him. "Do we have to decide all this now? Right now?"

Jane took his cup out of his hand and put it on the counter behind him as she enveloped him in an embrace. He smelled her hair. She was home to him. The home that he'd tried to forget but the one that he now needed back.

"I love you, Jane."

"I know."

David could feel desperation creeping its way up his throat. "And I'm sorry that I let you down. I'm not that guy anymore."

"I know." She squeezed him tighter.

2

"No cop then, huh?"

Giovanna took a seat at the roof terrace table across from Kathy. Kathy shook her head and took another drag on her cigarette.

"Can I?" Giovanna tapped Kathy's pack of cigarettes that was on the table between them.

"I thought you quit."

Giovanna lit the cigarette she'd taken without waiting for permission. "That didn't take. Anyway, you saw me smoking last night."

Kathy shrugged. "Yeah but I forgot."

Giovanna shrugged. "Once a smoker." She exhaled her first lung full and then re-focused her attention. "So why is there no cop?"

"Just isn't. Just, you know… didn't want to do anything last night." Kathy tightened herself at Giovanna's furrowed brow.

"Is everything okay?"

She hadn't called him. Waited long enough to straighten herself out before calling a cab and then just ducked off with her tail between her legs. It made her sick to think about it.

Kathy forced a smile. "Yeah, I'm good. Just didn't…"

"Did something happen?"

"No. Like what?"

"I don't know. Anything. You just seem…"

Kathy reached across the table and touched her friend's hand as she pushed out a bigger, better smile. "I'm fine. You've got to stop worrying about me. I think I drank more than I realised 'cause I'm feeling a little used, that's all."

Giovanna relaxed. "Just not in the right way. Right?"

"No."

"So what's happening then? Are you going to see him again?"

No. "I don't know. Maybe."

"You should." Giovanna stood and made her way past Kathy, touching her shoulder as she went. "He likes you."

Kathy reached up and gave Giovanna's hand a squeeze before it left her shoulder and then removed another cigarette from her pack.

3

Suspended for less than twenty-four hours and already ordered to come in to the station – 'And bring Radley with you!' No real explanation, but Jenny Wieze's name had been mentioned. Andrew's head was not yet working properly. No Kathy. So he'd hit the town hard. No warm body to fuck away his troubles, so he drowned them instead.

Andrew turned on the shower and recoiled at the squeak sound the tap twisted out. One hour. Andrew stepped into the regulated stream of water. He'd have to make it quick. This was clearly about the Harris case, and he was going to need a couple of strong cups of coffee in his system if he was going to be able to face it.

* * *

Five minutes to go and that meant he'd be at least ten minutes late. The skinny girl in the stained green apron handed him his coffee with an apologetic smile. He waved her off with a smile of his own even though he really wanted to punch her in the face for being so cack-handedly slow. Out of the door and back into his conveniently adjacent car. He might have been on suspension but he still had his tags. Andrew wedged his takeaway coffee cup in between the two front seats as he got the car started and back into traffic.

David had actually been around to answer his own cell phone, which had made for a nice change, and the message had been passed on with as much clarity as Andrew had available to him. No notable reaction at the mention of Jenny Wieze's name. Just a cool calm, 'I'll be there'.

Andrew freed his coffee with tried and tested skill and took another sip.

4

The idea of going in alone did not sit well with David. It had been clear from Andrew's call that he wasn't ready, so David knew he would be the first to arrive and there at the entrance to his old station was where he anxiously waited.

He saw Andrew's car go past, headed round the back to the parking lot. David was tired of resentment. He and Andrew were partners but had never been close, never been friends. He didn't care to think about whether or not his partner should have been there for him, whatever that could have meant. None of it mattered. Right now all he needed was a friendly face to stand by him.

"David."

David looked down the concrete steps to see Andrew coming up, a takeaway coffee in one hand and the other extended out in front of him.

David shook his hand. "Do you know what this is all about?"

"No, but if Jenny's here then it's about the Harris case." Andrew stepped past him and opened the door. "Come on."

* * *

Up the stairs to the top floor, through the swinging doors and into his old place of work. It had only been less than two weeks since his suspension, but as David walked past the lines of desks, most of them empty on this Sunday but some peopled by faces that he didn't really know, it felt like he'd been away for a lifetime. David caught himself smiling. This type of – what was it – abstract thinking? It wasn't him at all. He really was changing.

Stacy Keen was in front of them. "They're all in the office. They've been waiting."

Andrew stooped conspiratorially towards her. "Who's in there?"

David looked at his watch. They were fifteen minutes late.

"Just get in there, Detective. You're already seventeen minutes late."

David looked at his watch again.

"Thanks Stacy." Andrew waved a dismissive hand at her but she was already gone.

"Right." Andrew was looking at him. "Let's go."

* * *

The office was full. The Chief was in his usual position behind his desk with Jenny Wieze seated in one of the two guest chairs opposite and Laura Stanwick from the prosecutor's office in the other. One of her lackeys was off to the side. David thought he'd seen him before but really, it was just another face in a long line that he didn't care to know.

The two chairs were turned slightly outwards away from the desk and pretty much facing each other so that when Andrew and David entered the office, all disapproving eyes were on them.

"Close the door."

Andrew did as he was told. The Chief didn't say anything else once Andrew had completed his task. He just slowly knocked his clasped hands continuously down onto his paper-strewn desk.

Andrew stepped forward. "What's happening?"

Jenny Wieze turned her head away from them. Her disgust was etched across her face.

Laura Stanwick stood and approached them holding out two folders for them to take.

"Do you remember your old partner, Detective Radley? Dan Carter."

David looked up from his opened folder, which had what looked like a statement inside. "He was my partner for eight years. I remember him."

"Part ways on good terms?" She waved him off before he could respond and continued in a now frustrated tone. "It doesn't matter. The fact is, your old partner has put himself forward as a witness for the defence, claiming that he saw you killing a man named Calvin Hargreaves whom you believed was responsible for raping your sister. And if I didn't know any better, it would have appeared that that didn't happen either."

All eyes were on him again, including Andrew's. There was nothing to say. Why would Carter come out with this? What was this? There was no body. Carter didn't have any proof. What the hell was this? What was it going to mean?

"Carter just came forward with this? Just like that?"

"Is it true?" Laura Stanwick's eyes were burning right through him. She'd

236

never liked him.

Again she waved off his attempted response. "Oh it doesn't matter if it's true anymore."

"What? How can it not matter? My partner has some kind of grudge against me." It made no sense. "So he comes out with this shit to damage me. It's pointless. He can't have any proof because there is none because it didn't happen! None of this happened."

It didn't make any sense. Carter had been a harder bastard than he could ever be and the son of a bitch had never been above palming a few dirty notes. If anything, David had it over Carter, but the guy did his job and they worked well together so nothing needed to be said. And when the time came, Carter had been there to help him but he never saw anything. Just another vagrant dying in an abandoned building that caught fire because he was drunk and careless. It didn't even make the papers.

"He spins a pretty good tale, Detective, and as I said, it doesn't matter if it's true. This case was on a knife's edge as it was thanks to your run-in with Garver Harris, and now this comes up to give the defence's accusations precedence. From a respected and decorated police officer who was your partner of eight years no less."

She threw her arms up. "It's over."

"Just like that. One day we're fine and then my ex-partner comes up with this lie and it's over."

"Oh, please."

Jenny Wieze said the words just loud enough for all to hear and they echoed in the silence that surrounded David's own. He forced himself onwards.

"Have you even talked to him?"

"It's over! I don't have to talk to him. The judge is going to have no choice but to throw this case out. Your reputation cannot be trusted." Laura Stanwick snapped around and grabbed her coat and purse from next to her seat.

She turned back. "All of you need to be in court tomorrow. Be there for nine."

David stepped out of her way as Andrew opened the door. She left.

Jenny Wieze stood. "Thank you sir."

The Chief stood and shook her hand. "I'll give your Captain a call. You take care."

She nodded her lacklustre acknowledgment and then collected her own coat. No purse, just a pencil skirt and a gun. She looked at the two of them standing on either side of the open office door and nodded again.

"Detectives." She left.

"You too, Bates."

Andrew turned away and left as well, pulling the door closed with him.

"Sit down, David."

"What does this mean?" David took his seat and waited for the answer he didn't want to hear. It wasn't about getting his job back anymore, but he knew there was going to be more to it than that.

"I don't think there's enough to Carter's story for anyone to go digging into any of it. But," the Chief was shifting uncomfortably in his seat, "there's no way you're going to be able to get your job back."

David nodded. "I know."

The Chief was still rolling. "Once the press get hold of this, which they will – hell they probably have it already thanks to a conveniently placed leak – they'll have a field day with it. It's all too much." The Chief paused. "You know that don't you? But if I was you I'd tell my sister to be ready."

Kathy. His mind had been on Jane and what all this meant for the two of them. Oh God. This was too much. It was exactly what he'd fought to avoid.

"David. I.A.D. probably won't care to dig into this, but with the papers on it, it may prompt them to take another look at the Garver Harris thing."

5

Andrew couldn't believe it. This hadn't come out of nowhere. Your partner doesn't just come out after so many years and decide to ruin your life. First Agent Webb gets killed, and now this. It was connected.

"Detective Bates. What brings you down here on a Sunday?" Bill was in the middle of a sea of white coats surrounding his workstation. "The first Sunday of your suspension, I do believe."

Andrew had been spotted as soon as he'd come through the swinging doors. He waited as Bill continued with whatever it was that he was showing the rest of his class. A few heads looked in Andrew's direction as Bill went on.

"This information was passed on to me personally by the man behind the big desk, and I don't mean God. I was told in no uncertain terms that I was not to provide you with any assistance whatsoever and that if you asked I was to then immediately run upstairs and tell on you."

Nobody was paying attention to the experiment and Andrew spotted that Bill's dark haired little helper was still there and her eyes were on him. Bill was still going.

"So, with all this knowledge available to you, it makes me wonder why you're still standing there. Because, as you know, I'm afraid of the man behind the big desk, and I am of course still referring to the one with actual power."

"Bill."

"Yes, Detective." He was continuing with his demonstration as though anyone was paying attention.

"Can I have a word with you?"

Bill's shoulders slumped in a dramatic sigh. "This isn't happening," he said to his students as he shoved whatever it was they were looking at aside. "Everybody can finish whatever it is they got going on and then head home. We'll try this again tomorrow."

There was a general sense of relief that seemed to wash through dispersing crowd, which Andrew tried to peer past and get a look at what was initially so

238

interesting. All he could see was a petri dish with nothing happening inside it. Bill came walking over.

"I wasn't kidding, Bates. I'm not getting into shit for you."

Andrew put his arm around Bill's shoulder. "I know, I know, and any other day that would be fine but right now I really need your help."

Bill laughed. "Oh God. You're unreal. No. No. There's no way."

"You remember I asked you to check out that stuff."

Bill stepped out from under Andrew's arm and walked over to another workstation to monitor one of his tech's progress, rushing to be done for the day. Andrew watched as the young Asian guy reluctantly moved aside on his low-wheeled chair to give Bill's large frame enough room to get in front of the big computerised microscope-looking machine, and take a look at the world at the sub-atomic level. Andrew wasn't sure if microscopes could see that small.

Bill fingered the device's automated touch screen. "I remember and I broke it down and all the rest, and you never came back for my findings, which I would have given to you when you were still technically on the job, but now you're not so..." Bill looked up from his view of the, at least, very small world. "I can't help you."

"Look Bill, this is important."

"It always is." Bill was on the move to hover over the next workstation.

Andrew took Bill's arm stopping him. "In private."

Bill's eyes showed his surprise at Andrew's hand. Andrew dropped it away before continuing. "I think I'm in trouble."

"Look Andrew, you know I'd help you but this isn't even your case anymore. Groder's laid it down for me and when he tells me that I'd get in shit if I helped you, I believe him. Just let it go, man."

Andrew could feel eyes turning their way again. He could feel the walls of this cluttered area moving in on him as his old friend, or as close to what he could call a friend, ran on. He had pulled David into it now too.

Bill continued as he settled over the next tech's station. "You're already suspended and if you keep this up you're going to get yourself fired."

"I know that!"

The whole room froze as Bill slowly looked back up at Andrew. This had never happened between them before.

"Let's go to my office."

* * *

The door to the overloaded but well organised office closed and Andrew turned to it. "I'm sorry Bill. I didn't mean to do that."

"What's going on, Andrew?"

Bill was looking at him as though he was crazy and needed to be placated. Andrew didn't like it.

"I don't know how much you've heard but I kinda stumbled onto something

239

in the Cartwright case which…" Andrew didn't like the way he was sounding. He began to pace. "Honestly, I don't actually know what I've found, but it's starting to look like it's made a target out of me."

Bill circled past Andrew and settled his large posterior against the edge of his desk as he sighed thoughtfully. "A target? What does that mean?"

Andrew sighed too. "I don't know."

"Look Andrew, I would like to help you, but…"

Andrew dove in. "The stuff we found at the scene that was mixed in with the whiskey. I know that it has something to do with some pharmaceutical company, something to do with some drug that still undergoing FDA approval. Apparently no one else has it…"

Bill tried to interrupt but Andrew pressed on. This was all he had.

"But I don't know the name of the company and I need that name." Andrew again ran over Bill's attempted interjection. "All I need is a name. This isn't about some crazy obsession that could cost me my job. This is about trying to find out who I think is going to try and kill me."

Bill looked more perplexed than shocked. It was not a promising look for Andrew.

"Have you talked to Chief Groder?"

"Just the name, Bill. Can you get it? Find out where that stuff came from?"

Bill sighed again. "Maybe." His face then screwed up as he looked past Andrew through his office window, which overlooked his domain.

Andrew turned to see what he was looking at and then saw the dark haired little helper turning her head sharply away as she pretended to continue working. Andrew didn't turn back and made for the door.

"Thanks Bill."

"You fucked her, didn't you?"

Andrew had the door open and was backing out, pulling the door closed as he went. "Give me a call once you have it and don't tell the Chief."

* * *

Andrew grabbed his now officially ex-partner's arm as he came out of the Chief's office. "We need to talk."

CHAPTER TWENTY

1

The courtroom was full and Andrew was sitting next to David two rows back from the prosecutor's table. Jenny was closer to the back and nowhere near them. After they had parted ways the evening before, David had told him that he was going to talk to his ex-wife and his sister and tell them what was happening. He'd looked rough when he came in and that had been the first thing Andrew had asked him about. David didn't respond but Andrew could tell that those two encounters had been put off a little longer.

Raped. David said none of it was true, but that clearly didn't mean anything. Andrew didn't know how he felt about it. He wasn't even sure he felt anything at all. Not that it mattered as she clearly didn't want to see him. Had she felt threatened by him? Christ, he didn't need this on his plate.

"All rise."

Everyone in the courtroom rose to their feet at the bailiff's instruction as Judge Amanda Bridgett entered and took her place behind the bench.

"You may be seated."

Her voice was tired. Tired at the pointlessness that was to come out of this long and overblown case. They all retook their seats.

"Council, approach the bench."

Each side's top dog went forward. Laura Stanwick in their case with an overly tall and overly bald sleaze in a suit for the bad guy's side. Damon was looking pleased with himself in the swanky suit that he clearly knew he was gonna be walking out of there in.

It didn't make sense. What could having Damon cut loose do for them? How could it help them? Two in the back of the head for Agent Webb, so they clearly had a better button man than Damon Harris could ever be. He was little more than a thug. It didn't matter. The fact was that it was too close to home to be a coincidence.

Carter, David's old partner, wasn't anywhere to be seen. Probably to be brought in dramatically through the large doors when his moment came. David hadn't exactly been totally sold on Andrew's theories but he did want to talk to Carter. True or not, talking to him would surely shine a light on something as out of the blue as his old partner suddenly jacking him in for no good fucking reason.

Judge Bridgett was done with the lawyers who returned to their seats. Andrew caught David catching the look Laura Stanwick gave.

"Detective David Radley."

Andrew could feel David's own blood running cold at the sound of the Judge calling his name.

"Stand up."

David rose to his feet and straightened himself out once he got there. Judge Amanda Bridgett just looked at him for a good half a minute before speaking again. Her voice was tired and her eyes were pissed off.

"Again, this whole case has been put into question and thrown into disrepute at the mere mention of your name. Do you have anything to say for yourself?"

David kept his head up. "No Judge."

"Sit down, then."

David sat down as Judge Bridgett raised her voice to include all the ears in the courtroom.

"New witness testimony has come to light which casts a dark shadow over this case and all procedures by which it was brought forward. I have just conferred with council and since there can no longer be any rational or logical objection, it has been decided not to draw this mess out any longer than necessary." Her gaze settled on Damon Harris. "Mr Harris."

Damon rose to his feet, dwarfed by his tall lawyer who was standing at his side.

Judge Bridgett continued in her tired tone. "It pains me to do this, but as I have no real choice I'm calling a mistrial. You are free to go."

Her hammer came slamming down and it was done.

2

No more words were said to them as everyone packed up and left. It was over. David watched Damon Harris. All smiles as he shook the hands of his relatively high priced legal team. *They* hadn't got him off. Damon's eyes met David's own.

He didn't even care about him. It was just a case. It was Garver who'd brought it to his home. He had been the only one David had cared to care about, and that was only when he'd decided to step into his life. This whole case had been nothing but a nuisance to him. He was a homicide cop and that was all that this case was supposed to be. If that was the way it had stayed then Damon would have gone down long before on a simple murder wrap. But then it gets folded into that Jenny Wieze bitch's case and it gets complicated and it has a chance to brew and then it has a chance to inject itself into his life and then...

Damon's eyes told David that he was going to have to start caring about him too. He'd have to tell Kathy before it all got to the papers. Today.

* * *

Carter may not have been in court but he had been in the building. Kept in waiting in case the prosecutor's office had demanded to hear the testimony, which would have obviously been a technicality. David was waiting with Andrew by Carter's old car, which was parked just round the corner from the courthouse. The case was over now and there was nothing legally stopping them from having a talk. The legality had of course been on David's mind, but it hadn't stopped him the night before from going to Carter's apartment. When Carter did end up at home he'd find that his door, which had been neatly pulled closed, now had a broken lock from the kick it had received.

Carter stepped round the corner and stopped in his tracks. David felt Andrew's hand on his shoulder and realised that he had just been about to lunge for him. Andrew was right, it was too much violence this close to the courthouse, which still had too much activity swarming about it as cops held back snapping reporters questioning the now vindicated Damon Harris as he made his indictment of the people, involved in what he'd spin as a set up.

"David." Carter was fat and old, a fact which his mismatched suit didn't help to disguise.

"Dan." David stepped forward as calmly as he could manage. The front of the courthouse might have been busy but the walled in little street they were on was very quiet. "How you been?"

Time had had its way with David's old partner. It had only been just over two years since he'd last seen him, but he was no longer the grizzled hard on he used to be. He looked weak. He looked brittle. Too much time to fill and nothing to fill it with. The idea of ending up like the old man who was taking half steps away from him made David's mind flash with images of his own gun deep inside his own mouth.

"This your car?" David indicated behind himself.

Carter nodded, fiddling with the keys he'd already had in hand to quicken his getaway.

"Then where you going?"

Carter halted in his retreat and let David reach him. "I had to do it, David. They…"

Carter was rocked sideways as his heavy frame carried him stumbling into the middle of their quiet little side street, where his knees gave and he went slamming down. David stalked over to him as his knuckles called out for more. Carter spat out the blood that was getting in the way of his words. He raised his hand.

"I'm sorry!"

David slapped Carter's outstretched hand aside and grabbed him by his coat to pull him to his feet. The old material tore under the force and weight and Carter went back down.

"David!" It was Andrew. "Get him in the car."

"Help me."

Andrew quick stepped over and they each took an arm.

"Are you going to kill me?"

"No Carter, I'm not going to kill you."

He was on his feet.

"Give him the keys."

Carter unclenched his fist and let Andrew have them.

David pushed Carter on as Andrew unlocked the car and opened the back door. "Just get in the car and tell us what you know."

Carter nodded, allowing himself to be manoeuvred into the back seat. David shoved him on and climbed in the back with him. The synthetic material of the back seat was full of holes with exposed foam poking through. Andrew got in the front and the doors closed.

"We're just gonna go for a swing around the block while you tell us why you decided to crawl out from under your rock and fuck me like this. Drive."

Andrew started the car and pulled out of their cosy walled-in narrow road and turned the corner away from the courthouse. David watched Carter as he pulled out his napkin from his torn coat pocket. His hands were shaking as he began dabbing his busted lip. This was not the man David had known.

"Talk!"

Carter shuddered in fright. "I don't know who it was Dave, or why or anything. I got a call from somebody late on Friday night telling me all this stuff. How he knows about you and your sister and the guy…"

David cut him off, his eyes on Andrew. "Okay… so what… just like that some guy throws a couple of names at you and you make up some bullshit story about seeing me kill some guy, about actually being there and seeing it happen. I read your little statement. How did you know you wouldn't get into trouble yourself? You put yourself in the same room as me. What…"

David's words got away from him. He could feel himself shaking now. He could see his old partner's head being put through the car window. He backed off letting Carter get the words out that his protectively raised hands were begging for.

"He had me, David, I didn't know what else to do. He knew names and dates and scores. He was gonna put me in jail man."

"So you just gave him everything. My sister…"

"He knew it all already man. He was picking dates out of a hat and where, as he said, something changed. Your work fell apart, your record became tarnished and then he just starts on about how it was to do with your sister being in the hospital. She was raped. I tried to deny it, man, but he said that you may have been able to pull a few favours to keep it quiet, but the fact was it's still on record. He just knew that something came of it and he wouldn't take no for an answer. I told him about Hargreaves… I had to."

David's eyes again went onto the back of Andrew's head, taking it all in. It didn't matter anymore.

Carter was still babbling on. "This thing with you… He said all it needed was to look bad. He told me what to write, who to take it to, what to say. There's not enough in there to put you in jail, just enough to make you look bad. He said that was all it would take."

"What did he have on you?"

Carter's shaky hand continued to dab away unconsciously with his napkin which was only serving to spread the blood around the lower half of his fat face. "My deal with the Trendle brothers… the thing with June, the fat one – you remember her?"

David nodded as Carter spouted out a couple more. The stuff on Carter wasn't that tough to get a hold of. All you needed was his name, his reputation and a little access to his case history and, after talking to the right people, you'd have it all. David supposed that was true of what they seemed to know about him too, but not since Friday.

"You spoke to this guy on Friday night. Not before. That was the first time."

"That was it. I never heard from him before."

"And what makes you think you're not going to hear from him again? Now that it's done." David didn't let him answer as he leaned in against Carter's retreating frame. "You sure you haven't suddenly found yourself in with enough money to skip town and find a new life?"

"What?" He laughed, it was bitter and hollow. "No David. All I've got waiting for me is half a bottle of cheap scotch." The smile dropped away along with his eye contact. "Any money I had is long gone. I got my pension and it gets me by and that's all there is to it. Not all of us have nice cushy divorce settlements to fall back on."

David's fist tore away from him almost on its own and found its mark inside Carter's gut. The old man wheezed as he hunched over, his face red and the veins in his neck bulging. David grabbed him and pulled him back against the seat. Andrew's eyes were on him in the rear view mirror. He hadn't planned on hitting him again. Carter was old and David knew that too much could kill him.

He had his breath back and a twitching smile on his face. "I just couldn't go to jail, old friend. I wouldn't survive it." He pulled in a deeper, more controlled breath. "No, I don't think anyone will bother coming for me. I did what they wanted and that's that. There's nothing left."

Andrew stopped the car. There was nothing else to get. His old partner knew only what they wanted him to and nothing else. David wasn't so sure they wouldn't send someone to finish him to tie off the loose end, but he couldn't focus his time on watching Carter on that slim hope.

"If there's anything else, you call me. I'm listed."

Carter nodded as he tried to regulate his breathing. He was covered in sweat now. David could only hope that he didn't die from a heart attack, or at least that no one would place him and Andrew in the car with him if he did. Andrew got out first. David took one last look at his old partner. His torn suit had blood on it. David got out the car and joined Andrew. They started walking back to their own cars.

"Okay Andrew. Tell me again. Tell me everything."

3

"Kathy, there's a reporter downstairs who wants to talk to you."

Cindy had her hand over the phone's mouthpiece. She was in her semi-office, which was little more than a two-by-four glass cell, holding the phone out to Kathy who was standing in the open doorway.

"A reporter? From where?"

Fashion correspondents didn't show up at the office. They either cornered you on location or, if they were coming to your office, called to schedule some face time. Cindy spoke into the phone to Toby who was recently hired to run their front desk which, since the very public success of their last show, they very much had a need for. Still Kathy didn't like the idea of an outside world reporter seeing the place. It was, after all, strictly a layover spot. Once their issues started going out and the money started coming in, it would be onto a far less exposed concrete themed location.

"He won't say. You want Toby to get rid of him?"

Toby was just nineteen, very cute, very gay and very insecure. He wouldn't be able to get rid of anybody.

"Ask him what it's about. If it can wait then they can make an appointment and talk to Giovanna."

Cindy relayed her instructions and then arched her eyebrows when the response came.

"He says the reporter wants to talk to you about the recent developments in your brother's case."

"My brother?"

"What should I say?"

That hollow feeling that had accompanied the mention of her brother was back. The court case – suspicion. She had made a conscious decision to let it go. What was the reporter here to tell her? Why her? Same name – hers being bandied about town lately. 'What's your viewpoint on the fact that your brother was possibly responsible for the death of a suspect in an ongoing trial…Now that you're famous, that is'.

"Tell him I'm on my way down."

* * *

Toby was there to meet her as she came through the stairway door into their buildings clean but sub-basic foyer slash reception area. Toby's station was, in fact, a small wooden desk.

He pointed to the couch by the far wall next to the tall pot plant where the attractive, slickly suited reporter had just stood up. He was whispering something which Kathy couldn't make out, past his nervousness. She squeezed his arm reassuringly and then patted him back in the direction of his station.

"Miss Radley?"

The attractive, slickly dressed reporter was walking over to her with his hand outstretched. The other one, Kathy could see, had a tape recorder in it. Better than a camera crew.

"That's right." They reached each other and shook hands. "And you are?"

"Mike Foster. I'm a reporter with *The Park Reader*."

She hadn't heard of it. "You told Toby over there that this has something to do with my brother."

He smiled – it was perfect. "Yes, that's right. I was actually hoping to maybe have a sit down in your office so we could have a little talk about it all."

Kathy didn't like him. "Look, Mike Foster, I don't like reporters showing up unannounced, making cryptic comments about my brother so they can demand an interview. Why don't you just tell me what this is about?"

"I'm sorry, Miss Radley. I did not mean to ambush you. Believe me that was not my intention. But I have to tell you, now that the Harris court case is over and with the information as to why, which will very soon become more widely known, I won't be the only reporter knocking on your door. So," he elongated the word before proceeding, "why don't you talk to me and we'll make sure we get the story straight before things get out of hand?"

Kathy found her voice coming out just above a whisper. "What are you talking about?" She cleared her throat.

The mini recorder was clicked on and held up between them. "Do you remember a man by the name of Calvin Hargreaves?"

Those eyes and teeth flashed their way through Kathy's mind and she found herself taking a step back.

"What?"

* * *

"Kathy, are you all right?"

Cindy was on the other side of the door and Kathy couldn't find the strength to tell her she was okay and to leave her alone. She splashed water on her face again and looked at her cracked reflection. She was in the cleaners' toilet where she'd hoped to go unseen, but Toby had obviously called up to Cindy again.

Did she remember Calvin Hargreaves? She'd just continued backing off as his questions kept coming. Was she aware of her brother's supposed involvement in his disappearance? Did she have any comment? *I didn't come here to ambush you.* Her reaction had been all he was after. *The Park*… whatever, my ass. He was from some trashy tabloid piece of shit and didn't want her to know its name before he fired away at her with his questions.

David had killed him. In her name. Was that so bad?

"Kathy!"

"I'm fine!"

Silence.

The face in the mirror was looking at her with hate in its eyes. She looked away.

"Cindy?"

"Yeah?"

"Is he gone?"

"He's gone."

"We're going to have to hire security. At least three guys."

247

Kathy snatched out four paper towels from the dispenser and wiped her face and neck. She saw that her shirt was wet.

"Security? Why?"

"Just do it. I want a team in place by tomorrow morning. One on the door, one on the front desk and one on the stairway door. Find something else for Toby to do."

She looked at herself again. She wasn't going to let them have her.

4

"So what? You think that means I owe you now? Is that it?"

They were in the office of Damon Harris's lawyer, who Cliff had sent the older cop's ex-partner to. Directly afterwards Anthony had placed a discreet and nondescript phone call to that lawyer alluding to what was now being queried. Just another crook like the rest of them. Anthony hated lawyers. This one had apparently lost his seating privileges as his client had chosen to take his seat and put his feet on his nice enough desk, which went along with his nice enough office, which was anonymously tucked away in the nice enough building.

Anthony wondered what kind of price range the lanky bloodsucker ran. Not enough to only have one client but judging from their surroundings, he did okay. Anthony could tell he was annoyed at having his rightful place being usurped by this stocky little weasel with the lopsided goatee. Anthony had his seat pushed away from the desk, keeping the two of them in his sights. Crooks were never to be trusted.

Damon was playing with his tie, a free man. "Because from where I'm sitting, it looks to me like you guys have already blown your load before you got a chance to make a deal. I'm out and I'm happy, but you ain't got shit on me so why would I help you? What's in it for me? Because I'm not that much of a giver, if you know what I mean?"

Nothing had been said. No questions asked and no demands made. Anthony had just let him ramble on.

Anthony smiled. "Mr Harris, we both know that your brother, may he rest in peace, was the brains of your operation."

The weasel's cocky smirk was slipping. Anthony continued.

"And since his death, your little organisation being leaderless has pretty much been stripped and sold for parts. So if I were you I wouldn't get too comfortable squatting in the chair of the lawyer you pretty soon won't be able to afford."

Damon's chair slowly swivelled beneath him as he removed his feet from the desk. Anthony could see it in his eyes that he was about to make things ugly. Anthony didn't think he was stupid enough to bring a gun into the proceedings, but from the way his lawyer was tensely stepping forward, Anthony wasn't completely sure.

Anthony kept his cool. He knew how to play this game. "Now, I'm not suggesting that you owe us and I know that you have business with the ones who put you in jail and who killed your brother, and I respect that."

Damon had settled again. He was listening.

"All I'm saying is that since our interests are similar, we might come up with a business relationship. One that will be both personally and financially satisfying to you."

"What do you want?"

* * *

Anthony sipped his Bourbon as he watched the shirtless Chester sitting on the coffee table watching whatever was on the TV. The curtains were closed with just a couple of shafts of sunlight coming through. One ran its way up Chester's pale body. He didn't seem to notice. He looked grey, wasted away with dark rings below his empty eyes. He was perfect.

"I need a girl this time. That plump one with the dark hair." Anthony lit a cigarette.

"When?"

"Soon."

Business was going to have to be put on the back burner for the minute. Things needed to be dealt with first. Chester was nodding. Anthony let his eyes drift about the dark apartment. It had become decidedly less well-kept and the air was sale.

"Where's that little girlfriend of yours?"

Chester changed the channel.

"Chester, where's Jamie?"

His eyes were locked to the bright flashes on the screen. "She took off. She's probably with friends. She does this – she gets straight and then loses it and disappears. She'll be back in a couple of days." Chester changed the channel.

"She took off?"

Chester nodded, his gaze still transfixed. Anthony's glass flew from his hand and smashed into the TV. Chester's hands went up instinctively as he fell backwards away from the eruption of sparks flying from the destroyed screen. He fell off the coffee table and landed on the crumb-infested carpet.

Anthony was on his feet and above Chester. He could not have that vindictive little cunt running loose, potentially with a mind to tell the cops that there was a bad man who was making her boyfriend become far less attentive than he used to be. Chester's neck was in his hands.

"Anthony…" Life had come back into his eyes.

Anthony lifted him up, his hands securely clamped around Chester's neck.

"What did I tell you about that girl, huh?"

Chester's head snapped back as Anthony shook him. His eyes were bulging as his head settled forward again. Chester's grip on Anthony's wrists weakened.

"I told you to keep her in check, make her respect you. I want you to get out there and find her and you bring her back here. You got me?"

249

Anthony swung Chester sideways, letting him bounce off the wall and fall to the floor. He rolled onto his back gasping for air. His eyes quickly locked onto Anthony again as he knelt down beside him.

"If you don't show me that you can control her, then I won't have any use for you or her." Anthony pulled a wad of notes from his pocket and then threw it onto Chester's chest, reminding him why he was there.

5

The husband was home. David watched the car pull up in front of what used to be his home. He was sitting in his own car. It was the flashy red mid-life crisis mobile that he'd bought once his divorce settlement had come through and which had then been kept in storage ever since. No more unmarked police car for him.

David's plan had been to go in and talk to his ex-wife before her new husband got home from work. To talk to her about what was happening. She'd said she could see a change in him, could see that he was a new man. She'd clearly known in her heart the truth about what he was capable of; what he'd done in the past and now. And if she knew all that then it coming out into the open shouldn't change the way she was now choosing to see him.

David took a sip from the small bottle of whiskey he'd brought along with him. His own little pre-emptive strike against his plans to go in and talk to her. If his will failed him, then at least he'd have something to numb the pain. Of course, David knew before he had taken his first sip maybe an hour before, that he wasn't going to go in there. It didn't matter that it shouldn't change things – the fact was that it did. A disgraced cop and a drunk. Her life was better than that.

David took out a cigarette. He'd bought the pack along with the bottle – two things he'd been avoiding of late. He lit the cigarette and breathed the smoke in. It went well with the bottle. David's hand went up to his forehead. If he couldn't face Jane then how would he face his sister? His teeth clenched. He took another sip through them and then breathed in, sharply savouring the burn that followed. His fist slammed into the dashboard. It hurt.

One last sip before turning the ignition and getting out of there before he ended up going to his old home and kicking the fucking door down.

* * *

David's knuckles were rapping against the once green door. The car had just stopped. He wasn't drunk. It was a small bottle and he hadn't even finished it. There were mints in the glove compartment. That had been the deciding factor. It had to be done. The door opened.

"David?"

"Jerry."

"What can I do for you?"

David could tell that he was threatened by him. David was physically bigger and had a presence that Jerry could never muster. But it was more than that. He just knew that his wife was still drawn to him. Jerry didn't know he was fucking her. David could tell that too.

"I need to talk to Jane."

Jerry's wide set frame was blocking the door to prevent David from inviting himself in.

"What about?"

There was a smirk waiting to form on that smug mug of his. David could have slapped him.

"I need to talk to my ex-wife to tell her something. It's…"

His finger was on David's chest, "That's right David. *Ex*-wife. Meaning she's not your wife anymore. Do you think I don't see what you're trying to do? Coming back into her life all of a sudden, into the kids lives." There was a poke. "You don't care about them. If you did you wouldn't have…"

David suddenly had two handfuls of Jerry's shirt and was moving him inside. Jerry's weaker hands were on David's. "Hey!"

"You do not know me Jerry, 'cause if you did you would never dare to talk to me like that."

"Get your fucking hands off me!"

"Or what?"

David had him against the wall inside the foyer of his old house.

Trying to pry himself free, Jerry screamed into David's face. "This is my house!"

The words hit David. "Your house!"

"David!"

Jane was behind him. David looked at his hands on her husband's chest. He loosened his grip and Jerry yanked his shirt free. Jerry was saying something but David wasn't listening. He was anticipating the turn he was going to have to make to face her. He didn't want to see that disappointment in her eyes.

"Jerry, please."

Her husband stopped his yammering and got out of David's face. David turned to her. She took his breath away more and more these days. Her eyes were sad and she had never looked more beautiful.

"Jerry, can you give us a minute?"

"I don't want…"

"Please, just one minute."

She was rubbing her husband's arm, soothing his frayed nerves. It was a hard thing to have to see.

"I'll be in the living room." He left an open door behind him.

Jane waited and then looked at David. Her arms folding protectively across her chest.

She spoke softly. "What are you doing here?"

David stepped towards her only to see her step back away from him. His heart sank and he slowly pulled his outstretched hand back.

He took a breath. "Damon Harris has been let off. That's why I came. I just wanted to tell you... I just want you to be careful because of..."

"I know, I know. I saw it on the news today." She turned away from him only to turn back with her arms out in a big sweeping gesture. She was no longer speaking quietly, "And do you know who else knows? Your sister."

What did he expect? There could be nothing to say in his defence.

"Is she alright?"

"Is she alright. Do you care?" It was her finger that was against his chest now, "She called me saying that a reporter came round asking her if she had any comment about the guy who raped her. He said all the papers are going to get wind of it eventually."

It was all undone. Jane had lost her momentum. She pulled her hand back from his chest before clasping both together in front of her mouth as if to shield him from what she had to say.

"What have you done, David?"

It sounded like goodbye and David didn't know if he could survive that a second time.

"I'll fix it, Jane." She was backing away from him, "I will. I'll make it right. Please just tell me this doesn't have to be it."

"David, don't." Her arms resisted his but she let it happen as his arms wrapped around her.

"Please just give me a chance to make this right."

"What's going on here?"

"It's okay, Jerry, he's leaving."

This was his wife, his house, his family, his life and he could feel it trying to pull free. He could hear its end over his shoulder as the new husband approached him.

"David you have to let go. Now."

His lips were at her ear, "I love you, Jane. Please don't make me go. We can start over right now. Together – right now."

She was shaking in his arms. "No."

No, no, get out and go. David squeezed her tighter.

"Hey! You heard her. Now get the fuck out of my house." Jerry's hand was pulling at his shoulder.

David let go of his ex-wife and spun around to face her husband. "This isn't your house!"

The coward immediately shrunk away as their eyes met. David's fist followed on from his turn and connected with that smug face, like it had always longed too.

"Don't!"

David felt the warm gush as Jerry's nose was smashed in beneath his fist. David watched in a cool state of ecstasy as the man's knees gave while his one hand shot up to protect the damage and the other went back to stop his fall. He went down.

"What have you done?"

David turned to her voice, which was coming up from where she'd fallen after he'd spun away from her. She didn't look at him as she crawled past to attend to her husband. David's eyes followed as she reached him. Blood pouring past his hand, his work shirt ruined. David unclenched his fist. The ecstasy was gone.

"I…"

"Just get out of here!" She wasn't looking at him.

He couldn't move. If he left now there would be no coming back. He couldn't just let it go. These mistakes were ones he'd already been forgiven for. It wasn't right that he should be forced to pay for them now.

David was down on his haunches, her back to him as she attended to her dazed husband. Her back jerked at his touch.

"You said you saw a change in me. You saw me change. You can't let it all go because of this."

"David." Her voice was weak.

"I've seen it in your eyes, I know you still love me. I know it – I know it, I've felt it. Jane…"

She was crying, "Just go, please."

"Jane…"

Jerry's bloodied hands crept their way onto her shoulders before sliding across her back and pulling her into him and away from David's hand. Her back rose as she took a breath.

"Just leave!"

The words vibrated through his every vein turning his blood to ice. He stood. His eyes were pulled up towards the top of the stairs where he saw the two children he didn't know looking back at the man who they didn't know either.

* * *

It didn't hurt. He punched the dashboard again. He punched it again. Again. The steering wheel got away from him and he quickly put both hands back on it. The road was dark and the night was empty. The suburbs were behind him now. His grip on the steering wheel was tight. He screamed. Again, louder. A hole appeared in the windscreen with the glass splintering around it. Another, and the steering wheel again got away from him. David looked to the two holes as the world tilted and the ground came rushing towards him.

CHAPTER TWENTY-ONE

1

"No comment."

Kathy put the receiver back into the cradle of the old chunky telephone that sat on her small desk in her small viewless office. Giovanna was standing in the open doorway.

"How you doing?"

Cindy had done her job well. The security staff hired, briefed and in place first thing in the morning and not a second too soon as apparently the reporter hadn't been exaggerating when he said that pretty soon everyone would know. Kathy had missed the flashes by coming into work early but many a staff member had had to fight their way through, with a few opting to turn back and call in sick. If your name wasn't on the list then you weren't getting through.

Kathy had since made an announcement of sorts and work was pretty much going ahead. Nerves were apparently frayed though, and Kathy could tell that the rumours were already starting.

Giovanna stepped in and took a seat. Kathy knew that she was worried about her friend.

"Who was it?"

Their number had gotten out there and the phones had been ringing non-stop with everyone looking to talk to anyone who might have something to say.

"Susan Sallenger from *Fashion Weekly*."

Kathy raised her eyebrows at her partner because she wasn't sure there was anything else she could say. Now the fashion world was calling because they too could smell blood.

"How you coping with all this?" Giovanna reached out and squeezed her hand.

Kathy knew that Giovanna could smell their blood as well. She cared about her friend above all else, sure, but the fact of the matter was that this little media flare up could wipe away everything. It was their gloriously successful show that should be the talk of the town. This was the kind of thing that could spook advertisers, their investors, their colleagues. It could all just fucking fold. Kathy wasn't doing too badly though.

"Is it really illegal for us to smoke in our own building?"

Giovanna sighed thoughtfully. "I think it's more of a rule than a law." She leaned back and pushed the office door closed. "And we all know what those were made for."

"So really more of a suggestion than anything else."

Giovanna was nodding in agreement. "Like the Ten Commandments."

The pack was in Kathy's hands with two cigarettes quickly being removed, distributed and lit. No windows. Kathy breathed it in.

2

Andrew cut the unanswered ringing off. Back to this already. He bounced his cell phone down onto his abbreviated kitchen counter before pouring himself out a cup of strong black coffee. Maybe David was right not to answer. What did they have? David had listened to all that he had to tell him and then… What? What did they have? What could they do? Effectively, neither of them were Cops so there was no power, and those who still had it didn't want to know.

After having laid it all out for David and seeing him then shrug his shoulders before leaving, Andrew had strongly considered giving Jenny Wieze a call: 'Hey, how you doing? Just thought I'd come and check on you. Better be careful now that Damon is back out on the street. By the way, do you think you could help me with my illegal investigation?' Andrew looked at his phone. He was still considering it. It started ringing.

Andrew snapped it up. "Hello."

"Andrew? Detective Bates."

It was Wilks. This was not a call Andrew was expecting.

"Wilks. Yeah, it's me. What do you want?"

It came out a little colder and more demanding than Andrew had intended. Wilks just seemed to bring out the best in him. The line was quiet for a second before Wilks started up again.

"Uh yeah. I just called 'cause I thought you should know." Andrew's hand tightened instinctively around his phone. He'd heard this tone before. Wilks continued. "They found Alex Staffridge and his brother dead last night."

Andrew's grip loosened. "What?"

"They were found at his place. Apparently the door was open and there they were lying on the floor for everyone to see. They'd both been done with a knife. I thought you'd want to know."

Christ! "Yes. Thanks. Wilks call Social Services – um – Jennifer… what was her surname, it's…"

"I already did. She's gone. She ran away."

"She ran away? When? Why?"

"I'm not sure. Sometime later last night. She must have heard about it from Stafbridge's P.O. He was just in here screaming to the rooftops about being set up and that this had something to do with us, with the whole precinct. I think he was just scared that he was gonna be next and wanted to let everybody know not to let that happen."

Andrew's mind was spinning. Wilks had finished talking. What was he going to do?

"Thank you, Mark. I know you didn't have to do this."

"I thought you should know."

* * *

It was too early. There wasn't even a guarantee that she'd be on this same spot. Roseberry Homes was just around the corner. Andrew couldn't believe he was back to this square. Sitting in his car watching an empty piece of sidewalk and looking for a whore who might not show.

Chances were that eventually Clarice would show. But time was ticking on for the other one, Frankie. He had to find her before they did. A figure came swivelling round the corner. This one was tall, blonde and skinny. It wasn't either of his girls. She'd have to do.

* * *

"Excuse me."

She swayed her narrow denim skirted frame around to face him but then stepped back at the presence she was obviously all too familiar with.

"What? I ain't done nothing."

She was wasted. Her arms were covered by the rib hugging white shirt she had on, but from the pinpoint bruises Andrew could see on her neck, it was pretty clear what she was on. Andrew grabbed her by the arm. Niceties would be a waste of time with this one and Andrew didn't plan on throwing any more money away.

"Hey. Ow."

She tried to raise her arm high enough to slip her head underneath in what Andrew could only imagine was an attempt to twist herself free. Her arm wasn't going anywhere. Andrew moved her back until she was against the wall. She hit her head.

"Ow."

* * *

Jasper had the sinewy body of a met amphetamine freak. Andrew had the long mop of hair that was restricted to the top of Jasper's head and was using it to swing him into the glass door that led to the pool. The glass cracked and Jasper slid down and thumped to his ass.

Jasper touched at the back of his head before examining the blood that his fingers brought back with them. "What do you want?"

Much better.

The door to what could only be described as a commandeered and pimped out inn had been opened by the big and black, who after refusing Andrew entry had taken the edge of the door square in the face. He was still out. Andrew had brought his Saturday night special along but had decided to confiscate the shotgun which had slid across the white tiled floor.

The screaming had ensued and the girls had begun to scatter. Andrew grabbed one of the small ones as she tried to scramble past. "How many guns in the house? Where's Clarice?" She'd just shaken her head in despair. Andrew let her go.

That was when Jasper had shown up. He had his gun trained but Andrew had seen him coming and had his newly acquired shotgun aimed squarely at Jasper's midriff. Jasper also knew full well what Andrew was and killing a cop was never something to be taken lightly, especially when it was in your home. Jasper had dropped his gun and then spat on his own floor instead of answering Andrew's question. That was when Andrew took hold of a clump of Jasper's greasy hair.

Andrew repeated his question. "Can I talk to Clarice?"

He was standing over Jasper with his gun aimed directly down at him.

"Why?"

"I just need to ask her something."

"Fucking cops. She probably ran off as soon as you busted in here and started shooting up the place."

"She wasn't one of the ones sitting in this lovely reception area of yours and I didn't see her coming down those stairs. And I didn't fire any shots so I'm thinking if she's here then she's still here."

"She probably went out the window whe..." Jasper's words were muffled out as the barrel of the shotgun went into his mouth.

Andrew went down onto his haunches being sure the barrel stayed where it was. "You know, all I ever want to do is talk to these girls. But since I knew I was again going to have to butt heads with the likes of you, I decided to take a different approach. And I know that's not exactly fair... Not giving you the benefit of the doubt and all, but if you don't stop giving me shit I'm going to rip this barrel out of your mouth and crack you across the teeth with it. Clear?"

The gun backed its way out and Jasper spoke, "Josie!"

From the corner of his eye, Andrew saw a short fat girl with orange hair and orange skin stand up from behind the multi-fabric sofa where she'd been cowering. Keeping his eyes on Andrew and the shotgun barrel that was still aimed at his face, Jasper continued.

"Go upstairs and find Clarice and tell her to get her big ass down here."

"Which one's Clarice?"

"Just get your ass upstairs and find her!"

The fat orange girl hopped to and quickly ran upstairs. Andrew stood back up straight and lowered the shotgun letting it come to rest at his side. Andrew stepped back, and taking his meaning, Jasper pushed himself up onto his feet.

"Now when Clarice comes down here I'm gonna take her with me for a little ride. Now what I have to talk to her about has nothing to do with you or your set up."

Jasper was examining the fresh blood that he'd just brought back with his fingertips. He refocused his attention at hearing that Andrew had stopped talking.

Andrew continued. "So once we're done with our thing and I let her go, I'm gonna be checking on her from time to time." Andrew stepped into his next words, "And if she has anything off colour to say about you, or if I can't find her when I need to, then you and me will have a serious problem."

Jasper was holding onto his eye contact, but Andrew could tell he understood him. The unconscious henchman was stirring so Andrew backed off to keep him in his sights.

"So if she ever decides she's had enough of your little set up, you'd better ask her nicely to call me so I can say my goodbyes and not spend my time worrying about you having accidentally misplaced her."

"Officer."

Andrew turned his head to see Clarice descending the steps. She was minus her S&M wig and wearing a green zip up sweat suit. Her hair was long and dark brown and it suited her.

"Clarice. I need a favour."

* * *

"Take me there."

With her handbag now in hand, Clarice got into the car. Andrew closed her door and made his way round to the driver's side, all the while keeping his eye and newly acquired shotgun on the closed front door of Jasper's luxury inn. Andrew got in the car and put the shotgun on the back seat. He started the car and they drove off. It was getting dark.

* * *

"So what is this place? Like a brothel?"

"If you want to call it that, yeah. The place is what it is. It's a whore house, but it's just cleaner and nicer and more expensive."

"You told her about this place. If it's so great, how come you don't work there?"

"I've been in the game too long to work in a place like that. Frankie's still young and her skin's still tight."

"And you figured it was the best the world could offer a girl like her?"

"Maybe. Look it ain't no Russian slave house. It's a nice place and it sure as shit beats working the corners night after night. This kind of place could actually put some money in her pocket."

"Hmm, sounds like paradise."

Andrew saw the shift in Clarice's eyes as she began to despise him.

"You know what... Fuck you. Stop the car." Clarice opened the front passenger door of the speeding car.

"What are you doing?"

Andrew resisted reaching out to grab her for fear of losing control of the car and shaking her out of the open door.

"I don't want to help you anymore. Stop the car. I don't care what you think. All you're going to end up doing is pulling that girl out and putting her back on the street." She turned away from the passing road to look at Andrew. "Stop the fucking car!"

"Just close the door, Clarice. We both know you're not going to jump out of a moving car." Andrew accelerated.

After a moment Clarice gave him her best evil look and then pulled the door closed.

After another moment she spoke again. "You got a cigarette?"

"Don't smoke."

Clarice spat out her disgust as she turned away to look to the darkening world beyond her passenger side window.

"Look Clarice, I have to get her out of there. I need to get her some place safe before…"

Andrew trailed off but he'd got her attention. She turned her head to look at him again. He considered how to put it. He didn't have the energy to answer whatever questions his following statement would probably elicit.

"That thing with the family. She saw something, and now whoever did them is after her."

Clarice sat back in her seat shaking her head. Andrew knew what she was thinking. It was the exact thought that had been screaming in his head since Wilks' call.

She said it. "And you're the reason they know that, aren't you?"

* * *

"And here we are."

Andrew pulled the car to a stop across the road from the large three-storey building that looked much like all the other ones that lined the quiet Brooklyn street they were on. It was late.

Clarice looked away from the building to give Andrew a scolding look. "Don't park it here. A cop car across from a whorehouse. I think they'll notice."

Andrew started it up again and rolled on down the street. He turned the car down another quiet road before doing a U-turn and parking it just out of sight while keeping their target in view.

"So what are we talking here. Heavy security, local boys on the take, all that and more?"

Clarice was nodding her way through his list.

Andrew suddenly felt very tired. "I need to get in there."

"You didn't really think this shit through, did you?" She was enjoying her smirk.

"Or maybe get you to bring her out."

"What? You expect me to go in there wearing this and ask to talk to my dear old friend, and then walk out the door with her and climb into your car and just drive off? That's your plan?"

"Why not? You said it's a nice place. If she wants to leave then…"

259

Clarice held her hands up waving off his smarm. "Okay, okay, they ain't no slave traders but they still fucking criminals with an investment, and Frankie's one of their girls so there is, shall we say, red tape of sorts."

Andrew was doing his own nodding now. He knew the score. This place did seem to be an anomaly of sorts, but when you broke it all down the end results were always pretty much the same."

"Okay, but like you said, it's no prison, right?"

Clarice shrugged her acknowledgment of her previous assessment.

"So you go in there, tell them you're an old friend of Frankie's and you've come to say hello. You get her to come down to see you. What's the layout like in there?"

Thinking. "Reception counter on the ri... left, and like a waiting area on the right. Pretty small. There will only be one guy behind the desk. There's this like heavy-duty bulletproof glass wall, which he controls the door to. One the other side there's a lift."

It would work. "You get her to come down and through the glass door, and then I'll bust in and grab you both. Easy."

Clarice didn't look convinced, but opened her door and started to get out anyway. Andrew touched her arm stopping her.

"You got a cell phone? Take my number." Andrew quickly scribbled it down on a scrap of paper and handed it to her. "Programme it into your phone."

Clarice searched through her bag and, once locating her phone, did as he said.

"Now keep it in your pocket or whatever, but out of sight and soon as she comes down you call my phone. I won't answer, it's just a signal so I know she's there and then – bam. So be ready."

"Uh-huh, and what if she's busy fucking somebody and can't come down?"

"Then you just wait." Frankie could have been sitting in the car with them by now.

"This is stupid. All this shit is starting to make me sound really suspicious."

For the first time, Andrew could hear fear in her voice.

He toned it back. "Clarice, this is important..." Andrew paused, he had it. "Just make it like this big surprise thing. Tell them to get her to come down because you're an old friend and you want to surprise her. She comes down and you call me. Got it?"

Clarice smiled. "I'll figure something out."

She stepped out of the car with her handbag slung over her shoulder and her cell phone in hand. As she began to close the door Andrew opened his mouth to tell her not to push it if it didn't look like it was going to happen, but he instead let the closing door cut him short.

* * *

The door opened and after a few brief words that Andrew couldn't hear, which accompanied her winning smile, Clarice was in. The door was closed behind her and Andrew started his car up again, shifted it into first and then quietly crawled it round the turn before bringing it to a stop some ten metres away from the front door. His cell phone would be ringing soon. Andrew shifted the car into neutral and left the engine running. The area was still quiet enough but Andrew decided against the overly conspicuous shotgun. He grabbed it from the back seat and stuck it down in front of the front passenger seat. The girls would be in the back. Andrew reached back and opened the back passenger side door. A lone passer-by's head turned as he climbed out the driver's side door, which he too left open. Andrew made his slow steady walk towards the front door of this high priced establishment. There were cameras about. This needed to happen now because it wouldn't take them long to realise something was wrong.

Gun now in hand, he examined the door he'd briefly looked at when they'd first driven past. Sturdy, but he'd been a cop long enough to know how… His phone rang.

Andrew let his shoulder take the lead as he charged for the door he'd specifically distanced himself from. With a final forceful lunge, his tensed upper arm connected. A splintering crash followed as the door tore its lock free from the doorframe and Andrew suddenly found himself stumbling into the golden hue of the building's small reception area. He saw Clarice on the wrong side of the closed glass door. Her hand was locked around the shocked Frankie's wrist. Andrew's gun was on the man behind the reception counter.

"Don't fucking move!" The primped and slight little man seemed to merely pause. "Open the door."

There was no reply from the man whose unseen hands had no doubt triggered a silent alarm. Andrew stepped up to him and once he had his tie, pulled his nose forward into the butt of his hammering gun.

"Now!" Seconds till the heavies emerged.

A shaky hand found the right button and the glass partition door slid open.

"Come on!"

Clarice rushed past him pulling the shocked but compliant Frankie with her. Andrew followed them out.

"Get in the back."

The whole thing had taken a good ten seconds longer than Andrew had hoped, but they were out quick enough for his exposed car to still be where it was supposed to. They were in and the doors were closed. Andrew shifted it into first and pulled off. Nobody in the rear view. If they ran his license then it'd just tell them to let it go. Andrew swung round the next turn and pushed down the accelerator.

* * *

Andrew looked at Frankie in the rear view mirror. She was clinging to Clarice for dear life. There were lights behind them but they were keeping their distance. Another turn. Andrew kept his eyes on the rear view mirror. The lights didn't follow them round the turn and quickly disappeared behind the buildings. Andrew didn't think anyone could have got onto them quickly enough. It was a clean getaway.

"Listen Frankie. I'm gonna get you to a safe place, okay? I'm not going to let anything happen to you."

The Chief would hear him out. Her boyfriend and his brother just happened to get knifed. Done just like the Cartwrights. It was too much to ignore. If all it meant was getting her shipped out of the state once and for all, then maybe that was enough. This wasn't digging, the Chief would see that.

The next turn brought Andrew out from in amongst the maze of buildings and onto an open road. He knew where the city was from here. A car passed them coming from the other direction. Andrew turned his head following as it went by before turning out of sight. There was another car ahead of them that was going too slowly on this deserted road. Andrew checked his watch. It was late. Theirs were the only two cars on the road and all the dark building to either side were closed and empty. Andrew didn't like this. The gap between them and the cruising car ahead was closing. What would happen when he tried to pass it?

Andrew eased his foot off the accelerator until they were cruising just that little bit faster than the car they were steadily nearing.

"Is everything okay?"

Andrew caught Clarice's eyes in the rear view. She knew the answer.

"I don't know. Put on your seat belts."

What was that? Andrew turned his head with his eyes adjusting just in time to see the black mass behind them suddenly speed up and ram into the back of his car. The impact blew out the back windscreen and rocked Andrew forward, his chest slamming against the steering wheel. As all the air exploded from his lungs, his head was whipped back round and he saw them slam into the back of the car in front.

* * *

A piercing hum cut through Andrew's darkness. He opened his eyes to see smoke rising from his car's buckled hood through the cracked windshield. He peeled himself away from the steering and the piercing hum of car horn was ended. He felt explosions of pain in his chest as the pressure subsided. He turned his head slowly, trying to think his thoughts one at a time. The girls. His gun.

"Are you girls hurt?"

A groan sounded out. It was Clarice. The thoughts started rolling. They'd been hit. His gun. The shotgun was wedged in the passenger seat floor space. He needed to move. His hands weren't moving fast enough. He pulled his Saturday night special out, safety off.

No movement at the front of the car. Undoing his seat belt Andrew turned his body round to avoid using his neck. Clarice's nose was bloodied and her forehead was cut from slapping into the back of his seat. She was trying to blink reality back into place. Frankie was strewn across Clarice's lap, unconscious but breathing. Her arm was badly broken. No movement at the back. Both the other cars were still in place. Andrew turned himself forward again. They were sitting ducks. They were waiting for him to get out.

"Clarice." Andrew shouted through his whisper.

"What?" She wasn't with him yet.

"We're in trouble."

"What happen…"

Andrew heard the double silenced shots as they smashed the back seat window in, cutting Clarice's words off. Energy jolted its way through Andrew's body as he pushed himself away from his driver's side window to lie flat across the two front seats. He let off two shots before seeing anything. Both tore through his driver's seat headrest. Clarice was slumped over, her reddened fringe obscuring whatever damage had been done. Frankie was still out.

Two more bullets broke through the driver's side door before going into the seat by Andrew's legs.

A rattling roar charged forth from Andrew's throat as he blew hole after hole into his own car door. Another shot from outside. The bullet hit his ankle. A scream sliced its way through Andrew's roar as his one hand instinctively pulled free of its grip on the gun and reached forward in desperation.

Andrew's constricted eyelids opened and in his head's tilted back position, Andrew saw movement behind him. The shotgun was against him, his handgun almost empty. Andrew let his gun go and twisted onto his side, grabbing the pump action shotgun and pulling it free. The door was being pulled open behind him. His hand was on the trigger. Andrew pumped it and directed the barrel past himself and squeezed the trigger.

BOOM! The noise was beyond deafening. Andrew felt a gust of air sucked away from him as the passenger side door was blown off its hinges. Frankie screamed from the back seat.

"Fuck me!"

The voice came from beyond the blown off door. Andrew pumped the shotgun and, with his head tilted back, not seeing much of the upside down world beyond, he fired again. The extreme slam of the blast hammered its way through his eardrums. Frankie screamed again.

He had too… Andrew felt his blood freeze. He knew this game and he now knew there was no way he could win it. The shotgun was uncocked.

Andrew raised his head slowly to look back down the length of his own body and through the, as yet, unbroken driver's side window. The man standing on the other side of it was masked and in black, with his pistol aiming squarely at Andrew. There was nothing to say.

"I'm sorry, Frankie."

The glass blew inwards and the bullet tore its way through Andrew's ribs snatching away his air. It didn't hurt. There was blood on the car's ceiling. It faded away.

* * *

"Take her."

Screams. The voices were far away.

"Are you going to shoot her?"

"Not here. I don't want to leave her blood all over the place. Put her in the trunk."

Screams. The blood on the ceiling began to come back. Andrew struggled for a breath. He found his hand. It was red. He was cold. He couldn't breathe. His other hand was red too. He could feel the hole in his chest. He could feel his warmth being monotonously expelled.

"He's still alive."

The voice was behind him. Andrew let his head flop back to see the figure standing above him.

"Go get Damon." It was the other one's voice.

The one above him disappeared from sight.

"You've been a real pain in the ass, you know that?" It was the one who'd killed him. He was above Andrew now. "A real pain."

He bent down, reaching past Andrew. Andrew tried to follow his movements but they were too fast. The Saturday night special. His killer was checking it. Any bullets left? One or two, probably.

"Almost jumped the gun before. Thought the first whore was the one, but then when you started heading this way I let it play. Thank goodness, huh?"

His hands were on him. Andrew could feel himself being shifted, lifted, propped up. His hand was being folded around his Saturday night special. Andrew let his eyes roll to where his gun was being made to point. Damon. It was Damon Harris. The driver's side door was open and there was Damon swaying back and forth on his knees, a thin line of blood running down his face. The gun went off and Damon flew back.

"He dead?"

"He's dead."

The gun dropped free and Andrew's body flopped back. There was blood on the ceiling.

CHAPTER TWENTY-TWO

1

"Do you mind if we move this outside, actually? It's just that I'm dying for a cigarette and this is a non-smoking apartment."

"Whatever makes you more comfortable."

Kathy stood up, immediately rubbing her clammy hands together as she watched and waited for Teresa Miller to collect her notes and the recorder that she'd organised across the low coffee table that sat between the two eclectic couches, which, of course, Kathy had originally guided them to.

So this was how it was going to go. A front-page piece for tomorrows *New York Times* and she was bouncing around like a crack addict. A cigarette was the ticket. Kathy could feel Teresa Miller taking in everything with her eyes. Her notes were together, and along with her small recorder, they were slipped back into her brown leather flat bag.

She was on her feet. "After you."

Teresa Miller looked nice – professional without being too straight or stuffy. Pencil skirted brown suit with a light pink blouse, and her hair down. It was the exact level of respectable cool confidence that Kathy had spent the previous three hours trying to evoke with her choice of wardrobe. She'd had mixed success and as she lead the way out to the roof stairs, Kathy was wishing she'd opted for the cream slacks and green blouse rather than the confidence insisting black jeans, black long sleeve top and black fuck me boots.

* * *

It was overcast but that was good because it kept the sun out of their eyes and the day was still warm enough. They took their seats at the table and as Kathy fumbled with her cigarette, Teresa Miller got out her recorder and re-organised her notes. Kathy lit her cigarette.

"You ready?"

Kathy nodded and hoped her smile didn't betray the fear she was feeling. The recorder was clicked on.

2

Blood in his mouth from hitting the steering wheel. It poured out when he opened it. David opened his eyes. The world was almost on its side. He was hanging. The seat belt. Two bullet holes. David felt his stomach. It hurt. He fought gravity to angle his heavy head and look to where he knew he'd taken a bullet.

He saw the hole and it was surrounded by black, which David knew beyond the darkness of his car would be blood red. Rapid tapping sounded out from above to which David turned his head and saw sand and small stones falling onto the closed driver's side window. They were being displaced by the dark figure standing on the road some two metres above. Another bullet hole, and with it David's head was rocked back as searing fire exploded at the back of his neck. He didn't scream. More displaced stones rattling on the window.

David kept his movements slight as he looked back up. The figure was gone. His left hand shot back, grabbing at the pain and finding that a piece was missing. Warmth flowed over his clamped fingers. The other hand found the seat belt catch and released it. Gravity grabbed David and he slammed painfully shoulder first into the passenger side window below. It rattled but didn't break.

The angle of the car was steep but there was enough room to squeeze out once he got the window open. Pain was everywhere and David's body wasn't letting him have the angle he needed. A slapping pressure was hitting him from above. He could smell it. David looked up and saw the gasoline splashing down onto the driver's side window and flowing down onto him through the bullet hole. The darkness that filled his car had covered his hanging absence. He found the handle and began to roll down the window, slowly. He twisted himself over and brought his other hand into play. He could feel his heart thundering away, which he knew could just as easily end up killing him. It was enough. David went onto his back. The world erupted into an orange glow as fire began to fall from above. Dirt got into his neck as he pulled himself free. He rolled over the fire that was spreading up his leg and then continued to roll away. Momentum took over as the earth descended and then he was falling. The hard stop came as quickly as the fall and as hot as he'd just been, he was now cold.

* * *

Beep... beep... beep... David couldn't hear anything past that noise... beep... His world was black and he couldn't find the light past that noise... beep... beep...

The white came. His body was there for him to feel again. David closed his eyes and then forced them to open again. It was the ceiling that was white. He was in a white bed.

...beep... He turned his head and saw the beeping heart monitor next to his bed. He was in a hospital and he was alive. Small consolation. He didn't have any specific pain but his whole body ached. His fingers came up and began clawing at the thing that was choking him.

"You've come back to us, Mr Radley..." Soft hands were on his. "No, no, don't do that."

David saw her leaning over him. Her face wasn't clear but her voice was the most soothing sound he'd ever heard. He let her hands have control of his.

"I'll just go find the doctor and let him know you're awake."

He turned his head to watch her leave and was reminded with crystal clarity, why there was a tight bandage around his neck. As the nurse disappeared past the dull green of his dividing curtain, David saw that the large room he was in was filled with beds such as his, each with their own incessant beep... beep... beep...

* * *

David was awake again, and it was Wednesday, and as best as he could figure it, he'd been unconscious for roughly thirty-six hours. The burning car had been found on the night but David was told that he hadn't been discovered until late the next day. He'd been hidden from sight lying at the bottom of an under construction run off for funnelling rainwater and had been in the hospital ever since, as a John Doe, as he was found without ID.

Shot three times and lying in a ditch and still breathing. David didn't know whether to laugh or cry. It hurt too much to do either. As the doctor had told him, his identity had only just been confirmed some two hours before he'd woken up. Gunshot victim, so the cops had been called in. His prints had been taken but nothing had come back. If the burned out husk had been his unmarked police car, all the dots would've been connected a lot sooner and his prints would have been run through a narrower database. As it stood now though, he was just another victim who had to wait in line like everyone else.

His phone had been in his pocket and when they had eventually found an appropriate charger, numbers were called and his identity had been confirmed. The Chief was on his way.

* * *

"What did the doctor say?"

The Chief looked tired. David's voice had come back to him and he'd settled into his pain enough to have his bed mechanically raise him into a seated position. After expressing his initial distress over what had happened to David, the Chief had simply sat on the bed side chair and seemed to become instantly distracted by his own questions. Something was wrong.

"Three bullets. The one in the leg is supposedly going to have to stay but it doesn't hurt at all. I didn't even know it had happened." David could tell from the Chief's vague nods that he was barely listening – he'd speak up soon. "The one in the gut's probably fucked me the worst, but it's the chunk that the last one stole from the back of my neck that's really killing me."

The Chief looked up from his chewed thumb. "Yeah, the doctor said you're lucky to be alive. The cold water saved you, slowed your heart rate."

"Something like that."

The Chief nodded. "David, I haven't called your sister or Jane about this. I haven't had the chance." He stood up. "I'll call them now."

"Don't. Leave it. I'll take care of it later. What's up, Chief? What are you not

267

telling me?"

The Chief sat back down. "We know who shot you. They shot you, you crashed, shot you again, set the car on fire and then moved on."

"You know? Who was it?"

"Damon Harris."

There was no expression behind the words. This was too perfect. Andrew was right. No one wanted to hear. David felt himself shift in discomfort as his skin began to flush. They make sure Damon gets off so that when they take pot shots at them everyone will... David's mouth was open in preparation to say all these things when...

"Andrew?"

The clarity in the Chief's expressionless face became clear.

"Last night. Andrew's car was hit on the outskirts of Brooklyn. Looks like he was trying to find his witness. There was another girl dead in the car with him. Andrew's partner says it was a whore who'd pointed them in the girl's direction before. Anyway, the girl wasn't there, so who knows."

Andrew was dead. David didn't know what to make of what he was feeling. His sister had liked him, David had seen it. The Chief was still going.

"The scene was a mess. The way it looks is that Andrew's car was hit from front and back by two cars. Only one was left on the scene. Damon's boys must have..."

"It wasn't Damon."

"David..."

"Chief, you know that Andrew fell into something. Whatever that was is what got us both shot. All this started..."

"David, we have Damon's body. Andrew shot him. He died at the scene and Andrew was the one who shot him. Those are the facts. We even have his lawyer's body. It was him."

Damon? Was that right? The Chief was standing.

"Whatever Andrew was into doesn't matter now. It's over."

"What about the girl? His witness."

David could see it in the Chief's eyes, which were now looking widely down at him, that his words had angered him.

"What about the girl? She ran away just like she'd done before. That's the end of it."

The end of it.

3

The interview was well into its second hour and more than anything else in the world, Kathy wanted another cigarette. And they were there to be had, but after stubbing out her last one maybe ten minutes earlier, Kathy had noticed that there were almost a dozen freshly stubbed out ones in the ashtray already. *Kathy Radley had chain smoked nervously throughout the interview.*

Ah, almost a dozen already. There was no taking it back now. Kathy slid another one free.

It had been the last question that had prompted this decision. What was it? Kathy lit the cigarette.

"Miss Radley."

Nervous, distracted, dressed all in black…

"I'm sorry. What was the question?"

It came back to Kathy before Teresa Miller answered her. They'd covered the basics. The fashion side, her childhood, a touch on her policeman brother, all to be edited down later as they reached the real meat of the interview. They'd been circling the issue for almost twenty minutes now and Teresa Miller had finally said it. You were attacked. But her question wasn't: How did you feel/or/Were you scared…? She repeated her question.

"Did it change you?"

Kathy wasn't sure how she felt about the question. It was a good one, designed to be expanded on, to make her search for the answer. It was probably the right question. Kathy placed her cigarette in the ashtray and then slid her left hand forward across the table.

"You see this scar?" Kathy turned her hand over slowly as Teresa Miller leaned forward to examine the angled pale line that ran half way over both sides of her hand. "It's a constant reminder of that cold day." Kathy's voice was steady. "I got it trying to stop what was done to me."

Kathy retracted her hand and picked up her cigarette.

"This is something I've lived with for four years and, until recently, have never spoken about. And I'm sure it's had its way with me over those years and maybe there's a lot of things I would do differently if I could, and I know that I haven't always been able to face up to things the way I would've wanted to." Kathy breathed in her favourite poison. "But for better or worse I've made it to where I am in my life, and I just pray, now that I've been forced to face this demon of mine, that I won't be punished for it."

* * *

Kathy had wanted it to end there. It would've been a nice cap, an ultimatum even: 'Dare you; the world of media keep on with this, lest you face the moral consequence of feeling really, really guilty for ruining my career'.

It hadn't stopped there though, and questions shifted towards the alluded-to actions of her former cop brother and how she felt about the rumours and did she think they were true, and so on and so on.

Kathy had taken some coaching from Giovanna for this inevitable section of the interview, where the key was not to seem elusive as though you're hiding something, but also not to come off as though you believed the accusations might be true. In other words, be just a little pissed off. Not so much as to cause offence, but enough to seem hurt that they'd dare to ask you. This kind of balancing act wizardry was why Giovanna was their spokesperson.

269

When it came to working with the industry pros, Kathy could do the dance with the best of them, but to be put out there and be witty for the world to see was not her strong suit.

After so many 'I don't knows' and a dozen more uncomfortable bum shifts, Teresa Miller had finally taken pity on her and clicked the stop button on her little digital recorder.

Teresa Miller was now gone, and Kathy was making herself a stiff drink at their temporary home's no longer fully stocked bar. It wouldn't be long before the owner was back and they had to find homes of their own. Kathy sipped her drink, her teeth exposing themselves at the sharpness of its bite. A new home. That would all depend on their magazine and that was most likely going to depend on how well her interview was received when it came out in the papers come the morning. Kathy took another sip and breathed in deeply to savour the burn that followed her strong daytime drink. It was still early enough and really she should have been getting sorted to go to work.

4

The recently closed hole in his stomach was the one that was giving David a hard time now. The tightly pulled together skin at the back of his bound neck was still thundering away, but it was the stomach wound that was forcing its way to the fore of his consciousness now.

David pressed on, one slow step after another. He had his saline drip stand for support. He needed a phone. No money. The Chief had left an hour before but his words had been buzzing around in David's head ever since. He needed a phone and if he could time it right he could use the one at the main reception desk.

A few heads had been turned at the sight of his partially hunched-over frame and it wouldn't be long before one of them realised that he wasn't meant to be out of bed. The three ladies behind the counter were chatting away amongst themselves, but two were facing his way and would spot him as soon as he reached over to grab the phone. This wasn't going to work.

"Excuse me ladies." This was the kind of thing Andrew would have been able to do with ease. Charm the ladies, despite an open back gown and a grimace of pain stretched across his face.

"Mr Radley?" It was the voice he'd first woken up to.

She was young and black with curly hair, beautiful eyes and wide lips. She was rounding the counter and headed in his direction.

"Mr Radley, you shouldn't be out of bed in your state. You're going to tear your stitches."

She'd reached him and the way her hands were going David could see her lifting up his only item of clothing to examine those potentially torn stitches there and then.

David took hold of her hand. "I need to use the phone quickly. I need to get hold of someone right away. It's very important."

She was nodding. David also noticed that it was now she who had a hold of his hand and that she'd already turned him away from the counter and was walking him back towards his bed. She was hypnotising him with her voice.

"Mr Radley, if you need us to call a family member for you, then you just need to give us the number and we'll take care of it for you."

David noticed that his return journey was happening a lot faster. She was supporting his arm... it would hurt too much to force them to stop.

"What's your name?"

She smiled. "Dallas."

"Dallas?"

Her smile broadened and David felt like he could fall in love with her.

"I don't want to talk about it. Now get back into bed and let me check those stitches."

David looked and saw that he was standing next to his bed again. He sat down against its edge and let the lovely Nurse Dallas help turn and guide him back in. Once under the sheets, which David then pulled up above his dignity, he let Nurse Dallas pull up his gown and expose the bandage that was taped down against the left side of his stomach. It was clean.

"Looks like you're okay, but I'm just going to..." She trailed off as she began rolling back the taped bandage with her fingertips.

David fought the sponge bath images that were trying to force their way into his head. She raised the bandage and David looked at the two intersecting rows of stitches there, one long one and one short. The longer one was clearly the result of the surgeon's knife.

"You've got sixteen stitches there that you can see, and a few more that you can't, so I'd be a little more careful if I were you." She set the bandage tape back in place.

"Dallas, I need to make a call. It's important. It's about why I'm in here and it's also why I need to get out of here."

"Mr Radley. You can't leave now. At least not for a couple of days. You've just..."

He took her wrist. "Please. I need my phone."

"I'm sorry, I don't have access to it, and besides..."

"What about yours?"

* * *

David punched the number into Dallas' cell phone. He was beginning to think that she was actually sweet on him. She had also said that once he was done with her phone that she was going to have to tell the doctor that he was planning on leaving and that he mustn't tell him that she'd let him use her phone, which wasn't meant to be used in hospitals anyway. It was all agreed to and Dallas was essentially standing lookout at the end of the large room.

"You're talking to Dana in the basement. What can I do for you?"

"Dana, it's Radley. I..."

"David. Oh my God. Are you alright? I just heard you were shot. Thank God you're alright."

David had never heard Dana's voiced pitched so high before and felt a slight well at the genuine concern that he heard there. He cut her off before she could delve into what happened in relation to Andrew.

"Dana, I'm fine, I'm fine. I'm calling 'cause I need to talk to the guy Andrew was partnered up with. Can you give me his number?"

It was silent on the other end. David could feel her thoughts turning over.

"Okay."

* * *

Wilks was on his way. The kid seemed eager to help. Andrew had obviously left an impression on him. David looked up at his doctor who was yammering away about the dangers of leaving the hospital so soon after major surgery, and that any wounds sustained because of leaving would undoubtedly cause issue with his insurance, all the while rattling meds he'd have to take and trying to arrange an appointment time for him to come in for a check-up.

David signed the forms and placated his doctor's worried assertions with a series of nods and 'Hmm' sounds.

"Just… try not to move around too much and don't stand up too straight. Okay?"

David nodded again and his doctor whizzed off in an arms up huff.

"Got some pants for you." Dallas held up the once white, elasticated pyjama bottoms that were covered in tiny, once yellow, pictures of little ducks.

"Thanks Dallas. You've been amazing."

"That's okay."

She was smiling coyly as she helped him swing his feet over the edge of the bed and pull himself up into a seated position. She did like him. She slipped the pyjama bottoms over his feet and then up his legs. Once they were fully over his feet she placed his hand on her shoulder and then eased him up to stand. She smelled good. David closed his eyes. Another time maybe. Maybe another life. He couldn't think about it now.

"Umm…"

The elasticated pyjama bottoms were sitting mid-thigh and it was starting to get awkward as to how close Dallas should allow herself to get.

"I've got it." With a slight dip and a little grimace, David hooked the elastic with his finger and raised them up beneath his open backed gown.

"Detective Radley?"

The two of them turned to the young, definitely a cop – obviously Mark Wilks, who was standing just at the end of the bed.

"It's just Mr Radley now, but call me David."

At this invitation, Wilks approached with a smile and his hand out.

Dallas ducked out of the way. "I'll go get your transportation."

A smile was shared between them as she turned and left.

David accepted Wilks' hand. "So you're Detective Wilks."

"That's right. Call me Mark."

David wasn't sure he was going to like him. He'd call him Wilks. The eyes were on his outfit.

"Thanks for coming like this."

The agreement was to come fetch him and drive him home so he could change before taking him to the station. The information that had prompted this was what David had forgotten about what Andrew had shared with him, but which he knew he knew. The whore – what was her story? Why did Andrew go after her? Why had she run? And then Wilks had said it. The boyfriend and his brother where she'd been staying had both been killed. Why? How?

How did they find them? Why did they kill them? They were killed to find out where she was, to draw Andrew out, to draw her out. How did they find them? Nobody had followed Andrew and Wilks on their first visit. It'd been too long before *they* had acted. If they'd known about this witness, they would have acted then.

No, this boiled down to the same thing as the situation with Carter. *They* knew more than they should have been able to. There was a mole.

* * *

They had him, a young stupid tech who quite simply didn't know any better. And there he sat, alone on the wrong side of the two-way mirror, staring into the blackness of his bad coffee. The Chief was shaking his head as he paced and looked to both him and Wilks, who had stood up pretty tall to get the Chief to stop yelling and listen to what he had to say.

The tech was twenty-three and from Dana's department. That was where the info was and where he had to be. Once broken down, the Chief had called in Dana, and before they knew it she had the kid by the ear and had him spilling his guts. The voice on the other end of the line had claimed to be I.A.D. and that was all she wrote. Had to be a Fed like the other one had told Andrew. Had to be, to be connected enough to know how to use that card.

A single tear as the kid had laid it out. He was telling the truth. Just a stupid rookie who didn't know any better. 'Don't tell anyone you spoke to us or you could be held liable for obstructing an ongoing investigation'. The way the kid told it, the voice wanted everything there was to have on Detective David Radley and his partner. All of it – past, present, future – all the info, all the files. The kid's computer was being checked for electronic footprints in the hope that they could trace where the downloaded files had been sent to, but it was all coming back stale. If it didn't come back as a dead end then, as Dana told it, the route would be far too twisted to ever reach the source. All under the guise of a discreet investigation which the kid had bought hook, line and sinker.

The Chief asked the question, "So what does this mean?"

"It means Andrew's hit was a cover up." David stood away from the desk he was leaning against and felt an instant twinge of regret. "The kid said the calls had just stopped and he'd figured that was it, but then they call back again to ask what Andrew's been up to. The case was cold as far as they were concerned. We'd been taken off it and the Feds had snatched it away, but then Andrew pops up on the dead Fed's phone and boom, they know something's up. The files are checked, the girl's name comes up and they think witness. They get Andrew, they get the girl and they thought they'd got me." David slapped his hands together.

"Okay, David. Let's say I think you're right. Then why the show? The Fed thought the Cartwright family was just a cover for Jack. You think Damon was just a cover for Andrew... But why? Why the big show? The Fed, Webb, was just popped, two in the back of the head. Why didn't he get a big cover up?"

"The pharmaceutical company, right?" David looked to Wilks who hadn't said anything for a while.

This was where it got shaky. He didn't know. All this information had been relayed to him second hand. It was the pharmaceutical company. Andrew had asked Bill to check into it.

"Bill knows something about it. Get him in here."

"Get Bill Dudley in here!" The Chief screamed in the direction of the open door after which a scuttle of compliant feet was heard.

Wilks stepped up. "He's covering himself."

He had everyone's attention. Swallowing, he went on.

"Webb said the first Fed, Jack... He said he thought there was a mole in the Bureau. Someone keeping this company out of harm's way. But he said he hadn't done anything with it." He swallowed again but hurried on obviously trying to hold onto his train of thought.

"Webb gets killed – no muss – he's not connected to them so it doesn't matter. But this Agent Jack gets killed and gets this big cover up job... But why? It can't be pinned to the pharmaceutical company. There's nothing saying they'd have a reason to have him killed. There's nothing on file... Nobody knows he's onto their mole."

The Chief again asked the pertinent question, "Okay?"

Wilks was rolling. "So why the cover up? Why the cover up with Andrew?" Wilks was looking at all of them waiting for them to get it. "Like I said, he's covering himself. He doesn't want anybody to know someone was onto him. He doesn't want the pharmaceutical big wigs to know he almost let them be exposed."

There was dead air as everyone tried to take it in. Smiling his 'don't you get it' smile Wilks pressed on. "Webb getting killed didn't make noise because he hadn't made any noise. But now with Andrew on the phone – Witness. Now killing him would make noise. Make the whole Cartwright thing shaky. The whole first Fed thing gets shaky, and why he died gets shaky. So he gets the cover up. Like Webb said, all this Agent Jack had was suspicion. So who benefits from this cover up? Not the pharmaceutical company. A law enforcement officer dies who has a vague connection to them. If they wanted him dead did it really need to be all that. It's the mole. There might have been evidence but more than that, this was about not getting the finger pointed. If Jack didn't find anything he still would've had to say that he suspects a mole. And if that got out then the mole would be the one who would need to be dealt with. Not by the Feds, but by the people who he's protecting. He needed time to go through Jack's back log and a reason that no one would want to touch anything he was involved in." Wilks took a deep breath attached to a deep smile.

He was right. When you stop being useful and you know too much you become a liability. Whoever it was was scared.

The Chief stepped forward, looking at him and Wilks. "Maybe you're right about all of it. But that still doesn't change anything. You're still no closer to knowing who any of these people are, and nobody at the Bureau wants to hear about it."

He was right. David felt his wounds burning.

"What about me? It's going to come out that I'm still alive and…"

"If you're right about all this then they've already blown their cover on that one. Damon's dead." The Chief sighed out the heavy weight of it all. "But we can look at covering you just in case. Until it all blows over."

The Chief's hand was squeezing David's shoulder. "I know this is bad, David, and I'd hate for this to be true and have it mean that Andrew's real killer gets off scot free. But if you let it go now then that will mean the end of all of this. You hear me David. You're still alive."

"All these people dead and I'm just supposed to let it go?"

The Chief's eyes flared and his voice followed. "If Andrew had listened and done as he was told, he'd still be alive. The whore who was with him and probably that little girl who he got everyone to sniff out too."

David felt his weakly hunched body flinching as the Chief's hand whipped up to point directly at his face.

"If Bates had listened to me, Damon would be in jail and you'd still be a cop. You think about that. Now let it go!"

All around had shrunk back. The Chief lowered his hand and turned to leave as Bill walked in through the open doorway into the stunned silence. He immediately stepped aside to let the intensity of the Chief walk past. The Chief turned to him as he did.

"I thought I told you not to give Bates any more assistance on the Cartwright case." He continued on, exiting the room before Bill could babble out his defence.

With the Chief's presence gone, Bill turned his eyes on David with a big 'Gee thanks' and a 'Fuck you' written in each of them. Then with a shake of his head he turned to leave as well.

"Bill."

* * *

275

Bill had simply pulled a folded up sheet of paper from his breast pocket and dropped it to the floor before making his silent exit. Coleman & Dean Blue Bird Pharmaceuticals. It was a print out of the substance found with details of its ongoing F.D.A. trial.

They were back down in Dana's basement division where she had accessed the company's website.

"What are you going to say?" Dana looked up at him from the computer screen on her desk.

Wilks was hovering. Both looked nervous as he plucked the telephone receiver from Dana's desk and began to dial the number listed on the pastel web page. They were both nervous but like him, they both wanted something to be done.

"As the investigating officer in the Cartwright case, I'm just going to call them up and ask them a few questions."

Dana touched his hand stopping it mid-dial. "You're going to identify yourself as a police officer?"

"They'll need a reliable source they can check out. They won't have time to go too deep, and even if they do find out I'm no longer on the force it'll still be enough to make them antsy... Force them to connect the dots."

"David, this is illegal. You said the FBI's watching these guys. If they hear this conversation, then you could go to jail for tampering with their investigation."

David gently shifted her hand aside and proceeded to redial the number. "Or maybe I end up forcing their in-house rat to expose himself, or hopefully get him killed, and then I've done them this huge favour and they won't be so mad at me." It was ringing.

"Good afternoon, Coleman & Dean Blue Bird Pharmaceuticals, this is Doris speaking. How may I help you?"

"Hi Doris. This is Detective David Radley. I'm a homicide detective with the New York Police Department. I need to speak with someone upstairs. It's important."

The music had vanished from Doris' lyrical voice as David heard her fumbling about on the other end of the line. "Um, yes – yes. Okay. Just one second, sir. I'm just going to put you on hold for a minute. Is that alright?"

"That's fine."

The music came up immediately. Both Wilks and Dana were looking at him anxiously.

"Hello Detective Radley. How may I help you?"

"Who am I speaking to?"

The voice had an elongated deepness to it that was full of the kind of self-assured confidence that came with knowing that right and wrong only mattered to those who still rolled around in the dirt.

"You're speaking to me, Detective. Now what can I do for you?"

"I was hoping to talk to one of the higher-ups and for now, at least, I'm willing to assume that is the case. Your company's name has come up a number of times in our investigation into the murder of a family."

"A family?" The ease had shifted to cautious curiosity.

"That's right. Our investigation shifted considerably when a Federal Agent by the name of Jack Griffin was connected to the murder. Does that name sound familiar?" David didn't wait for a response. "Several sources have linked Special Agent Jack Griffin to your company, sir, and with the evidence collected so far, there is reasonable cause to suggest that somebody working for your company may have been complicit..."

Click.

5

"You said you'd killed him!"

They were standing over the phone at the side table in the living room. Leon had it on loudspeaker. Cliff hadn't shown up for the meeting to discuss their next target but it hadn't been long after Anthony's arrival that the phone had rung.

Anthony watched Leon throwing caution to the wind, sipping his Bourbon from one of his prized crystal tumblers as he listened to Cliff's rant. The Cop had survived and their golden goose was in a panic. Leon was drinking but all in all he didn't seem the least bit fazed.

"He fucking called the people I killed Jack for. They..."

Leon set his tumbler down and leaned closer to the speakerphone. "You mean the ones you had us kill Jack for."

There was a moment of silence and then...

"What fucking difference does it make? They know!"

"I thought they always knew, Cliff. Wasn't that the point, or was it maybe a little mess that you'd fixed for yourself?"

More silence. Leon picked up his tumbler and took another sip before continuing.

"You brought us in and you kept the details quiet because you figured we might not be too keen to help if we knew the kinds of people you were messing with. The kind you were having us mess with. Am I right?"

"You're in line to make a lot of money with me Leon, so don't get all self-righteous. I..."

"I suppose this latest development means our little venture is over, correct? No more money?"

Cliff could be heard gathering his breath on the other end of the line. He was on the verge of a breakdown.

"We still have the pictures of the judge. There's a lot of money to be made there. Leon... I need that money. I need to get out of here. I need to..."

"Of course you do. You need to leave the country, start a new life somewhere. I tell you what." Leon left the words hanging as he finished off the last of his Bourbon.

"Leon..."

"I think what we'll do is buy you out. How does twenty thousand sound?"

"What? Leon, we can get at least a quarter million out of this guy. I…"

"Twenty thousand. It's been nice doing business with you, Cliff, but I don't think there's anything left in it for me. Come to…"

"You son of a bitch!"

"Tick-tock, my friend. That's my final offer. Consider it a favour."

"There's a restaurant…"

Leon snatched up the telephone receiver cutting off the speakerphone. "Give the details to Anthony. Time and place and I'll make sure he gets the money to you. Goodbye." The receiver was away from his ear and into Anthony's hands before any response could be heard.

Anthony raised the phone to his ear. "Cliff. Anthony here."

Anthony took down the details as Leon walked off to the kitchen with his cane in hand. The sound of another glass being poured was heard before Leon reappeared. He had a yellow Post-It note between two of the fingers in the hand with which he was holding his overly full glass of Bourbon.

Anthony clicked the phone off and put it back into its cradle. "So what now?"

Leon handed him the Post-It note. It had a telephone number and the name of some company: Coleman & Dean Blue Bird Pharmaceuticals, written on it in blue pen.

"That's the name of the people Cliff's working for. I want you to drive into the city, find a pay phone and call that number. Mention the whole cops calling them thing. Leave the number of the phone box. They'll call you back on a clean line." Leon turned and walked over to the couch and sat down before turning on the TV.

He clicked through the channels till he found some boxing. "Then when they call back tell them everything. Everything pertaining to our little job for Cliff and then give them the details of when and where he's expecting to meet you."

Anthony could feel himself smiling slightly. He should never have doubted the old man.

"And I want that other cop dead too. Do it tonight and then tomorrow we'll get out of town, set the wheels in motion to getting our money from the judge and find ourselves another gig. Something a little less complicated."

* * *

The old man had it sussed. Anthony felt almost foolish for his lack of faith as he drove into the city for that one last loose end. Corner the sister and call the brother. He'll gladly trade his life for hers. As Leon put it, it's just the way it works.

Anthony had been keeping one of his eyes on her and in all likelihood she'd be at that little makeshift fashion building of theirs. She and her partner tended to work late. Anthony checked his watch. It was after seven. She'd still be there. Her

278

and maybe a handful of others. The security staff were just for show and would've left already. He'd need another pair of eyes for this one. Anthony pulled out his phone and selected the number of his little helper.

6

Kathy watched in agonising anticipation as Giovanna nodded and 'ah-ha'd' into the cell phone. Kathy was sitting at one of the random empty work stations trying to seem more interested in the photos and letters clipped together in a mock layout for one of the magazine's pages.

The desk creaked as Giovanna sat her posterior down onto its corner and then aimed her furrowed brow down at Kathy. Kathy looked away and started touching things causing them to separate and turn into a mock pile. She stood away from the desk and took a couple of steps.

The whole day, her interview with Teresa Miller had been playing on her mind and the whole day, Giovanna had been watching her with concerned eyes. Finally Giovanna had just said, 'do you want me to call her and find out how it went?'

At first it had sounded like the worst idea in the world, but as the day drew to a close, Kathy let her protests soften. With the last of the staff gone for the night, Giovanna had decided to make the call, and with an 'okay, thanks' – she pressed the red button and pocketed her phone.

No more pretence. Kathy was biting her thumb and staring directly at Giovanna. "What did she say?"

The cheap desk creaked again as Giovanna stood up and stepped over to Kathy with her hands out beckoning for hers. Kathy let her have them.

"I'm so proud of you, Kathy."

"She said it went well?" Kathy could feel herself smiling.

"She said you have nothing to worry about. She said it's a great piece about a brave, strong, successful, independent woman who has flat out refused to let the world keep her down."

Kathy felt her heart rise and fall with each word. Giovanna was wearing her big sister smile and Kathy couldn't help but love her for it. Kathy laughed and hugged her friend. He whole world seemed to instantly feel lighter.

"Don't cry."

Kathy couldn't help it. The shuddering had just come out of nowhere and the tightening embrace was only making it worse.

"Oh Kathy. Shh…" Giovanna's hand moved to stroke Kathy's hair.

7

"Hmm… what have we here?" Anthony paused at the slightly ajar door to look at the scene he was about to burst in on. The girls were hugging. It was allowed, he supposed, but he had to smile at the gutters his mind instantly began digging.

The sister was crying. Anthony could see the shudders as the other one,

Giovanna, stroked her hair. Would she recognise him when he burst through? Would she scream because she'd know his intentions, or would it simply be because of the knife in his one hand and the gun in his other?

Anthony wanted her to recognise him. He wanted to see that shift in her eyes the second they looked into his.

Two of them. Anthony would have to be on his game to keep them under control. He didn't want to have to shoot either of them outright. Both his and Chester's guns had silencers and there was no one else in the building so it wouldn't be an issue, but it'd be a real waste.

Anthony creaked the door open a little wider. Getting in hadn't been a problem. Security was a joke. The downstairs toilet window was hidden from view by a nice dark alley and didn't even need to be broken. It had simply popped open. There had been a car parked across the street but the local rag hound waiting behind its steering wheel hadn't seen them.

The door creaked that much further and that much louder. He saw those shoulders tense.

"Ladies."

8

Wilks stopped talking when he saw David fish out his ringing phone. He was a good kid who was now being good enough to drive him back home again. And he obviously had his head screwed on, putting that last puzzle piece together. But he was a little too green and good natured for David to stand. David smirked, remembering how that was almost precisely how he'd felt about Andrew when they'd first been lumped together.

He didn't recognise the number.

"David Radley here. Who's this?"

There was gravel in the voice that replied and David instantly knew that he was talking to one of the main players on the opposite team.

"I have some information for you, Mr Radley."

"Who is this?"

"My name isn't important but I will say that I'm one of the people who has been affected by you and your partner's persistent digging."

David could see Wilks looking at him. He could tell something was happening.

"You killed him."

"I arranged for it to be done and now I've arranged for the same thing to be done to you."

A silence followed those words, but before David could ask the obvious question the gravel echoed through again.

"But with your call today, which I will tell you yielded fruit, I'm being forced to cut certain ties and move on. Now listen carefully because this is important to both you and your sister."

Kathy.

280

"The man who killed your partner. He's my associate but he's recently become something of a liability. He's become a risk taker in the indulgence of his newly acquired tastes."

"You leave my sister out of this."

"You're not listening to me David. It's not me who's a threat to your sister, it's him. And that's exactly where I've sent him."

David could feel his cell phone shifting against itself in his tightening grip. This couldn't happen.

"Where?"

"This is how it's supposed to work. He corners her and then calls you. Tells you to come alone, and then kills you both when you get there. It's the way these things are done."

"Where?"

The tone didn't change. "But he won't call. Not for a little while at least. Not until he's indulged."

The car was too small. David's whole body was tense with every inch of him wanting to thrash out.

"I'M GOING TO FUCKING KILL YOU! TELL ME WHERE SHE IS!"

"David calm down. I don't want you to miss my point. You go there now, alone, quiet. No cops, no noise – just you. He won't be ready for you and then you can kill the man who killed your partner and stop him from hurting your sister. Sound fair?"

"You tell me where."

"Your sister's little aspiring fashion house."

David cut the conversation off. He couldn't bear listening to one more second of that voice. It could be a trap. It sounded like a trap and it felt like a trap, but David didn't think it was.

Wilks was looking at him. "What are we doing?"

Wilks was in it. There was no getting around that. He needed the car. He needed the gun.

"Drive."

9

No-no-no-no-no-no-no. Kathy couldn't breathe. He was standing over Giovanna. He had made them both sit in chairs. Kathy couldn't move. His leg was between Giovanna's knees. Kathy had just frozen, no use to anybody. The door creaked and there they were – there he was. He'd smiled at her. Giovanna had seen it in her eyes before she'd seen the gun, the knife.

The knife was against her friend's swollen cheek. Kathy had never seen her scared before. Giovanna had screamed for them to get out as she'd moved herself directly into harm's way. Kathy couldn't move. Her friend was crying. He'd just hit her and slammed her back into the chair. Kathy had just done as she was told and sat down.

The boy was standing in front of her. There was very little behind his eyes

281

but Kathy couldn't see any lust in them as he watched the other slice another button off her friend's top.

"Help us."

Kathy barely heard her own words but it turned the boy's head in her direction. The gun in his hand was shaking. He didn't belong.

The words trembled out again. "Help us."

10

"You can't go in there. Look at yourself, you're a fucking mess."

They'd just pulled up to the sidewalk with the fashion house just ahead. There were lights on the third floor. The itching stitches in his stomach and the pain beneath them were crying out in agreement with Wilks.

"I need a gun."

"Jesus Christ. You and Andrew sure know how to fuck with a guy's career. Let me call for back up."

"Now, Wilks! We gotta go in now."

He needed a gun but he'd go in with or without one. David opened the door and eased himself out.

"David, wait."

He couldn't wait. He had to go. This wasn't going to happen again.

11

"What did you say?"

Kathy felt her body go limp beneath her. The boy turned to the one who was in charge. The one standing over her friend. The one with the knife.

"What did she fucking say?"

The boy's voice began to shake along with his loosely held gun, "I don't... I don't know. I didn't hear her."

He was glaring at the boy but the knife was still pressed against Giovanna's neck. Kathy met her eyes. No, no, no, no – this couldn't happen.

"Are you going to help them?"

"I just don't..."

"You didn't help the girl did you, Chess? Or that little whore. You've got a gun. You can do things differently this time."

Kathy saw the boy's hand tighten around the gun that was hanging limply at his side. It was on his mind. Kathy looked at the other one, his gun tucked away and securely clipped in his shoulder holster. There was only a metre between them.

"What are you going to do, Chess? Save the day? Save these ladies and then go to jail for the rest of what will be a very short and miserable life for a pretty little boy like you?"

Kathy could see the steel melting away, ...and so could Giovanna, "Please!"

The boy's eyes snapped onto Giovanna's at her crying plea, but it was gone. The other one saw it too and turned back to Giovanna.

282

The knife was suddenly away from her neck and she screamed as Anthony's hand had her under her shoulders, yanking her out of her chair. Giovanna was flipped over as her chair was kicked aside and she was slammed down face first onto the desk behind her. His elbow was in her back as he used his knife to raise her skirt.

Giovanna's scream shattered its way through Kathy's mind.

Kathy was out of her chair. "No!"

She shouldered past the boy with ease and was on Anthony's back before he could turn. Her nails were in his cheeks, clawing to find his eyes.

"Argh … You fucking bitch!" His hands were fumbling desperately for her fingers. Kathy heard the knife fall to the floor. He had her finger.

"Chester! Get this bitch off of me."

He was going to break it. Kathy tasted blood as her teeth pinched the skin at the back of his neck. He screamed again and then his other hand was in her hair. She clawed for his throat. His hand was away from her finger and then Kathy felt all her air vanish as his elbow slammed back into her stomach.

She was being pulled back and twisted round as the boy took her down to the floor with him.

"Fuck! Fuck! Ah… Shit. You're gonna fucking pay for that, you bitch!"

Kathy opened her eyes, catching her breath and found herself looking directly into the boy's eyes who she'd fallen on top of. His gun was pushed into her hand. It was being put on her now. Her finger found the trigger.

"Jesus, bitch, I'm gonna make you sorry for that one."

She'd wait for her moment.

"And don't you fucking move!"

He was talking to Giovanna. He'd be on her soon.

"You're in trouble now. Come here!"

His hand stung her as it slapped onto her back and grabbed for a handful of her top. Only one hand. He had his knife. He'd only give her one chance at this. Her top stretched and dug into her as he yanked her back. She let herself be pulled to her feet. Both hands on the gun. She should have just turned over and shot him while she was still on the ground.

What was going to happen when he turned her around? Was she going to turn into a knife being slammed into her gut? Would he see the gun before she could aim it? Take it away from her. Rape, stab and kill them both. Why was this happening?

Kathy realised that her eyes were squeezed tightly shut as he used her momentum to spin her round. No room to move, no time to aim. Kathy felt the pressure of the gun's silencer barrel connecting with him.

"What?"

She felt his body shift. Kathy squeezed the trigger. She couldn't open her eyes. Did she get him? He still had her. Kathy felt herself being pulled.

He screamed. Kathy opened her eyes and raised the gun at the enraged figure stumbling back away but pulling her with him. She saw blood on his leg. He was

283

too fast – only one chance and it was gone. His knife was up and gliding towards her. It slipped easily into and then across the length of her forearm. She heard her own scream as the gun slipped from her hand and fell to the floor.

His grip on her top faltered as she pulled back and they both tumbled away from each other. Her arm covered in the red that she could feel ebbing from the deep line in her arm. She hit the floor. He didn't. Anthony stumbled against the desk he'd tried to have Giovanna on. Kathy saw her on the floor behind it.

He was still standing. His bloody knife still in his hand. The boy was on his feet again, his gun on the floor to the middle of their skewed triangle. He was looking at the boy. He knew. Kathy could feel the light slipping away. She looked round to find her friend's eyes again. They were there looking at her. Kathy tried to smile, to ease the terror in her friend's eyes – the friend she wasn't able to save.

12

Voices, screams – they were running up the last flight of stairs. No gun for the civilian so Wilks had the lead. Wilks was at the top waiting, checking through the door leading to the third floor. David could feel blood running down from his leg and stomach as he took the last few steps to catch up.

Wilks looked and gave a nod before stepping into the dark corridor. There was a thud. Yelling. There was light at the end of the corridor. One more door.

David could have killed Wilks for that gun. "Let's go."

Wilks made quick for the door before David could pass him. Was that a gunshot? No, no, no. A scream of rage and pain. A man. David heard Kathy's scream. Wilks was at the door. He kicked it in.

"Freeze, police!"

David reached the open doorway and had to fight to stop himself from shouldering his way into the room past Wilks. There she was on the floor. Alive. Her arm – blood. She was alive. She was bleeding badly.

"Drop the knife!" Wilks stepped into the room.

Two men. One young with hands up and his back to them. The other one was the one he wanted. His leg was bleeding.

"Drop the fucking knife! It's over!"

David eased into the room behind Wilks.

She saw him. "David!"

"It's okay, Kathy. I'm here."

She was still bleeding. He could see her slouching into the support of the desk behind her. There was the other one. David could see the relief in her eyes.

Wilks stepped into his words. "Drop the knife!"

"No."

Then in a blinding second he was out of Wilks' sights and behind the boy. David saw the flash before he recognised it's muffled sound... Again. Wilks screamed, taking the second bullet. Blood splashed onto David's arm from the hole in Wilks' ribs. Another shot.

David pushed himself into Wilks and brought them both down behind a desk

284

and a cubicle wall.

"You okay?"

Wilks didn't answer. His clenched teeth and strained neck prevented this. David reached over him grabbing his gun. No time to waste. He was up on his feet again keeping low. His stitches were gone now but David barely noticed.

"Come here, bitch!"

A sharp scream. No time. With a lunging sideways dive, David put himself back into the open, his gun trained. Kathy was being yanked to her feet by her hair. The boy was in the way, scuttling for his gun. David pulled the trigger sending two bullets tearing into the boy's hunched-over back.

The gun forgotten, the boy's hand shot back, reaching uselessly for the two gaping holes there. His head snapped back as his spine inverted, pulling him all the way back over. No scream as his body hit the floor, only a jet of blood forced from his mouth with the slam of the impact. Another was coughed loosed as he tried to take his last breath.

The boy was out of the way but the other one had her. David rose to his feet, keeping his gun on the man now shrinkingly hiding behind his sister. The gun was to her head and David didn't have a shot.

"You okay, Kathy?"

She nodded over the taut forearm that was around her neck. The bloodied knife was still in the grip at the end of that forearm, pointing down the front of his sister's body. She was still bleeding.

"You still with me, Wilks?"

There was a deafeningly long silence before the strained reply came. "I'm still here."

David stepped forward focusing his attention on the man behind his sister. The man who'd killed his partner. Who'd shot him – the one who David knew had been behind the knife from the start of it all.

"This place is going to be surrounded by cops any minute. Just…"

"How bad do you want me?"

"Just let her go."

David found himself side stepping over the boy's corpse as his sister was being manoeuvred sideways, her captor moving to circle their position past him. David knew he was moving for the door.

"You going to stop me from leaving this place?" He'd found his line with the open door and was backing his way towards it.

"Just let her go."

"I'm taking your sister with me out this door," he was moving faster, "and if you try and follow me, I will shoot her."

"David."

"You're not taking her anywhere!"

He was at the door. No, no, no, no. His head turning to check.

"David!" Her eyes bulged as her head shook frantically.

"No!" David felt his feet move. "Don't you take her!"

Kathy screamed as she flopped forward. David caught her in his arms. She was alive. His gun went onto the empty doorway. He could hear the fading footsteps. His sister's arms were around him too tightly. He couldn't follow.

"Oh God, David, thank God."

She cried in his arms and he comforted her.

"I'm so sorry, Kathy. I'm so sorry."

CHAPTER TWENTY-THREE

1

Cold. Anthony breathed in sharply through his nose as his head pushed itself back against the driver's seat headrest. A few more deep breaths. He couldn't afford to pass out. Anthony looked down. His seat was black with blood but the bleeding had been stopped. With his hands shaking wildly, he began shifting, tucking and securing the end of the belt he'd just tightened around his damaged thigh.

The bullet hadn't hit the artery so he knew he'd be okay for a while. He looked at himself in the rear view mirror. He was pale and covered in sweat. Leon had set him up, he had no doubt. Just like that. Just like Cliff. He started the car up again. He had nearly taken out a lamppost as he'd swerved it off before. Back onto the dark road. He had to make sure.

* * *

He'd expected no less. Anthony re-holstered his gun and limped a little further into the house. Leon had seen it all coming. In some variation or another, he had known that it would all come crashing down. The furniture was all still there, but anything that was Leon's was gone.

Anthony wiped the gathering sweat from his brow, immediately realising that some of the sticky blood covering his hand would be left there. He'd find him. Leon was smooth but he'd find him. Make him pay. Anthony turned and limped back to the open front door he'd kicked in.

2

She opened her eyes and found herself looking into the darkness of her bedroom. She was warm and comfortable. Her eyes began to close again. Wait – why had she opened them? What had woken her? She strained her ears. She could hear something. Movement in the living room. She'd heard the front door.

She threw the covers aside and swung her legs over the edge of the bed, arching her head forward trying to tune into any more potentially revealing noises. There came a clank and a chink and a slam. It wasn't her man. It was him.

3

Anthony watched the ice shift and crack as the Bourbon rushed and splashed over the three cubes. He needed a second to figure out his next move. Glass and bottle in hand, Anthony limped his way into the living room before slumping down into the armchair. Cigarette. Putting the glass and bottle onto the side table, Anthony reached into his pocket and manoeuvred the red stained pack free. He was a mess.

Anthony pulled one cigarette free, staining it too in the process, and then lit it with his equally red smeared lighter. Long day. Anthony bypassed the glass and took a swig directly from the bottle. It had never tasted better. Biting down on the cigarette filter, Anthony leaned forward and poured it over the gaping hole in his leg. The burn shot straight down his leg before rushing out his toes.

"Ah, God."

Anthony felt a fresh layer of sweat spring into being. He didn't want to look at it just yet. He wiped the sweat away, taking a nice cool crisp sip of Bourbon from the glass. It tasted even better than the first.

"Where's Chester?"

4

He looked ridiculous. Blood covered his one leg and there was a big streaking smear across his forehead. Add to that the big smile that had just spread across his face at seeing her. He looked ridiculous, but it was blood he was covered in.

Switch had to hug herself because she already knew the answer. "Where's Chester?"

5

She was wearing that same tummy-revealing top of hers. A little more meat on her now though. Hugging herself – she still didn't like him looking. Small shorts. This was just what the doctor ordered.

"Little Jamie Nuemyer. Back again. Good girl. You know you had us worried for a little while there."

"Where's Chester, you fucking scum bag! Tell me!"

There it was. That fire. All her muscles had just become taut as she leaned into her words. Just what he needed. Anthony's cigarette left his fingers as he flicked it across the room at the disrespectful little bitch. She gave a short sharp squeak trying to swat it away as it bounced off her arm in a spray of sparks.

His gun was out the holster and aiming at her, but she'd already turned and stepped into the darkness of the corridor before seeing it. That's it – go to your bedroom, keep things nice and simple. Anthony picked up his glass and knocked back the last of his Bourbon. Then the glass flew across the room and shattered against the wall where Jamie had just been standing. Anthony pushed himself out of the chair. His leg was hurting but he still had enough blood to go round. Just what he needed. This little bitch had been asking for it from day one.

"Where you going, Jamie? Come back here."

Anthony reached the darkness beyond the corridor and…

6

One, two, three – the four-inch switchblade went in and out, in and out of his stomach so easily. That look on his face as he staggered back, not even realising that he'd dropped his gun. Switch kicked the gun away. He just stood there looking from her to his blood covered hands clutching his gut.

"I want to hear you say it!"

He didn't understand. He would.

Switch quick stepped over to the entranced figure of Anthony and slapped aside the weakly flaying hand that reached out to fend her off. Her free hand went straight for the belt, ripping it free. The force pulled Anthony to his knees. Switch felt all her muscles tighten as she shoved the blade hilt deep into that ready-made hole. Warmth gushed up over her hand as Anthony threw his head back in a desperate howl of shock and pain.

"Where's Chester?"

7

Anthony's world was plunged back into full colour as his hand shot out to lock around her wrist. Her eyes – he couldn't look – they were sapping the life out of him. No, no, no, no. His blood. No, no, no. He couldn't move her hand. She was shouting again but he couldn't hear her. Her hand was moving. He reached out for her neck but his hand was just slapped away. He saw his other hand slip away from her wrist and immediately felt the knife go ever deeper. It didn't hurt.

Anthony felt the back of his head hit the floor. She was still yelling. She was asking about Chester.